DO NO HARM

*A Forge Book

DO NO HARM

MAX ALLAN COLLINS

A Tom Doherty Associates Book

New York

DO NO HARM

Copyright © 2020 by Max Allan Collins

A Forge Book
Published by Tom Doherty Associates
120 Broadway
New York, NY 10271

www.tor-forge.com

Forge® is a registered trademark of Macmillan Publishing Group, LLC.

Library of Congress Cataloging-in-Publication Data

Names: Collins, Max Allan, author.
Title: Do no harm / Max Allan Collins.
Description: First edition. | New York : Forge, 2020.
Identifiers: LCCN 2019046684 (print) | LCCN 2019046685 (ebook) |
ISBN 9780765378293 (hardcover) | ISBN 9781466860797 (ebook)
Subjects: GSAFD: Mystery fiction.
Classification: LCC PS3553.O4753 D6 2020 (print) |
LCC PS3553.O4753 (ebook) | DDC 813/.54—dc23
LC record available at https://lccn.loc.gov/2019046684
LC ebook record available at https://lccn.loc.gov/2019046685

Our books may be purchased in bulk for promotional,
educational, or business use. Please contact your local bookseller
or the Macmillan Corporate and Premium Sales Department
at 1-800-221-7945, extension 5442, or by email at
MacmillanSpecialMarkets@macmillan.com.

First Edition: March 2020

Printed in the United States of America

0 9 8 7 6 5 4 3 2 1

For Dr. Alyas Chaudhry
and his Trinity team,
who made this book possible

AUTHOR'S NOTE

Although the historical incidents in this novel are portrayed more or less accurately (as much as the passage of time and contradictory source material will allow), fact, speculation, and fiction are freely mixed here; historical personages exist side by side with composite characters and wholly fictional ones—all of whom act and speak at the author's whim.

Richard Kimble has been tried and convicted for the murder of his wife. But laws are made by men, carried out by men, and men are imperfect.

—**Roy Huggins,** *The Fugitive* **TV series**

Our justice system is human and therefore it is apt to err.

—**Erle Stanley Gardner**

Although this case was about a 1954 murder, those involved were real people with real hopes, dreams, and emotions. . . .

—**Jack P. DeSario and William D. Mason**

Be careful, then, and be gentle about death
For it is hard to die. It is difficult to go through
the door, even when it opens.

—**D. H. Lawrence**

– BOOK ONE –

LIE DETECTING

1957

CHAPTER 1

Like a police car's siren, the shriek penetrated his slumber.

Startled from a deep sleep, but still groggy with it, Dr. Sam Sheppard pushed up on his elbows as the siren became a scream, a woman's scream, Marilyn's scream, from their bedroom above.

Then: "Sam! Sam!"

He clambered from the daybed, positioned against the stairway wall, and started quickly up. The last he knew, he and his wife had been entertaining another couple, good enough friends to understand that after twelve tough hours at the hospital, he might crap out on the couch like this, no harm done. So the house was dark, company had gone home, with Marilyn off to bed.

Nothing unusual about any of it.

Even the cries from above, however concerning, did not alarm him. Marilyn, four months pregnant, might have been having convulsions, as when she carried their son Chip. The boy right now was in the bedroom beyond theirs, a sound sleeper like his dad.

These thoughts flashed through his mind in a few seconds.

But as the screams continued, and his thoughts came into focus, he knew something much worse than convulsions was wrong. He took the several steps to the landing, then at the top of the stairs, which rose vertically to meet the horizontal hallway, he found the door to their bedroom open. The screaming had stopped now, replaced by a raspy gurgling, and a figure in the darkness—a night-light from behind Sam providing scant illumination—was hovering over Marilyn, who was on her back. The figure was flailing, but then moved across his vision, in a blur of almost glowing white.

A T-shirt?

Sam rushed inside the bedroom to help his wife, who was moaning now, but first there was an intruder to deal with. He grabbed at the formless figure with its white torso, grappled with it in a fashion Sam hadn't experienced since high school wrestling days. The grunting of their struggle joined the bubbling groans from the bed, when something struck him from behind.

Struck him hard.

The world went red, then black, as Sam fell to the floor.

When he awoke, he had no idea how long he'd been unconscious—a minute? An hour?

*Feeling punch-drunk, he was on his stomach at the foot of the bed, his feet out the door and in the hallway. His dazed condition eased while the throbbing pain at the back of his neck—*had that been a judo chop?*—did not, and he pushed himself up, noticing his open wallet flung nearby, his badge (he was the local police physician) catching the dim light and winking at him. Absentmindedly, he stuffed the wallet in his pocket and he got shakily to his feet.*

Even in the near darkness, he could see Marilyn, on her back, in her diamond-pattern pajamas, almost floating in blood, a damp veil of it covering her face, its coppery smell all pervasive. He checked her neck for a pulse that wasn't there. Just enough illumination came from the night-light across the hall to reveal the unsettling shimmer of blood splashed on the walls.

He backed away from the horror and hurried to the room next door, Chip's room, finding him deep asleep. Before he could even feel a sense of relief that his son had been spared, from violence, from the screams of his mother, the boy slumbering and blessedly unaware of their loss, Sam heard movement downstairs.

Lithely muscular, a thirty-year-old six-footer, Sam—in the T-shirt, slacks and moccasin-style slippers he'd sacked out in—ran down the stairs. In the darkness but silhouetted against the windows onto the lake, no glow of white now, was a nonetheless discernible form, a dark human form that must have heard him coming, because it, he, moved quickly across the living room and to and through the door onto the screened-in porch, facing the lake.

Sam followed the dark figure outside, through the screen door and across the narrow backyard, then down the thirty-six steps to the bathhouse on its platform eight feet above the lakeshore. As before, this was just a silhouette, but a silhouette of what appeared to be a man, a big man with a good-sized head and bushy hair.

Rattling down the remaining few steps, Sam caught up with him, and tackled him to the sand. Waves were hitting the shore as violently as the struggle on the strip of foamy beach rolling in nearby. Again, Sam found himself wrestling with an attacker, but when strong fingers gripped his throat and squeezed and squeezed, unconsciousness took him a second time.

When he awoke, he was belly-down on the beach, his feet and legs in the water, where the waves kept churning. His head was on the bank, out of the water, or he might have drowned.

Staggering to his feet, he came slowly to his senses. Was this a nightmare or reality? The cascade of surreal events could only make him wonder. He made his wobbly way up the many steps to return to the scene of horror on the second floor of the house looming above.

At the very least, Marilyn had surely been badly injured by the intruder—intruders?—and the husband, the doctor, went to his wife quickly, through the house, up the stairs. Again he found the scent of copper and the splash of blood and a woman with no pulse.

In a daze, he began to pace aimlessly, first upstairs, then down, and up again, and every time he re-entered the bedroom he hoped he would wake from this bizarre bad dream. But one final examination confirmed Marilyn was gone.

There would be no waking from this, for either of them.

He wandered downstairs, disoriented, sleepwalking through the kitchen, *through his study and living room and finally he became focused enough to find the phone and call for help.*

But what good had crying for help done his wife?

"What," Erle Stanley Gardner asked me, "do you think of his story?"

The story, of course, belonged to Dr. Sam Sheppard of Bay Village, Ohio, whose wife Marilyn had been murdered in the early-morning hours of July 4, 1954. Dr. Sam, as many called him (including the Cleveland media who'd crucified him), was found guilty of her murder on December 21 of that year. He was currently in a maximum-security prison in Columbus.

"It stinks," I said.

I had followed the case, which had made the Chicago papers— it got a lot of national coverage—and the accused husband's account had been repeated again and again.

"I mean, your melodramatic touches improve it," I granted, "but it's still about as believable as a flying saucer sighting. I mean, who the hell gets knocked out twice in one fight?"

We were seated in Gardner's knotty-pine office in the sprawling main house of his thousand-acre ranch outside tiny Temecula, California. The creator of Perry Mason and so many big-city mysteries was a would-be Westerner, with a tanned, weather-beaten oval face and snap-button open-collar tan shirt with black trim as evidence. He was one of those men of average height who seemed taller because of wide shoulders and a stout build, his brown hair going gray but the dark eyes retaining a boyish twinkle behind round-lens glasses with dark plastic frames.

"That's what the jury thought," Gardner said, between puffs of his pipe. "But much as I prize our system of justice, sometimes juries do get it wrong."

"Sometimes it's *given* to juries wrong," I said.

I was not a Westerner, and my suit was strictly big city, a dark brown Botany 500 with a brown-and-yellow silk tie. I'd been more casually dressed when I'd driven the near two hours plus down from Los Angeles.

I'd never been to the writer's Rancho del Paisano before, described to me as halfway between L.A. and San Diego, and got a little lost. Back roads, stretches of desert and grassy rolling hills brought me to a modest mountain where, about halfway up, the scattered buildings of the ranch awaited, almost hiding in a grove of oak trees.

My host had given me a quick tour of the eight guesthouses and the main building before depositing me at my own quarters, which were outfitted with a liquor cart, assorted Gardner novels, a thermos bucket of ice, and an electric heater for the morning cold.

I gussied up for dinner, which Gardner did not, and found myself seated at a long, narrow, well-polished slab of wood that passed for a table. Gardner had a small army of young women (younger than he was anyway) who were live-in secretaries. At least one of them had other duties—Jean, who cooked the meal (steak with salad and baked potatoes, simple but delicious) and joined us.

I didn't read mystery novels, but I knew Della Street from TV and Jean might have been her.

This trip to California had been chiefly to see Gardner—specifically, to deliver three reels of tape recordings and other materials from a polygraph examination of Sam Sheppard's two brothers and their wives that I had supervised at the John E. Reid and Associates lab back in Chicago.

I was not myself a polygraph examiner, but I'd had a longtime relationship with one of the machine's inventors, the late Leonarde Keeler. Gardner and Keeler had both been part of the Harry Oakes investigation in Nassau, a decade or so ago. That was one of the famous cases that put my business, the A-1 Detective Agency, on the map.

And frankly I was fairly famous myself by now, with articles in *Life* and *Look*, as well as the true detective magazines, for whom I sometimes wrote up my cases. Well, we in the trade call them "jobs," but the public who bought Gardner's mysteries—*The Case of the This*, and *The Case of the That*—had long ago made their choice.

That minor-celebrity fame, and a friendship born in Nassau, where Gardner had been covering the Oakes murder for Hearst, got me roped into being an investigator for the so-called Court of Last Resort. Pro bono work, but the publicity was good. More newspaper and magazine articles for Nate Heller meant more business for the A-1, which now had Los Angeles and New York branches; home base was in the Monadnock Building in the South Loop.

I didn't share this ulterior motive with Gardner, who was a millionaire book writer and could afford to be philanthropic. He kept on filling the paperback racks with his novels, plus had the Mason TV show going with Raymond Burr, who got courtroom confessions on a weekly basis. I bet Gardner's weekly take was even more impressive. A Court of Last Resort series was coming soon, too.

Most people understood the premise of the Court—a bunch of experts—ex-cops, criminologists, lawyers, private detectives—looked into credible claims from men behind bars who felt they'd been wrongfully convicted. But the Court wasn't some bustling legal office where, in some posh suite, specialists in crime-solving gathered in conference before polishing their magnifying glasses and scattering to balance the scales of justice.

No.

It was basically a monthly column by Gardner in *Argosy*, a men's magazine of the guns and cars variety. Me, I preferred *Playboy*, but that I kept to myself also. The editor/publisher of the magazine, a longtime pal of Gardner's, funded the expenses for the public defender–type work of the experts and investigators who did the author's bidding by phone and telegram.

And, like I said, I was one of them. In a way I didn't mind, because it got me back out into the field. The A-1 had grown so big lately that I really was the "President" I'd claimed to be in 1932 on the door of my one-room office on the fourth floor at Van Buren and Plymouth over a speakeasy. I'd been the only employee and slept there, too, on a Murphy bed. Now I was mostly supervising and doing PR, sleeping in a double bed in my modern townhouse, thank you very much, not always alone.

The trouble with the Good Old Days is you don't know when you're in them.

If you've done the math, you should know that the storied private detective seated opposite Erle Stanley Gardner was not a kid. I was in fact a well-preserved fifty or so, some gray at the temples of my reddish brown hair, six feet and two hundred pounds and handsome enough to play myself in the movies, though that had never come up.

And they were going to fictionalize me on the Court of Last Resort TV show. Meaning any money I got for it would be fictional, too.

"So what did you think of the Sheppards?" Gardner asked, as he rocked slightly in his swivel chair, periodically puffing at his pipe.

The desk was a massive mahogany thing edged with cowboy knickknacks, an anomaly in the knotty-pine space with its Indian rugs on the floor and Western paraphernalia on the walls—knives and spears and guns and ropes and framed pulp magazine paintings. Countless reference books crowded built-in shelves and a Dictaphone machine hugged the desk like a frightened time traveler.

I was lounging in an overstuffed leather chair I'd pulled around, an ankle on a knee.

"The middle brother seems to be in charge," I said. "Both brothers are articulate, though Steve—brother number two—is more intense. Richard is there for the family, cool, quiet, a cheroot smoker. Steve is there for his brother Sam."

"Some say they're aloof," Gardner said.

"I can see that. To me, I'd call it guarded. Your experts—Hanscom, Snyder, Gregory, Reid himself—say the whole damn clan passed with flying colors. Wives and all."

Perhaps I should mention the small menagerie in attendance, a sort of ad hoc jury, milling about (when they weren't lounging on sofas and comfy chairs like mine), were various dogs, of the stray variety, looking like Rin Tin Tin's illegitimate offsprings; also a chipmunk, who could roam the desk at will, where right now were piled the tapes and original graphs of the polygraph exams, plus a list of the questions asked and answered.

"The chance that all four Sheppards could deceive experts like this," Gardner said, absently scratching the chipmunk's neck, "is about one in a million."

I shrugged. "If that. But people *have* done it."

With the pipe in hand, he waved that off, making a trail of smoke. "Not with experts like these. And not with a psychological hotshot like yourself looking on."

I sipped a rum and Coke I'd been provided by Jean, who had since disappeared. "I appreciate that vote of confidence. But that doesn't make a polygraph test admissible in court."

"In the Court of Last Resort, it does," he said, with a confident squint. He was a lawyer himself, and back in his criminal defense days, that must have been the look he trained on witnesses he was out to spook.

I grinned. "The court of Gardner, you mean."

"The court of public opinion! My cynical friend, the polygraph is a scientific instrument. Does its job like a camera does its. A piss-poor photographer will give you a lousy picture. A top-notch polygraph operator will give you a *real* picture . . . and we used the best four in the country."

A little dog hopped into my lap. When I got over being startled, I said, "What the hell kind of canine is this? Or is it a fox?"

"It's not a dog, or a fox. It's a coyote. A runty little one. But you can pet him like a dog. Name is Bravo."

I petted it and the damn thing purred or something.

Gardner was right, of course, about the polygraph (I was careful never to refer to it as a "lie detector" in his crusty presence). The graph the machine made showed respiratory variations, as well as blood pressure, pulse, and skin resistance.

"You can't beat the polygraph," Gardner said, relighting his pipe with a kitchen match. "Unless you're a psychopath. But you *can* beat the operator. Only, not *these* four."

"Agreed." I flipped a hand. "But what have you proven? Nobody ever suspected any of *those* Sheppards of murder."

He sat forward and pointed the tip of his pipe at me like it was a .38. "No, but they've been suspected of covering up for Dr. Sam. To have helped him conceal evidence . . . or remove it. To have exaggerated his injuries so he could be whisked away to the nearby family hospital and dope him up so he couldn't be properly interrogated."

I nodded toward the pile of tapes and graphs and such on his desk. The chipmunk, finding them of no particular interest, jumped down and scampered off somewhere.

"All that stuff says they didn't do anything of the kind," I said. "Also shows that all four, wives included, believe in Sam Sheppard's innocence. How about you, Erle? Do *you* think he's innocent?"

Gardener thought about that. Bravo the miniature coyote on my lap watched its master as if in anticipation of his response.

"I think he deserves a better hearing," Gardner said finally, "than he got. Now, I'm not saying he didn't have a fair trial. That the jury didn't do their best to be careful and impartial, despite all the publicity. His lawyer hasn't been able to get the verdict set aside, you know."

That was how the case had become the baby of the Court of Last Resort—all other options seemed closed to Sam Sheppard.

"General opinion," I said, "was that he did it."

"At the time," Gardner said with a nod. "But a steady stream of letters from those who feel otherwise have poured in to *Argosy* and editor Harry Steeger, and directly to me, as well. A sizeable public out there feels the widespread publicity *did* adversely affect the outcome."

"People also voted for Adlai Stevenson. That doesn't make him president."

"And others," he said, ignoring that, "including a good number of attorneys, feel the evidence—almost entirely circumstantial, by the way—was not sufficient to prove Dr. Sam guilty beyond a reasonable doubt. And that's the standard required in our courts."

"Fine," I said, after a sigh and another sip of rum and Coke, "but now it's in your lap. If you have any questions about what's on those tapes, or the other material, I'll be in L.A. for the rest of the month. You can catch me at the Beverly Hills Hotel."

The squint was gone but the friendly smile worried me almost as much. "Well," he said, with a tiny shrug, "I know you have to check in with the A-1 branch there, time to time."

"There will be some of that. But I'm also planning to pry my son loose from my ex-wife and have a little fun. We haven't been to Disneyland yet."

"How old is Sam now?"

"Eight." Like he was interested.

Now he got a sly look going, with a pipe stuck in it, puffing away like the Little Engine That Could.

"Did you really think, Nate, that all I had in mind was recruiting you as a delivery boy?"

Bravo jumped down, sensing trouble.

I said, "Well, one can always hope."

The sly look disappeared and something as grave as the expression on a judge, about to pronounce a sentence of death, came over the pudgy face. "Do I have to tell you that the polygraph test we *really* need our four experts to administer is of Sam Sheppard himself?"

"It's the obvious next step," I said. I wiggled a forefinger at him. "But that sounds like where *you* come in."

He nodded. What is it about a nod from a guy puffing a pipe that gives it extra weight?

"I have to approach the warden where Dr. Sam is incarcerated," he said, "to request the test. He's likely to say no—he wouldn't want every prisoner in the place to start asking for such testing— but that's where I have to start."

"Then what? The governor?"

Another weighty nod. "The governor of the great state of Ohio is almost certainly where we'll end up. He can make it happen."

"Frankly, Erle, I'm not sure I see where you're going. Like I said, lie tests are inadmissible. Remember?"

"Of that I'm well aware. But if Sheppard passes, then the Court of Last Resort will throw all its resources at the case. And, remember—

in a situation like this, it's the public who ultimately pushes the legal system into doing the right thing."

"The *real* Court of Last Resort."

He jabbed the air with the pipe tip, putting a period on my sentence. "Precisely. Of course, it would be nice to have something to back up these polygraph results."

"Such as?"

"Some fresh investigatory results."

Which was where *I* came in.

"You want me to go to Cleveland," I said, "and dig into this thing."

He smiled just a little. It was disarmingly boyish coming from such a grandfatherly type. "Why, are you volunteering, Nate? Don't you have enough crime on your hands already?"

"Don't you?"

The boyish look left. "I'm not some commanding officer, who tells a man to volunteer. I understand you're busy, and this is pro bono work, much of it coming out of your own pocket."

I waved that off. "No, I volunteer, all right."

That made him blink. Not an easy thing to do with this guy. "You *do*? I was expecting to have to do some arm-twisting."

"Actually, Erle," I said, regretting only a postponement of the Disneyland visit with my son, "I've been interested in this thing from the start."

Another blink! "Really?" he asked. "Why is that?"

I shrugged. Two dogs, a chipmunk and a coyote looked at me, intrigued. "The murder happened in the early morning hours of July 4, 1954—correct?"

"Correct."

I shrugged. "Well, I was there."

"Where?"

"Cleveland. But to be specific, I was in that house—the *murder house*—later that morning."

Gardner's eyebrow climbed.

"Nate," he said, "if I were writing this? This is where I'd end the chapter."

CHAPTER

In years to come Cleveland would be known as "the Mistake on the Lake," but in July 1954 it was still "the Best Location in the Nation."

The latter designation had been coined in 1944 by a PR guy working for the Cleveland Electric Illuminating Company, in a longer, uncapitalized version that included "for many industries." The Cleveland papers trimmed the slogan to what was a familiar one for years—especially in the early 1950s, as the seventh-largest city in the United States enjoyed an economic boom fueled by such civic projects as a rapid transit system, a lakefront airport and a thousand miles of street and highway lighting. Flourishing fossil fuels, steel and textiles, with exports racking up record sales, turned Cleveland into one of the world's great industrial centers.

In 1947 my friend Eliot Ness ran for mayor of Cleveland. He'd been a popular and highly publicized public safety director there in the '30s, in charge of the police and fire departments, youngest in the nation to hold such a post, continuing a kick-the-door-down crime-busting style he'd begun in Chicago as one of the key feds who put Al Capone away. But that hadn't kept him from getting his butt handed to him in the 1947 mayoral race.

In 1944, he left law enforcement to be chairman of the board of Diebold; soon he and his third wife, Betty, were living among other business executives in Bratenahl, an exclusive area on the east side of Cleveland. When I visited him ten years later, he was still on the east side, but in a modest bungalow on Ford Avenue. He'd been shown the door by Diebold in '51 and, since then, his fortunes could be said to have fallen.

He'd been doing whatever it took to support his wife and son—electronics parts wholesaler, bookstore clerk, and frozen hamburger salesman.

"This is going to be the next big thing," Eliot said.

He was talking about home alarm systems, which he was hoping to get the Cleveland police to help him promote. We were sitting at the kitchen table in his small house, which was crowded with the expensive contemporary furnishings of his former spacious digs. The glass-topped dining room table and its chairs were white wrought iron and looked like money.

Wife Betty was a good cook and vivacious hostess, a lovely apple-cheeked dark-haired gal who wore a crisp yellow-and-white dress as she served us up. She had a certain elegance about her, and seemed to adore Eliot. But I noticed a tiny frown that disappeared as quickly as it came, when Eliot spoke with enthusiasm of this latest "big thing."

Eliot may not have shared his wife's elegance, but he still dressed well: dark tailored suit, light-color tie snugged in place, hair trimmed and neat. But the man sitting across from me was not the lean lawman I'd known so well in Chicago, twenty years ago. His puffy face might have belonged to a man of sixty-five. He was about fifty.

I was staying in the guest room of the three-bedroom house. Eliot had asked me to come. He had called me at my A-1 office in Chicago and invited me for a visit.

The voice I knew so well said, "Come celebrate the Fourth with Betty and Bobby and me."

It was July second.

"Can it wait? I was flying out today to see my son."

"You tell me. I have news about our friend in Sandusky."

I said, "See you tomorrow."

Our friend in the Sandusky Soldiers and Sailors Home was one Lloyd Watterson, the so-called "Mad Butcher of Kingsbury Run," the Jack the Ripper of Cleveland in the '30s. Eliot and I had caught him, and subjected him to Leonarde Keeler's lie detector; but Lloyd's influential father had pressured the then public safety director to allow a quiet institutional commitment rather than a highly public arrest and trial.

Years later we learned Watterson had been signed in voluntarily, and was taking holidays that sometimes seemed to include murder. One of these was a famous one in Los Angeles that I had worked, calling in Eliot to stop the Butcher again, and return him to a padded cell. With Lloyd's father now deceased, these homicidal holidays should have stopped.

Apparently they hadn't.

But Eliot hadn't said a word about why he'd invited me since I'd arrived by car late afternoon. We enjoyed his lovely wife's company—their adopted son, an eight-year-old in glasses, was shy—and Eliot and I spent the evening in his tiny study, listening on the radio to the Indians beat the White Sox five to four, while Betty and Bobby watched television in the living room.

There was no Cleveland/Chicago rivalry between Eliot and me, because I was strictly a fight fan—both baseball and football left me cold. My host, however, was an all-around sports fiend—I was convinced he'd gone to the University of Chicago chiefly for the football tickets.

Through all this he said not a word about the Butcher.

When the game was over, I followed Eliot into the living room where he told Betty he and I were going out for a few drinks to "talk some business." She merely smiled and returned her gaze to the TV. A movie was on—*Strange Holiday*, appropriately enough. Bobby was already off to bed.

This was the University Circle area, near Case Western Reserve University and various museums and parks, with a lagoon bordering a long parkway. We had to drive a while, in Eliot's 1950 dark blue Ford convertible, to find a bar. I had to smile when we turned onto Mayfield Road to do so—Eliot had run a good share of the old Mayfield Road Mob out of town back in his public safety days.

The little working-class joint was hopping—Saturday night with July Fourth around the corner. The cigarette smoke hung like London fog and a jukebox gave out with "Sh-Boom," to which younger couples were slowly rock-and-rolling.

We got lucky and snagged a booth in back to tuck into. A pretty, pretty bored waitress took our orders—a rum and Coke for me, and a Manhattan for Eliot, "With Cutty Sark, please." When the drinks came and we'd sampled them, Eliot reached into his inside coat pocket and withdrew a handful of what appeared to be postcards.

"You may recall," he said, "me telling you, some years ago, that I got the occasional taunting missive from our friend Lloyd Watterson."

"I do."

"Well, they've started again."

He spread them out before me, five postcards, like a demented poker hand. One—addressed to "Eliot. Am. Big. U-Ness" at the Union Commerce Building, where he kept his office—had a pasted-on newspaper clipping of an advertisement for five pansy plants for twenty-five cents with an oddly sinister floral image and printed remarks about "good cheer" and "spring."

More overtly sinister was a card with a clipped ad for *Handbook for Poisoners*, and a message about Eliot's "paranoidal nemesis" catching up with him one day. Another, from "your mental defective," was mostly a clipping of a rustic comedian in a tugged-down hat sticking out his tongue.

A card with no pasted-on image was addressed to "Eliot Direct-Um Ness," with rambling thoughts about "the eminence of the Reaper" and seeing Eliot in an appeals court one day (though there had never been a trial). A photo from the recent film *Riot in Cell Block 11* depicted two angry prisoners behind bars on a card addressed to "Eliot (Head-Man) Ness," a grisly joke since the Butcher's victims were often left headless.

One *Cell Block 11* prisoner was actor Neville Brand, who like Audie Murphy was a highly decorated soldier in World War II; Brand would one day memorably play Al Capone on *The Untouchables* TV show.

Of course neither of us knew that; it was in the future—five years from now.

I asked, "Has Betty seen these?"

He nodded. "Since these came to me at work, I considered withholding them. But, damnit—she has a *right* to know. These are threats to our family! I've played them down, but . . ."

I was sorting through, reading them. "Nothing here that would impress the police."

"Nothing at all."

"But as long as he's locked up good and tight—"

"He isn't."

"Hell you say."

Eliot sighed as he gathered the cards up and tucked them away. "You'll recall I got Lloyd committed to a veterans hospital in Michigan, after we coraled him in L.A. But about a year later, I've learned, he was back at the Soldiers and Sailors Home. And with his father dead, he can sign himself out."

"Any indication he might be up to his old tricks?"

My friend's nod came slow. "One recent murder here in town has the Butcher's fingerprints . . . but not literal ones . . . all over it—last year, a body cut up exactly like the torso victims turned up on the East Side."

"The East Side as in . . . *this* East Side? The where-you-live East Side?"

He gulped some of his Manhattan, then nodded again. "A vacant lot within walking distance of my place. Witnesses reported seeing a man matching Watterson's description near the crime scene."

I swirled my glass of rum and Coke. "We should have buried him in the desert like I said."

"You're telling me."

Doris Day was singing "Secret Love" on the jukebox and couples were clutching to it. You could have sliced the smoke in here and sold it for bacon.

I sighed. "So what do we do about it? We kind of lost our chance back in L.A."

"I still have some standing in this town, and you've got a national reputation in the detective business. We request an audience with the director of Soldiers and Sailors and make our case that Lloyd be recommitted, with no ability to sign himself out. I have a couple of Cleveland dicks who will join us."

I was already nodding. "Sign me up."

A smile twitched on Eliot's lips. I could see the old warhorse still in there somewhere.

Then the smile vanished and he said, "But, uh . . . nothing to Betty about this, at least not till we arrange a hearing. I don't want her getting tied up in knots over it."

He had drained his glass.

"You know," he said, "I could use another drink."

My glass was empty, too. "You know, so could I."

The plan had been to sleep in, so when Eliot shook me gently awake in his guest room, what I said was, "What the hell time is it?"

"Quarter to seven."

"Little early for fireworks, isn't it?"

"Apparently not. Get dressed. There's been a murder."

My first thought, typically cynical, was in a town Cleveland's size, there's always a murder. But Eliot's grave expression made saying that out loud inadvisable.

"Suit and tie," he said, as he went out.

So this wasn't an early morning holiday event.

When I got to the kitchen, he had coffee going and was writing something, leaning over the counter to do so. Looking over his shoulder, I saw he was leaving Betty a note that he'd be back soon but not to wait breakfast.

We both threw down some coffee and then were in the Ford convertible. We seemed to be heading downtown, but I was no expert on Cleveland geography. The open air was riffling our hair, hats on the backseat floor so as not to blow away. It was early enough to be almost cool. Traffic was light—people were in church or just lazing around till parades and hot dogs and firecrackers kicked in.

"Remember that little cottage Edna and I lived in?" he asked, in what seemed a non sequitur.

Edna had been wife number one. She'd been his secretary in Chicago days.

"On Lake Erie? Your pal Chamberlin rented it for you, right?"

"Right. A woman's been brutally murdered in the house next door, just west of there. Past that park."

"Jesus. Anyone you know?"

He shook his head. "I knew the people who lived there before this young Sheppard couple and their boy moved in."

A sick feeling came over me. ". . . Is it the Butcher?"

"That's one reason we're taking a look. All I know is it's a savage thing—butchery if not the Butcher."

"Last I looked," I said, lifting an eyebrow, talking over the wind the Ford was rustling up, "you weren't a cop anymore."

He gave me a quick sideways glance. "You remember Frank Cullitan?"

"Sure. Prosecutor you worked with. He was in on the Harvard Club raid."

"Right, and plenty else. Well, he's still county prosecutor, has been for all this time. He asked me to have a look at the crime scene."

We drove a while, or anyway Eliot did. When we got to the downtown, I think I saw tumbleweed blowing through.

I said, "Bay Village is its own suburb. What's Cullitan got to do with it?"

"As county prosecutor, he's got jurisdiction, if he wants it. And the local police chief called for help. There are fifty-nine suburbs and that many little departments. Bay Village has a force of five."

"Sounds like the makings of a real bureaucratic stew."

"And not a bit tasty," he said. "Nate, we're strictly ex officio here, doing a little observing for Cullitan."

"Fine by me. I'm not in Cleveland looking for work."

We were about halfway to our destination—Bay Village was sixteen miles west of downtown. With its eight-thousand-some, mostly affluent residents, Bay Village sat on a bluff high above Lake Erie, houses often facing the beach below, which was narrow but nonetheless convenient for swimming and boating.

I asked Eliot, "Does Cullitan call you in like this often?"

He shook his head. "Only now and then. Frank's been keeping me posted about any crimes that have the smell of the Butcher on them."

"He thinks this is a new torso victim?"

"He didn't know much more than I've already told you. But he said Gerber is on his way to the scene, and he may want me to keep an eye on our estimable coroner."

That was about as close as Eliot came to bad-mouthing anyone he'd worked for or with. But I knew Dr. Samuel Gerber, Cuyahoga County coroner, was someone who'd rubbed Safety Director Ness the wrong way during the original Mad Butcher investigation.

A little man with a big voice, Gerber had been coroner since 1937. He'd arrived during the height of the torso killings and began spouting off to the press, giving public lectures on the case, and writing articles about it, for *True Detective* magazine among others. This was exactly at the time Ness and his chief assistant Robert Chamberlin were doing their best to tamp down public panic.

A Democrat, Gerber was as political as nominal Republican Eliot was not. The coroner stayed readily available to the boys of Cleveland's three daily newspapers with quotes, tips and even scoops. He was a one-man PR machine who often took reporters out to dinner.

"If Gerber is interested enough to spend a holiday on this," Eliot said, hands tight on the steering wheel, "he must think it's something big."

"Like a Butcher victim?"

Eliot shrugged. "Cullitan doesn't know. But he wants my take on it."

The spacious backyards of the Bay Village homes were more like front yards, with lovely trees and well-tended lawns, facing the two-lane highway, Lake Road, where we now cruised.

"We're looking for 28944," Eliot said. "Sheppard residence."

As we glided along the lakefront neighborhood, we were in an idyllic *Father Knows Best* world, dads with good jobs, moms who were happy homemakers, kids, dogs. On this early Fourth of July morning, the members of these households would be snug in their wee little beds, God in His heaven, all's right with the world.

So it seemed, at least, until we neared 28944 Lake Road, where a crowd of neighborhood gawkers milled on the lawn among the maples and an old elm, some rubberneckers in bathrobes and slippers, with uniformed officers here and there looking over-whelmed. Patrol cars, an ambulance and various other vehicles crowded into the driveway and along the road. Everybody was staring at the sprawling two-story white Dutch Colonial house as if it were on fire.

We parked in front of a cemetery several houses to the west. Neither of us reclaimed our hats from the backseat, a nice breeze coming off the lake, the sky clear. Lovely day. For a murder.

We made our way through the bathrobe-and-slippers brigade to the front door, or anyway the back door that served as one. Standing on the cement slab porch with a two-pillar overhang were a young uniformed officer, maybe in his mid-twenties, and a heavyset guy with baggy eyes and a baggy suit.

Eliot had an honorary Public Safety Department badge he could flash, and he did, saying, "County Prosecutor Cullitan sent me."

The young cop, a handsome kid, said, "You can go on in."

"Just a second," the older man said. He had heavy black eyebrows and a chin or two to spare. "Let me have a look at that."

Eliot showed it to him.

"Eliot Ness," the lumpy guardian-at-the-gate said, obviously impressed. "I'm Marsh Dodge—mayor of Bay Village. Also public safety director myself."

They shook hands.

"This is my friend Nate Heller," Eliot said, nodding to me, "the well-known investigator. He's visiting from Chicago and I asked him along."

Dodge beamed in hale-fellow-well-met fashion. "Well, that's fine! Fred here—Officer Drenkhan—was first on the scene, if you'd like a word. Really, I guess *I* was *really* first on the scene . . . live just down the street. Sam called me, and Mildred and I came right over." He shook his head, shuddered. "Hell of a thing."

"We don't know anything," Eliot said, "except that there's been a brutal murder of a young woman. The wife, is it?"

Dodge nodded somberly. "Marilyn. Lovely girl in every way. We were friends, the Sheppards and Mildred and me. I was the first person Sam thought of to call."

He seemed a little proud of it.

I asked, "When was this?"

"Early. About twenty till six. Still dark. We drove over here, the wife and I, even though we're only a few houses down. I've had a bum leg since I was a kid."

The young cop put in, "I was here by a little after six. Dr. Sam was kind of half sitting, half reclining on a red leather chair in his den. He told me he heard his wife scream and remembered going upstairs, of fighting on the stairs, of waking up in the water, and going back upstairs. None of it tied together. I didn't know what to make of it. He didn't say anything after. He was holding onto his neck like it hurt. Face looked like he'd been hit. He was in trousers but no shirt."

I said, "You call him 'Dr. Sam' . . . ?"

Dodge answered for the young cop. "Sam Sheppard's an os-teopath, a surgeon. His family runs a hospital about a mile from here—Bay View. Father and two brothers are osteopaths, too. Very successful."

Eliot nodded toward the house. "Is 'Dr. Sam' inside?"

"No," the cop said. "His brothers, Richard and Steve, they came right away."

"I called Richard," Dodge said. "He was the one who declared Marilyn dead. Then he and Steve hustled Sam to the hospital for treatment and observation."

"Hustled?" Eliot said, with a frown. "Were they trying to get him away from the authorities? And into the family hospital?"

Drenkhan said, "They cleared it with Chief Eaton. Chief's around here somewhere. It's been a madhouse! People in and out. Neighbors and friends and reporters and photographers, and even some little kid who wanted to make sure he got his turtle back."

Eliot and I said, *"What?"*

The cop nodded. "Yeah, he went up and got it out of Chip's room."

Eliot frowned. "Chip?"

"The Sheppard boy. He slept through everything. The murder. The comings and goings this morning. Didn't even wake up when the kid retrieved his turtle. Chip's uncle Richard carried him down and got him out of here, right before they took Dr. Sam to the hospital."

A voice cut through the crowd: *"Excuse me! Coming through!"*

In a crisp summer suit and a straw fedora with a checkered band, a pocket hanky in his breast pocket, dapper little Samuel Gerber moved through the crowd, a knife through warm butter. Gray-haired, his glasses rimless, a tie pin holding his already neat four-in-hand in place, the county coroner strode toward us like Judgment Day in a five-foot-three package.

When Eliot and I turned toward him, he broke his stride momentarily, and when he started back up, it was more an amble. Then he came to a stop like a car that almost ran a light.

Hands on his hips, he gazed up at Eliot. The cement landing gave us a foot on him, and he looked like a well-dressed Munchkin.

"Well, Mr. Ness," Gerber said. "What brings you here?"

"Frank Cullitan asked me to size up the scene. Hope you don't mind, Dr. Gerber."

Their profound dislike for each other was plastered over with polite smiles and respectful appellations.

Gerber turned his sharp gaze on me. "You're Heller, right? Been a while."

I had done a few jobs for Eliot in Cleveland in the '30s; for a while, the department had been so corrupt, calling in outsiders like me had been a necessity. So Gerber and I knew each other a little. But not enough for him to call me "Nate," or "Heller" minus a "mister," for that matter.

But I decided to have more class than this little shit.

"Nice to see you again, Dr. Gerber," I said. "I'm tagging along with Eliot. Just happened to be visiting an old friend."

"Well, I'm not sure I can approve you joining us inside," he said to me. "It's a crime scene, after all. Closed off."

The young cop chimed in. "Oh, uh, we haven't closed the house off, Doctor."

I managed not to laugh as Gerber frowned. It was eight A.M. and this had been a crime scene for over two hours and hadn't been sealed off yet.

"Sir," the young cop said awkwardly, "I was the first responder. Perhaps you'd like me to fill you in."

"Well, that would be a start."

Drenkhan did so, quickly, efficiently.

"Where do you have this doctor?" Gerber asked testily. "Please tell me you have a man watching him."

Dodge answered for the young cop, saying, "Well, he isn't here. His brothers came and said he needed immediate treatment. They took off to Bay View Hospital for—"

"You allowed our best suspect to be spirited away to that

family's excuse for a hospital? Before he could be properly questioned?"

"Chief Eaton cleared it," Dodge said lamely.

Drenkhan, perhaps realizing he'd stepped in it, said to the coroner, "I'm sorry we haven't known how exactly to handle this. I'm the one who called this in to the Cleveland PD. I knew this was too big for us. We haven't had a homicide in Bay Village in eleven years! And that was way before my time."

Gerber, seldom speechless, didn't know what to say to that.

Eliot said, "Dr. Gerber, I would like Nate here to accompany us. You probably know he's an investigator of some national repute."

Gerber drew in a breath, then apparently decided this wasn't a battle worth fighting, particularly since everybody and his duck still had access to this place.

The little coroner took the lead and then we were inside, in a hallway with closets to the left and a wall to the right. Toward the far end of the hall, a runner seemed to lead to a black leather medical case, upended, yawning open, much of its contents scattered—prescription pads, vials, blood pressure sleeve, stethoscope.

A little bird-like woman in a yellow T-shirt, pedal pushers and sandals introduced herself as Mildred Dodge, playing hostess at this Fourth of July party. She showed us through the kitchen to the living room. This was just the opposite of Eliot's small house with so much furniture crammed in; the Sheppard home was large but sparsely furnished, if with attractive antiques.

Mrs. Dodge positioned herself like a sentry at the bottom of the three steps up to the landing and the stairs, blocking the way. Then she pointed up there and said, "It isn't pretty."

She stood aside and, Gerber in the lead, we went up, leaving her at her post.

The bedroom was to our right and we stepped in gingerly, arranging ourselves along the foot of the nearest of two wooden non-canopy four-poster twin beds. We kept at as much of a respectful distance as possible. Just behind us in the corner was a rocking chair with some clothes on it—white shorts, bra, a sweater slung over the back; on the floor nearby were white panties and some white moccasin slippers and a pair of blue tennis shoes. Between the twin beds was a small nightstand with a phone and clock; over at our right against a wall was a dresser. The other twin bed had its quilt and covers turned invitingly down. The shades were drawn. Nothing here seemed to have been touched.

Except the woman on the bed.

And Mrs. Dodge had been right: it wasn't pretty. More like something out of Hieronymus Bosch.

Marilyn Sheppard lay on her back, the top of her wreathed in red on the blood-soaked bed, head to one side as if she were looking at us as we entered, only her face was not really a face anymore, just a blur of clotted blood, her skull battered from a welter of savage blows. Her legs dangled over the foot of the bed, at the knees, as if she'd been pulled up, perhaps caught under the wooden foot rail. Her top was pulled exposing her breasts, her midriff exposed, too, seemingly untouched, but the rest of her was naked, though draped by a sheet, her pajama bottoms pulled off of one leg and bunched at the knee. Bruises on her forearms and hands, and broken fingernails, said she'd fought back. The walls bore so much blood, sent flying there, it might have been a modernistic wall-paper design.

Gerber approached the corpse. He had a look, but soon turned and nodded to us to leave, which was fine with me. The coroner wore a naturally pallid look. But right now so did Eliot, and I'd wager so did I.

On the first floor, the daybed against the staircase had a neatly folded corduroy jacket on it. This immediately caught the coroner's attention.

Gerber made a disgusted face. "This 'doctor' woke up to screams, and ran to his wife—but first folded his jacket?"

A Cleveland police officer came over and told Gerber a man from the fingerprint unit had arrived. The coroner went over to deal with that while Eliot and I conferred.

"Not the Butcher," I said.

"No. *A* butcher . . . but not *the* butcher. The poor woman was hit twenty or thirty times. But did you notice? Her skull wasn't crushed—just gashes, crescent-shaped, made while someone tried to . . . obliterate her face."

I frowned. "She was naked from the waist down. Rape, you think? Attempted rape that enraged the attacker, turning him into a madman?"

"Possible." Eliot let out a deep sigh. "A madman or someone who really hated her."

"She may have got in a few good licks, judging by her arms. Good for her."

He nodded.

Gerber was coming over. "I'm taking a look at the beach. Care to join me? This 'doctor' supposedly fought the intruder, presumably all the way down there . . . since that's where he says he woke up."

"Lead the way," Eliot said.

The yard was only thirty feet deep till the slope of the bluff cut it off. Wooden steps through the thick brush and tall grass descended to a platform with a modest bathhouse, then a shorter staircase jogged down from there to a narrow strip of beach, maybe four feet wide. Gerber started down the steps, at a quick pace, though like us he was easily fifty.

As we took our sweet time, I whispered to Eliot, "What's that odd English he puts on the ball every time he says 'doctor?'"

"Oh, like a lot of medics, Gerber has a thing about osteopaths. To him they're not real doctors."

At the bottom of the second, shorter flight of stairs, we were on the very narrow beach, waves rolling in gently.

"If the good doctor," Gerber said, quietly acid, "struggled with the killer here on the beach, where are the signs of it?"

Eliot said, "Erased, possibly. It can get choppy out here at night, even this time of year. Wind off the bluff howls, and in the moonlight you can see the whitecaps. Thirty-, forty-foot waves can break on this beach."

Gerber gave him a look.

A little embarrassed, Eliot said, "I used to live next door, with the park between. My wife and I walked this beach many times, in all kinds of weather."

His first wife.

Right now the picture Eliot had painted seemed absurd, the sky still clear, the morning cool. That would change, and the day would heat up; but now it was as idyllic as the life the Sheppards seemed to have been living.

I said to Gerber, "How about those?"

I was pointing to footprints in the sand, close to where the bluff rose, heading west. The right foot seemed to have a heavier tread.

Gerber bent over to have a look. "Well, *that's* no damn struggle. And none of those are deep enough to make plaster impressions. I'll get some pictures taken." He looked around, squinting behind the rimless glasses. "See any sign of a T-shirt ripped off in the so-called struggle? He was bare-chested, Officer Drenkhan said."

"No," Eliot said, and I shook my head in agreement.

Gerber grunted. "Let's head back up."

We did.

The coroner toured the first floor and we were allowed to tag along. Two Cleveland homicide dicks had shown up while we were beach-combing, and they fell in on either side of Gerber. Beaky, narrow-faced Bob Schottke was a veteran detective in his mid-thirties, his boyish oval-faced partner, Patrick Gareau, noticeably younger.

The living room, otherwise undisturbed, had a desk whose top two drawers were emptied out, the lower drawers pulled out halfway. Stacked in the den were five desk drawers, one emptied out. A green metal box had been tipped over, spilling tools and a woman's wristwatch. Several shotguns were leaned against one wall, unsecured.

Gerber's disgusted expression underscored his assessment: "Staged. No real burglary is this neat, this careful."

"Usually," Schottke said, "the place is trashed. Ransacked."

Gareau said, "That medical bag, sitting on its end like that? How do you drop something and have it land so perfect?"

I said, "What about the broken sports trophies in the study?"

Schottke said, "Just an afterthought. To make it look good."

"*Sam Sheppard* did this," Gerber said to the homicide dicks. "Open-and-shut case. I'll go over to that sham hospital and get a confession out of him. Meantime, you two stick here and supervise . . . start by sealing off the goddamn house."

Then Gerber turned to Eliot and me. "I'm going to have to ask you to leave, Mr. Ness—I hope you've seen enough to satisfy the county prosecutor." He said nothing to me.

Just then, the fingerprint man came up and said, "No signs of forcible entry, so far anyway."

Gerber grunted. "Doesn't surprise me. Of course, these suburban types don't even lock their doors. Sheppard'll use that to say there *was* a break-in."

As we headed out, I said to Eliot, "Maybe after this you can sell some of those alarm systems out here."

"This isn't how I hoped to build a business."

Mrs. Dodge, who was near the steps to the landing, talking to a dark-haired teenage boy, smiled and nodded to us as we passed. *Thank you for coming!*

Outside the crowd hadn't thinned any. We edged through and strolled to the Ford.

"Gerber's going to railroad that poor son of a bitch," I said. "I didn't see a damn thing in there that wasn't circumstantial evidence at its thinnest."

"Agreed," Eliot said.

We'd been driving in silence for a while, heading back, when I said, "Somebody ought to do something about that smug little prick."

"Gerber? Well, at least he's pinning it on the right man."

"What? How can you say that?"

Eliot shrugged. "It's a typical domestic homicide. Crime committed at home, a spontaneous act. Victim's body isn't concealed.

Death made to look like it's part of a robbery or rape. Partial removal of victim's clothing, but victim rarely left completely naked. Victim positioned to suggest a sexual assault's occurred. Real offender receives nonlethal injuries. Crime is reported to a friend or neighbor. Blunt force trauma, usually to head and particularly the face. Straight out of the FBI manual, Nate."

"Maybe. But I still say Gerber's a smug little prick."

He didn't argue with the point.

CHAPTER 3

Eliot and I, with the help of two Cleveland police detectives who had worked the Torso Murders, were successful in arranging a hearing at the Soldiers and Sailors Home in Sandusky, Ohio, re: Lloyd Watterson. No longer would the Mad Butcher of Kingsbury Run be given free passes to commit homicide, when he was in the mood.

In some respects, this was a great success for Eliot, despite how long it took to well and truly put this maniac away. But for many years the Torso Murders would be considered his greatest failure (as it had no official outcome), far overshadowed by the efforts he and his Untouchables made battling Capone in Chicago.

A small irony, though it resonated in a large way with me, came from a phone call I received at Rancho Paisano the day after I'd relived for Perry Mason's creator my tour through the Sheppard murder house with Cleveland's former public safety director.

The call, from my friend and A-1 partner Lou Sapperstein, was to pass along the sad news about another good friend of mine.

Eliot Ness was dead.

A few days later a brief memorial service was held at a funeral home in tiny Coudersport, Pennsylvania, where Eliot Ness had been involved in the latest—the last—of his attempts to make it big in the business world. His law-and-order acumen had made him a natural to be the face of a company marketing a watermarking process designed to battle forgery and counterfeiting problems.

But the top man had been a huckster planning to leave investors holding the bag, and Eliot—recently diagnosed with heart problems—fought hard to save the company. The stress proved too much. He died on his kitchen floor, where he'd collapsed, near a bottle of Scotch he'd just bought.

I didn't attend the Coudersport service. Betty Ness told me many in the little town turned out for it—Eliot in a short time had become well known and well liked in the community.

I did go to Cleveland on May 20 for the bigger service at the Presbyterian Church of the Covenant. Betty and Bobby Ness were present as well as longtime Ness friends, including his onetime assistant, Robert Chamberlin, who had once rented him a small house on the Lake Erie shore. An honor guard from the Cleveland PD was in attendance, and the reverend spoke of Eliot's public service, courage and integrity, "his youthful and vital spirit, his warmth and understanding and his concern for people."

Did I shed a tear or two for my old friend?

It's possible.

Less than a week later, I was sitting with Flo Kilgore in a banquette in New York's famed if overrated Stork Club. I had just told her about attending Eliot's memorial service back in Ohio when she shook her head and laughed a little.

"I realize," I said, "that I'm consistently a laugh riot, but I fail—"

She raised a gloved hand. Flo and I had been friends and occasionally more than that since she was a girl reporter and I a fledgling private eye, both holed up in a small hotel in Flemington, New Jersey. I'd been there to testify at the Bruno Richard Hauptmann trial, which she was covering for Hearst.

"It's just the bittersweet irony of it," she said. "Your friend is probably about to become famous. I ran an item in my column just last week."

Flo's "Voice of Broadway" for the *New York Journal-American* was widely syndicated by King Features. Though it was mostly show-business fluff, the column occasionally got into politics and organized crime—she'd started out working the crime beat, after all.

She was saying, "That memoir of his that's coming out soon? Desilu just bought it for TV."

The Untouchables, written with sports writer Oscar Fraley, had been something of a desperation move by the money-strapped Eliot, who had never been one to boast about the Capone days, much less try to profit from them.

"Well, I hope his family makes a few bucks." I lifted my vodka gimlet. "To absent friends."

She raised her martini glass. "Absent friends," she said.

In her early forties, Flo was a pretty thing with a heart-shaped face and big blue eyes, somewhat compromised by the weak chin her ex-pal Sinatra liked to make nasty jokes about. Her hair wasn't short nor was it long, but back from her high forehead, and typically a pink hat with a cloth rose perched on it. A string of pearls caressed her neck, her trimly curvy shape shown off nicely by a black dress with a scoop neck and an absurdly large pink ribbon, like she was a package waiting to be unwrapped.

I wouldn't have minded.

"Say," I said, "didn't you cover the Sheppard murder trial?"

Her smile was pixie-ish. "Well, *there's* an icebreaker for you. You know darn well I did. It got play all over the place. Of course, after the guilty verdict, the *Cleveland News* didn't run my column about it."

"Why?"

"Oh, I said the trial was a major miscarriage of justice."

"Was it?"

She shuddered. "It's the first time I was ever scared by the jury system . . . and I mean *scared.*"

We'd already had lunch—her the chicken a la king, me the fried scallops and oysters. Not bad, but highway robbery at these prices. You could make a sawbuck disappear faster than Mandrake the Magician, tip not included.

She was narrowing her girl reporter eyes at me. "What brings the Sheppard case to mind? That's very old news."

I gave her a brief rundown on Gardner's interest in the case, and how I'd be heading back to Cleveland soon to poke around some. I was only in New York for a few days to check in with the A-1 branch in our Empire State Building suite of offices. And, of course, to see her.

She sipped her martini through a tight little smile. "To pump me, you mean."

I gestured around us to the mirrored walls and the various famous faces, bathed in the flattering low lighting. "That sounds a little dirty, for a classy joint like this."

She was lighting up a cigarette with a silver lighter that probably cost around what my first car did. "Well, if you're about to dig back into the Sheppard mess, I can give you a rundown on the trial, if you like. I was there for most of it, and when I wasn't, a stringer covered for me."

"You had to go back weekends for the show," I said.

Flo nodded. She was a regular panelist on the Sunday night game show, *What's My Line?* I would never have told her, but I found that program about as compelling as watching flypaper catch flies. If there had been anything else on worth a damn, I wouldn't have tuned in.

"Before and during that trial," she said, "the local press and radio and television *blanketed* that town with distortions and exaggerations and outright lies. You know who Louis Seltzer is?"

"Editor of the *Cleveland Press*, isn't he?"

"He is. A self-important little tyrant. He was convinced Sam Sheppard was guilty and made no secret of it. He tried that case in the pages of his paper and found for the prosecution. And, of course, where did the *real* jury come from? From the citizens of Cleveland who were already tainted by this scurrilous drivel!"

"The jury could have found Sheppard guilty of first-degree murder," I pointed out, "which likely would've meant a death sentence. They settled instead on second-degree, and life in prison."

Long lashes batted over the baby blues. "Nate, those prosecutors only proved Dr. Sam guilty of one thing—failure to keep his trousers zipped. And if every man, and woman, who committed adultery got life in prison, we'd have no room for the real criminals."

I grinned at her. "Maybe we'd get lucky and they'd put us in the same cell."

She took some smoke in and let it out. "If you'd been in that courtroom, lover, you'd know what a farce that trial was."

"So take me there."

"Where?"

"That courtroom. That trial."

All right.

It was small and ugly, those chambers, and crowded with press, which this Judge Blythin blithely allowed. He was starstruck around the likes of Bob Considine, that Scotland Yard inspector, Fabian . . . and of course, moi. Sometimes it was so noisy you couldn't hear!

When they brought the defendant in for the first time, I could tell he was working hard to maintain his dignity. He was in a dark blue suit, white shirt, black tie, black socks and shoes. Might have been going to a cocktail party. Broad-shouldered, tall, athletic-looking. Handsome but in a soft, pampered-baby way. You could see why some could say he was a ladies' man.

He didn't let the presence of the press throw him, at least not that it showed. He sat staring straight ahead as the photographers crouched or climbed on chairs to get their shots, and the newsreel boys brought their cameras around. Did all right for himself—till later, when he took the stand.

But I'm getting ahead of myself.

His brothers and their wives were always in court, very proper, very dignified. When the trial got into lurid territory, they seemed out of place, like they'd wandered in thinking this was church only to find out it was the circus.

Sheppard's attorney, Bill Corrigan, a white-haired, fatherly, almost elderly gent with a reputation as the city's leading defense lawyer, tried for a change of venue and got nowhere. The jury came from a list of seventy-five that had been made available to Cleveland's three newspapers. For a month these jurors, knowing they were in the pool, had been exposed to the press. Marilyn Sheppard wasn't the only victim who got bludgeoned—Seltzer and his competition bashed Sam Sheppard every bit as bad.

When the trial got under way, Dr. Sam sat straight and emotionless as Prosecutor Mahon, another white-haired paternal figure, told the jury how thirty-five vicious blows had ended the life of the defendant's wife. He enticed them with talk of Sharon Kern, the Bay View lab tech who'd been Dr. Sam's partner in adultery.

Then Sam's story of that terrible night was retold in a way that made it seem even more ridiculous than it was.

Oh, dear! Another martini, please! And extra olives.

The defense painted a different picture of the Kern relationship. It was over—Marilyn was pregnant, again, and so Sam had ended the affair, his wife forgiving his infidelities as he became a loving husband again. These recent months had been their happiest.

The first witness for the prosecution was Dr. Lester Adelson, the deputy coroner, a cocksure little mustached man in an askew red bow tie. He set up a screen and subjected the jury to color slides of the dead Marilyn Sheppard, pointing out and explaining her ghastly injuries. Contused abraded this, ragged lacerations that. Darling Nate, it was a horror show!

Corrigan did a number on this testimony, though, establishing the autopsy was perfunctory and error-ridden, that many tests usually conducted in homicides were skipped. And they had failed to identify the murder weapon!

The next-door neighbor that Dr. Sam called that morning—Marshall Dodge? Mayor of Bay Village, the hometown butcher? He looked terrible—tired and washed out. Skin hung on him like he'd lost weight in a hurry. His eyebrows were black and overgrown, coming to curled points like the devil in a cheap movie.

This Dodge character spoke slowly, haltingly, not recalling much of anything. Much of what he said tallied with Dr. Sam's story, but he roused

*the courtroom with the claim Dr. Richard had come down from the mur-
der scene to ask his brother, 'Did you do this, or did you have anything to
do with it?' The response had been 'Hell, no!'*

*But the notion that the defendant's own brother thought it possible
Sam had killed his wife hung like a dark cloud over the proceedings.*

*I'd interviewed Dr. Richard the week before, when he told me how
close the family was, how they worked side by side and lived close to each
other—that he knew what Sam was like, and that he was incapable of
violence.*

*Next came Dodge's scrawny wife, Mildred, who'd gone along with her
husband when Dr. Sam called saying something terrible had happened
to Marilyn. She went up to see the awful crime scene, then came down
and offered Sam a glass of whiskey, saying it might help. Sam said, 'No, I
don't want it. I can't think clearly and I have to think.'*

*Mildred said Dr. Sam complained that his neck hurt. That he'd been
hit at the top of the stairs, and then chased someone. He had a bruise over
his right eye. She put a hand on his bare shoulder to comfort him, and his
skin was dry.*

*On a note more helpful to the defense, she mentioned seeing a puddle
of water on the porch, and wet footprints on the stairs. This tallied with
Sam's story of waking up on the beach.*

*Testimony from several friends indicated Sam had been in a good,
relaxed mood on the evening of July third. That no one remembered ever
seeing a fit of temper from him, or knew him to ever strike his wife or indeed anyone. The neighborhood children considered him a hero, and the
Bay Village police knew and liked him.*

*Marilyn, on the evening before her death, had been in an upbeat mood,
having confided to friends that the couple's problems were behind them.
Her big complaint? That she wanted more furniture in the house—Sam
could be tight with a dollar—while he'd bought himself a little sports car.*

*When the Lords, their neighbor friends, left at 12:30 A.M., after a
pleasant evening with the Sheppards, Sam was sleeping on the daybed in
his corduroy jacket. Later that jacket was found neatly folded on one end
of the couch. Hearing his wife's screams, would Sam take the time to take
off his jacket and carefully fold it before going to his distressed spouse?*

Dr. Lucas Hardmann, a friend from when Sam and Marilyn had lived in California, was a houseguest who'd gone off on an overnight trip on July third, absent during the tragic events of early July Fourth. He'd once advised Sam not to send Marilyn a letter about wanting a divorce, but also said he'd never seen Sam in the company of another woman.

Visiting Dr. Sam at Bay View Hospital the day after the murder, Hardmann said his friend had burst into tears, saying, 'My God, I wish they'd killed me instead of Marilyn. Chip needs his mother more than he needs me.' The defense had to like hearing that, but prosecution witness Hardmann also reported hearing Dr. Steve say to Sam, 'Let's go over the sequence of events, so you can get your story straight.'

While he was staying with the Sheppards, Hardmann had gone out on several dates. In each case, when he returned, he found the Lake Road door unlocked. On one occasion Marilyn had told him specifically not to lock it, because the housekeeper was coming the next day.

Officer Drenkhan testified that the murder bedroom showed no sign of struggle or forcible entry—dust on the sill of a locked screen window was undisturbed. A small light in the dressing room across the way seemed to have burned all night.

Under cross, Drenkhan said that Dr. Sam, as Bay Village's unpaid police doctor, had never lost his head. That he seemed an 'honest, hard-working, even-tempered man.' While he'd seen no pedestrians patrolling the neighborhood, the officer admitted the nearby public park gave easy access from the beach.

And Drenkhan reluctantly confirmed he'd heard Cleveland police officers and Dr. Gerber himself discussing such topics as the possible sterility of Dr. Sam—calling into question Chip's parentage—and that getting a confession out of their suspect was all it would take to get a conviction.

Defense attorney Corrigan also brought out the ineptitude of the police investigation—for one thing, a cigarette butt that had been seen in the upstairs toilet bowl had disappeared. Marilyn had stopped smoking because of her pregnancy and Dr. Sam didn't smoke at all.

The bald, elderly police chief of Bay View confirmed Dr. Sam had been whisked away by his brothers shortly after police had begun to arrive. Sam's story of being robbed was called into question by the chief *stating the defendant's waterlogged wallet contained three twenty-dollar bills, three ones, a credit card and a thousand-dollar check.*

The chief confirmed earlier descriptions of the murder scene, but added a disturbing note: blood had soaked through the window drapes to stain the wood beneath.

When the chief first went down to the beach in the morning mist, he found the waves high, every third or fourth one washing across the sand. The implied question was, If Dr. Sam had been unconscious on the beach, why hadn't he drowned?

Dear! One more martini, if you please. And don't forget the extra olives!

But the real bombshell came from Coroner Gerber, who flatly said the murder instrument had been 'a two-bladed surgical instrument with teeth on the end of each blade.' The coroner claimed to see the impression of the weapon on Marilyn's bloodstained pillow. The weapon, Gerber insisted, was a plaster cast cutter, fourteen and a half inches long, of stainless steel with cutting handles and a 'powerful jaw, serrated and grooved.' Dr. Sam owned such an instrument, Gerber insisted.

Despite heated defense objections, color photos of the pillowcase were passed around the jury. To me, it was just a Rorschach blot, and might have just as easily suggested a lobster's claw as a surgical instrument.

The coroner downplayed Dr. Sam's July Fourth injuries and said he 'appeared normal and had no difficulty talking,' his pulse strong, blood pressure fine. On cross, Corrigan had his own medical objection: Why hadn't Marilyn Sheppard's body been thoroughly examined for signs of sexual assault? Had Gerber ignored the prowler/rapist theory because he was biased against Dr. Sam from the start?

The lead homicide detective, Robert Schottke, read a statement Sam Sheppard made early on in which he denied having an affair with Sharon Kern. His wife, Sam had said, became 'insanely jealous' when he bought a wristwatch for Miss Kern. Marilyn also accused him of having other affairs, Sam admitted, though he considered the marriage 'ideal' after his wife grasped that a doctor comes in contact with many women.

Sam had said it was ridiculous to think he would kill his wife, that he'd devoted his life to saving lives, and besides, he loved Marilyn.

A medical doctor who examined Sheppard at the request of the coro-

ner on the afternoon of July Fourth found him conscious and alert. The only injuries the doctor noted were a swelling over the right cheekbone and temple, and a black eye. He was dismissive of the more severe diagnoses at Bay View Hospital, revealing the contempt felt by doctors about osteopaths, and the shared belief that the Sheppard clan closed ranks around Sam to protect him in the days following the murder.

When 'the other woman,' Sharon Kern, appeared at the courthouse, newspaper and television photographers swarmed. She was a pretty, rather thin brunette, in a black dress with a white Peter Pan collar, her hair short and bobbed. The former Bay View Hospital lab technician—she wore little or no makeup and looked pale—confirmed a sexual relationship with Dr. Sam lasting over two years. They would make love in Sam's car and in an apartment he kept at Bay View Hospital. He'd spoken of divorcing Marilyn. He loved Sharon. He gave her a ring.

But he'd also told her that he still loved Marilyn, if more like a sister than as a wife, and feared his father would not approve of divorce.

Finally, as the Sharon/Sam relationship continued on its steady course to nowhere, the lovely lab tech had quit at Bay View Hospital and moved to California. But Sam had seen her there last March, where for a week she shared a room with him at the home of a doctor friend of his. After Sam went back to Bay Village, the two lovers briefly corresponded. But no talk of divorce, she said.

Sharon and Dr. Sam did not look at each other while she testified—not so much as an exchange of glances.

Cross-examination of 'the other woman' was swift and brutal, ending with Sharon being asked if, during their intimate relationship, she was always aware Sam was a married man.

She said yes.

The defense began by calling Stephen and Richard Sheppard, who depicted their younger brother as a devoted husband and model citizen. Youthful despite his gray hair, the well-tailored, cool Stephen insisted his brother's neck injury had been serious, and the absence of certain reflexes—which had been shrugged off by the prosecution's doctor—signified brain concussion.

When he arrived at the murder scene, Stephen said the notorious corduroy jacket had not been folded neatly, but lay crumpled on the floor. And he'd found his brother sitting on the floor, murmuring confusedly, hands clasped behind his neck, in obvious pain. A quick examination revealed stiff tissues, tense muscles and ongoing spasms. His brother, he said, was cold, clammy, shivering, shaking.

On the way to the hospital, Sam had blurted, 'How did this happen? My God, Marilyn's dead! Why couldn't this be me?'

Stephen took full responsibility for keeping the coroner and police away from his brother for the four days after the murder, after initially allowing them interviews with no lawyer present. But Dr. Steve had clamped down, after seeing that every time anyone came in with questions, Sam would relive that terrible night and get agitated.

On the stand, Dr. Richard indicated Marilyn's real jealousy was over her husband's work and the demands it brought. Marilyn, he testified, 'was very much in love with Sam, and Sam was very much in love with her.' But being a doctor's wife was difficult for Marilyn. Their arguments were limited to such banalities as with whose family Thanksgiving and Christmas would be spent, and Marilyn having a new dishwater put in while he was away.

The elder Sheppard brother insisted—despite what Mayor Dodge said on the stand—that any notion 'Sam might have been connected with the crime never crossed my mind.' Instead, he spoke of delivering the tragic news to Sam, who said, 'Oh, God, no!' and fell to the floor.

The climax came, of course, with Dr. Sam Sheppard's own testimony. His story was by now familiar, and had more clarity than the aftermath, which Sam still had trouble remembering. For example, he had trouble 'visualizing' the Dodges coming to the house in response to his call. Or the police arriving, either, though he remembered his brother Richard telling him Marilyn was gone. And he remembered falling to the floor.

Attorney Corrigan asked him, 'Doctor, have you in your lifetime ever submitted to sin?'

And Dr. Sam said, 'I have succumbed to human frailties, yes.'

Mahon for the prosecution took the cross. He was prone to red-faced anger and indignant shouting. This didn't work with Dr. Sam, who was quiet and composed and not apt to shout back.

But that self-control did cause a problem for Dr. Sam Sheppard. This was a defendant who spoke with care, and used high-flown language (describing his attacker as 'a biped'). A certain lack of passion in him melded with an aloofness.

His wife had 'lost her sexual aggressiveness' after the birth of their son, he said. Nonetheless, he never considered divorcing her. When Dr. Hardmann suggested Sam should divorce Marilyn, Sam told him Marilyn was the finest girl he ever knew.

'But sexual intimacy was painful to Marilyn after the birth of Chip,' Sam said. 'There was an extreme psychological factor based on prolonged labor and extreme pain.'

Mahon pressed the defendant about orthopedic wrenches. Sam said these were called brace adjustors, for use with post-surgery patients having back problems, and admitted carrying a pair of the tools in his car.

Don't you think it's strange, Nate, that neither the prosecution nor the defense pursued that line of evidence?

Then Mahon asked Sam if he'd injured himself 'jumping or falling off the beach house onto the beach.' Sam said that was impossible, and Corrigan objected to the question, saying there wasn't a shred of evidence that his client's injuries were self-inflicted.

As the cross-examination wound down, Mahon asked Sam about lying at the inquest regarding his intimacy with Sharon Kern. The defendant said, 'I felt Miss Kern's reputation justified that answer, sir.'

Asked why he had grabbed no weapon, knowing an intruder had assaulted Marilyn—weren't there shotguns in the study? Sam said he'd never in his life gone after anyone with a gun.

On the stand, Dr. Sam had admitted to being a sinner, but in a none-of-anybody's-business manner. And nothing had come out that directly connected him to his expectant wife's killing.

The opening defense summation paraphrased something I'd written—that five months after her murder, the state did not know how Marilyn Sheppard was killed, or with what weapon and why. Yet the prosecution wanted this doctor sent to the electric chair on the flimsiest of evidence.

Corrigan got melodramatic, holding on to Sam's hands and saying, 'These are the hands the state would have you believe killed Marilyn

Sheppard. Look at them. These hands. These hands that just a few hours before had worked with skill and devotion to save the life of a child.'

And he begged the jury not to see the affair between Sam and Sharon Kern as one of 'evil intent, but of moral frailty.' Dr. Sam had succumbed to sex, yes, but wasn't sex the strongest lure in the human body?

Corrigan spoke of the police working in teams to interrogate Sam, giving him the virtual third degree, throwing pictures of his dead wife in his face. And the attorney concluded, rather desperately I thought, by reminding the jury the Christmas season was upon them, given us by God 'to set man free and establish on earth the principle of freedom.'

The prosecution's wrap-up was a reiteration of all the unanswered questions, from how could the athletic Dr. Sam have been knocked out twice in one scuffle to why hadn't the murderer killed Sam, too? All the unanswered questions, so many of them . . . but it all boiled down to Sam had done it because he was there. .

The judge did his part in trying to nudge the jurors toward giving Dr. Sam the electric chair for Christmas. He explained how circumstantial evidence can be enough to convict—if a neighbor reported seeing George Washington walking away from your yard with an ax on his shoulder, and your cherry tree had been chopped down, that would be weighty circumstantial evidence in a charge against George Washington for chopping down that tree.

"By the end," she said, "I wouldn't have convicted Sam Sheppard of anything except maybe negligence in failing to keep his back door locked."

"Twelve people disagreed."

She laughed a little. "Twelve people tainted by the guilty verdict the Cleveland press already pronounced, again and again."

I had a sip of my second gimlet.

Then I smiled and said, "If you don't embarrass easily, I'll compliment you on a remarkable performance. How could you remember all that, in such detail, two years later? I mean, I know it was a memorable trial, but—"

"I've been working on a chapter about it," she said. "It's all fresh in my mind."

"Chapter in what?"

She'd been saving her latest pair of olives. She kissed one of them off its little spear and chewed and said, "I'm collecting and revising pieces I've written over the years—murder cases I've covered. *Murder One*, I'm calling it. Bennett is keen for it."

"Bennett Cerf you mean?"

Cerf, the publisher of Random House, was another regular panelist on *What's My Line?*

"I don't mean Tony Bennett." Her mouth made a wicked little smile; one might even call it sly. "So. You're heading to Cleveland soon to do this pro bono job for Perry Mason's daddy. Find out new things about the Marilyn Sheppard murder. Maybe solve it."

Now I knew why she'd given me this performance.

"I am," I said. "Would the girl reporter like to come along?"

CHAPTER 4

Just west of downtown Columbus, on Spring Street, the Gothic monstrosity known as Ohio State Penitentiary took up eight square blocks, like a nightmarish relic out of some other century, which is what it was. Behind its timeworn granite walls, with their expected glassed-in towers for blue-clad guards cuddling high-powered rifles, the prison housed five-thousand-some inmates—about twice its supposed capacity.

I pulled my rental Chevy into the front drive, past a guard booth, and into an unmarked spot in a small parking lot where a sign said: FOR OFFICIAL USE ONLY. A trusty in khaki stepped from the booth with a clipboard and a frown. I flashed my Illinois private operator's badge at him, and at a distance it passed muster, or maybe he just didn't care, but in any case he returned to his hut.

I made my way up the stone steps of the administration building and into a lobby where visitors waited on benches at left and right for the short precious visits that had often taken a long dreary trip. At an information desk I was guided to a lieutenant's office, where I presented my identification for a prearranged visitation with one of the institution's most famous inmates.

Erle Gardner, with the help of Sam Sheppard's attorney, William J. Corrigan (who I had not yet met), arranged the visit, which I'd made a requirement of my involvement in the renewed investigation into Marilyn Sheppard's murder. I wanted to size Dr. Sam up. If he didn't pass my inner lie detector, I would find something better to do with my time. Like make a living.

Flo Kilgore was not along for this leg of the journey. The plan was for her to join me in Cleveland in a few days—this was a Monday and she'd had her TV show last night and her column was due today. I'd flown into Port Columbus International Airport, and would drive the two-plus hours to Cleveland tonight, where a room was waiting at the Hotel Cleveland.

A guard with a billy in his belt escorted me past cell-block buildings through the large prison yard and its shops, water tower, vegetable gardens and baseball diamond. Our destination was the hospital, where number 98860 was lucky enough to be housed in the dorm. After moving past ancient brick structures, we seemed to be moving toward a new, modern one.

I automatically turned in that direction, but the guard said, "No! That's the prison personnel offices. *That* one's the hospital."

He nodded to a dilapidated four-story affair nearby.

The best you could say for the hospital dormitory was that it had plenty of windows; otherwise it was brick walls, creaky wood floors and hospital beds that looked like they dated to the Civil War. But the patients did have bedside tables and—for those who were mobile, and not using bedpans—toilet facilities. That, of course, wasn't the case for the exposed commodes of seven-foot-square cells designed for two and inhabited by four in cell-block buildings nearby.

The guard escorted me to the far end of the long narrow dorm, where a broad-shouldered figure—in hospital whites—was seated with his back to me. You know—a biped.

Sam Sheppard glanced back at us and smiled tightly as he got to his feet. He was smoking a pipe. About my height and in his mid-thirties, he had boyish features on a rounded square face with a dimpled chin and high forehead, his short dark hair thinning slightly. Already I could tell he didn't blink much.

The guard took a position at the opposite end of the ward, which was only half full, the beds nearest us empty. We had more privacy than could be expected.

The convicted wife killer extended his hand and we shook; his grip was firm and perhaps tried a little too hard. Under those whites, which made him look like the doctor he used to be, was a fullback's build, the short-sleeved shirt revealing muscular arms.

"I'm pleased to see you, Mr. Heller."

His voice was higher-pitched than I'd expected.

"Pleased to see you, Dr. Sheppard. Is it all right to still call you that? Doctor, I mean."

"Not only all right, but proper. They can take away my license, but not my medical pedigree. Sit. Please."

A wooden chair was waiting opposite where he again sat himself on the side of his bed.

"I'm very pleased that Mr. Gardner has taken an interest in my case," he said, with a pipe-in-hand gesture. "And I've read about you in some national magazines, so I'm obviously grateful that you're offering your investigative skills."

I rested an ankle on a knee. "Well, this is a preliminary meeting, Doctor. So far I've only committed to taking this meeting with you."

The puckish smile went well with the boyish face. "Perhaps you should call me 'Sam,' or 'Doc,' as most people around here do."

"All right, Sam. And it's 'Nate.'"

He sucked smoke from his pipe, held it in a few moments, let it out. "You need to make your mind up about me. That's only natural. I can tell you about that night, that morning I should say, if you like."

"Mr. Gardner had a fairly thick file for me to go through—newspaper clippings, magazine articles, excerpts from trial transcripts. So I'm familiar with your story."

"It's not a story," he said, but there was no edge to it. Maybe a bit of whine.

"Only you know that for sure," I reminded him. "The only other witness to the crime is dead."

I was trying to blindside him but it didn't work.

Very coolly, he said, "No. At least one *other* person knows—the real killer. Or perhaps there were two of them."

I nodded. "You did tell your friend Marshall Dodge that 'they' killed your wife."

He nodded, pipe in hand. "And I often find, when I try to talk about the incident, that the pronoun 'they' jumps to mind."

That stilted, slightly pedantic way of phrasing things had hurt him badly in court.

"We'll get to that," I said. "My understanding is we don't have the usual visitation time limit."

"That's right. Mr. Gardner is now officially one of my attorneys, if only as a formality. That enables you, as his investigator, to spend as much as an hour with me. Of course, I'm on call, and might be needed in surgery, for some emergency. So we should keep that in mind."

"It sounds like you still *are* a doctor, and not just because you hold a degree. Like you're on staff."

"I'm afraid," he said, "the only degree I hold behind these walls is for Second Degree Murder. Technically, I'm a male nurse, making beds, folding linen, mopping up, checking pulses, preparing surgical packs. But in reality I'm still a surgeon."

"Is that legal?"

The puckish smile again. "I doubt I'll be thrown in jail for it. When I first took this position, which pays a generous one dollar a week for sixty-hour days, I was limited to administering anesthesia. But then the visiting physicians started requesting my assistance during surgery. And taking consults with me beforehand. Soon I was put in charge of the postoperative division, since the doctors here only work during the day."

"They're mostly volunteering their time?"

"That's right." His pipe was out and he relit it, puffing it back to life. "At least in here . . . I can do something constructive . . . with myself and education . . . and get some regular exercise." The pipe bowl was glowing again. "I do five hundred push-ups a day. Spend a lot of time lifting weights—a person has to know how to defend himself in a place like this."

"Have you had problems? With your notoriety—"

"When I first got here," he said, with a flicker of smile, "they marched me down to chow, and a con yelled out something like, 'Tell us about that broad you were shacked up with.' I merely smiled and said, 'Some things a gentleman doesn't discuss in public.' I got quite a laugh from everyone on that, getting me off to a good start."

"And now you're one of the boys?"

He frowned, though his voice remained calm. "Not really. I could never speak the language of the professional criminal. I have no bank robberies or holdups to reminisce about, after all."

"I guess not."

He shrugged. "So I've staked out a position as a loner, what they call a 'solid square' inside. Someone who can keep his mouth shut—no danger to my fellow inmates."

"Not a squealer."

"Not a squealer. You learn to stay away from the rapists and child molesters, because they are more likely to be informers—finks. Punks. Badasses and motherfuckers, as I've come to know them." He gave a little comic shudder. "The language in stir is *not* for the delicate of nature."

"Neither is prison life in general."

"Exactly right. An individual must learn to withstand the indignities administered by sadistic guards, the constant clanging of bells and slamming of iron doors, the long, sleepless nights that come if you allow yourself to think. It's difficult to hold up under the loneliness, Nate." He sighed some smoke. "To suffer the lack, frankly, of female companionship."

My smirk had scant humor in it. "Plenty of prisoners find another form of companionship."

An eyebrow went up. "If that is your way of introducing the subject of homosexuality, let me say right now that I do *not* indulge. If anything, I am known as a protector of young men, not their defiler."

"How so?"

He shrugged. "Well, take the time an immature young newcomer was threatened by a burly Negro—either satisfy him sexually or get beaten with a hammer. I told the Negro in no uncertain terms to lay off the boy. He laughed at me—he was bigger than I, younger than I, too."

"How did you handle it?"

He gave me half a smile. "I sucker-punched him and used karate on the back of his neck. He dropped like a bag of cement."

That oddly recalled the way Sheppard said he'd been knocked to the floor when he ran to help his screaming wife.

"As I say," he went on with unconcealed pride, "I keep in shape to be able to handle myself in these circumstances. I participate in most of the prison sports—basketball . . . I'm a hell of a point guard even now . . . and I'm chief trainer for the football team. Play baseball, and of course wrestle. I wrestled in high school and college, you know."

"You seem to have a very positive attitude," I said, "considering."

"My strength comes from my family. From the support my brothers give me. You know, my mother killed herself within days of my guilty verdict. Shot herself. And my father died, oh, a week later—of cancer they say, but really of a broken heart. This sorrow has only brought Steve and Dick and myself closer together. And I console myself with the thoughts of the many happy years of my marriage, when we led the best of lives."

He nodded toward the framed photographs of his wife and son on the bedside table. "Even in my cell, I kept Marilyn's picture, and Chip's, prominently displayed."

That struck me as an odd way to put it. Like his handshake, that was trying a little too hard.

"A normal person," he said, "has to work to stay sane under these conditions. Take this hospital—the first-floor ward, used for quarantine of new 'guests,' makes no allowance for cross-contamination. Nor does the tuberculosis ward, which is on the same floor as surgery and two surgical wards. Madness!"

"And yet you seem to have preserved your own sanity."

Nodded. Puffed. "I have. But it's a struggle. I once had a prison bureaucrat advise me, confidentially of course, to let a prisoner die after a stabbing incident. Because he deserved it, I was told."

"And?"

"And I refused! It would be a violation of my medical oath—to do no harm. Another of these public servants asked me to plant drugs in a prisoner's mattress! The object? To have a guard find the contraband and throw the uncooperative convict in the 'hole.'"

"You have access to narcotics?"

He nodded. "And that sometimes puts me at odds with other male nurses, who steal morphine to use or sell, primarily to jockers who want to bait young men into homosexuality."

A jocker, in prison lingo, did the "pitching," a queen "the catching."

"Of course I don't squeal on them," he said with a one-shoulder shrug. "That just isn't done. But they soon learn I'll slug them senseless if I spot them filching narcotics. They'll switch much-needed medicine with a syringe of distilled water! Unconscionable."

Time to get into more pertinent matters.

I said, "You understand that Erle Gardner and his Court of Last Resort, and that includes *Argosy* magazine, are not taking a position on your guilt or innocence."

"Understood. This is about the undeniable unfairness of my trial, and the Roman holiday the press had at my expense."

"Yes. But a key component of Gardner's effort is getting you a polygraph test—are you comfortable with that?"

"Hell, I insist upon it!"

"Yet you refused a lie detector test when you were first being investigated."

He waved that off. "Of course I did. That test would have been conducted by the Cleveland authorities, in a climate of public clamor for my arrest. How could I trust them under such circumstances?"

"You'll sign a waiver for a test by the same experts who questioned your brothers and their wives?"

"Absolutely. Wholeheartedly, unhesitatingly. I'll abide by whatever their examination and conclusion might show."

"You'd risk that?"

He gestured with pipe in hand. "To a guilty man, it could spell catastrophe. For an innocent man, there's no risk—it's a godsend. Mr. Heller . . . Nate. I was just the 'logical suspect,' though little of what was said about me was logical at all. For example, that I might have killed my wife and then, in remorse, thrown myself, head first, off the beach house landing, to kill myself."

"Well, isn't that possible?"

His eyes flared. "It's absurd! Me, a medical man, seeking a means of self-destruction, would choose *that* as the method? It's second only to the ridiculous notion that a doctor, committing homicide, would use a bludgeon."

"But you were a husband found alone in a house with a murdered wife. You *were*, forgive me, the textbook logical suspect."

"To a lazy constabulary, perhaps!" He pointed at me with the pipe. "Within two hours after I was taken to the hospital, *two hours*, witnesses heard Coroner Gerber loudly express the opinion that I was the murderer of my wife."

I knew this was the truth—I was one of those witnesses. But I saw no benefit to telling Sheppard I'd been in his house that morning.

"Since you're not from Ohio, Mr. Heller, you probably aren't aware that Coroner Gerber was a highly publicized player in regard to the so-called Torso Murders that plagued Cleveland for years on end. A dozen or more slayings, never solved. So embarrassing for him. Is it any wonder the watchword of the Sheppard investigation was 'wrap this one up fast!'"

"How soon did you realize that?"

He let out a small, hollow laugh. "Well, I was in my hospital bed, a few hours later, when both the coroner and two Cleveland detectives questioned me at length. I complied freely and completely, as best I could in my dazed state . . . even though one of the detectives began with, 'I believe you killed your wife.'"

I shrugged. "The best remedy for that—to your entire situation,

Dr. Sheppard . . . Sam . . . is to find the real killer. What are *your* suspicions?"

His pipe had gone out again. He got it going while his forehead tightened in thought. Finally, he said, "You're right to say 'suspicions,' because I have no single answer to this question of questions."

I nodded. "Has the picture of the intruder, the 'form' you encountered and struggled with, grown any sharper in your mind, over time?"

He nodded back. "Somewhat. I'd say he was on the stocky side, medium build, average height. His head was large, his hair dark and unruly."

"The 'bushy-haired man.'"

"Yes. I have a sense that his features were either heavy or coarse, or that he was unshaven. Not a beard, but a day's growth, which makes sense in the early morning hours. But this was in the semigloom, remember. He wore a white or light-hued upper garment and dark trousers. Whether this was the white blur of the form I saw hovering over Marilyn, I couldn't say."

"Because there may have been two of them."

"There may have been two." His eyebrows went up and the pipe was in his teeth. "My brother Steve seems convinced I saw Marshall Dodge and his wife, Mildred, in my wife's bedroom that night . . . or rather morning. That the reason the Dodges' telephone number came to mind, in my frazzled state, was my subconscious speaking."

"Why the Dodges?"

A sigh of smoke. "Well, not long after Marilyn's funeral, Marsh and Mildred Dodge invited Steve over to their house for a gathering of my friends who, Marsh said, wanted to help 'my cause.' The friends included a former FBI agent whose idea of helping was to tell Steve I should confess. That if I did so, I would likely be charged with manslaughter, not murder, and have the full support of these . . . these great friends. Steve left mightily irritated, thinking Marsh calling this meeting seemed highly suspicious. Why hadn't Marsh, as mayor, summoned the police when he first got my call? Why did he haul his wife along to a murder scene? And why go unarmed, when a killer might be somewhere about the premises?"

"Dodge seems an unlikely suspect," I admitted. I had met Dodge, who was an older man, heavy and unattractive in a Droopy Dog kind of way.

Sheppard's eyes narrowed. "Spen and Marilyn were very friendly—he was a kind of father figure to her. You know, Marilyn was in the first grade when her mother died, and she and her father were never terribly close."

"How does that make Dodge a suspect?"

He shook his head. "I don't say he is. That's Steve talking. Marsh and I were friends—had a boat together. He used it for fishing, and I used it for waterskiing, mostly. Of course, he and Mildred *did* do us kind of dirty in court."

"You mean Dodge claiming that your brother asked you if you had anything to do with the murder."

"Right. Which was either a lie or perhaps he misheard something. And Mildred claimed in her testimony I told her that head injuries were easily faked. Which was a lie, too, unless I'm just not remembering. Why would that even come up?"

I let some air out. "I don't see a motive."

"I don't really, either. The idea of Marilyn having an affair with Marsh? Just doesn't tally. Oddly, though, he did have something of a reputation as a ladies' man."

"You're kidding."

"No, he did. I believe he ran around on Mildred . . . and if you've seen her, who could blame him? And I know he would come over from his butcher shop and have coffee with Marilyn, and deliver meat to her."

If the double entendre of that had occurred to him, he didn't show it.

"Somebody," I said, "committed this murder. You must have some ideas."

The eyebrows went up again. "Well . . . my friend Lucas Hardmann was staying with us. He had the guest room. I was trying to help him get on staff at Bay View. He was something of a . . . well, you'd have to say a rounder. He would encourage me to stray, actually. Talk about the kind of fun he and I could have, out on the prowl. Y'see, he knew Marilyn had become, uh, frigid after Chip's birth. Funny thing, though—he seemed to have a thing for her himself."

"For your wife?"

He smirked. "Well, I never really noticed it, but Marilyn would complain to me that Luke would flirt with her, get 'handsy,' as they say . . . make a play for her, now and then. She said she rebuffed him, but . . . well."

"Is it credible he did that? Came on to her?"

"Maybe. But it's more likely she was just trying to get me riled up with Luke, so that I wouldn't see him or have him stay over. Luke is kind of a slob, and Marilyn liked things neat. She once said he 'repulsed' her."

"He was out of town the night of the third and morning of the fourth."

A nod. "He was. Visiting Paul Robinson in Kent. Paul's a doctor, too."

"How far away is Kent from Bay Village?"

"Oh, thirty miles, give or take."

Not much of a drive.

I asked, "What sort of doctor is Robinson?"

A shrug. "General practitioner. He was an intern at Bay View for a while. I'm not exactly his favorite person."

"Why's that?"

His smile was vaguely embarrassed. "Oh, well . . . he and Sharon Kern were engaged for a while."

I sat forward. "What? Was this Robinson her fiancé *before* your affair with the Kern woman began?"

"Uh. Before and, uh, after, actually."

I was shaking my head. "Why didn't this come out at the trial?"

"It just didn't. What importance could it have?"

"Are you kidding? A houseguest who has the hots for your wife goes off for an overnight with your mistress's ex-fiancé? Half an hour or so away? On the night of your wife's damn murder?"

"I'm sure Luke and Paul were talked to."

Well, they would be.

"Anyway, it's much more likely," he said, "that Marilyn was killed by a stranger. Our beach is easily accessed from the nearby park. My wife was a lovely girl. She went swimming and waterskiing, and in the summer wore sexy little shorts and tops. Some sick soul may have admired her, watched her, frankly lusted for her."

"And just traipsed into your house and killed her."

Sheppard leaned forward. "No. Let's say he'd been watching her. He sees her at the door saying good night to our guests. No sign of me. And it was well known that I was a doctor and frequently away from the house on calls. He enters through the unlocked door. He goes in with a flashlight, doesn't see me sleeping on the daybed, tucked against the stair wall. Heads upstairs to find Marilyn, perhaps with a flashlight in hand. . . ."

He lowered his head.

"You can guess the rest," he said softly.

The intruder pulls down her pajamas, they bunch at one knee, her other leg bare, pushes up her top over her breasts, tries to begin his assault but she fights back. He puts a hand over her mouth and she bites down, hard—two pieces of her teeth are found in the bed. His perverse passion turns to rage and he wields the flashlight like a club, again and again and again. . . .

"And you rush to help Marilyn," I said, "and the bushy-haired man does battle with you."

Several nods. "Several witnesses saw such a man, remember, in the A.M. hours of the Fourth."

"But he doesn't *have* to be a stranger," I said. "He could be a neighbor or friend, who'd watched Marilyn and longed for her."

He gestured with the pipe and smoke curled in a near question mark. "It's possible. Marilyn was a warm person. She would treat a deliveryman as a friend. There was a window washer she struck up a friendship with, for example."

"Do you know his name?"

"No." He shrugged. "There were many such persons."

"We only need to find the right one," I said.

5
CHAPTER

On either side of Euclid Avenue, the sprawling yet cluttered Western Reserve University, where many former residences served as college buildings, had few of the endless lawns and tree-sheltered lanes of most campuses. With Wade Park at the west, University Circle did have its share of elms, and some typical limestone and sandstone structures, among which the modern two-story bunker of a building of the Cuyahoga County Coroner's Office seemed an anomaly.

Several statues were nearby—one of Marcus Alonzo Hanna, who got President McKinley nominated, another of Louis Kossuth, a Hungarian statesman whose bronze likeness Clevelanders of that descent honored with an annual patriotic display. Near the university hospitals, the Coroner's Center (as it was nicknamed) similarly honored Dr. Samuel R. Gerber, not with a statue but an edifice, housing a modern crime lab, X-ray and photographic facilities, and an up-to-the-minute autopsy room. Oh, and—almost as a footnote—a refrigerated room with cubicles for dead people coming and going.

I found Dr. Gerber in the auditorium, where he was wrapping up a lecture on homicide investigation to a packed house of students. The Coroner's Center was also a teaching institution, enlisting as an instructor the nationally known medical examiner whose work on the Torso Murders and the Sam Sheppard case had made him a star. That one of these famous criminal cases was unsolved, and the other questionably solved, seemed beside the point.

"Remember what Sherlock Holmes said," the little man with the big voice intoned as he leaned against his podium. "'Eliminate all other factors, and the one which remains must be the truth.' That's all for today. You have your assignments."

The young men and women—a good number in this amphitheater—began to file out. I eased my way down the stairs past them, admiring a coed or two (or twelve) and took a seat in the front row. Gathering his notes and books, the small figure, who loomed only because of the riser with podium, wore a white lab coat and might have been your family doctor.

Glancing up at me, he said, "May I help you?"

"I hope so," I said.

Then the eyes behind the rimless glasses studied me. "Ness's friend. The Chicago detective. Nathan Haller."

"Heller. My apologies for ambushing you like this. I called your office and was told you'd be here. I wondered if I could steal just a few minutes."

He leaned against the podium, looking down at me, as if he were the six-footer and I were five foot three. "I do have an appointment in fifteen minutes. What's the occasion?"

I quickly told him that I was looking into the Sheppard case for Erle Stanley Gardner and the Court of Last Resort.

He did not come down and join me, preferring the professorly advantage of the podium. "'Court of Last Resort' sounds rather official, Mr. Heller. But we both know it's just a monthly feature in a cheap magazine."

"Not that cheap. It's up to thirty-five cents."

He gave that a tiny smile, which was about what it deserved, then his expression turned serious. "I heard about Eliot's death. Very sad. A young man, relatively speaking. My condolences."

"Thank you." I didn't ask why he hadn't been at the memorial service. Strange, in a way, since the Kingsbury Run slayings would forever link him with Eliot.

Still leaning across the podium in a casually condescending manner, he said, "May I be frank? About this effort of yours?"

"Please."

Now he stood to his full height. He began to pace before the big blackboard, with reading assignments on it, as if to remind me who was schooling who.

"Mr. Heller," he said (and at least I now rated a "mister"), "your Court of Last Resort would seem indeed to be the last resort for Dr. Sheppard. The efforts of counselor Corrigan's forensics man— after we turned the house over—were not found convincing by the Eighth District Ohio Court of Appeals, who denied the motion for a new trial."

He returned to his podium and resumed his patronizing stance.

"And," he lectured, "the Ohio Supreme Court affirmed Sheppard's conviction just last year—a decision the Supreme Court of these United States chose to let stand. So why should I talk to you about this very much decided case?"

"Because," I said, "there's one court remaining to hear it."

"What court would that be? The one of 'Last Resort'?"

"In a way. The court of public opinion. And the man who gave the world Perry Mason, patron saint of unfairly accused defendants in murder cases, is just the person who could embarrass you royally."

He thought about that. Straightened. Smoothed a side of his already perfect white-gray hair; he was balding some, giving him a high forehead, not unlike Sam Sheppard.

Then he said, "If so, why on earth should I help you, Heller?"

Ah. Back to the Good Old Days when I didn't rate a "mister."

"Because," I said, "you have a basic misunderstanding of what Gardner, and I, are up to. We're not saying Sam Sheppard is innocent. We have no opinion on that. The idea of my looking into this old case is to see whether new evidence does exist that might get the not-guilty verdict overturned. And, if so, pave the way for a new trial."

"Well, he's guilty as sin, man."

"Then what do you have to worry about? Gardner's biggest concern is the unfairness of the trial in the context of a smear campaign by the press in general and the *Cleveland Press* in particular."

"That's greatly exaggerated."

I thought back to my morning in the murder house, where reporters ran rampant. Later, photographs stolen from frames and family albums would appear in their papers.

"Perhaps," I said. "But I want you to understand I have no ax to grind here. I'm just an unbiased investigator making sure justice was done."

He slowly took the several steps down from the riser and came over and sat next to me.

This small man was a big deal in the world of criminology. He had traveled worldwide, lecturing. Had assisted Scotland Yard. Written the standard textbook for physicians giving testimony in court. Served term after term, his reelection automatic, no matter which party was otherwise in power. As a practicing physician and licensed attorney, he had been called "the most powerful figure in Cleveland's criminal justice system."

"I have no desire to be made a fool of," Gerber said, with surprising honesty. "But if there's been a miscarriage of justice—which I severely doubt—I will do everything I can to cooperate."

"Thank you, Doctor. Along those lines, I would be grateful if you would spread the word among your colleagues on the police department that my inquiry is neither pro Sheppard, nor against."

"Understood."

"But if I may be frank—there are those who say you had a bias against Dr. Sheppard, and his whole family. That their Bay View Hospital rankled."

"Are we off the record?"

"Certainly. I'm gathering background, nothing more."

"I won't be quoted in Gardner's column?"

"No."

We were sitting side by side, and I'd angled myself to face him;

but for the occasional glance, he looked straight ahead, at the empty podium and the looming blackboard.

"The Sheppard family has always been a shady operation," he said, the pun of that apparently eluding him. "I, of course, like most physicians, feel none of these osteopaths, these charlatan bone crackers, should be performing surgery. That should be a crime in and of itself."

"The American Medical Association doesn't recognize them, I understand."

A nod and a glance. "That's correct. And these Sheppards . . . for one thing, they ran an abortion mill."

That was a new one on me.

But all I said was, "Is that right?"

He nodded curtly, his eyes on an invisible lecturer. "Many hospitals perform 'legal therapeutic abortions,' should a woman's life be threatened. But at the Sheppard father's first clinic, here on the East Side, starting in the '30s? All a woman had to say was that she would kill herself if she didn't get an abortion. And that was all Sheppard and his staff had to hear."

"Would abortions of that kind be considered illegal?"

"Most certainly! It's a serious crime, for an abominable, immoral practice! Any doctor knowing of such a procedure has a responsibility to report it to the police."

I frowned. "Wouldn't that violate the confidentiality between doctor and patient?"

"No! It's a crime. We had many, many reports of criminal abortions taking place at the Sheppard Osteopathic Hospital on the near east side. We were told that countless fetuses were buried under their parking lot! And we dug it up."

"And found?"

"Well . . . nothing. Apparently they disposed of the tiny corpses in some other fashion. But it was well known that a woman wanting an abortion simply had to go to Richard Sheppard and say she wanted one."

"Dr. Sam's brother?"

"No! The father. But the man's *offspring* are just as bad. We have reliable word that five to ten abortions are performed monthly at Bay View Hospital."

I wondered if it was the same reliable source who advised him to dig up that parking lot.

"They are a sleazy bunch, those Sheppards," he was saying. "They're ambulance chasers—Sam Sheppard was the Bay Village 'volunteer police physician,' going along to accidents—and what hospital do you suppose accident victims were shuttled to? And his brother and late father had the same arrangement with Rocky River and Westlake, among other West Side suburbs!"

I decided not to say that ambulance chasers and abortionists weren't necessarily wife murderers.

"Such an unprofessional pseudo-branch of medicine!" He was ranting now, lost in quiet rage. "They're glorified chiropractors, and the idea of them performing operations and prescribing drugs makes me shudder." He shuddered. "And these Sheppards, they virtually *market* themselves—use the press for promotion! Issuing self-serving press releases to the papers and even medical journals."

This coming from a man who played the Cleveland media like a kazoo.

He seemed to have run out of steam, so I said, "I really appreciate your frankness. I had no idea what kind of people these Sheppards are."

"Well, they are," he said, rather childishly.

"You seemed to know that Sam Sheppard was guilty from the start. But weren't his injuries real? My notes say he had a spinal cord contusion and a concussion, combining to cause a nervous-system malfunction."

"Ridiculous," Gerber said, with a smirk. "Our physician said Sheppard's so-called wounds were superficial and probably self-inflicted. And the X-rays Bay View Hospital provided were either faked or switched. That leather neck brace 'Dr. Sam' wore to the funeral, and the inquest? An obvious fraud. Blatant play for sympathy."

"Of course," I said, "you brought him down a peg by testifying about the murder weapon being a 'surgical instrument.'"

"Yes," he said, with a thin smile, "it left a blood signature."

He'd used that phrase in court: "blood signature." It appeared to have real weight for the jury.

"I have a couple of questions," I said, "about other evidence."

"Certainly."

"Later examination of the murder room turned up a tiny leather strap, a chip apparently of red nail polish, and another tooth fragment."

"Random items," he said with a shrug.

"But the tooth fragment didn't belong to either husband or wife."

Another shrug. "Every murder scene has unanswered questions. Those little evidentiary bits didn't necessarily date to the time of the crime. Anything else?"

"At the trial, you gave the probable time of death as three A.M."

"That's correct." He turned his head to look at me, one eyebrow raised above a rimless eyeglasses lens. "And what was the good doctor *doing* for the three hours until he called Mayor Dodge, at around five forty-five?"

Dr. Richard Sheppard, the first physician to examine Marilyn's body, put the time of death at between 4:15 and 4:45 A.M., and Gerber's top deputy put the death between 3:30 and 5:30.

"We believe," Gerber went on, "that one or both Sheppard brothers were called by Sam Sheppard, in the aftermath of the sudden murder, to help him clean up and stage that bogus robbery and generally get a story together."

I gestured with an open hand. "A polygraph taken in Chicago recently, with both brothers and their wives, indicates otherwise. The examiners were top people and unbiased."

He bristled. "It sounds like a stunt to me. Do I have to tell you that Dr. Sheppard refused a polygraph test *before* and *after* his arrest?"

"No, I'm well aware of that. And we're insisting that he take one now . . . but certain permissions have to be obtained—from the warden of the prison, perhaps the governor. How would you feel about Sheppard finally taking a lie test?"

His expression brightened. "Why, I'd be all for it, of course! It would certainly bring this Court of Last Resort inquiry to a rightful conclusion."

With a pleasant smile, I said, "Well, you certainly seem to have been the driving force behind the original investigation."

"Someone had to be. Five police agencies were involved, and chaos was ensuing." He sat straighter, his chin rising. "So I called a meeting of the county prosecutor, county sheriff, the Cleveland chief of police, the Bay Village chief . . . and myself, of course. We met right here—in this auditorium."

He smiled to himself, reminiscing.

"We had a dozen photographers and as many reporters. Radio and TV. I used that blackboard and a slide projector, to show the color shots I'd eventually bring into court. It was a most successful event."

Much like the Torso Clinic that Eliot Ness had thrown for the press in 1937, and that Samuel Gerber had milked for years.

I said, "And you were chosen to head up the inquiry?"

"No," he said, the smile disappearing with a hint of embarrassment. "We didn't come to an official arrangement. But *someone* had to show some leadership."

The newsroom of the *Cleveland Press* was a vast space occasionally interrupted by pillars with prominent round clocks keeping deadlines looming. The metal desks gave it a modern feel, but the past hovered by way of typewriters chattering and cigar and cigarette smoke drifting like a battlefield haze. Occasional shouted questions or orders were peppered with profanity, as if someone had spread the word that a Chicagoan had come calling and creating an atmosphere out of Hecht and MacArthur's *The Front Page* was only polite.

The office of editor Louis B. Seltzer was at the far end, but on my way there, I ran into him, seated, jutting into the aisle with his little well-shod feet on a reporter's desk as he read copy, one stem of his glasses in his mouth. I'd met him a few times back in Ness days, but there was no reason for him to recognize me.

"Be with you in a moment, Nate," he said, without seeming to have noticed me frozen there.

I recognized *him*, all right. He might have been Dr. Samuel Gerber's rich brother, similarly short, but his baldness had taken over all save the sides of his oval-faced head. Typically dapper, he wore a crisp gray pinstripe suit with a starched shirt and a darker gray tie with a gold stick pin and a matching breast pocket handkerchief.

"Good job," he told the reporter, tossing the copy on the desk, then springing to his full five six to say to me, "Heard you called. Only have fifteen minutes for you, though. That time of day."

His stride back to the glassed-in office was quick and sure. He went in first, leaving the door open for me to go in through and then close. A visitor's chair was waiting, the office itself rather spare, a wall of wooden file cabinets at his back, other wall space taken up by the usual framed award certificates and photos of poses with the famous—mostly entertainers, local boy Bob Hope, Danny Kaye, Frank Sinatra, Jack Benny.

Seltzer was "Mr. Cleveland," after all.

A window to one side made a living seascape of Lake Erie with freighters going by at their own regal pace. The sky was clear with just enough clouds to add artistic touches. All was right with the world, when you were the editor of the flagship paper of the Scripps-Howard newspaper chain.

I knew a little about this man. That he'd been brought up poor. Dropped out of the sixth grade to become a copy boy. Was a police beat reporter by twenty, perhaps explaining his interest in the Sheppard case. An editor at thirty.

Had once gotten himself incarcerated at the Ohio State Penitentiary to do an exposé on the institution's terrible conditions. Sam Sheppard could have told him not all of those conditions had been improved.

"Your friend Ness," he said, as if we were already in the middle of a conversation, "was a great public servant. Honest as hell. When my man Lausche went in as mayor, a Democrat, Frank was pressured to drop Eliot, a Republican. Frank refused. And Eliot set about to wipe out every gambling den and racketeering place he could. Good men, both of them. Sorry for your loss. Now, what's this about?"

I gave him the rundown on Erle Gardner and the Court of Last Resort's interest in his case.

"I just came from seeing Dr. Gerber," I said. "I wanted both of you to know that this effort is open-minded. We're not setting out to prove Sheppard's innocence, or his guilt, for that matter. Just to determine if he got a fair shake at the trial."

Seltzer served up a smile, then put a cigar in it and lit up, after pushing a humidor my way. I declined the offer.

"I suppose I'm the bad guy in this latest Perry Mason," he said jovially, adjusting his glasses. "Well, that's fine. Every good mystery needs one. But as far as I'm concerned, it already has its villain, in one Doctor Samuel H. Sheppard."

I crossed my legs, got comfortable. "What made you so sure of that, so early on?"

He leaned back in his swivel chair. "What I knew from the start, Nate, was this was a great story. Again, a mystery, with fragmentary clues, painstakingly assembled by modern scientific methods, lovely young woman for a victim, handsome young husband for a prime suspect, a rich successful family for my working-class readers to envy."

His frankness made me smile. "Let's go back to that prime suspect," I said. "Didn't Gerber and the cops kind of rush to judgment on this one?"

He shook his head. "Marilyn Sheppard was brutally murdered.

At the time of the killing, only two other persons were present—her husband and a sleeping child of seven. I think we can safely rule out the child as a suspect."

"Agreed."

"And then there's another element that sets this murder case apart from most others—there was a deliberate effort to prevent law enforcement authorities from finding the killer."

I frowned. "You mean, because Sam Sheppard's family rallied around him?"

"That's part of it, and not an unexpected part, obviously. But you have to understand Bay Village to really see what was going on here. It's a tightly knit community, socially active, with a population of mostly younger people, who make a good living, to say the least."

The kind his "working-class readers" might readily resent.

"They're very loyal to each other," he was saying, "when any form of trouble occurs. Take this Dodge fellow—the local butcher, a close friend of Dr. Sam's—they owned a boat together! Dodge rejected Dr. Gerber's advice to arrest Sam. And quickly a protective wall went up around Sheppard, designed to wait until public interest waned, and investigators had turned their efforts elsewhere."

"Why, were there signs of that happening?"

Dark eyes flared behind the glasses. "Damn right there were! All the other papers in town were losing interest—but not the *Press*. We kept the case on page one. We stayed at it, prying, trying to break down that wall. I finally put together a list of questions for Dr. Sam, which he answered . . . with the help of his lawyers no doubt."

Why, should he have done otherwise?

"His responses were non-informative and inconclusive," Seltzer said, waving that off, disrupting his cigar smoke. "So I published a page-one editorial—wrote it myself—headlined 'Somebody Is Getting Away with Murder.'"

"And you kept at it, I understand." I didn't allow any disapproval into my tone.

"Oh, yes! The next headline was 'Why No Inquest, Dr. Gerber?' I admit feeling a little bit bad about calling out Sam Gerber like that—we're good friends, as you may know. But a newsman must do what newsmen must do."

"And then Gerber called an inquest."

Flash of a smile. "He did! How much do you know about that?"

"Not much," I admitted. "Just that it was held in a high school auditorium with a full audience and a lot of press, and that Sheppard lied under oath about the affair with the Kern woman. And didn't Gerber throw Sheppard's lawyer out?"

Seltzer nodded vigorously. "He did, and rightly so. Corrigan was causing trouble. It wasn't a trial—it was a damn inquest! That shyster had no right making objections and causing trouble. After that, my next editorial was headed 'Quit Stalling—Bring Him In.' And Gerber and the Cleveland PD did just that. Put him in handcuffs and hauled him away, like the murderer he is."

I shifted in the chair, crossing my other leg. "You've been praised for your role in the Sheppard case, in some quarters. But in others—"

"We . . . I . . . have been vilified. Yes, as I said at the outset, some view me as the bad guy in this yarn. I'm well aware that the *Press* and I have been criticized by those who believe we 'tried' the case in our pages before it got to a courtroom. That we inflamed public opinion."

That made him laugh and shake his head.

"Well," I said, risking a raised eyebrow, "even the Ohio Supreme Court, when they turned down Sheppard's appeal? Remarked on the 'Roman holiday' atmosphere the media brought to the party."

He took in cigar smoke, let it out quickly. "I know that better than anyone. And when the United States Supreme Court declined to review Dr. Sam's case, Justice Frankfurter raised the question of whether the defendant had been denied a fair trial because of that."

So this was something he *had* given real thought to.

"But," he said, lifting a forefinger, "both courts refused the appeal. Don't forget that."

"No," I said, nodding. "And my job is to find new evidence, not raise this old issue. Which is why I wanted to assure you of the impartiality of this investigation."

Now he was nodding. "And I appreciate that. Understand, Nate, that my philosophy, where the newspaper business is concerned, rests on the ultimate best interests of my community. To help it grow and prosper, and fight those things that are harmful to it. To do battle to make the community a better place to live."

I gave him a bland smile. "Well, that sounds just fine."

He turned to the window with Lake Erie in its view. His voice grew reflective.

"A newspaper," he said, "is properly concerned about the state of law enforcement in its community, and cannot permit a protective wall to go up, shielding a murderer by saying or doing nothing. We must move in with all our heavy artillery." He turned back to me and his smile and nod were dismissive. "Now . . . I have a paper to get out."

He gestured toward the door, and turned to his typewriter on its stand, and started right in, clickety-clacking. Perhaps he had an editorial to write, if he had any juice left after all the editorializing he'd subjected me to.

Louis Seltzer was a guy who, if he got his balls in an uproar, could shake the walls of City Hall like Sampson in a bad mood. If you were chief of police, or the mayor, you wanted to keep Louis Seltzer happy.

Even I wanted to keep him happy, at least temporarily.

I went through the endless newsroom to the elevator and down to the parking garage. As my footsteps echoed, my mind pondered.

This was a dangerous man. I hoped I'd kissed enough ass to keep him out of my hair while I did my job in Cleveland. But this was a man who knew that taking the likes of the Sheppards down a notch was just what his blue-collar readers would relish. After all, Sam Sheppard made thirty grand a year! Seltzer had printed that in his paper.

But not that the editor made seventy-five grand himself.

I was getting keys out to unlock the driver's side of the rental Chevy when I felt the finger poke in my back.

Only it wasn't a finger.

Somebody besides Louis Seltzer was bringing out the heavy artillery.

CHAPTER

Right there in the parking garage, with no one around to notice, I was escorted to another car, parked nearby—a brand-new Olds 98, white with black trim, a snazzy number I knew to have electric windows and power steering, because my partner Lou Sapperstein drove the identical model, color and all. Would have been nice if Lou had driven here to pull a practical joke, but that didn't seem to be the case.

Yet I couldn't help feeling a nostalgic twinge for the days of bulgy black sedans and bent-nose gangsters who knew what they were doing.

The three taking me for a ride—some kind of ride, anyway— were disconcertingly young. What kind of hoods wore gabardine bomber jackets, in shades of light blue and tan? Hell, there was hardly anywhere to tuck a gun.

I was in back with the kid who had ushered me here, between him and a pudgy one, who looked like the next-door neighborhood kid on *Ozzie and Harriet*. Wally, was it? The kid who'd walked me over with a gun in my back had the kind of acne that would leave him pockmarked one day. When he grew up. All I saw of the driver was the back of his head, black hair shorn as close to the scalp as if a military base barber were responsible.

In fairness, none of them—and I had soon glimpsed the narrow, slit-eyed, sharp-jawed driver's face in his rearview mirror, cigarette dangling from tight lips—was really a kid. They were at least mid-twenties and maybe more. But I was a guy in his fifties and guys this young were dangerous. I would have to pick my moment carefully.

I said, pleasantly, conversationally, to the pockmarked junior hood, "Where are we headed?"

"Somewhere," he said in a high-pitched, Henry Aldrich-ish way. *Coming, Mother!*

It would really piss me off to be killed by brats like these.

Really, though, I was the one who deserved a spanking. This was a murder case, a not fresh one admittedly, but one of my standard rules was to always carry my nine-millimeter Browning under my arm in *any* murder case. Murder cases, after all, always had murderers in them.

The barrel of what proved to be a snubnose .38 was jammed in my side now.

I said, "Do us both a favor. Take that gun out of my side. Whoever you're doing this for wouldn't like me getting killed here in the car."

He thought about that, for a sullen few seconds, keeping the snout of the pistol poked in me, then withdrew it but still kept it pointed at me. A snubnose is kind of an insult. A little toy-looking thing that can kill you.

"Don't point that at me," I said sternly. "Don't point it at anybody. Aim it there, why don't you?"

I nodded toward the empty rider's seat up front.

His pimply brown forehead tightened, and he seemed to be about to argue with me, when Wally, also with a high-pitched voice, said, "He's right. Careful with that."

This told me something interesting. These punks were not workaday hoods, used to carrying guns. Mob guys, even the Junior Varsity, weren't as inclined these days to go around packing heat all the time, as we senior citizens put it. But I had a hunch hauling any kind of hardware was not a usual thing with this trio.

In a way, that made them more dangerous. Getting accidentally killed is still dead. Having some spooked amateur shoot you still puts a bullet somewhere.

The drive my new friends and I had made from the *Press* building and the Playhouse Square theater district was less than ten minutes, but we were in another world—the world of the Flats.

To some, the Cleveland Flats, situated on the bottomland of the river's floodplain, was an industrial wonder—shipyards, foundries, oil refineries, chemical plants, lumberyards, flour mills. To me, the Flats would always be a hellish collection of gin joints and warehouses, where sailors and working men wandered in a dank, dark world lit by flickering neon and open flames from gas runoff, the silence broken by honky-tonk music and the fingernails-on-blackboard screeches of factories across the river. Some of these dives dated back to the turn of the century, piles of brick held together by sweat, sawdust and swill.

We pulled in the alley behind one such establishment, the Harbor Inn, a dingy dive loomed over by the Center Street Swing Bridge on the west bank of the Cuyahoga River. Wally politely held the car door open for me and his pockmarked pal nudged me inside with the snubnose. The driver took up the rear, after parking against the side of the building behind some garbage cans.

We were in a back room, or anyway the middle of one, within a fortress of stacked cartons of beer and booze. The floorboards creaked like whining women and the ceiling was high and ornate, peeling light brown paint, like the ugliest suntan in history, set off by one long dangling light bulb, which was already switched on as we came in. A small square table was centerstage, with four chairs around it, as if waiting for somebody to show up with a deck of cards.

On that table, though, was a coil of clothesline, which suggested someone might get tied up with it. Maybe someone who was going to get worked over. That was good news of a sort, because nobody hauls you into the back room of a working bar to kill you. There were plenty of places, indoors and out, to do that in the Flats. But this wasn't one of them.

Still, I was in no mood to be tied up. I was in no mood to be questioned by a trio of somewhat grown-up Dead End Kids at all, even if clothesline wasn't involved. I quickly got my bearings.

The table was between me and a pathway through stacked boxes to a door, apparently into the bar, from which bled rock 'n' roll—"All Shook Up." Jukebox, of course. I didn't figure the Harbor Inn could afford Elvis Presley. Standing half-blocking that path was the driver. He was wearing a blue car coat with a grinning red Cleveland Indians "Chief Wahoo" patch; also jeans and tennies. The rearview-mirror glimpse hadn't revealed that the close-cropped black hair was part of a crew cut.

Were hoods these days getting young or was I growing old? Don't answer that.

Behind me was Henry Aldrich with the .38 in my back, and over to my left, by the table near one of the empty chairs, stood a grinning Wally. He had a hand in the pocket of his light blue bomber jacket, maybe holding a gun. He had a crew cut, too, brown-haired variety. He might have been high on booze or pills, or maybe the glassy-eyed unblinking stare was excitement or nerves or something.

The kid edged from in back of me, at my right now, the gun pointed at my gut.

"Sit down," Henry said. His hair was long and blond with a Vitalis-dripping pompadour. "We're going to talk."

"I can talk standing up," I pointed out.

"Listen, old man! I said sit *down*."

"You don't need to tie me up," I said reasonably. "I'm happy to answer your questions. I just don't have any idea what it is you want to know."

With his free hand, he shoved me toward the waiting chair. Not hard, but making his point.

I raised my hands, as if noticing for the first time he was armed. "All right. It's just that you don't need to get tough. I'm happy to cooperate."

Elvis said, *I'm all shook up!* and I grabbed the chair and hit

Henry with it. The thing shattered into kindling, but wood is wood and it knocked him down. He wasn't out but he was good and stunned, his hair back like a cheap wig, and I plucked the .38 from his loose grasp and took the two steps needed to reach Wally before his fumbling fingers got the gun out and I slapped him with the .38, holding it tight in a palm like the hunk of metal it was. The driver was coming at me, also with a gun out, another snub-nose, and he looked scared, but that didn't stop him. He didn't fire his weapon, though, which I'd kind of counted on, because these imbeciles had chosen an open-for-business bar and not one of the countless warehouses in the Flats to do their roughing up and en-forced questioning.

I kicked the table at him, and it slid roughly across the slatted floor, but it did slide, and the edge of it caught him in the midsec-tion and folded him over, till he was sprawled on it. I could smell the Butch Wax holding his hair up in front. I yanked the table back, like a magician pulling out a tablecloth without disturbing the china and silverware on it, and the driver hit the floor in a pile. His gun I kicked away, then kicked him in the head.

Behind me bloody-faced Wally was scrambling on the floor toward his gun, which had been half out of his pocket and had fallen from his fumbling fingers onto the floor. He was like a jelly-fish washed up on the beach. I kicked him in the head, too. Both he and the driver were out cold, very damn cold, and I knew a kick like that could kill somebody, but I hadn't started this, had I?

Henry was on the floor, like a high school girl looking for a con-tact lens, and what the hell, I kicked him in the head, too. They'd kidnapped me and waved guns at me and I can only take so much.

While the Everly Brothers sang "Bye Bye, Love," I went around gathering things—guns, car keys, billfolds. They were all asleep and breathing hard, little men who'd had a busy day. Nobody seemed dead or anything.

In the alley I dropped two of the weapons in a garbage can, and the clunking sent some animals scurrying. Cats maybe. Or rats. After dropping one snubnose in my suitcoat pocket, I got behind the wheel of the Olds, used the key in the ignition, and drove. In a few minutes I pulled in alongside The Flat Iron Café.

Whether the Flat Iron got its name because of its steam iron–like shape or because it resembled New York's Flat Iron Building has been the source of pointless controversy for years. If you're wondering how a Chicago boy knew that, I was fairly well familiar with the Flats, having done an extended job for Eliot in these environs back in 1940. The area hadn't changed much. Neither had I, apparently; this I realized as I sat looking through the wallets I'd lifted off three younger men whose heads I kicked into unconsciousness.

Driver's licenses, with names that meant nothing to me, union cards, a total of three hundred and seventy-five dollars, some of which had probably been their pay for their botched mission tonight. I shoved that in my pocket, of course. But the only thing of any real interest was the business card in one wallet.

WILLIAM J. CORRIGAN
CIVIL AND CRIMINAL LAW
Williamson Building
200 Public Square

In addition to a phone number on the front, another number in pencil was scrawled on the back. Home, most likely.

This was starting to make a little sense, but just a little. Corrigan, Sheppard's lawyer, had represented mob defendants any number of times, and was known around town as organized labor's attorney. But I'd had some friendly long-distance contact with him already, so he was aware I was working with Gardner and the Court of Last Resort, with a new trial for his client the ultimate goal. He knew I had a Cleveland trip in the offing. Were those Bowery Boys somehow his welcoming committee?

In a phone booth down the street, I fed in coins and dialed. It rang only a few times before a slightly tobacco-and-age-ravaged voice came on the line.

"Bill Corrigan," it announced.

"Nate Heller."

"Mr. Heller! A pleasure. Are you in town?"

"Oh, I'm in town."

"When can we get together, sir?"

"Right now."

"Well, uh . . . I'm in for the evening. I don't live in the city, you know. I have a farm, and—"

"How soon could you get to the Flat Iron Café?"

Everyone in Cleveland knew the Flat Iron Café.

"Could you give me half an hour, sir?"

"Sure. I haven't eaten. I'll have a bite while I'm waiting."

"Splendid. Could you, uh, tell me what this pertains to, beyond the Sheppard case?"

"Frankly, Bill, I'm not sure. You see I just took three guns off three young characters with union cards who snatched my ass and tried to grill me in back of the Harbor Inn. They're sleeping that off, but in the meantime I've worked up an appetite."

"Oh, my lord . . ."

"See you soon."

I hung up.

The Flat Iron Café had begun as the stable of a four-story hotel. Many decades ago, the top two stories had caught fire, and the remaining two stories became a fabled drinking and dining spot. Odd as hell, the place was half cafeteria, half bar. Steam from the buffet trays mingled with cigar and cigarette smoke. I did as the Romans do, or the Rumanians or the Irish or what have you. I got my tray and took my place in line. I was pretty sure the size of the servings dished out to you was according to your size. I got corned beef and cabbage, with sides of boiled spuds and carrots. This was mostly a tradesman joint, iron workers, longshoremen, pipe fitters. The bar was thirty feet long, the tables banquet style. You sat by whoever you sat by. On a bench.

I plopped down at the unpopulated end of one table, so that Corrigan and I might have a little privacy in this most un-private of establishments. I had finished my third beer and my second plate of corned beef and cabbage when a small, white-haired, bespectacled gent came in. He wore a fedora with its brim turned up and a blue vested suit with shades-of-blue striped tie. He paused inside the door just long enough to pick me out among the overalls and dungarees.

At lunch you might see lawyers and businessmen among the working men, but this time of evening the presence of two business suits was rare. He got a few looks but no remarks; neither had I, but then my suit was a little rumpled from getting kidnapped. He hustled down the aisle between long tables, a man in his early seventies with some spring in his step that belied a time-ravaged face.

He sat across from me.

Counselor Corrigan must have known me from my press coverage, because there was no questioning tone when he said, "Mr. Heller," and reached a thin, bony hand across for me to shake.

He removed his hat and glasses and lighted up a cigar. It had a sweet, pungent aroma—Romeo y Julieta? A waitress came over and we ordered beers—they had Hamm's on tap. Waving out his match, he lifted his light blue eyes and smiled a little. More like a fold in his face, on a wrinkled puss like that.

"I made a phone call," he said, "and was able to ascertain why you were subjected to that undignified roust, earlier. And I couldn't be more embarrassed."

Then why was he smiling?

He leaned close. "You see, I have an associate, who worked with me on the Sheppard trial, who has some . . . we'll call them unsavory clients. These include a certain 'Big Al.'"

He didn't mean Capone—he referred to Alfred "Big Al" Polizzi, who Eliot had jailed from time to time.

"And as I'm sure you're aware," he said, "I have represented a few unsavory sorts myself."

"Of course you have," I said. "You're the top criminal defense lawyer in town."

A bus boy was clearing my plates.

"The thing of it is," Corrigan said, his expression good-natured but his eyes holding me, "my associate happened to be at the coroner's office this afternoon, on business."

"Is that right."

"I had made my associate aware that you were headed to town to look into the Sheppard case for Mr. Gardner. He saw you speaking with Dr. Gerber, recognized you, and became . . . concerned."

"He knew me? Do I know him?"

The fold of a smile again. "There's a case to be made that private detectives should perhaps not seek your level of publicity, Mr. Heller. At any rate, he waited and followed you to the *Press* building, where he saw you going into Mr. Seltzer's office. He misinterpreted those visits as being counter to our efforts. Rather rashly, he made a phone call, and you know the rest. You have my apologies, although this is nothing I would have countenanced."

I swigged some beer. "Well, no hard feelings. I would like to meet your associate and shake his hand."

"Very decent of you."

"Then throw him down the stairs. What kind of 'associates' do you have, anyway, Mr. Corrigan?"

He was looking past me, toward the cafeteria line. "Pity I've already eaten. An old Irishman like me has trouble resisting a steaming plate of corned beef and cabbage. That's what you were having, wasn't it?"

"Skip the blarney. Doesn't your associate know I have friends in Chicago?"

I had a not entirely undeserved reputation for being "mobbed-up," going back to Frank Nitti days. Which I leaned on, when it benefitted me.

"I didn't get into that with him," Corrigan said. "I can tell you I let him know, in no uncertain terms, that I didn't approve of what he did. He's not a *partner* of mine, understand."

"But he was co-counsel on the Sheppard trial?"

He sighed cigar smoke. "Mr. Heller, whatever friendships you may have with certain individuals in Chicago, you are also known to have been associated with Senator Kefauver, and his investigations into labor unions and such."

I showed him some teeth. "Just as you are known to have represented various racketeers at Kefauver's hearings. That's no license to grab me and shove guns at me. Who were those punks, anyway?"

The beers came.

"They are overenthusiastic youngsters, and I do apologize. You won't be bothered again. You have to keep in mind what my associate and I were up against in the Sheppard case. The police arrest this man on a charge of first-degree murder, and only *then* do they try to find evidence to make the charge stick."

I shrugged. "Sheppard was the obvious suspect."

He shook his head and the white shock of hair in front bounced. "I know. And I will ruefully admit to you, Mr. Heller, that I started out thinking Sam Sheppard guilty. Imagine my surprise when it turned out I was defending an innocent man!"

"Now and then it happens. Was your assumption of Sam's guilt why you advised him against taking a lie test?"

The fold in his face indicated distaste. "Perhaps in part. But chiefly because it would have been implemented in an adverse environment by police already satisfied that Dr. Sheppard was guilty. Not to mention that my client's thinking may have been somewhat muddled due to his spinal and cranial injuries, suffered during the struggle with Mrs. Sheppard's murderer."

"But if Sam had passed the test," I pointed out, "the case against him might have collapsed, in that early stage."

He shook his head, white shock bouncing. "Not a risk worth taking."

"But you do realize a polygraph is the first step toward getting full support from the Court of Last Resort."

He nodded once. "With Mr. Gardner's top polygraph experts, I'm convinced we'll have a worthwhile outcome."

He sipped beer, then sat forward.

"What, Mr. Heller, if I may ask, was Dr. Gerber's reaction to the notion of Sam Sheppard submitting to a lie detector test at this late stage?"

I shrugged. "He seems all for it. And claims that, even at the cost of his own embarrassment, if an injustice was done to Dr. Sam, then let the chips fall where they may."

"Do you believe him?"

"Oh hell no. From what I read in the file Gardner prepared for me, Gerber was the first to make a snap judgment about Sheppard's guilt." Actually, I knew this from witnessing it myself, when Eliot and I toured the murder house, but I didn't go into that.

"And," I went on, "the little half-pint's been Sheppard's adversary ever since."

The blue eyes got wide for a moment. "I should say. Take that circus of an inquest—where yours truly, counsel for the defense, got thrown out bodily for speaking up for my client. And for having a stenographer keep a record! I was in the hallway at the close of that travesty, when our illustrious coroner came strutting out of that gymnasium, surrounded by mooning young females wanting autographs."

Dr. Samuel Gerber seemed an unlikely teen idol.

Corrigan ranted on: "But the trial was little better. Reporters standing on tables, sitting on railings, hanging from the chandeliers! Movie cameras taking pictures of the jurors—when the prosecuting attorneys weren't stepping in front of the lenses for their own glory. Did you know the jurors were given a tour of the murder house, including the bedroom and its bloody walls?"

"That I hadn't heard."

"Well, my client was hauled along in handcuffs under heavy guard, as if he were Baby Face Nelson planning an escape. Even the damnable weather was against him. No July Fourth holiday this— but an overcast gloomy day with an icy November wind cutting through. Lake Erie's waves swallowed the little strip of beach— how could I ask the jurors to picture the murderer fleeing along it? Or to imagine Dr. Sheppard struggling with an assailant, much less lying unconscious for God knew how long, his body half on sand, half in the water. But on that day there was no sand!"

"Sometimes you can't catch a break."

He was shaking his head, lost in frustration. "All of my objections about TV cameras in the courtroom were overruled. Thanks to Louis Benson Seltzer, a voracious beast had been unleashed."

"The press, you mean?"

"The press. The *Cleveland Press* in particular, but the press in general. Under the guise of news, the local papers and national ones as well covered the case in the most tasteless, rumor-mongering terms, including rabble-rousing editorials. Dr. Sam Sheppard was convicted in the minds of the public even before he was arrested and charged!"

"It was Seltzer who pushed Gerber into action in the first place, wasn't it?"

He huffed a humorless laugh. "Oh yes. The police department, the prosecutors, even Gerber himself, they're all just pawns on Louis Seltzer's chessboard. You spoke to him today."

"I did. His attitude on Dr. Sam's guilt is unchanged and unapologetic. I called on him only to . . . keep him at bay. I told him Erle Gardner was an unbiased observer in this, and not taking sides. Just taking stock."

"Is that true?"

I shrugged again. "If real doubt hadn't been raised about your client's guilt, I wouldn't be here—Gardner is as straight a shooter as you'll come across. And there's little doubt that Sam Sheppard was denied a fair trial."

The hypnotic blue eyes looked past me into nothing. "He should have had a new trial by now. I admit my shortcomings in this. You see, I wanted access to the house, but the court wouldn't allow that unless I was supervised by the police. I wanted complete and free access, to bring my own forensics man in."

"So instead all the jury got was the prosecution's experts."

He nodded glumly. "And their forensics were shoddy—no microscopic examination of the blood from the blows, which could've indicated the weapon's composition. No test made for seminal fluid on the body or bedclothes. No effort by the fingerprint man to lift prints from the second-floor banister, doorjambs or bed."

Another round of beers came.

"Finally, after the verdict," he said, "we were able to take control of the house. I brought in my man—Dr. Paul Leland Kirk. Are you familiar with him?"

I nodded. Kirk was a top criminologist who had founded a lab in Chicago. Currently he was a professor at the University of California in Berkeley, the author of the respected *Crime Investigation: Physical Evidence and the Police Laboratory.* He'd been an associate of Eliot's old mentor, August Vollmer.

"Dr. Kirk's findings should have gotten us a new trial," Corrigan said, after another sigh of smoke. "Consider what he was able to prove! That the killer was left-handed when Dr. Sheppard is right-handed. That injuries to Mrs. Sheppard's teeth indicated she had bitten her attacker's hand, with her husband showing no such wound. That the lack of blood on the ceiling indicated an attacker of limited power, as did the skull not being crushed despite so many blows. Most importantly, that a large bloodstain on the closet door, likely from the assailant's bloody hand, did not match the blood types of Dr. or Mrs. Sheppard."

"Which means a third person was in that room, and almost certainly the perpetrator."

He waggled a lecturing finger. "Also, the murder weapon was cylindrical—a flashlight or a length of pipe—*not* a surgical instrument, as Gerber insisted, in a blatantly calculated way to make Dr. Sheppard appear guilty. And if Mr. Gardner provided you with photos, you know the physical evidence—the manner in which Mrs. Sheppard's pajamas were disturbed, exposing her breasts and genital area—indicated the crime involved sexual assault."

I nodded. "As did the way she'd been pulled down to where her legs were hemmed in under the bed's foot rail. And, Mr. Corrigan—I saw more than just photos."

He frowned. "What do you mean?"

"I was in the murder room that morning. Of course, so was everybody from the Mormon Tabernacle Choir to the New York Yankees."

The blue eyes were wide again. "Why in the world—"

I explained.

He was shaking his head at the coincidence. "You're aware the county prosecutor was your late friend's close associate? And there are others in this case who knew the former safety director well, worked with him. . . . Is that a conflict of interest for you?"

I shook my head. "If anything, it'll open some doors. As for Prosecutor Cullitan, I met him a few times in the late '30s, but that's as far as it goes. Dr. Kirk and I are friendly acquaintances. I've used his Chicago lab from time to time."

His eyes narrowed. "Then you must know what Dr. Gerber did to him."

"I don't, no."

He shifted on the bench. "Dr. Gerber has effectively black-balled Dr. Kirk—kept him out of the American Academy of Forensic Science. Our coroner is an officer of that group. Lost him a research grant, as well."

Kirk knew forensics, but Gerber knew politics.

Corrigan was saying, "When we went before Judge Blythin with our new evidence, Gerber joined the prosecutors to savage Dr. Kirk's findings. And Blythin said the evidence could not be considered because we could have learned all this before the trial, if we'd only been diligent."

I snorted a laugh. "Like Blythin would have overruled himself."

"Precisely. We kept at it. And we still *are*, Mr. Heller. That's why I'm happy to see you opening a private investigation of the case. And why I wholeheartedly support Mr. Gardner's involvement."

"Good to hear."

His eyebrows lifted. "Of course, we both know a good polygraph result won't be admissible as new evidence. But it *would* build positive public opinion. And any new evidence you turn up, well . . . that will be most appreciated. Right now I'm working up a writ of habeas corpus to file in the Supreme Court of Ohio."

"On what grounds?"

"That the prosecution withheld evidence from the defense. Having to do with a missing or misfiled laboratory card with blood evidence. It's as thin as the missing card, frankly. I'm just exhausting the last legal remedy in Ohio. I have my eye on the Supreme Court."

I finished my beer. "Mr. Corrigan, I would appreciate it if you would help me line up some interviews—in some instances arrange them, and in others just provide addresses."

"Most happy to, Mr. Heller. And I do apologize for that little joyride you were taken on by those overeager younger members of the labor movement. . . . You know, I think I *will* have some of that corned beef and cabbage."

CHAPTER

The E-shaped, thousand-room hotel on the corner of Superior and Public Square had seen better days, but it remained a first-class hotel. It was part of the Union Terminal complex, which included Higbee's department store, the post office, a trio of office buildings and looming Terminal Tower itself. For me, however, the Hotel Cleveland was just a great big haunted house.

Others agreed with me. Built over the site of the city's first hotel, where any number of unhappy things happened, the hotel's ghostly activity over the decades centered on the fourth floor. Water runs from faucets on their own, lights turn themselves off and on. But for me, a different kind of ghost was tugging at my memory.

In the grand ballroom, Charles Lindbergh had given a speech not long after his solo transatlantic flight, before the kidnapping of his child brought me into his life. Eliot and his second wife, Evaline, a fun and lovely gal, often dined and danced in the still-going Bronze Room upstairs. And Eliot and Leonarde Keeler had, in a suite on the fourteenth floor, made a polygraph examination of Lloyd Watterson, confirming him to be the Mad Butcher of Kingsbury Run. President Truman, with whom I'd once eaten lobster in D.C., had stayed here. So had Eleanor Roosevelt, though not with Harry.

I'd left the rental Chevy in the hotel garage and was now trooping through what had once been an elegant lobby, still boasting a majestic fountain fashioned from marble out of the same quarry as Michelangelo's *David,* or so the management claimed. But the vaulted lobby ceiling now ruled over bright-green-cushioned chairs, sea-foam couches built around the bases of gray marble columns, orange overstuffed faux-leather chairs, and a green-and-white paisley carpet that looked like the upholstery of your least favorite aunt's couch. No wonder the ghosts stuck to the fourth floor.

Having checked in earlier, I was making my way to the elevator when a rather unsteady voice called out to me. "Mr. Heller! Nate."

I turned and another ghost was walking toward me on legs even more unsteady than his voice. He hadn't been young fifteen years ago, but now he was old. Eighty or nearly so. He had been one of those quiet men who could summon a powerhouse voice when raiding a gambling club or giving a summation that would send a man to the chair. He'd done the latter perhaps a dozen times.

County Prosecutor Frank T. Cullitan—who'd been Eliot's good friend and ally in both men's primes—had been a rather fleshy man, not exactly heavy but sturdy-looking, a somewhat imposing six-footer. Now he looked like a stiff wind could take him down. He swam in his brown suit, his once salt-and-pepper hair pure salt now; the small chin still jutted, but the neck that had bulged with a second chin was currently as loose and wrinkled as the suit. The dark eyes behind dark-rimmed glasses looked rheumy.

"I'd just about given up on you," he said.

That was as if we'd had an appointment, which we hadn't.

"Frank," I said. "Good to see you."

We shook hands. It was like grasping a handful of twigs.

"Better than the last time," he rasped.

He meant Eliot's memorial.

"I was told you were in town," he said, "and took a chance you'd head back here. The desk confirmed that—this always was one of your haunts."

"Who told you I—"

The oval face, a bag in which his skull was loosely held, showed embarrassment. "Dr. Gerber called me, and said you'd stopped by to speak to him."

Was that what this was about? Was Cullitan part of the anti-Sheppard squad?

"Let's get a drink," I said, and he thought that was a good idea. We headed to the bar off the lobby.

We hadn't quite gotten there yet when I said, "How long had you been cooling your heels out here, Frank?"

He checked his watch. "Not quite two hours."

That damn near startled me. "Most people aren't willing to invest that much time in a chance to talk to me."

"Well, to be honest . . . I fell asleep." A little grin appeared above the jutting chin. He was as gray as wet newspaper. "I frankly just woke up and was heading out when I spotted you."

A booth in the under-populated bar would give us all the privacy we might need. An attractive brunette waitress in form-fitting black-trimmed-white took our order—bourbon on the rocks for him, rum and Coke for me. The waitress and I exchanged flirty smiles that we both knew wouldn't lead anywhere.

"Before we get started," I said, trying not to sound too defensive, "you need to know something."

The watery eyes took on an alertness. "What is that?"

"I know you and Dr. Gerber go way back. If he, or his pal Seltzer, think maybe I was selling them a bill of goods about being unbiased, then let me assure you otherwise."

He frowned, leaning forward; he looked like he might cry. "Nate, please . . ."

I raised a palm. "Erle Stanley Gardner and his associates are beyond approach. When they decide to look into a case, they do so impartially, objectively."

He was shaking his head. "I'm sure that's true."

Our drinks arrived. We both sipped them, regrouping our thoughts. Mantovani was providing a soft, piped-in soundtrack for us. "Three Coins in the Fountain" right now.

"I'm afraid you've mis—" He began to cough, covering his

mouth with a napkin; it lasted a while. He cleared his throat. "Sorry."

"Are you all right, Frank?"

The smile in the haggard gray face was a terrible thing. "No. Not really. I've been in and out of hospitals . . . and that has no bearing . . ." He coughed again, shorter but just as nasty. "Or really . . . to be honest with you . . . I guess it does."

"I heard you had heart trouble. It kept you out of the court-room on the Sheppard case."

He nodded. "My doctor forbid me going anywhere near that trial. What you need to know is . . . I tried to stop it."

"The trial?"

He nodded, not looking at me.

I shifted in the booth. "Frank, forgive me, but that's ridiculous. You are . . . or anyway were . . . the top elected official in charge of prosecuting criminals in Cuyahoga County. You could have stopped it any time you chose."

His eyes were half-lidded, as if he might fall asleep again. But the voice stayed alert, if ragged. "I still hold that office, yes. But it's not that simple. You see, at first? *All* of us felt that Sam murdered his wife. I had conversations with Eliot about it. You were in that house that morning, weren't you?"

"Because you sent Eliot there to get his take on the crime scene, yes. I happened to be visiting."

His nodding had a slow-motion feel. "Well, to him the crime fit all the standard signs of a domestic homicide."

"I know. He told me."

He gestured with an open hand, as if to a jury. "And we were *all* sure Sam would crack, if we could just get our hands on him. Not for any third degree . . . just have him in custody. When his brothers fought that, it only strengthened our resolve."

"Well, that's pretty clear. But Sam *did* give interviews to Gerber and a couple of homicide dicks on July Fourth, just hours later."

His eyebrows rose above dark-rimmed lenses; it looked like it took effort. "Till his doctor brothers started claiming he was injured too badly to withstand further questioning. Which was an obvious ruse."

I shrugged. "The docs and their wives held up under polygraph testing a few weeks ago, when asked if Sam's injuries were real. Top examiners said they passed."

"Still, the way they circled the wagons was suspicious." He cleared his throat again, but it reached down into his chest, as if looking for something. "But by the time the trial came around, I *knew*."

"What did you know?"

A gravelly sigh. "I knew we didn't have a case—not a legal leg to stand on."

He almost seemed to be shrinking further into the suit.

"Yet you went on with it?"

A weary head shake. "I had to, Nate. Do I have to tell you, a Chicago boy, that a man in my position sometimes gets marching orders from above? Anyway, we all felt there was no alternative but to go to trial—things had . . . well . . ."

"Gotten out of hand?"

A glum nod. "Whether we had the evidence or not, whether the legal niceties were honored, whether Sam Sheppard was guilty or innocent . . . the trial must go on. We felt confident, despite the lack of any real proof."

"Why?"

He took a good swig of the bourbon. "Prejudice would take care of the verdict."

"Trial by newspaper."

He managed to lift a shoulder and put it down again. "And television and radio and simple word of mouth. Everybody hates rich successful people. Even other rich successful people."

"The Sheppards aren't rich. Success isn't wealth."

"Tell that to an hourly worker. Tell it to one out of a job."

I leaned in. "The way you'd come to feel about the case . . . is that the real reason you stayed away from the trial?"

". . . To a degree. But I really haven't been in fit shape for the courtroom in some time." He sighed and it was like sharp finger-nails were tearing him somewhere inside. "I go back in tomorrow."

"To the office?"

He shook his head. "The hospital."

"Why the hell are you telling me this? Are you willing to go on the record?"

He held up a hand as if swearing in at court. "I'm telling you this in confidence, and maybe a little bit to honor the memory of a good, very honest man we both knew and revered." His upper lip curled. "I think what happened to Sheppard stinks, and I hate that I was part of it. But, damnit, the pressure was too great! And I'm telling you . . . well, when Gerber called me today, about your visit? It was a kind of warning. He hears 'Court of Last Resort' and gets very nervous. Sees his reputation getting tarred. So he tells me to watch myself. Not to trust you. And guess who else called me?"

"Seltzer."

His smile showed teeth as gray as the rest of him. "Yes. Mr. Cleveland himself. Everybody wants to remind me that Sam Sheppard was convicted on *my* watch, and that any effort to get our verdict overturned would be a stain on *my* record. My . . . 'life's work.' I got those friendly calls because those two know your friendship with Eliot might lead you to me, a mutual friend."

"Eliot has plenty of those in this town."

"He does. Hell, Chief of Police Story was Eliot's man, and he was hip-deep in sending Sheppard up himself."

"Do you know if Eliot kept tabs on the case?"

"He did, at least a little. He never changed his mind about Sam doing it, but he was sick over the press campaign to convict that man before the trial even started."

"Sounds like him."

Cullitan leaned toward me. "Look, today, after I got those calls? I decided this time, to *hell* with the pressure. I'm a sick man, sure, but not *that* sick—I have *some* shred of decency left. You need to know that digging into this again is the *right* thing to do. Get

Sam the fair trial he never had, and if they convict him, so be it. But otherwise let the poor bastard loose."

"Will you come forward, Frank? Say all this on the record?"

He drew in a deep breath and let it out slow—I was surprised he didn't rattle. "Let's see what you come up with, Nate. Then we'll talk again."

He finished his bourbon, gave me a ghastly smile, slipped out of the booth and, like any good ghost, faded.

Flo Kilgore said, "If Frank Cullitan would go public, you'd have Sam out in a flash."

She was in a black silk short-sleeved blouse with gray skirt and little gray hat that sat at an angle on her head, like the Coca-Cola Sprite's bottle-cap cap.

I'd picked her up late morning at the Cleveland Hopkins International Airport, and on the eleven-mile drive to Public Square had started catching her up. We got her checked into a room on the same floor as mine, and had her bags sent up while we strolled over to Higbee's department store, where we took an elevator to the tenth floor and the Silver Grille.

Flo had an affection for department store "tearooms," perhaps because the largely female clientele would show their enthusiasm for her with wide, impressed eyes and shared whispers but rarely stepped over the line for an autograph. That would be simply gauche.

The Silver Grille was known for its homey dishes with occasional exotic touches. But also for—as Flo had pointed out while we were perusing the menu—its art moderne decor, reflective of its early '30s origin.

"A pity," she said, "that Higbee's allowed changing times to creep into this charming little tearoom. Look at how they've dulled the original look by adding banquettes. And they've painted over the silver grilles along the ceiling and floor! Well, at least the aluminum chairs and tables are still here. And the bronze chandeliers."

I had fully expected Flo to want to be escorted somewhere where wine and liquor were served. So this choice had been a surprise, at least until she discreetly poured something from a silver flask into her 7-Up. After a white-gloved hand tucked the flask back in her purse, she smiled and said, "A girl needs her pick-me-up."

"Until she falls down, at least."

She gave me a pucker-kiss of a smile, said, "Oh you," and sipped her sparkling glass. "You see that hideous gazebo over there?"

"I'm a detective. I notice everything."

"Remember that red marble fountain? You've eaten here before."

"I have. I don't."

"Well, it was simply a marvel. Before this place was *improved*, and that gazebo thing got erected over it, the red of that lovely fountain was picked up in the columns and carpet. Delightful."

That conversation was before we dined—Flo had the Indian chicken curry on rice with fresh coconut and toasted almonds; I had the broiled whitefish with scalloped potatoes and buttered Brussels sprouts, which was what I'd always had when Eliot and Evaline and a girl named Vivian and I used to lunch here. Vivian died in a boating accident in 1943. Another ghost.

By the time I was diving into my butterscotch cream pie and Flo was working on her strawberry sherbert and macaroon, we'd come back around to what had brought her to town.

"So what's the plan, Sherlock?" she asked.

"Never call me that," I said. "I also don't answer to Sam Spade."

"I promise to avoid it. So what's the program?"

"We have a two o'clock with the Sheppard brothers—the two that aren't in stir, anyway."

"You do sound like Sam Spade sometimes."

"And you sound like Brenda Starr sometimes, but let's be good to each other and not mention it. Counselor Corrigan is lining up some interviews for us—former Bay Village mayor Marshall Dodge and his wife, Mildred, and of course the Lords, who were guests at the Sheppards' house the evening of July third. And, I hope, the missing houseguest, Hardmann."

"I can only stay for around three days."

"With any luck, that'll do it. I wouldn't mind getting back to making a living myself."

"Do you . . . anticipate any more excitement?"

I'd told her about the pimple-faced trio that took me for a ride.

"No," I said. I patted my left side. "But I'm packing."

"At least you didn't say 'a rod' or I would have had to break my Sam Spade pledge."

I leaned toward her. "We have to remember this is a murder case. It's an old murder case, but to whoever really did this crime, it's still got that new-car smell."

"If Frank Cullitan would go public, you'd have Sam out in a flash."

Which is where you came in, but don't leave just yet.

"I think to get Cullitan off the dime," I said, "we'll have to come up with something *really* new. But it's a very good sign that he sought me out and spilled."

"'Spilled,' Mr. Spade?"

"Eat your sherbert. It's melting."

Bay View Hospital, at 23200 Lake Road in Bay Village, was a renovated mansion on the Lake Erie bluffs, a sprawling Gothic, many-turreted edifice of yellow-tan brick with a reddish brown roof. Sam Sheppard's father, the late Dr. Richard Sheppard, Sr., had purchased the Victorian-era mansion in 1948. Now its twenty-four rooms had 110 beds and forty-seven doctors, two of whom ran the place—Drs. Stephen and Richard Sheppard. Flo and I sat across a tidy desk from the former while the latter stood at his brother's right hand.

Stephen had a mild, almost soft look about him, but that was deceptive. In his late thirties with a full head of prematurely white hair, he was the middle brother but the natural leader of the clan, now that their father was gone. His office had cream-color walls, with a few framed diplomas as decoration, though his desk had an array of family photos.

Dark-haired, dark-eyed Richard—a gynecologist and obstetrician—was husky, with a slight paunch, and in his early forties. He wore a doctor's white jacket while the seated Steve was in a well-tailored lightweight tan summer suit with brown bow tie; he had a natty, *Esquire* magazine fashion layout look to him.

We'd exchanged pleasantries and performed the handshake ritual, and both men seemed especially pleased to see the famous Miss Kilgore.

Flo had been a rare and important positive voice in the raucous orgy of press coverage of the case, the trial in particular. She'd been given the first exclusive post-trial interview with Sam. Right now Dr. Richard was telling her why.

"That article you wrote on Sam and Sharon Kern pleased all of us, very much."

"Well, thank you. It was sincere."

"It's hard to swallow," he continued, "that a doctor, a man, would take a heavy weapon and batter his wife to death because of, what? An uncontrollable passion for a girl he hadn't seen or talked to in four months? It makes about as much sense as saying my brother killed Marilyn because she baked him blueberry pie that night when he'd distinctly asked for apple."

Steve said, "And blueberry was his favorite."

I almost laughed at that, but I managed not to, because I wasn't sure it was a joke. Doctors.

I said, getting fairly familiar since we'd met a number of weeks ago at the polygraph testing, "Dick, you're not claiming that Marilyn and Sam never had a spat?"

A quick head shake. "Of course not. What married couple doesn't?"

"Right. But when there *was* friction, what was it about? And please don't say whether to spend Thanksgiving or Christmas at which in-law's house."

"Nate," he said, answering my familiarity with his own, "you need to understand—Marilyn was very much in love with Sam. It was just . . . difficult for her."

"His running around?"

The older brother stiffened. "Difficult for her to adjust to the life of a doctor's wife. Especially difficult when he was interning and frequently spent all night at the hospital. Sometimes volunteering his help."

Steve said, "Naturally, Marilyn wanted Sam to spend all his free time with her."

His brother said, "I think she was a bit . . . jealous of his profession."

"That's not uncommon," Steve said. "At any rate, we are pleased to see both of you. Miss Kilgore, during the trial, you were a most welcome antidote to Walter Winchell."

Winchell's nationwide, outrageously prejudicial coverage of the case had been featured on his TV show as well as in his widely read columns. And some members of the jury admitted having been exposed to it.

"And, Nate," Steve said pleasantly, "we couldn't be happier that you're re-opening the case."

I shifted in my chair. "Well, it's not me re-opening it—it's Erle Gardner and his Court of Last Resort, and *Argosy* magazine, for that matter. You do understand that I've been tasked with pursuing new evidence with an open mind. That includes the possibility of demonstrating your brother's guilt."

Steve's smile was barely readable. "The jury only *guessed* that Sam was guilty. If he *is* guilty, I'd like to know it. In that case, I would want him to *stay* in jail. If Sam were really guilty, it would be a lot easier on all of us on the outside."

Flo was frowning. "Why is that?"

"For one thing," he said with a restrained shrug, "my mother and father might still be alive. I'd have been able to leave this goddamn Cleveland area years ago and set up my practice somewhere else. We'd have folded up our tents."

Richard put a hand on his brother's shoulder, but his eyes were on me. "That's what the police wanted us to do, you know. They urged us to pressure Sam into confessing."

"But because I know Sam didn't do this," Steve said, "I had to stay here and raise my kids. And Sam's."

I asked, "Chip is with you?"

"He is. But now he insists on being called 'Young Sam.'"

Flo, a mother herself, said, "This would be so hard on a child."

Steve said, "He believes one hundred percent in his father's innocence."

Another unbiased opinion.

"I've heard," I said, "that Sam was offered a deal and turned it down."

"That was part of the confession routine," Steve said, with bitterness that also was hard to read. Like most doctors, he played his feelings close to the vest, but his words gave him away. "You know who this Schottke is?"

I nodded. "Homicide dick."

"He said to me, 'Your brother is guilty as hell and you know it.' I said I knew no such thing, and so did he. He told me to get Sam to confess. Said, 'Goddamnit, he can plead insanity.' Said Sam would do six months in a hospital and come out cured. Go back to medical practice, no more police problems."

Richard said, coldly, "Would you go to a surgeon to use his scalpel on you, when you knew he was a murderer? Or a supposedly 'cured' psychotic?"

Flo said, "I'm so sorry. This has been so very hard on the two of you . . . and your families. . . ."

"We've had no time to feel sorry for ourselves," Steve said. "Or to mourn our parents, or look back fondly on better days. Days when I guess we, or at least I, was a little smug in my perfect life."

Much the same perfect life had been Sam Sheppard's.

Richard said, "We had to get about the business of living, and making a living. We've devoted ourselves and our time to this hospital, to our clinic, to our patients, to our separate families."

Steve said, "Special, personal problems come up when you go through a series of tragedies. And, of course, all of that was secondary to planning and taking steps to get a reversal of Sam's conviction."

Flo asked, "Has all the nasty publicity had any impact on the hospital?"

With a head bob indicating the door at my back, I said, "Certainly seemed to be bustling on our way in today. No shortage of patients or doctors, apparently."

Richard said, "There's been little if any effect on Bay View. Of course, we have one less surgeon on staff—one less gifted, talented surgeon, at that—so the volume of our work has increased."

I said, "Perhaps we should let you get back to it."

"I do have to go," Richard said, with a glance at his watch, then he smiled and nodded at us, and—without taking time for another round of handshakes—slipped out.

"I have a few minutes," Steve said, still ensconced behind his desk, not going anywhere.

I had a feeling he always had time for his brother Sam's cause.

He went on: "I wonder if you might tell me what you have in mind. How you intend to proceed."

I told him about the interviews we had arranged, or in an instance or two were still being lined up.

"I invited Miss Kilgore along," I said, "because, frankly, her television fame can be useful. People are both intimidated and caught off guard by it."

Flo smiled and nodded in agreement at that.

The surgeon's frown, like his smiles, was barely perceptible. "Why is that, do you think?"

"Well," Flo said. "They on the one hand know I'm a celebrity, and on the other are used to inviting me into their homes every Sunday night. Understand, if anyone wants to go off the record— or ask me to leave, fearing publicity—I'll scurry off to the car and wait there for Nathan, like a good little girl."

Like a good little girl reporter, she meant. She'd likely find a window to listen at.

"Nate," Steve said, "pay special attention to Marshall Dodge, and his wife as well. To me they are excellent suspects. I tried to get the police interested, but didn't get anywhere. And that character Hardmann, too."

"I plan to. Anything to add on either score?"

"Well, Dodge spent a lot of time with Marilyn. Very friendly."

"Do you suspect an affair?"

"It's possible. He's much older than Marilyn was, and, frankly, he's not much to look at. But Marilyn told me herself that Dodge was in love with her. He seems to have served as a father figure to her."

And some fathers have been known to turn to incest.

I said, "Understood. And Hardmann?"

"Marilyn hated him. Hated him! He was a slovenly sort and more than once Sam inflicted his old friend on her as a houseguest. I'm fairly certain he made passes at her that were *not* warmly received."

"The police cleared him," I said.

This time the bitterness in his smile wasn't hard to read at all. "And why not? They had their man from the start, didn't they?"

CHAPTER

The setting was unusual for the white gloves, pert hat, high heels and other feminine attire of Flo Kilgore, as she sat on a stool in the chilly back room of the Bay Village Meat Shop with its butcher block, meat grinder, assorted saws, stainless steel sinks, hanging smoked meats, and double-door meat locker.

I was seated next to her on another stool, and our host was similarly perched but facing us, a bloodstained apron and white beanie (no propeller) over gray coveralls. Marshall Dodge, former mayor of Bay Village, heavyset, baggy-eyed, droopy-faced, looked only slightly more healthy than the hanging beef carcasses that awaited his attention.

Right now he had our attention and we had his.

"We were friends, certainly," he said, meaning his family and the Sheppards. "We'd been neighbors a while, six months or so. This was, I think . . .'51? But only to nod to—they were younger than Mildred and me, a good ten years. Then out of the blue Sam wrote me, offering his services as police physician."

"Because you were mayor," I said.

He'd shown no signs of recognizing me from our brief meeting at the murder house back in 1954. Of course, he was dazzled by the presence of TV star Flo in his little shopping-mall meat shop.

"Yes," he said. "That Bay View Hospital of the Sheppards', they were trying to get a leg up on emergency services in all these West

112

Side suburbs. Bay Village would be a prize catch. So Sam became friendly with me, the two families became friendly, and maybe in retrospect that was a little bit political of him. But I liked the guy. And Marilyn, of course."

With a winning little smile, Flo said, "You bought a boat together, I understand."

He nodded. "Sam and I went out fishing, and he and Marilyn used it for waterskiing. They were both real athletic. Sam liked to take that little boat out and let 'er rip, bought a top outboard motor for it. Kind of a speed demon, Sam. But about all *I* used it for was fishing."

I asked, "Was it a genuine friendship, d'you think, or was he using you?"

He shook his head, giving me a facial shrug. "You'd have to ask him. I know I went to *bat* for him, getting him that police physician position. It didn't pay anything, but that hospital sure did benefit. You know, a lot of the city council members were against Bay View Hospital even opening here. We had an M.D. on the council who really fought Sam getting the police surgeon slot." His chin came up, lording it over the creped neck. "But I appointed Sam, and that was that. As mayor I could do that."

"And you stayed friends," I said.

"Oh yes. The two families got together all the time, for a while there anyway. My mother was living with us, and she was something of a hypochondriac—Sam would stop by to humor her, and she loved the attention. Sometimes he came over and watched sports with me, just kicked his shoes off and leaned back and had a beer."

Flo asked, "Where did Mrs. Sheppard fit into this?"

"Well, Marilyn was just a swell person. Just a hell of a nice person. One hundred percent straight. She knew, well . . . she knew Sam was playing around."

I asked, "And *you* knew? Before she mentioned it?"

"Everybody knew. He was kind of shameless about it. Lovely girl like Marilyn . . . just no excuse for it."

"You've had similar criticism, though, right?"

That blindsided him. I thought he might fall off the stool. "Have you been talking to that . . ." He almost spit out the rest. ". . . Stephen Sheppard?"

Actually I had. He'd given Flo and me chapter and verse before we left.

"We've been asking around," I said vaguely. "Am I wrong that some of the guys in town call you 'Lover Boy'? That you're considered something of a Romeo?"

This overweight, baggy-faced butcher being a well-known local ladies' man seemed absurd; but that's what Sam's brother Steve had claimed.

"That damn Stephen Sheppard's been going around telling all kinds of lies," he said, shaking a fist. "I should have punched out that S.O.B. a long time ago . . . pardon the language, Miss Kilgore. . . ."

Flo put a sympathetic smile on her famous face. "Then it's just idle gossip that you had an affair with her?"

"It's nonsense! Marilyn and I were friends, that's all. I was like a . . . a big brother to her."

"How so?"

"Well," he said, and he gestured around him, to hanging carcasses and phallic smoked meats. "When she ordered special cuts off me, I'd deliver them. If she had a bowling league match that ran long, I'd pick up her boy Chip when the school bus dropped him off. And she'd stop by for a cup of coffee now and then, for a heart-to-heart. At her place, of course, but sometimes she'd sit right here in this back room with me."

Flo asked, "Heart-to-heart about what?"

"Sam, of course. He was neglecting her. He was selfish. It was all his career and his own interests. Including the kind that wear lipstick."

I said, "But rumors *did* fly around about you and Marilyn?"

He shrugged too elaborately. "It's a small town. What do you expect?"

"Did Sam ever confront you about it?"

The butcher took that like a slap. Finally he said, his voice softer, "He asked me once."

"Asked you . . . ?"

"If I was sleeping with Marilyn. I said, no—*hell* no! He accepted that."

Flo, still giving him a sympathetic gaze, said, "Were these rumors why you took a lie detector test?"

Another slap—he drew in a deep breath and let it out. "Those rumors were part of it, yes . . . but mostly the garbage Steve Sheppard was spreading around town about me. You *bet* I took a lie detector test. I had nothing to hide!"

"But you didn't pass it," I said.

That slap he took wearily, like he had it coming. "I . . . on a couple of questions . . . they said I showed deception. So I took another test a while later. Passed that fine. Flying colors. Nerves the first time, I guess. And it's *Steve Sheppard* who's the liar!"

"How do you feel about Sam at this point?"

His eyes tightened. "Let's just say . . . I'm comfortable with the verdict."

Flo leaned forward. "Did you ever witness anything that might indicate your friend was capable of such a terrible thing?"

"I didn't," he admitted. "But Marilyn once said they'd had a real 'battle' the night before. I said I couldn't imagine Sam getting mad at anybody! She said he never showed that side of himself to anybody but her. That where she was concerned, he was a real 'Jekyll and Hyde.'"

Flo gave me a quick sideways look.

"So," I said to him, "your friendship with Sam was over by the time of Marilyn's murder."

"Not . . . over. Cooled, maybe. I was always a good friend to Sam. I was who he thought of to call, right, that awful morning? You know, if I hadn't been mayor . . . and also public safety director? He'd have been arrested *much* sooner. I resisted it. Finally had to recuse myself."

Flo said, "But you testified for the prosecution."

He frowned and the deep-set, baggy eyes seemed suddenly sinister. "They *subpoenaed* me! What else could I do?"

I said, "On the stand, you claimed you heard Richard Sheppard ask his brother if he'd killed Marilyn. That his own brother's first thought was that Sam did it . . . which *had* to weigh heavily on the jury."

His mouth was a thin firm line. "It's not a claim, Mr. Heller. It's what I heard."

"Richard and Sam say otherwise. And you'd never mentioned it before that moment."

"I was under oath!"

He'd been under oath at the inquest, too, where he'd said Richard had said something to Sam but he couldn't hear what. I didn't confront him on that, but noted the disparity.

Flo said, "Mr. Dodge, we don't mean to sound like prosecutors ourselves. We're just trying to take another, honest look at this case. Certainly if Sam Sheppard didn't do the crime, you wouldn't want him to stay behind bars?"

"Of course not! But I don't see that you're turning up anything new here. Just plowing old ground." He patted his thighs, or the bloodstained apron covering them, anyway. "All right. I've answered all your questions. I really should get back to my customers. There's only one man behind the counter out there."

"Some questions," I said, "have never been answered, Mr. Dodge. Like why you didn't call the police immediately—if not from your house after Sam phoned, but when you discovered Marilyn had been battered to death?"

Flo picked up. "Weren't you afraid the murderer might still be there?"

I asked, "Why didn't you take a weapon along?"

He blinked at the barrage of questions. Then he sighed deep. "It's easy to ask things like that when you didn't live through it. I answered my friend's call, we ran over there, and Mildred rushed upstairs and found Marilyn, and I tended to Sam. The police got called. I really don't want to discuss it further."

I said, "I have just one other question."

". . . All right."

"The Sheppards were your friends. You and Marilyn were particularly close. I'm not accusing you of an affair, but you've indicated you had a warm, personal relationship with this young woman."

"That isn't a question."

"This is: Why didn't you go to your friend Marilyn's funeral?"

That made him shake, just a little, as if the room's chill had suddenly got to him. ". . . It was just too much. Detectives, reporters . . . too much."

I nodded. "Had you already been hospitalized?"

His eyebrows climbed. "What?"

"I understand you had a nervous breakdown and were in an East Side hospital for a month."

"That's . . . that's incorrect."

"Oh?"

"It was . . . nervous exhaustion. That's all. And it wasn't till August."

"Right before the trial?"

He nodded.

Then he got to his feet and gestured toward the front of the shop. We got up and Flo smiled at him and thanked him for his time and frankness. I just smiled and nodded in a perfunctory way.

We were out in the shop, where a few customers were lined up along the glassed-in counter, when he said, "I know you from somewhere. Have we met?"

"Just in passing," I said.

The Dodge house, three doors west from the Sheppards' in this affluent neighborhood, was surprisingly shabby, a frame cottage worth much less than the lot it sat on, crying out for remodeling or perhaps demolition. The interior was no better, and as Flo and I sat in the living room on saggy chairs, our hostess—Mildred Dodge— sat across from us on the edge of an easy chair she'd pulled around. The furnishings were right out of the Sears showroom circa 1938, and the floor itself was at an angle. Curtains, not doors, separated the adjoining rooms.

Thin, petite, with a long face just shy of being pretty—her nose too long, her forehead too prominent, thanks to short graying dark curls—Mrs. Dodge said, "I do apologize for the state of this place."

Her eyes were her best feature, large, dark, wide-set, with some sparkle. Her eyebrows, unfortunately, were drawn on. She kept her hands folded primly in her lap.

"Don't be silly," Flo said, both her smile and voice sounding absolutely sincere. "You're obviously a wonderful housekeeper."

Flo's celebrity presence, I was sure, was the reason Mrs. Dodge had granted this interview. And Flo was right—the place was picked-up and pleasant, with a minimum of knickknacks and a few framed starving-artist oil paintings. But still a non sequitur in this well-heeled neighborhood.

"We bought it quite reasonably," Mrs. Dodge said. "It had been a summer cottage for East Siders. The plan had been to remodel, but we've never got around to it. Marsh was mayor until recently, and that was *so* time-consuming."

She had put on Sunday attire for her famous guest, a navy dress with white collar and cuffs, a cultured pearl necklace, and small white hat. Her husband had worn a white hat, too. That and a bloody apron.

Flo said, "Oh, I understand. And, of course, your involvement in the Sheppard case can't have been easy."

Mrs. Dodge just smiled her pinched smile, and turned to me. "We've met."

"We have," I admitted.

"You were at the Sheppards' that morning. With Eliot Ness,

who lost his mayoral bid. He was quite the golden boy when he was public safety director."

"Yes he was."

She trotted out a wider smile with some smugness in it. "Of course, my Marsh was both mayor *and* safety director."

"A big honor. Big responsibility." In a tiny town.

She frowned. "Let's get one thing straight. This nonsense about Marsh and Marilyn being an item is . . . nonsense. Marsh is just one of those men who likes to flirt, particularly with the young ones. Means nothing."

Flo's smile was sympathetic. "Small-town rumor mills are a fact of life, I'm afraid."

"Oh yes. And Marsh, he thought if he parked his car, right out front, when he dropped by to see Marilyn? That would let people know he wasn't having some sort of *secret* affair with her. But all it did was tell people he was seeing her!"

Still laying on the sympathy, Flo said, "Even if it was entirely innocent."

"Exactly!"

I asked, "And what did you think about it?"

The mouth pinched again but not in a smile. "That he was making a darn fool of himself. Anyway, she wasn't interested in that kind of thing."

"What kind of thing?"

The drawn-on eyebrows went up the prominent brow. "Sex. She wasn't interested in that at all. I'll tell you what fueled all the talk. The Sheppards had this once-a-week housekeeper who came in, and she was vaccinated with a phonograph needle, that one. A few months before the tragedy, Marilyn was sick in bed. Influenza or some darn thing. Anyway, Marsh went over and fixed her breakfast and took it up to her on a tray."

"Breakfast in bed," I said.

"Yes. But he came right back down. And then it got all around town he'd served Marilyn Sheppard breakfast in her own bedroom.

The heck of it was, Dr. Sam had *called* Marsh at the meat shop and asked him to look in on her! No good deed goes unpunished, they say. Anyway, it spread around town like wildfire. I was born and raised here, and you're right, Miss Kilgore—it's a rumormonger's paradise!"

"One rumor I've heard," I said, "is that Sam and Marilyn fought." I didn't mention that it was her husband I heard it from.

"Well, all old married couples do that, even the young ones. Marilyn was always wanting to buy more of that antique furniture for the house and Sam didn't like it—the expenditure, not the furniture. And he complained when he came back from a convention to find she'd bought a new dishwasher without asking. Well, he hadn't asked *her* permission when he bought that little *sports car*, had he?"

Flo said, "That does sound like typical husband-and-wife squabbling."

I said, "You and your husband were the first people to get there—to the crime scene."

"People made a fuss over me knowing where to go," she said. "Running right up to a bedroom I'd never been in. But I knew Marilyn slept upstairs, and it was right up there off the top of those stairs. So that's a bunch of hooey."

Flo frowned sadly. "Seeing what happened to Mrs. Sheppard—that must have been just *terrible.*"

"Horrible. I went up to that bedroom, and . . ."

She shuddered. "I impulsively grabbed her wrist, then just . . . let go of it! This isn't real, I thought. It was like something out of a chamber of horrors in a wax museum."

"After you saw what happened," I said, "you went down and poured Sam a stiff glass of whiskey."

"Yes. He was slumped in his chair, moaning, real miserable. I thought it might help. He didn't want it. He said he needed to be able to think straight. I downed it myself. I guess I was hoping to pass out or wake up. I wished I could do one or the other. *It just was not real.*"

"Seems to me," I said, "you composed yourself most admirably."

She smiled the pinched smile. "Thank you, Mr. Heller. I tried to keep my wits. To stay alert, keep my eyes open. I pointed out a puddle on the back porch and some smaller wet spots on the stairs that were like . . . you know, footprints. Those police didn't even take pictures."

"You were the one who woke Chip up?"

She nodded. "Some people think it was unusual, the boy sleeping through screams and all. But he was always a deep sleeper, like his daddy. Also, there were two back-to-back closets between the two bedrooms. That Chip, his closet was piled with funny books. He's a nice boy, Chip."

"Right," I said. "When you testified, you only mentioned one thing that really hurt Dr. Sam's case."

The eyebrows rose again, not as much. "The head injury thing?"

"The head injury thing."

She drew a breath, let it out. "Well, I took my sister to see Dr. Sam. She'd been in an automobile accident. He treated her, and just in passing mentioned how hard it was to diagnose brain injuries. Head injuries were easy to fake, he said, which was the bane of insurance companies."

This had come up when Steve Sheppard was filling us in about the Dodges. He'd said that faking a head injury was actually difficult, and Sam had only been advising Mildred's sister not to make a quick settlement. But of course the implication to the jury had been that Sam Sheppard had faked his own injuries after the murder.

"If I might make one observation, Mrs. Dodge," I said, "that I hope you won't take wrong."

The pinched smile again. "We won't know unless you ask, Mr. Heller."

"There were a lot of people in that house, the murder house, that morning. You acted as a kind of . . . you sort of directed traffic."

Curt nod. "I did. Wife of the mayor. Wife of the safety director. That was a way I could help."

"Well, I saw a young man there. You were talking to him. He seemed to be a neighbor kid, or even . . . ?"

Another nod. "Our son Jerome. Yes, Jerry was there for a short while."

"Excuse me, but . . . why did you allow that?"

Her chin came up. "I not only allowed it, I encouraged it. Much the same way I once instructed Marsh to take Jerry to the scene of a terrible car crash. He was a little younger, but a teenager. Thirteen, fourteen. He needed to see what death was. What the world was like. The aftermath of that automobile accident—two were killed— was instructive for a growing boy, a boy growing into a man."

My own eyebrows took a ride. "You're not saying you sent him up to see the murder scene?"

"I did exactly that. He needed to see what people are capable of. What life and death are really like. What the consequences are."

Flo looked pale. I think the blood ran out of my face, too.

"You need to understand, Mr. Heller, Miss Kilgore. Jerry and the other neighbor kids thought the world of the Sheppards. Their place was a regular hangout for the boys and girls. There was a kind of clubhouse in the loft over the garage—the driveway was their basketball court, a hoop above the garage door. Jerry *idolized* Dr. Sam, and Mrs. Sheppard was a kind of big sister to him."

She had been like a daughter to Jerry's father.

"Jerry is doing very well at school," she said. "He's in pre-med at Case Western. Not doing anything much this summer, helping me around the place, handling a few hours at the meat shop, but mostly just having a good time."

I asked, "Is he around today?"

"Well, he and a friend of his took the boat out."

"The boat your husband and Dr. Sam bought together?"

"Yes, that's right. Do you think I was wrong to send Jerry up to see what happened to that young woman?"

"Frankly, I'm not sure I understand what lesson you hoped to teach," I said.

"That life is a fragile thing, of course. That one must take care."

"You spoke of consequences."

"Well, Marilyn was a lovely girl, and while she didn't like sex, she . . . she rather radiated it. She was friendly and some might say flirtatious. She wore daring little tops and tight little pants, short little pants. I don't mean to be unkind, but in a way you might say she . . . flaunted what she had."

Flo said, "You're not suggesting she brought this on herself?"

"Oh, no! No. Just that life is as dangerous as it is precious. Drive too fast, too reckless, you get in a car crash. If you walk in the forest in the sunshine, you'll probably be fine. If you do so in the dead of night . . . who knows?"

We walked to the Sheppard house and skirted the place, not want-ing to disturb the new owners. Discreetly we made our way down the thirty-six steps to the beach, feeling a little lucky not to get yelled at. The waves were not at all angry today, the sun a buttery thing, just warmth, not heat, and the water was in competition with the sky over whose shade of blue was lovelier; the handful of clouds seemed an afterthought, God in a watercolor mood.

Two athletic-looking young men, barely out of their teens, were sitting in their bathing trunks on the wooden slats of the little boathouse landing, which looked out over the narrow stretch of beach where a struggle between Sam Sheppard and a bushy-haired man may or may not have taken place.

The two boys, their backs leaned against the side of the boat-house, had cans of Falstaff and looked alarmed that two adults had found them. Their reaction told me they were under twenty-one, drinking age in Ohio.

"Is one of you Jerry Dodge?" I asked. "I'm not a cop."

A younger, handsomer, darker-haired version of his father got to his feet, smoothed the sides of his red trunks, and said, "I'm Jerome Dodge."

The other boy, who was taller though neither was short, scram-bled to his feet, pulled up his dark green trunks a little, and grinned and pointed. At Flo.

"You're that lady on TV," he said. Not as handsome as his

friend, blond with close-set eyes, but with the same kind of slimly muscular build, he sounded a little drunk. My shrewd detective's eyes quickly spied, on a scrubby piece of the bluff near the boathouse landing, several more Falstaff cans, empty. Some cigarette butts, too.

Flo smiled and gestured to herself with a white-gloved hand. "Yes, I'm Flo Kilgore, from *What's My Line?* Pleasure to meet you . . . ?"

The trail-off invited the blond youth to provide his name, although probably not a national TV show he appeared on regularly. "I'm Dennis Lord. Denny. Jerry's friend."

Good thing he clarified that.

"My name is Heller," I said. "I'm looking into the Sheppard case for Erle Stanley Gardner."

Since Flo's celebrity had impressed at least one of them, I threw that in for good measure.

"The Perry Mason guy," Jerry said.

Denny frowned and said, "On TV?"

Jerry said, "Yeah. The lawyer thing. Mr. Heller, what can I do for you?" The way he said that reminded me that he sometimes worked behind his father's meat counter.

"We've spoken to your dad and mom—your dad at work and your mom at home, just now. I have a few follow-up questions for you. And maybe Denny, too."

"Well . . . okay," Jerry said.

"Okay," his friend said with a bare-shouldered shrug.

"Jerry, I understand, on July Fourth the year of the Marilyn Sheppard murder, you and some other local boys who pal around together were enlisted for a search of the hill and beach."

Jerry nodded, and Denny said, "Me, too."

Jerry said, "There were around a dozen of us boys, who hung around together. We were looking for the murder weapon or anything else that, I don't know, might be a clue."

"You found some items in a green bag, is that right?"

"Yes," Jerry said, "it was a tool bag from Dr. Sam's study. I guess he kept it in a desk drawer. Green cloth, maybe, I don't know—six inches wide, thirteen inches long?"

"I was with him," Denny volunteered.

Jerry went on: "We undid it, dumped it out there on the hill—it was some jewelry, a watch with a broken band, a yellow chain with a football charm on it, gold. Another charm from some hospital, I think. A frat ring, stone kinda cracked up. Maybe a few other things, I dunno."

Denny said, "The cops took everything. Didn't find any prints."

"Not even you two's?"

Jerry and Denny shrugged at each other, then at me, the former adding, "Not that I know of."

Flo said, "I hear the Sheppards' place was a kind of hangout for you kids."

"Well," Jerry said, frowning a little, "not their house. The two rooms over the garage."

"Sometimes we even spent the night," Denny said, grinning a little. "One time, Mrs. Sheppard got mad at us, because some guys and girls stayed over at the same time. She said, 'No funny business!'"

I said, "But she was usually nice?"

"Oh yes," Denny said. "The girls and some of the guys, too, would talk to her about school problems and dating and stuff."

"How about Dr. Sam?"

"I really looked up to him," Jerry said. "I still do, sort of . . . I mean, if he isn't a murderer. Some people don't think he is."

"Do you?"

"I really don't know."

Denny said, "He wasn't as nice as she was. About a year before he killed her, if he killed her? We took the boat out. We had permission, and had done it lots of times. But . . . we were roughhousing around, and a kid almost drowned, and Dr. Sam got really mad. He never let us use the boat after that."

"Was he nasty about it?"

Jerry shook his head. "No, sir. He was quiet. But really firm. He found out . . . uh, listen. I'll . . . I'll tell you something else, if it's in confidence."

"Sure," I said.

Jerry looked at Flo. "You're a writer. Is this . . . what's it called, 'off the record'?"

"Off the record," she said with a nod and a smile.

His nod seemed more for himself than us. "We were goofing around the summer before junior year. We were . . . well, we got into shoplifting. Daring each other to swipe this and that from the dime store or record shop or whatever. Just for a little thrill and to get away with it, you know? We'd come to the clubhouse with our loot and laugh and brag, if we got the most expensive item. Which was probably worth just a buck or two. Anyway, Dr. Sam got wind somehow, and he took me aside and let me have it."

I frowned. "Hit you?"

"Oh, no. He'd never do that. He just talked to me about right and wrong, and values and stuff. He didn't even tell us we couldn't use the clubhouse over the garage. Still played basketball with us and everything."

"He was a nice guy," Denny said. "I suppose he still is."

Jerry frowned at me. "Is this going to start up again? All of it?"

I shook my head. "I don't think so. Not unless Dr. Sam gets a new trial."

"Could that happen?"

"Could. Maybe a long shot. We'll see."

Jerry huffed a sigh. "I'm glad I live in the dorm during school."

"Why's that?"

"Maybe I wouldn't have to put up with having all that under foot again."

"What do you mean?"

"Don't you know? During that whole thing, that coroner guy, Gerber? He turned our living room into a lousy *command* center. Worked out of our house for, like, six weeks! My dumb parents invited them in. Mom served that guy meals!"

The boys asked if that was all and we said yes. They left their beers by the side of the bathhouse and went down to the beach, kicking at the water, then going in for a swim.

Flo looked at me like she didn't know what to think.

Like I did?

CHAPTER

Our final stop of the afternoon was a few houses west of the Dodges'—the home of Denny Lord's parents, Betty and George Lord. This was another Cape Cod not unlike the Sheppard place, and nothing at all like the almost shabby former summer cottage Jerry's parents inhabited. The Lords lived in a white double-story affair with an attached garage and the usual short front lawn, well tended, by the street that was also a highway. Around back was a real yard, equally well maintained with the expected bluff and steps down to the beach.

Dusk was threatening to descend into that nice twilight the moviemakers call magic hour, as we sat on the screened-in porch in white wicker chairs, Flo and I with our backs to the wall and getting the entire Lake Erie view, with Mrs. Lord—who said we should call her "Betty," and used "Flo" and "Nate" right off the bat—seated on another white wicker chair to our right, angled toward us. She'd seen the view.

In cat's-eye glasses behind which big dark blue eyes almost filled the lenses, her dark hair a permed rounded frame for her pretty face, she was in her late thirties and reminiscent of the adult Shirley Temple. Her nice full figure, stopping just short of voluptuous, was made for the light blue shorts and pink blouse. Like Mildred Dodge, she wore a string of pearls, but these looked real. Her shoes were beaded moccasins. Her fingernails were red. Her tan was just getting started.

We were all drinking the lemonade she'd provided, herself included. We were past the laughter and excitement of her bringing a star from *What's My Line?* into her house. Her husband was out of town at an insurance convention, so meeting us so late in the day was no inconvenience—she did not have supper to make. She'd have a sandwich later and Denny was going out with some friends.

"We met your boy on the beach," I said, nodding toward it. The water was staying calm, the gentle blue waves shadowed now. "He and his pal Jerry were swimming."

And drinking beer and smoking, but mentioning that would have set the wrong tone.

"Jerry's a nice young man," she said with a smile as white and as pretty as the rest of her. "He and Denny played football together at Bay High School."

Flo said, conversationally, "Is Denny in college, too?"

She nodded. "Yes, he's in junior college."

That seemed to embarrass her a little.

As if to justify that, she said, "They have a basketball team, and he's a starting forward. I think Jerry regrets going to Case Western, in a way, because he so loved playing football, and was too small for the team."

"Mrs. Lord," I began, "I know—"

She stopped me with a hand and a blurted, "*Betty!* Mrs. Lord is my mother. Don't make me feel awkward using *your* first names, Nate." She smiled at Flo and said, "Flo."

"Thank you, Betty," I said. I sipped the lemonade. Nice, sweet but tangy. Kind of like our hostess. "I know you've had to go over this time and again, and are surely sick of it."

She nodded, half smiled; her lipstick was the same red as her nails. "Actually, it's been a while since I've talked about what happened. Oh, for a while, it was just wall-to-wall police and reporters around here—I had to testify at that inquest, you know. That Gerber is a terrible little man. So full of himself!"

Taking a chance, I said, "This porch is very similar to the one at the Sheppards'. Isn't that where your two families had supper on the evening of July third?"

Didn't throw her at all. She sipped lemonade and nodded as she swallowed. "It was a kind of holiday ritual we'd fallen into. Either we'd go to the Sheppards, or they'd come here—one couple served up drinks, the other supper. As you noted, Denny and Jerry are practically blood brothers, and Chip would play with our smaller two, boy Mark, girl Helen—they must have been, oh . . . four and seven then. But, you know, we started out here—right here on this porch."

"Is that right?" I said, Flo and I sharing a glance, a little uncomfortable with sitting sipping lemonade at the extended crime scene.

"Yes," Betty said. "It was Marilyn's turn cooking, so we started here, with cocktails. George made martinis for Sam and himself, and whiskey sours for us girls."

She paused, frozen in reflection for a moment. "Such a lovely girl, Marilyn, so athletic, so fresh-looking. You could mistake her for a teenager! Hair so thick, lustrous—she wore it shoulder-length, you know. Those eyes, those wide-set hazel eyes of hers . . . and you should have seen *her* tan!"

She swallowed hard. She'd been so upbeat in all of that rhapsodizing about her dead neighbor that I hadn't noticed her tearing up.

"Sorry," she said, wiping each eye with a little paper napkin. "She was a wonderful girl."

Flo said, "You were good friends?"

"Oh, yes. Like sisters."

Everybody on this street seemed to feel like part of somebody else's family.

"We were in the Women's Bowling League together, two afternoons a week," she continued. "We would sit and talk—right out here, in summer, with lemonade. In the kitchen, in winter, coffee. George and I and her and Sam, we were all in the Junior Club."

I asked her what that was.

"A ballroom dancing group, for younger couples. You know, George and Sam were pretty close, too. We two couples went on a vacation once where, to save a little money, we all four slept in the same room."

Flo gave me a glance but I ignored it. But not the implication of what Betty Lord had said.

She was saying, "When we were having drinks that night, Sam unloaded on George, right where you're sitting. Marilyn and I were over by ourselves, by the window, looking out at the sunset. But George told me later that Sam'd had a particularly rough day. Emergency room duty. Little boy, about Chip's age, hit by a truck. Sam massaged the child's heart, got it going again, but then it failed. He was blue, really blue."

For a moment I thought she meant the boy.

"Sam said he tried his best. Felt awful about it. Anyway, about eight twenty Marilyn left to go start dinner. We started over, fifteen or twenty minutes later. Sam had some other work at the hospital, setting a fractured leg I believe. But he got back in time for dinner, around nine or nine thirty. All the kids, except the teenage boys who were out with friends, ate in the kitchen. We let them stay up late sometimes, on holidays. The grown-ups were out on the porch. It was sort of . . . idyllic. Hard to think that . . ."

She paused again. No tears, but her eyes bore a haunted look.

"You know the funny thing?" she asked.

"No," we said.

"With Sam being accused of murdering Marilyn? Just a few hours later? They were almost . . . *lovey-dovey* that night. We were all watching a movie on TV, *Strange Holiday*, Claude Rains, he's always good. Anyway, George had the radio on, turned low but where he could hear—there was an Indians game, they were chasing the pennant that summer. And Marilyn crawled up in Sam's lap! Sitting kind of sideways? He put his arm around her and they watched like that. I was almost . . . jealous. I said to George, 'I need a little attention, too!' But he was lost in the game. You know men!"

"Sam was asleep when you left," I said.

She nodded, frowned a little. "Actually, so was Marilyn. Sam must have had a really hard day—he didn't seem to be able to keep his eyes open, and he stumbled over to that daybed and flopped down. Marilyn dozed off, too, in her chair. Around midnight, we tried to sort of sneak out, George and I, without waking them? But that roused her and she walked us to the door."

"Did she lock it behind you?"

Frowning deeper, she shook her head. "I don't think so. This is Bay Village. People don't lock their doors. Or anyway . . . they didn't *used* to."

"But on July third, three years ago, they didn't."

"No. And we're still very social here, along Lake Road."

That gave me my opening. "Is that why there was so much talk, d'you think, in the papers at the time? About wife swapping and key clubs and so on?"

If I'd expected a reaction from her, defensive, or indignant maybe, I was wrong.

With a flip of the hand and a little half smirk she said, "Oh, that was probably some prudes down the beach. Old folks, you know? They'd roll their eyes and complain about orgies on the sand! We went swimming—in our bathing suits! Big deal."

"One rumor," I said carefully, "was that someone at one of these wild parties got Marilyn Sheppard pregnant. Someone who was *not* Sam."

She huffed a laugh. "Ridiculous. It's always the ones with dirty minds who call you dirty, right? Of course . . . there's some truth to Sam not being, uh . . . delighted, shall we say, about Marilyn getting pregnant again."

Sitting forward, her white-gloved hands in her lap, Flo said, "Oh?"

"George told me . . . you know how husbands and wives talk, kind of confide in each other? He told me he congratulated Sam about the blessed event and Sam just kind of . . . grunted, and said, 'That's what happens when you don't use a rubber.' Sorry, Miss Kilgore."

That remark couldn't be followed by "Flo," apparently.

"Joking maybe," I said.

"Maybe."

I sipped lemonade. "You said they were 'lovey-dovey' that night. What about the rest of the time?"

That made her frown; she was still pretty. "The *Press* somehow got hold of letters where Steve Sheppard and Dorothy, his wife? Wrote Marilyn asking her not to divorce Sam. Telling her about all his good qualities and how smart and talented he was, encouraging her to stay with him. You know, that family hated the idea of having a divorce in it. Their hospital had enough trouble with all the abortion talk."

Flo sat forward and said, with the same smile as when she guessed the occupation of a contestant on her show, "Well, dear— you and Marilyn were obviously quite close. Did she ever confide in you on that topic?"

"Divorce, you mean?"

"Divorce, yes."

She sighed. "You're *right* that we were close. I was probably her closest confidante. She told me that Sam had a girl in California that he was . . . how did she put it, not in *love,* but . . . 'enamored with.' I said, 'You have got to be kidding,' and she said, 'No, it's true, and there was *another* one before that.'"

"The girl in California would be Sharon Kern," I said. "Who moved away from here to try to break it off."

The big blue eyes got very wide. "But then Sam shacked *up* with that woman in California—right in front of some friends he was staying with! And this was in the middle of a vacation with Marilyn!"

"Oh dear," Flo said, as if she'd never heard anything shocking before in her whole life.

Betty nodded. "It was some kind of wedding trip having to do with relatives of hers. Marilyn stayed with family while Sam took a side trip to see a doctor friend . . . although I guess we know what 'friend' he was *really* off to see. I asked her how the rest of the trip went, after Sam joined back up with her, and guess what she said? 'Oh, it was wonderful. I think Sam fell in love with me all over again, and we had the best time.'"

Flo said, "Did she ever talk of leaving him?"

Her single shake of the head spelled certainty. "No. He was her first love, going back to high school. Maybe he was still just . . . growing up, she said. She would sigh and say, 'I guess I just love the guy. I would *never* leave him.'"

No wonder the prosecution had seized on the "Other Woman" murder motive.

"Sam told George, once," she said, "that he and Marilyn had an agreement, because she didn't really like sex. That it kind of . . . hurt her having it. That they had . . . have you heard of this? An 'open' marriage. But it seemed to me it was only open on one side."

"And yet she put up with it," I said.

"Well, they *did* argue. But nothing violent. She was particularly unhappy when she found a receipt for a watch he'd bought the Kern woman. He had some stupid excuse, and it kind of blew over." Betty shrugged. "Marilyn just . . . loved him."

Flo said, "Sounds like she really did."

"Oh, yes, very much," Betty said. "But you know what?"

She turned toward the screened window, the lake still calm but burning orange, the horizon edged with purple.

"I was never quite sure," she said, "about Dr. Sam."

The Rib Room at the Hotel Cleveland was less than hopping on a weekday evening. The place was so dominated by a near-scarlet red— red tablecloths, red-black plaid carpeting, even red wallpaper—that right away you got the point: the prime rib would be served and eaten rare.

The menu itself was insistent about the specialty of the house, with only two entrées (variant sizes of, you guessed it, prime rib) offered on the menu, and a footnote ("Available on request") for sirloin steak, whitefish or lobster.

The dining room was divided by a see-through wall of colonial spindles, along which Flo and I sat at a table for two, both looking rather jaundiced thanks to the yellow glow of lantern chandeliers.

A few heads had turned at the sight of a celebrity from television, and I gave the maitre 'd a couple of bucks to seat us off by ourselves, which he did.

Flo was clearly amused by the Midwest's idea of fine dining, but she communicated this only with little smiles and subtle eye rolls. When I ordered the Adam's Rib, served on the rib, she commented that it sounded "a little cannibalistic to a female." The waiter didn't get the joke, but I smiled. She ordered the whitefish only to be told tonight it was salmon. Pinkfish, then.

Flo looked lovely, despite the yellow cast, her dress a light pink with an almost daring neckline and bare arms, a gold necklace hugging her throat, a pink cloth flower in her brunette hair. We chatted about her kids and my son, and she mentioned in passing that she was back with her husband, Broadway producer Frank Fenton. They had started up their morning radio show again. *Breakfast with Flo and Frank* on WOR, always very popular.

By the time we were using two spoons on one order of cherries jubilee, I was thoroughly confused. What signal was she sending me? That hanky-panky was off the table? She and her husband had always had an understanding—she could be with any other man she chose, as long as she was discreet. And he could be with any other woman, or man, he pleased, employing similar discretion.

The dessert dish was cleared and we sat with coffee and, in her case, a cigarette. I didn't smoke, or anyway hadn't since the war, except in certain tight situations that recalled combat. I was fairly stuffed—the original Adam lost weight, giving up his rib, but I'd taken some on.

"So do we like the Dodges?" she asked.

"As people or suspects?"

"I don't particularly like either of them as people," she said, with a shrug, cigarette smoke trailing out her nostrils. "But as suspects? I certainly don't rule them out."

"Both of them?"

"Why not? If your friendly neighborhood butcher was having an affair with his little surrogate daughter, who looked like a teenage girl in her tight white shorts, then Mildred might well like to see Marilyn Sheppard out of the picture."

I made a face. "Can you really see Mildred bashing Marilyn thirty-five times?"

She nodded, letting the smoke out of her mouth this time. "Considering all those blows, and all that savagery, there wasn't much force displayed. The skull wasn't crushed. Could easily have been a woman who did the deed."

Probably a good thing nobody was seated near us.

"So," I said, "Mildred is your suspect."

"No. A suspect. I said before I liked both of them for it. Marsh might have done it, too."

"Why?"

She shrugged. "Perhaps Marilyn threatened to tell her husband about the affair. Or worse, his wife."

"Why not both?" I said with a nod. I sipped the coffee. "Maybe Marsh didn't know Sam was home—if he came in through the kitchen, he wouldn't have seen Sam on that daybed along the staircase. That light left on upstairs was a sort of signal that Sam was away, and Marilyn home."

"It's the night before a holiday," she said, cocking her head, "a lot of parties, a lot of drinking. Marsh might have gone upstairs and thought he'd surprise Marilyn with a little impromptu roll in the hay. . . ."

"And, woken from a deep sleep, finding a fat old drunk climbing on her—even if it *was* her lover—she said no. Resisted. Things got rough and rougher and she cried out."

"Very possible."

"Sir," someone said.

A stunned-looking waiter was there with the check. I took it and nodded to him, and he went off in a daze. You heard people talking about the damnedest things at these tables.

Flo was lighting up another cigarette. "How do you like our dedicated little coroner setting up his command post in the Dodge living room?"

That rated a laugh. "Most likely invited by the Dodges for that privilege. Where they could keep an eye on Gerber, and tabs on the investigation."

"Of course," Flo said, "there's always pretty Betty and her husband George. Who slept in the same room with Sam and Marilyn on vacation. What kind of fun was *really* going on in the homey homes along Lake Road? And on the beach they all shared?"

I shrugged. "Wife swapping, key parties, maybe—rumors are smoke that sometimes lead to fire. But that's consenting stuff. Husband and wives who like to fool around. The swinging set."

She raised a slender finger; her nail polish was pink. "But sometimes when wives and keys get passed around, it turns into something more. Sometimes a wife and a husband—who are not married to each other—do *more* than just have a sanctioned little romp. Sometimes they find they like what the other guy or gal has to offer. Like it better than what they have at home. Sometimes they fall for each other."

"Which makes a suspect out of both of them."

She nodded once. "Right. Betty may have fallen for Sam, George for Marilyn. That makes any number of scenarios possible, including George misreading the situation and assuming Marilyn would welcome a post-midnight surprise visit."

"What about the bludgeoning being more likely a woman's handiwork?"

She shrugged. "Could be a man who's three sheets to the wind. Could be he held her down with his right hand, assuming he's right-handed, and wielded his weapon—a flashlight maybe? With his left."

"Less power," I said, nodding. "But both the Lords knew that Sam was in the house."

"Knowing *also* that he was a heavy sleeper, dead to the world after a long hard day. If we're talking about an inebriated assailant, his judgment would likely be impaired."

I grunted a laugh. "And we're just getting started. There are a number of other good suspects."

"All well and good. But unless you can prove one of these suspects did it, Sherlock . . . excuse me—Mr. *Spade* . . . how does that get Dr. Sheppard out from behind bars?"

"A good lawyer," I said, "can convince a jury of reasonable doubt, if another solution can be shown to fit the facts. You don't need evidence."

Her eyebrows rose. "Maybe, but it helps. And you don't have a new trial *yet*."

I sighed, weight-of-the-world. "Well, we would if Frank Cullitan would just come forward."

She ground her cigarette out in a Rib Room ashtray. "Do you think he will?"

"That's the rub. I don't think he will unless I can show him new evidence. Damned if you do, damned if you don't."

The blue eyes narrowed. "Maybe not. Maybe what you said about juries might convince an honest prosecutor, too. That there's reasonable doubt, here. Too bad that . . . nothing."

"What?"

Her eyebrows went up and her eyes went down. "I just wish I . . . nothing."

"Stop it. What?"

"Well, it's just . . . I know something I can't talk about."

"Then by all means talk about it."

She leaned so close, she almost crawled across the table. "In confidence? You promise, Nate? You have to promise."

"Hope to die."

She sighed and then, though no one sat at a table near us, she spoke very softly.

The jury hadn't even been impaneled yet when I had a private conversation with Judge Blythin. The day I got there so did a lot of other press, including photographers, and there was a big fuss over my arrival. Lots of pictures. You know how it is.

Anyway, the judge's secretary approached me and said the judge would like to see me in his chambers. This was before court had been called to order. So of course I said yes. I was shown in.

The judge was very friendly. He shook hands with me and said, 'I'm very glad to see you, Miss Kilgore. I watch you on television every Sunday night and enjoy the program. What brings you to Cleveland?'

And of course I said, 'Why, Your Honor—this trial.'

And he asked, 'You came all the way from New York to Cleveland to cover this *trial?'*

I said, 'Well, it has all the ingredients of what we call in the newspaper business a good murder. It has an attractive victim, who was pregnant, and the accused is an important member of the community, a respectable, very attractive man. Then, added to all that, you have the fact that it is a mystery as to who did it.'

The judge smiled and said, 'Mystery? Why, it's an open-and-shut case!'

I asked him what he meant—I was a little taken aback, because I've talked to many judges in their chambers and never before had one given me an opinion on a case. Not till it was over.

'Well,' he said, 'he's guilty as hell. There's no question about it.'

"Flo," I said, and now I took her hand, "you need to come forward with that. That alone might get Sheppard a new trial."

She seemed to be frowning at herself. "Do you think I don't know that? That I haven't lost sleep over it? But I'm a journalist, Nathan. And I *never* give up a source."

"But you're not using that judge as a source!"

"No, but I consider what he told me to be in confidence. And anyway, if I came forward, it would be he-said-she-said. Since I'm a known critic of the verdict in the Sheppard case, I'd be ignored and held up to ridicule . . . even if I *did* feel free to tell."

I smirked. "Are you sure you're not just saving it for your book?"

Some women would have slapped me for that.

Flo just said, "Well, as slow as it's going, the judge might be dead by then. And I'd feel more comfortable sharing."

I shook my head. "It's a hell of a thing. Cullitan could come forward and put an end to this, and now I find out *you* could as well."

She reached out and clutched my hand. "You promised, Nate. You gave me your word."

What was my word worth, compared to a man serving a life sentence for a crime he may not have committed? And in a trial that was clearly a travesty?

But she was my friend, my good friend, and a little more.

"It's your decision," I said.

"Thank you. . . . Now. Shall we go upstairs?"

Soon we were getting off the elevator on the seventh floor, where my room was across from hers but two down, which sounded like something host John Charles Daly would have said on her game show. I walked to her door, and there was an awkward moment while we paused and decided whether or not to share a kiss, and if so, what kind. What I gave her was a friendly one, maybe a little more than friendly but not much more. Then she slipped inside.

Ten minutes later I was reading on the couch in my T-shirt and boxers and black socks, my feet up on a coffee table, when a knock came to the door. I placed the *Playboy* facedown on the table next to my nine millimeter. After my experience with Corrigan's little union card–carrying punks, I thought I'd better take the Browning along, and I did. Opening the door but leaving the night latch on, I saw Flo's sweet face.

She got a glimpse of the automatic in my hand, and smiled and said, "Is that a gun or are you glad to see me?"

"Is this a bribe to keep me quiet?"

That hurt her a little, so I added, "Or maybe you just want a cup of sugar."

I let her in. She was in a baby blue terry dressing gown, floor-length; being seen in the hall wouldn't have been a disaster for her, unless someone recognized her and saw her slip into my suite.

Which is what I'd booked, since I might need to interview someone and an outer room would be more businesslike. A panorama of the city's bustling streets with Lake Erie in the background filled the windows behind us as we sat on the couch. I didn't reach for my trousers or anything—they were in the next room, after all, and of course Flo and I knew each other well, including in the biblical sense.

"Something occur to you?" I asked.

She was sitting close to me.

"I was thinking," she said, "you might not be in the mood for company tonight."

"Is that right?"

"I was thinking," she said again, "that the nature of this case might have . . . put a damper on things."

"In what way?"

"Well. A sex murder. Adultery. An open marriage that may have gone tragically awry."

"*May* have gone tragically awry?"

"Well, yes. So I thought . . . did I mention that Frank and I, uh . . . you know."

"Are in an open marriage? Yes, you mentioned that." I'd never heard the term before Flo used it, a few years before.

"But I also thought," she said, "that you might *like* a little company tonight. Such an intense, troubling case."

"Job. We call it a job."

"Ah. Job. Would you? Like some company?"

She stood, turning toward me, and untied her dressing gown and let it hang open, revealing pale flesh and curves and more.

"Company might be nice," I said, standing, then took her hand and walked her into the bedroom.

If this was a bribe, I didn't mind.

I'm from Chicago.

She was sitting up in bed, the covers around her waist, the nice handfuls of pertly tipped breasts seeming to read along as she perused the paperback copy of *79 Park Avenue* by Harold Robbins I'd started on the plane. The light on her nightstand was on, mine was off, and I was almost asleep when the phone rang. On my nightstand.

"Nathan Heller," I said.

"Nathan," a familiar, friendly but gruff voice said, "it's Erle Gardner. How's the Cleveland trip going?"

"Well, it's Cleveland, all right. I'll write you a detailed report when I get back to Chicago, but for now I have to say I don't know if I've picked up anything new."

At least nothing I hadn't pledged to keep to myself.

I went on: "Did you know Dr. Gerber set up shop in the front room of the Dodge house? That the investigation was conducted from there?"

"No! Interesting."

I filled him in on a few other things, when he interrupted, sounding almost impatient, "I need you to make a trip to Florida."

"All right. When?"

"Tomorrow. I've already booked you on American Airlines to go out at eight A.M."

"Like the traveling salesman said to the farmer's daughter, this is a little sudden, isn't it?"

"We have a confession, man." Excitement colored his voice. "To Marilyn Sheppard's murder."

I didn't figure it was Cock Robin's.

"Erle, there have been something like twenty-five of those, over the years, and they've gone nowhere."

"This one's credible. My man Alex Gregory went down there and gave the suspect a polygraph examination and the guy passed it. I want to question our confessed killer myself, but I want you there. At my side."

"Why?"

"Because the polygraph is one thing, and the opinion of somebody who's been down in the mud with these kind of people for his entire career, well, that's another."

Should I be flattered?

"This could be the break we've been waiting for," he was say-ing. "I've had word Governor O'Neill is favorably impressed with the Sheppard family passing those lie tests."

That would be William O'Neill, who'd been Ohio's state attor-ney general during the Sheppard investigation, before his guber-natorial win.

Gardner said, "I am told O'Neill is giving serious consideration to allowing Sam to take a polygraph at the prison at Columbus. We'll all be there with Steeger's photographers and the works. NBC is excited. They're paying the freight."

Steeger was the *Argosy* editor. NBC was the network the upcom-ing *Court of Last Resort* TV show would be on.

"Hell, Erle. Sounds like we might be in the home stretch."

"It does at that. If we come back from Florida with something solid, a new trial is a damn near certainty."

We exchanged goodbyes and clicked off.

My naked bedmate had the paperback in her blanket-covered lap. She looked at me with big blue eyes; her breasts seemed to stare at me, wide-eyed, too.

She asked, "Was that Erle Stanley Gardner?"

"Yeah." I grinned at her. "And guess who you're in bed with? Paul Drake."

CHAPTER

Gary Weed—twenty-three, his slick-backed hair long and accompanied by endless sideburns—probably had an inch on my six feet. He was skinny, no more than 150 pounds I'd estimate, and almost good-looking, like a would-be rock 'n' roll idol dropped by his record label after one too many flops.

Hands cuffed before him, he shuffled in and, as directed by a uniformed jailer, sat in a straight-back chair next to a desk behind which sat Sheriff Rodney Thursby, broad-shouldered with a narrow oval of a face emphasized by his thinning dark hair's widow's peak. The sheriff wore glasses with dark plastic above the lenses and metal below, and no uniform or pinned-on star, no tie with his white short-sleeved shirt, cigarettes in the breast pocket. He had the unflappable look of a naval officer, which I'd been told he was during the war.

The sheriff had welcomed us to his domain, Gardner thanking him for his willingness to allow the Court of Last Resort to conduct a polygraph examination of Weed.

"Happy to have you here," Thursby said, affably professional. "Frankly, I don't have the funds available to do it myself."

Weed and the sheriff had a sizeable audience. Squeezed in the office of the jail, adjacent to the police station, were eight reporters from as far away as the *Chicago Tribune*, all standing, taking notes, forbidden to take part in the questioning conducted by two men seated in chairs across from the sheriff and his prisoner. One of those men was Erle Stanley Gardner, in a brown suit and darker brown tie. The other was me. I was in a short-sleeve shirt with no tie, having left it with my suitcoat in my rental car in the parking lot.

It was hot in DeLand, Florida, in June.

And, like I said, it was crowded in that office. Among the reporters and photographers were a few non-journalists, including Alex Gregory, the polygraph expert from Detroit who I'd met when he was one of the group examining the Sheppard brothers and their wives back in Chicago.

Getting here from Cleveland had taken three stops, including Tampa, with a connection to Daytona Beach, half an hour by car from DeLand. The latter was an idyllic little burg of six thousand or so, a college town with a village square, bandshell park, lots of oaks and the occasional palm. A block or so off a business district—where you might run into Judge Hardy and his family shopping for wholesome presents at Woolworth's or J.C. Penney— was the jail and police station.

Also nearby sprawled the Hotel Putnam, a six-story building in the Mediterranean Revival style with two wings, two towers, and flat roofs. I was surprised to find something so grand in such a small if picture-perfect town—apparently the hotel dated to the Florida land boom, and was only starting to show its age. Gardner, Gregory and I had dined in the restaurant off the lobby.

"I did two long sessions with Weed," Gregory said.

In his late fifties or early sixties, the polygraph examiner might have been a high school principal with his steel-gray hair, wire-frame glasses, and steady gaze. Age had given a softness to his face that was contradicted by sharp cheekbones. At this point all of us wore our suitcoats—the restaurant was air-conditioned.

We'd ordered and were waiting for our lunches.

"Three and a half hours yesterday," Gregory was saying, "and again today for four. He was cooperative, our young convict."

Gardner said to me, "He ran away from a prison work camp not far from here. Recaptured a day later. Sitting in jail awaiting trial on escape charges. Already faces ten years for a holdup in Tampa."

I asked, "How did we get from a Florida holdup to an Ohio homicide?"

Gregory said, "Weed told one of the jailers he wanted to get something off his chest—a crime he committed in Cleveland."

"Marilyn Sheppard's murder," I said.

"Yes and no. He never mentioned her name, just said he'd been in Cleveland early July '54, and that he'd driven to a western suburb in a stolen car. There he entered a big white house and beat a woman to death with a pipe, when she woke up as he was rifling a dresser."

Gardner said, "The sheriff, a modern type, no rubber-hose Southern lawman, interviewed this Weed boy, got more details, put it all down in a three-page single-spaced document. Then he got in touch with the Cleveland homicide bureau, sent them the statement. They showed no interest in following up."

"Which is where we come in," I said.

"Yes. And with us on the scene, the sheriff released a statement to the press, which is why we'll have so much company today. This little town is crawling with reporters—print and TV both."

"Anyone from NBC?"

"Oh yes." Gardner sipped iced tea. "This should give our new program a boost."

I wasn't sure whether he was talking about the TV show or the Court of Last Resort's efforts for Sheppard. And I didn't ask, too distracted by lunch arriving, including my grilled Florida pompano with buttered almonds.

I had just finished my apple pie with rum sauce when the conversation got going again.

"So the Weed kid is telling the truth," I asked the polygraph expert, "in your opinion? And the machine's, of course."

"He's telling the truth," Gregory said, after dabbing his mouth with a napkin, "or what he believes to be the truth. The reason I spent so much time with him is the seriousness of this thing. Giving Sam Sheppard false hope would just be cruel at this point."

And now Gary, who might have been James Dean's younger, less talented brother, was sitting there in his checked short-sleeve shirt and dungarees, cuffed hands in his lap. He seemed at once shy and eager to please.

"I'm Erle Stanley Gardner, Mr. Weed. And this is Nathan Heller, my investigator."

"Mr. Gardner," he said with a nod, his voice thin and with no discernible accent. He nodded to me, said, "Mr. Heller, sir." I nodded back.

"Mr. Weed," Gardner began, but the boy grinned bashfully at him, holding up a timid hand.

"Call me 'Gary,' please. I'm no 'mister.'"

"All right, Gary," Erle said with a grandfatherly smile. That round face of his had a way of suggesting warmth one moment and dead seriousness in the next. "Suppose you tell us a little about yourself."

The slender convict's eyebrows went up, though the eyes themselves stayed half-lidded; a good trick. "I figure it's the bad things you'd like to hear about. The good things don't really apply in this here situation."

I gave him a little help. "Where were you born, Gary?"

"Washington, D.C., sir. My pop ran off before I can remember. My mom was a waitress and . . . well, a prostitute is what you call it, in polite terms."

I'd never thought of "prostitute" as a polite term, but he had a point. "Whore" and "hooker" were definitely worse, and "courtesan" probably wasn't in his vocabulary.

"I dropped out of school at fourteen. Went to the reformatory for stealin' a car when I was fifteen. Did jail time as a vagrant, which I guess is a bum with no visible means of support or such. Got took in the air force, though! That was pretty cool, till they kicked me out. Stealin' from the PX. Did prison time for a gas station holdup. Escaped a couple times. I got slippery ways. Got a dime for me to do waitin' in Tampa for robbery."

I said, "Tell us about Cleveland."

"Well, I got out of stir around March of that year—'54. I hung out at my grandmother's in Virginia for a couple of months. That was boring and she wanted work out of me, so I took off hitch-hikin'. I was everywhere from Colorado Springs to Cheyenne, even L.A. a while, then took off east. Wound up in Omaha."

Erle said, "Cleveland, Gary. Tell us about Cleveland."

"That's where things got a little out of hand. I was dead broke, and I didn't have a piece or anything, so a stickup was out of the question. Anyway, I was hopin' to stay out of stir for a while. So I slept in alleys and parks and such. Then I broke down and helped load some fella's truck . . . and come away with fifty bucks! Man, that was real sweet."

I asked, "What did you do with all that money, Gary?"

"What do you think? I picked a girl up in a café, and went up to her place. Stayed the night. I gave her a few bucks, but she wasn't a whore or anything."

More like a courtesan.

Weed lurched forward, frowning, his sleepy eyes waking up. "Don't you ask me what her name was! I won't tell you. She was a nice girl and I don't wanna get her in no trouble or embarrassment or that. Anyway, I wandered around, took in a movie—ever see *Three Coins in the Fountain*? I saw that. That was good. Girls was pretty. Then at a bar I met a guy named Harry Freeman. Ex-marine with a disability pension from Korea. I stayed with him a couple days."

I asked, "What kind of guy was Harry?"

"Oh, a good guy. Great guy. Of course, he had a habit, 'cause of his war wound and all? Anyway, he fixed me up with some heroin that night, and I shot up at his apartment."

I saw Gardner flinch, just a little bit, then I asked, "What night?"

"This night we're talkin' about, sir. July the third. I sat all dreamy a while, lookin' out the window. You could see this bright glow in the sky! I got kind of excited, like maybe it was a flyin' saucer from outer space. Harry said it was just the Indians playin' the White Sox. Must be goin' extra innings, Harry says, 'cause it was around midnight. I felt dizzy, like I was floatin'.'"

I asked, "Did you pass out, or fall asleep maybe?"

"No. I got it in my head it was time to get out of Cleveland. Earlier, Harry was sayin' if I was gonna keep bunkin' with him, I really oughta kick in some dough. But I run through most of that fifty, so . . . well, I grabbed these two grips of mine and just went out in the night. I wasn't in no kind of mood to hitchhike, so I walked along some side streets, lookin' for a car to boost. The second one I tried was unlocked and had a key in the ignition. I got behind the wheel and took off."

I asked, "What color car, Gary? Do you remember? Old? New? Beat-up? Nice?"

"Oh, nice enough, but not new, not *brand*-new. Could've stood a wash. Four-door. A '49 maybe, or '50 or '51. It was a smooth ride, though. Man, I never had that feeling before or since—seems like somethin' was urgin' me on! I drove west out of Cleveland and wound up in some suburb, a very good part of town, right on the lake."

I asked, "How did you settle on a particular house?"

"Oh, I spotted one with the front door ajar, no lights on. It was a big two-story, built right down to the ground. There was a big tree in the yard and a driveway to a garage 'long the side of the house. I drove down a couple of blocks and parked, come back and just walked in the front door."

I asked, "What were you wearing, Gary?" This I did because he was starting to rush and I wanted to get it slow and in detail.

"Uh . . . a dark blue shirt," he said. "Khaki pants, tennies, yellow-and-gray socks, you know, what do they call it? Argyle? And underwear—just shorts."

Gardner asked, "Were you armed, Gary?"

"Not with a gun! I never carry no guns. That can get you in

trouble. What I had was this curved piece of pipe I found in California. It was square all around, not round like a lot of pipes. Had a flange on each end. I'd say it was one inch by one inch, with sharp corners. About nine inches long. I can make a drawing for you, if you like."

"Maybe later," Gardner said. "Go on."

"I was in a kind of hallway and past a kitchen, then it opened up into a room with a staircase to the left and a man in a couch up against the side of it. He was snoring. Really sawing logs. I just kind of crept past him and went upstairs—went into a bedroom. I was in there such a short time, it's hard to remember every little thing. A woman was asleep on a bed. Kind of on top of the covers. Slippers were on the floor and some clothes on a chair. Light come in through the doorway of the bedroom from a bulb burnin' somewhere outside the room."

He paused, drew in several breaths that he let slowly out.

I said, "Take your time, Gary."

"I went to a dresser and started lookin' for something to steal. Money, I hoped, but didn't find nothing worth takin'. I was closing the drawer, and maybe it made a noise because I heard a sound from the bed. It was like a woman coughing, like she just waked up. Not a scream. The iron pipe was stuffed in my pants. I got it out and went over to her. She was about thirty years old. Not fat or anything. She looked right at me. I thought she was going to . . . to do something."

"And what did *you* do?"

"I hit her with the pipe, three or four times. I know they say she got hit more times than that, and I maybe I did, but I don't remember it. If she screamed, I didn't hear it. But I was, you know . . . excited. And there was a lot of blood. It got all over me."

The reporters behind us were murmuring.

Gardner said, "Then what?"

"Then I heard somebody comin' up the stairs! I went out there and a guy was at the top of them. I hit him once, with the pipe, on the side of the head. I figured it was that guy sleepin' on the couch.

He started to fall and I shoved him out of the way. Just pushed past him and ran downstairs."

I asked, "What did you do then, Gary?"

"Well, I got down there and kind of got my, you know, my bearings. And I realized nobody was after me. That guy upstairs, I musta knocked him out. So maybe I could score something down here. I saw this leather satchel, you know, a doctor's bag? I dumped it out, but I didn't see nothing worth taking, tongue depressors, pill bottles. I tried to see what kind of pills they was, read the labels, but the only light was the moon through the windows. But then I heard that guy comin' down the stairs. I ran across the living room and onto a porch and then out a door to the bluff. There was all these wooden stairs and I run down them. Toward the water."

I asked, "Were you followed down those stairs?"

"I don't know. I never saw that guy again. I just ran along the beach, oh, maybe four, five hundred feet, in the direction of where I parked my car. I stopped and hurled that damn pipe into the lake. Then I went out into the water, a little ways, to kind of wash the blood off. After that, I climbed the bluff up to where I parked that Ford."

Gardner asked, "Where did you drive next?"

"Nowhere! Not right away. I just got out of those wet, bloody clothes, right there in the car. Got fresh clothes out of one of my grips, put the bloody clothes in the other. Then I drove back to Cleveland and dumped the car."

"Leaving the clothes behind, son?"

He shook his head. "No, I figured them clothes was evidence, and I best dispose of 'em, far away. And, anyway, having suitcases to carry is the best way to hitchhike. Anybody thinkin' of picking you up knows you're for real and not some fiend lookin' to rob or kill them."

Neither I nor Gardner knew quite how to react to that.

"Anyway," he went on, unprompted, "I got a ride right away, with an elderly man—fifty or sixty years old."

I guess that put both Gardner and me in our places.

"He let me stick the suitcase in back," Weed was saying, "and I climbed in front with him. We went east and, after about fifty miles, he said this was his stop, and let me out, and he turned off the highway down a dirt road."

I asked, "What then, Gary?"

"Well, I was there with my suitcases and I figured I best dispose of the one with the bloody things, pronto. I walked along and come to some road construction. Thought maybe I could put that grip somewhere where cement would go over it. Then I saw some tools that hadn't been put away, including a shovel. There was a wooded area and I walked back in there, dug a hole, and buried those bloody clothes, just leavin' 'em in the grip."

Gardner asked, "Could you lead us there, Gary?"

He shook his head, the slicked-back hair coming loose a little. "Not in a million years. I don't know that part of the world that well. Anyway, I went back to the highway and picked up another ride, just a few miles later. A sailor picked me up. He was in uniform, so I told him how I'd been in the air force. Left out the part about the PX and the brig and all. He was a good guy. Bought me some food at a diner along the way. Even played my favorite song on the jukebox for me—'Sh Boom.' Nice fella. Drove me on into Norfolk. That's where I saw it."

"Saw what?" Gardner asked.

"Saw it in the papers that this woman named Sheppard got killed. I was sorry to hear she was dead. I had no intention of killin' her."

Gardner and I exchanged glances.

"After that, I stayed with some relatives, in this place and that, wound up in Tampa. Got busted for vagrancy, and when they turned up my record, they left me in the can for two whole weeks. I went in a café, wrote a note to the cashier saying I had a gun, which I didn't, but he gave me the money and I got ten years. Sent to a road camp. I did some time, then just last month I busted out—road camps are a cinch, if you can just play model prisoner long enough to build their trust up."

Sheriff Thursby spoke for the first time, addressing Gardner and me: "We picked him up here in DeLand."

And also for the first time, Weed frowned. "I wasn't *doin'* nothin'!"

"No, but your face was," Thursby said. "It was looking right at me from a wanted circular."

Gardner asked, "Are you a drug addict, Gary?"

He shook his head and the hair loosened further. "No, sir. I use them sometimes, for . . . you know. Fun. Or, you know, relaxation purposes. Sometimes I get really low, so it's nice to get high. But I ain't no junkie."

I said, "How about you draw us that picture, Gary? Of the pipe you say you used?"

"Sure."

Thursby got the suspect a piece of white typing paper and a number-two pencil. Weed turned to use the side of the sheriff's desk, to support the paper, and began to draw.

He was left-handed.

Erle Gardner, Alex Gregory and I sat on a wrought-iron bench in the courtyard of the U-shaped hotel. Once again, early dusk made everything seem more beautiful, the well-manicured grounds with their greenery and occasional palms conspiring with a breeze from the nearby ocean to make the evening almost tropically pleasant.

Gardner was in his shirt sleeves and no tie—all three of us were. But Erle wore a Stetson. I wondered if he knew the inventor of the definitive cowboy hat had lived in DeLand, which had been the Wild West only during land boom days. The university here was named after him. Stetson, not Gardner, who was leaning back, enjoying a cigar.

I sat between the two Court of Last Resort board members. We'd just had dinner in the restaurant, but I was digesting more than that.

Gardner was saying, "Back in the '20s, this hotel was a frequent stop not just for tourists, but celebrities and entrepreneurs and even foreign ministers. That famous radio bellboy who cried, 'Call for Phillip Morris,' was employed here, not to carry your bags but as an entertainer. Many a famous actor and actress, in town for dates at the Athens Theater, just down the street, bunked in here."

Maybe he did know the Stetson connection.

"I heard," I said, "the guy who created Perry Mason once stayed here."

"I know you're pleased with our results, Erle," Gregory said, having none of such foolishness, "but there are obvious discrepancies in our man's story."

"I know," Gardner said, cigar in his teeth like a cocky politician, "and I made it clear to Governor O'Neill, when I called him late this afternoon, that this was only the beginning. That a new line of investigation needs opening up."

The governor, hearing Gardner's account of the Weed interrogation, had approved a polygraph examination of Sam Sheppard at the Ohio penitentiary. This was a major victory and the mystery writer was feeling good.

I was feeling okay. "Good" would be overstating it. And if I had to characterize Gregory, I wouldn't go past "fair."

"Weed believes what he's saying," Gregory said, leaning out to get Gardner's gaze. "But that he used narcotics on the murder night is . . . worrisome."

I said, "Our boy Gary may have read about the murder later. Hell, he *said* he did. I don't know that he's given us anything that wasn't in the papers. He could be looking back through a dope haze of a night and fantasizing he was responsible."

"Again," Gardner said, raising a palm like an Indian about to say *How,* "our results aren't definitive. But the subject passed the polygraph and told a logical, compelling story. And that should be enough to get an inquiry reopened, and that's all we're after."

"I agree," I said, "but the Cleveland PD may not. They'll seize on the discrepancies, like pointing out Weed said Marilyn was struck three or four times, not thirty-five. No sign of a bureau drawer being disturbed, either. Or the white form attacking Marilyn, seen through the open doorway by Sam, before he was struck. And what about the stolen items in the green bag? Gary has no memory of a struggle on the beach with Sam. And then there's the sexual aspect—he said not a word about pulling her pajama top up and the bottoms down."

Gardner gestured with cigar in hand, like Churchill making a point. "Mr. Weed gets the general layout of the yard and house right. He remembers dumping out the doctor's bag—perhaps during the drug-addled episode, he forgot or lost track of that. The same might be true about how many times he hit her."

"If explaining things away because he was on dope is our best course of action," I said, "we're in more trouble than Weed."

Gardner's frown was frustration-edged. "Nate, are you saying you don't like this boy for a suspect?"

"I like him fine. He's just the kind of petty repeat offender who might take advantage of an open door on Lake Road, to walk in and help himself to somebody's else's money and possessions. Of course, if Gary knew ahead of time Sam was a doctor, that kind of home invasion makes even more sense—he *is* a drug user."

Gregory said, "Don't forget that Weed describes a blunt instrument consistent with the crime. And that he recalls the blood-soaked clothes such a crime would induce. Additionally, he's about the right size, *bigger* than Dr. Sheppard."

"And that hair of his," I granted, "minus the Wildroot Cream-Oil, might make a bushy-haired man out of him . . . or bushy-haired kid, anyway. A little skinny to get the best of Dr. Sam, though."

Gardner, frowning in thought, said, "Not necessarily. He's young. Probably damn agile. Sam, waking up from a deep sleep, ten years older, might well have met his match."

Gregory said, "I *am* bothered by the boy saying nothing about the robbery downstairs, other than a passing reference to the doctor's bag."

I said, "Let me offer a possibility that a mystery writer might appreciate."

That made Gardner smile a little. He took a puff from the cigar he'd forgotten, then said, "Go on."

"What if Weed's story is true, in almost every detail? Let's allow that he may have gone batty, doped up as he was, and bludgeoned Marilyn Sheppard in some kind of frenzy. So he knocks Sam out, and, waking up and finding Marilyn dead, Dr. Sam knows immediately he'll be a suspect. With all of his screwing around with other women, the prime suspect. The *only* suspect. So he quickly fakes the robbery himself. And concocts a story about chasing the intruder and doing his best to stop him. Painting himself a hero, not a cheater in a bad position. And once he tells this tale, he's stuck with it."

Gregory was thinking about that, but Gardner was grinning. He liked a wild plot. "Not bad, Nate. Not bad. I'll have to remember that one."

I turned over a hand. "Here's another—perhaps Weed's confession lacks some details because he wasn't alone. What if he had an accomplice on his break-in—that Freeman character, possibly. And he's either protecting his accomplice, or himself *from* that accomplice."

Gardner's eyes narrowed behind the lenses of his glasses. "That would explain such missing elements as the absence of a struggle with Sheppard—it might have involved the accomplice, not the Weed boy."

Gregory was slowly shaking his head. "For all my probing—and yours, gentlemen—our suspect has raised as many questions as he's answered."

We all thought about that as the warm saltwater breeze did its best to lull us. It had been a long day for all concerned.

"To me," I said, "the biggest problem is not a few flaws in this Weed kid's account—it's the unwillingness of the Cleveland cops and prosecutors and the whole mess of them to admit to maybe making a mistake. A bad one."

But Gardner shook his head. "Nate, you're more cynical than I. I truly believe the authorities, at least in general, mean well. Mean to dispense justice in a fair-minded manner."

"Even if I give you that, Erle," I said, "in general? It's the specific instances that give me this cynical view . . . and the flawed human beings who appear to populate this world."

When Gardner had finished his cigar, we got up and strolled into the lobby, on our way to the bar for a nightcap.

"Now that we have the governor's okay," Gardner was saying to Gregory, "I'll assemble our team and fly everyone into Columbus. Nate, I don't think you need to make that trip. We'll be limited to just our polygraph experts."

"That's fine. I should go back to Chicago and earn a little money, anyway."

"You'll be the first call I make," he told me, a big grin on his big face.

"Erle," I said, and put a hand on his sleeve, stopping him. Gregory had already thrown on the brakes. I nodded toward the front desk.

Nattily dressed in a seersucker suit and sporty hat, Dr. Samuel Gerber was checking in. With him, in a baggy suit, looking not at all sporty, was Detective Robert Schottke, the first cop to interview Sam Sheppard about the murder.

"Gerber's a friend," Gardner said, gently pulling away, smiling, though not so big now. "He's a good man. I'll say hello."

He strode over and I followed him, feeling like a bodyguard. Gregory stayed planted where he was, like Lot's wife after she got a good look.

"Sam," Erle said, extending his hand, grinning.

Gerber turned from the register, froze momentarily, then smiled the way a father does to his daughter's first date at the door. The Cleveland coroner shook the offered hand, briefly.

"I guess I know what brings you here," Erle said pleasantly. "This is quite a development."

"Is it?" Gerber asked, the smile gone. "That's your man Gregory over there, isn't it? You might tell him that Gary Weed is a psychotic, which a *real* expert would know invalidates any lie detector test."

Awkwardly, Gardner said, "Have you already been to the jail here, to interview the prisoner?"

"No. We're doing that tomorrow."

"Well . . ." Gardner seemed stunned by this less than warm welcome. ". . . if the Weed boy is psychotic—that's something a psychiatrist would have to ascertain, wouldn't you say?"

Gerber's chin came up. "I would say he's a faker, looking for notoriety and a way to avoid going back to the Tampa jail."

I took a verbal poke at that chin: "Going to Ohio for a shot at death row seems like a funny way to avoid jail in Florida."

Gerber ignored that, saying to Gardner, "You and your so-called Court of Last Resort 'experts' are busybodies interested only in increasing the circulation of some cheap men's magazine . . . *and* feathering their nests with profits from another of your sensationalistic TV shows. Now if you'll excuse me?"

And Dr. Samuel Gerber went off with his police detective companion, carrying their own luggage. Apparently the bellboys were off calling for Phillip Morris somewhere.

As for Gardner, he looked so white and ready to pop, his face might have been one big blister. Gregory walked up and joined us.

"Nice of him spending Cleveland taxpayers' money," I said, "to come down to Florida and . . . how did you put it? 'Dispense justice in a fair-minded way?'"

The color came back to the writer's face and he said, "Let's have that drink."

"Sustained," I said.

CHAPTER

For the first time in over a week, I was in my inner sanctum at the Chicago branch of the A-1 Detective Agency, seated behind the old scarred desk dating back to the early '30s and my one-room office over the Dill Pickle on Van Buren.

Those digs, which for several years (thanks to a Murphy bed) served as my apartment as well, lacked what success had brought the A-1 and me. This spacious office sported a leather couch, leather client chairs, wooden file cabinets, and walls where framed famous faces from my past and present—including Flo Kilgore—smiled at me, flaunting their personal inscriptions. My son Sam shared a double stand-up frame on my desk with my ex-wife, Peggy, who I hated and still loved.

My partner, Lou Sapperstein, who went back even further than my desk, had left a stack of reports for me to peruse while his wife, Gladys, our office manager and my former secretary, provided a pile of letters for me to approve and sign. These I encountered upon getting to the office at ten A.M., which was a prerogative of being the boss. In half an hour we'd have our weekly staff meeting. Beyond my door was a bullpen of modern desks with mostly modern young operatives, stolen away from various police forces and the occasional rival agency.

Such was the life of a successful private detective in June 1957.

I was finished with the letters and getting ready to dig into the reports when the phone rang. Our receptionist, Millie, was on the line with a call for me.

"It's Erle Stanley Gardner!" she said.

Millie was new. Our previous girl had taken any number of calls from Gardner, relating to jobs I've done pro bono for the Court of Last Resort.

"Put him on," I said.

"I watch *Perry Mason* every week!" she said.

"Tell him that, then put him on."

"And I've read tons of his books."

"Tell him that, too."

She went off to do that, then Erle was on the line.

"If I fly to Chicago," he said, skipping any greeting, "can you have supper with me this evening?"

"Sure. What's up?"

"Make a reservation. George Diamond's?"

"George Diamond's it is, Erle. Seven o'clock?"

"Six."

"Sheppard case again?"

"Yes, goddamnit."

He said goodbye and hung up.

This was probably not good news—he'd been scheduled today to go to the Ohio State Penitentiary in Columbus for the polygraph examination of Dr. Sam. With him were Alex Gregory, John E. Reid, C. B. Hanscom, and Dr. LeMoyne Snyder, the group that had made the lie tests with the Sheppard brothers and their wives. With Gardner himself present this time, I hadn't been needed.

So a little before six, I was shown to a booth in back reserved for my guest and me in the legendary Chicago steakhouse on South Wabash. The place had a decidedly masculine feel with its dark paneling and rich red carpet, chairs and booths, although the framed paintings by Walter Keane of sad-eyed kids and sadder clowns seemed more inclined to please the fairer sex. Colored chefs were broiling steaks over charcoal in brick ovens, right out in the restaurant, providing a smoky aura that swallowed up tobacco fumes.

I ordered a vodka gimlet, which arrived just before Gardner, shown to the booth by a red-jacketed waiter.

"Bring me a bourbon straight up," Gardner told the waiter. "Four Roses Single Barrel."

"Yes, sir."

The mystery writer, normally rather genial, wore a sour expression; also a brown suit with a tan shirt and a Western-style bolo tie, with a golden horse's head gripping the rawhide strands. He looked like a rancher who'd just been grossly underpaid for his herd by George Diamond himself.

"They turned us away, Nate," he said, sliding in across from me. "The whole damn team!"

I blinked at him. "Why in hell?"

He tossed a hand in the air. "The governor withdrew his permission, without notice. We were on the damn *grounds* of the place when they kicked us out!"

"Getting tossed out of prison," I said, after a sip of gimlet, "is a pretty good trick. I thought you said Governor O'Neill was enthusiastic about the polygraph—happy to give Sam a chance to prove he'd been telling the truth all along, and maybe help bring the real killer to justice."

The waiter returned with Gardner's bourbon and took our order. We both got the filet mignon.

"All I know for a certainty," Gardner said, then paused to toss back some bourbon, "is permission was withdrawn. Warden Alvis himself turned us away, and he'd been all for it! These distinguished men, experts in their fields, invited by the governor personally, traveling hundreds of miles to get there . . . only to be turned away."

"Pressure from Gerber?"

His grunt wasn't exactly a laugh. "Not just Gerber. The original judge in the case, Blythin, made a public statement. A friend at the

Associated Press told me it was going out on the wire—Blythin said something to the effect that Court of Last Resort was putting itself above the Ohio and United States Supreme Courts."

Blythin. Who had, in his chambers, told Flo Kilgore that the case was open and shut—that the man who would momentarily be standing before his docket was guilty as sin. I wanted to share that with Gardner, but without betraying Flo, I couldn't. Damn. Shit!

"Don't give up hope, Erle," I said. "I told you about my talk with Prosecutor Cullitan. Maybe we can convince him to come forward."

He frowned, cocked his head. "Nate, haven't you heard? Frank Cullitan died last night—in the hospital. Heart attack."

Hell.

Our salad came. This was my favorite salad in the Loop—half a head of lettuce, crisp and cold, coated with crushed croutons and particularly delicious when drenched by the three house dressings mixed together. But I ate slowly, with no enthusiasm. Gardner, however, attacked his half a head as if it were Gerber's.

We ate in silence, and then I asked, "So what next? I'd like to talk to Hardmann, who seems a good, overlooked suspect. He's in California. While I'm out there, I could talk to Sharon Kern. She's no suspect, but as the 'other woman,' she would be—"

He raised a fork. Like a gladiator raising a trident. "No," he said.

"No?"

He lowered his fork and leaned in. "That's why I wanted to speak to you in person. I had no other reason to make a stop at Chicago. You've worked hard on this matter, and it's cost you time and money. You have a right to hear me say it."

"Say what?"

He swallowed a bite of nothing, which seemed not to taste good at all. "That we have no alternative but to withdraw. I'm officially announcing the Court of Last Resort is dropping its investigation into the Sheppard case until or unless it becomes possible to examine him by polygraph."

"Erle, don't take this personally. This is just Ohio politics. More than just Gerber and Blythin weighed in on this thing, behind the scenes, you can bet on it."

His jaw was set, his eyes piercing. "But I *do* take it seriously, Nate. My integrity, and that of my colleagues, has been unfairly maligned. Some damn Ohio politicians cussing me out doesn't bother me. But the Court of Last Resort itself has taken quite a lot of undeserved abuse. We're left with picking up the pieces and going back to making our respective livings."

Not meaning to malign him unfairly even further, I had to think part of his funk came from the embarrassment the affair would mean to NBC and the new *Court of Last Resort* TV program. But I kept that to myself.

"We will fold our tents like the Arabs and noisily steal away," he was saying. He finished his bourbon. "You know, Nate, no one on the Court of Last Resort ever announced a belief that Dr. Sheppard is innocent. We *did* state we felt the case should be investigated thoroughly. We *did* give our opinion that his two brothers and their wives had absolutely no knowledge that would indicate Dr. Sam is guilty. Nor did they do anything to obscure evidence."

"An opinion," I said, "based on rigorously controlled polygraph testing."

"Right! And the conclusions that were reached were either true, or else we'd better throw all of our polygraphs in Lake Michigan and forget about them."

Our steaks arrived, as well as baked potatoes with butter and sour cream. Gardner was definitely a meat-and-potatoes man. When he carved into the rare, football-size filet, the blood ran, and his attack on the thing showed he'd not lost his appetite for the fight.

But this round was clearly over.

I heard from Gardner a few times by phone in the coming weeks.

He reported that Sam's lawyer, Corrigan, had gone to DeLand and brought back a signed confession from Weed.

And a couple of things had come up that seemed to support the young convict's story—he'd claimed he hocked one of the suitcases he'd hauled along on his hitchhiking; a bartender who had then been working at the pawnshop in question remembered both Weed and the "grip." The "elderly man" remembered picking Weed up, hitchhiking. A woman recalled seeing a dirty dark blue car parked down from the Sheppard place.

None of it carried any weight with the Ohio authorities. Gardner talked to the press about the Cleveland police and their uncooperativeness. It didn't go anywhere.

As for Gary Weed, Sheriff Thursby reported to Gardner that the young man had been a model prisoner in his jail, before heading to Raiford Prison, where he'd be eligible for parole in five or six years.

For now, the kid who wasn't an addict but shot up on heroin, from time to time, was working in the prison hospital.

Like Dr. Sam was, back in Ohio.

– BOOK TWO –

FACT FINDING

1966

CHAPTER

12

"When Sam Sheppard first stood trial," F. Lee Bailey said, "I was flying Sabrejets for the Marine Corps."

The attorney, bull-necked, broad-shouldered, bore a burly form worthy of a football guard, mitigated by a three-piece tailored navy blue pinstripe suit and gold watch chain.

"At the time," he went on, "the case, despite its notoriety, made no particular impression on me. And Sam had been in jail six years by the time I was licensed to practice law."

With his resonant voice, shrewd squinty eyes, and a self-confidence too cool to be considered arrogance, Bailey made fascinating company. And with his widow's-peaked dark hair and squared-off oval of a face, his brow almost permanently creased in thought, he had the bearing of a defense attorney in a Hollywood film, though much younger at thirty-three than Jimmy Stewart in *Anatomy of a Murder* or Charles Laughton in *Witness for the Prosecution.*

"It's been a long road," he said, with the slight smile that was his equivalent of a grin.

Shortly after the death of Sam Sheppard's defense attorney, William Corrigan, in July 1961, Bailey became Dr. Sam's new lawyer. I had made the recommendation to Steve and Richard Sheppard myself, based on my acquaintance—friendship might be overstating it—with Bailey, who worked out of Boston but made a trip to

Chicago every other month to lecture at the Keeler Polygraph Institute. When I met him in '61, the young attorney was already a well-established examiner in that field.

That recommendation, and a few minor related jobs for Bailey, was the extent of my involvement with the Sheppard case, over the last nine years. Erle Stanley Gardner, though he made occasional public statements about the unfairness of Sheppard's incarceration, had divorced himself not only from the case but the Court of Last Resort itself. Pro-Sheppard articles continued to appear in *Argosy*, but without Gardner's input. The failure of the Court's TV show, added to the Sheppard debacle, had put a damper on the entire enterprise.

Meanwhile, Bailey had been doing battle with the Ohio authorities ever since he took Dr. Sam on as a client. In April 1963, the attorney filed a habeas corpus petition in U.S. District Court, asserting that prejudicial publicity before and during the 1954 trial violated Dr. Sam's due process. In July '64, a District Court judge declared the 1954 trial a "mockery of justice," in violation of Sheppard's Fourteenth Amendment rights, and ordered his release. In March 1965, the State of Ohio appealed the ruling, which was reversed.

But earlier this month, by an 8–1 vote, the United States Supreme Court concluded that Bailey was correct: Sam Sheppard had not received a fair trial, and the murder verdict was declared invalid.

"I have to admit to being surprised," Bailey said, "that the state intends to retry Sam."

He was alternating between puffs of his Pall Mall and sips of his Scotch and water. We were in a booth on the third floor of the Playboy Club, in the VIP Room, which provided the only real privacy in Hugh Hefner's Walton Street monument to his magazine's lifestyle (*Argosy* would have had a hunting lodge).

"I really didn't think they'd bother trying Sam again," the attorney went on, "but the prosecutor—John Corrigan, no relation to the late William—was ready with a speech to read in front of the cameras the moment the Supreme Court decision was made public."

In a way the prosecutor's manipulation of the press was Bailey's own fault: for years the defense attorney had fought for Dr. Sam not just in the Ohio and U.S. courts, but in the court of public opinion. He'd lectured at colleges and before civic groups; sometimes accompanied by Steve Sheppard, Bailey had gone on radio and television, stirring up petitions and letter-writing campaigns to several Ohio governors.

Early on, when he was trying to land a polygraph test for his new client, Bailey had gone to see Louis Seltzer to ask for fair treatment and support in return for press access. He met Seltzer in his office, flanked by the man's city and managing editors. He said his piece, then was subjected to derision by the two editors, Seltzer just listening and smiling as Bailey was told he was "a fresh kid" seeking publicity, who wouldn't "last two weeks as Sheppard's lawyer."

Ignoring the editors, Bailey reminded Seltzer, "You're an old man," while Bailey was a young man. For all the publisher's influence and money, the lawyer intended not only to beat him, but humiliate him. Seltzer had better die before then, because his public image would be destroyed when Bailey was done. This was the price of turning away an attorney who only asked for reasonable treatment for himself and his client.

At least that was the way Bailey had described the encounter to me.

In the years since I introduced him, by letter, to the Sheppard brothers, Bailey had risen from a civil litigation attorney fresh out of law school to the most famous criminal defense attorney on the planet, representing such notorious clients as Albert ("the Boston Strangler") DeSalvo, accused wife killer Dr. Carl Coppolino, and the Plymouth Mail Robbery suspects. He owned and flew his own planes and made use of the latest James Bondian security and communications gadgetry.

We'd had a late supper—trout for me, filet for the attorney—and now were getting around to why Bailey had wanted this audience.

"You may wonder why I haven't called upon you and the A-1,"

he said, "more often in the Sheppard case. After all, you started the ball rolling, introducing me to the Sheppards."

"I haven't wondered," I said. And hadn't cared. I'd had my fill of that mess.

"We're both marines," he said, "and I'm an ex-PI myself. So I know who you are and what the A-1 represents."

I lifted my gimlet and worked up a smile. "Semper fi, mac."

His mouth formed kind of a kiss of amusement. "After all, they based *Peter Gunn* on you, didn't they?"

"Wouldn't go that far. Got a consultant credit and small check per episode, though. Is Sam getting anything for *The Fugitive*?"

The wildly popular David Janssen TV show about a doctor wrongly convicted for killing his wife, only to escape on his way to prison, had debuted in 1963.

"The creator denies it," Bailey said. "He claims it's a modern-day *Les Misérables*, but everyone knows what it's really based on."

"Why don't you sue?"

Now the smile turned small and sly. "Because that program has done more for Sam in the arena of public opinion than all of my efforts put together."

I sipped my gimlet, smiled a little. "Did you know *The Fugitive* and *The Untouchables* are produced by the same guy?"

"I hadn't really thought about that," Bailey said. "You *knew* Ness—toured the damn murder house with him."

I nodded. "And Eliot lived on the other side of the park from the Sheppard house, essentially next door, during his Cleveland days. Now they both have TV shows from the same source. Try selling a coincidence like that to a jury."

His eyebrows briefly rose. "No thanks. But what I'm getting around to, Nate, is that I haven't been neglecting you in this matter."

"I didn't think you had. I gave you all my case notes—I knew Erle Gardner wouldn't mind. But all of that work was pro bono, and I don't imagine the Sheppards have much money to spend at this point. And I'm not anxious for a contingency job."

He raised a hand as if swearing in. "Wouldn't ask that. I'm bank-rolling this thing myself, except for expenses. When the time comes, I'll charge Dr. Sam a whopping fee. There's already a book, being ghostwritten for him, and I just know a movie will come of all this."

"So you do want to hire me?"

Unspoken, the word "finally" seemed to attach itself to the end of that question.

He let out smoke in a moody stream; he was as good at that as Bogie. "I haven't really needed you till now, in any major way. Would you agree with me that Steve Sheppard is the brains and backbone of the family?"

"I would. Richard is no dummy, not by a long shot, but Steve's the aggressive one. The fighter."

Several small nods. "Right. And if his brother had killed Mar-ilyn, Steve would know it. He would have gotten the truth out of him. Sam is very intimidated by Steve."

"Agreed."

His head tilted down and his eyes came up. "And if Steve se-cretly knew that Sam had done this thing, do you believe for a second that Steve would put himself and the whole family through all this?"

"No."

"Neither do I. That's why I've known from almost the start that Sam is innocent. So you might wonder why I haven't spent more time on finding out who the real killer is—why I haven't turned somebody like Nathan Heller loose on it."

"Sure," I said with a shrug, though I hadn't really given that any thought.

"From a legal standpoint," he said, with a smile so small and quick it barely took hold, "the fact of Sam's innocence is of no help at all to him. All the factual questions were settled by the jury that convicted him. If a jury errs, their mistake can't be corrected, not on the basis of fact. New evidence, at that particular stage, was ir-relevant. The only way Sam could slip out from under that verdict was through an error of law."

I nodded. "It was all about the way laws had been applied in his case. And *not* applied."

"Yes! And in this case, by way of an outrageous violation of the Constitution. Actually, twenty-two of them."

I knew many of them.

Sam had been arraigned without his attorney present. The Cleveland Press had maliciously implicated Sam in the murder, and criticized law enforcement for not making an arrest. A change of venue had been denied. Motions to postpone the trial until the prejudicial atmosphere had waned were denied. The names of jurors were published a month before the trial began. The jurors were not sequestered. The judge neglected to warn jurors to disregard rumors, opinions and other pressures. Both the judge and prosecutor were running for reelection and bowed to the wishes of the press. Sam's home was impounded, keeping the defense from attaining evidence there. And two police officers had testified that Sam refused a polygraph exam, prejudicing the jury further.

"Did you know," Bailey asked, after another sip of Scotch, "that our old friend Samuel Gerber has gone public with a recommendation to the state attorney general that Sam be granted parole? I must be making him nervous."

"And Sam didn't jump at that?"

One eyebrow went up. "He was seriously tempted. But that would mean never practicing medicine again, and implicitly admitting guilt for a crime he didn't commit. He asked me if I could guarantee that I'd get him out. I told him no, but just the same, he said, 'I'll hang on.'"

"A tough call."

"Sure as hell was. The prison chaplain has been passing along messages saying if Sam filed a plea for clemency, it would be accepted and he could avoid retrial. After Sam didn't take the bait, the chaplain told him the state would commute his sentence to manslaughter, and let him out with time served—and all he had to do was fire me as counsel."

That got another smile out of me. "Sounds like Gerber isn't the only nervous one."

"No—another old friend, Louie Seltzer, is now suddenly compassionate, and the *Press* has suggested editorially that the penal authorities should match Dr. Gerber's 'compassionate objectivity.'"

A brunette bunny whose name badge ribbon on her hip was Dolly stopped by to dip and deliver a fresh Scotch to Bailey and another vodka gimlet to me, and smiles to each of us. We thanked her.

I sipped the fresh drink and asked, "Where do I come in?"

He gestured with cigarette in hand. "Now we're not thumbing through law books looking for loopholes. *Now* we have a second trial. Suddenly new evidence of Sam's innocence is paramount. That's where Nate Heller comes in. You can pick up where you left off for Gardner. You have insights into this case that no other investigator has. I want you back in Cleveland and anywhere else that will be helpful."

I shrugged a shoulder. "Both Sharon Kern and Lucas Hardmann are in California, or they were."

"They still are. But my office did some checking on their availability, and both Kern and Hardmann will be in Cleveland, visiting relatives, over the coming July Fourth holiday."

Fittingly enough.

"If you're willing and available," he said, as he lighted up a fresh Pall Mall, "I'll have a packet sent over to your office with various addresses and a few interesting facts my investigators have turned up—investigators not in your league, of course, but useful nonetheless."

One PI was a blond beauty who Lee liked to exit his planes with, for the reporters. He would take off his aviator's jacket and put on his mink topcoat first.

"Now you're blowing smoke," I said, which he literally was.

Half a smile now. "Flattery is always the cheapest bribe, even in Chicago. Did you recall that Hardmann's alibi that night was that he was away visiting a friend?"

"I do."

The biggest smile so far—still not terribly big, if awfully sly. "But are you aware that his alibi is another doctor who had been

Sharon Kern's fiancé prior—actually, initially, *during*—her affair with Sam?"

"I did. But I don't know that anybody's looked into it seriously."

"Also," he continued, "I have some interesting leads to share with you where the Dodges are concerned. They're divorced now, by the way, Mildred and Marshall. I won't insult you by telling you how to do your business, but I think putting your focus on the Dodges makes the most sense. I've built a theory around them that I hope to introduce in court, and create reasonable doubt."

"I'd rather hear about that theory, Lee, than read about it in a report."

His smile was a curtain that lifted only slightly above his teeth. "Good, because I haven't put it in writing yet. Try this out."

With no sign of forcible entry, we know that the doors at the Sheppard house were either unlocked or the killer had a key. In any case, no evidence indicates a strange intruder. The downstairs disorder seems more a cover than a search for valuables—only worthless things taken, and what burglar, what stranger, would hit a woman twenty-five or thirty times?

And if that were somehow the case, what stranger—having murdered Marilyn after she interrupted him—would pause before fleeing, solely to find a thing or two of value? It's also likely a stranger would take in the entire first floor, upon entering, before going to the second. He would almost certainly notice Sam sleeping on the daybed, in which case he'd hardly climb to the second floor to look around, or attack Marilyn, without disposing of Sam first. More likely he'd slip back out and find another objective. On the other hand, someone familiar with the floor plan, who entered through the Lake Road door and the kitchen, might go up the stairs, if he already knew where Marilyn slept. With the lights out, and the avenue of approach, this individual very possibly might not have seen the sleeping Sam.

It's reasonable, then, to say that the killer or killers demonstrated familiarity with the home. Both Marshall and Mildred Dodge were familiar with the layout of the Sheppard home, including Marilyn's bedroom.

Now let's consider motive. A frenzied killer of this nature is either a psychotic with an urge to kill anyone he came upon, and vent his mindless rage; or, more likely, a person who was angry as hell at Marilyn for personal reasons. The circumstances speak out against some wandering psychotic homicidal sex maniac.

So Marilyn was killed by someone she knew—who hated her.

The first trial focused on "the other woman," and in a roundabout way, I think they may have been right—but Marilyn Sheppard *was the other woman! Mildred Dodge may very well have killed Marilyn when she caught her husband, Marshall, in the act of sexual intercourse, or in a manner indicating he and his willing partner were about to engage in such an act. . . . Yes, one more Scotch, Dolly. Thank you, dear.*

In an eight-month period preceding her death, and probably for longer than that, Marshall Dodge was having an affair with Marilyn. This seems to be more than a lust-driven tryst—Dodge may well have been in love with her. We have a new witness, Nate, who you will read about and interview yourself, who saw Dodge with Marilyn, when her nightgown was off her shoulders and below her breasts, in the front hallway. Dodge was kissing her breasts. This new witness also saw Marilyn hand Dodge a key.

Another new witness, a young woman who you will interview, Nate, was a close friend who visited Marilyn every morning. And also every morning, Dodge would drop by for coffee . . . and probably something more. A routine was established where, when Dodge arrived, the young woman would leave.

As you might recall, Dodge served Marilyn breakfast in bed, at least once. So he clearly knew the short route to Marilyn's bedroom. He had a key to the house, we now know. He was also aware Sam left a night-light on across the hall from the bedroom when he went out on nighttime calls. He would have known that the houseguest, Hardmann, was not there, because Hardmann's car was not in the driveway, where during his stay it regularly was. Dodge might have assumed Hardmann, also a doctor, had gone to the hospital with Sam.

Now, you'll recall that Marilyn's pajama tops were pushed up over her breasts. . . . Thank you, Dolly. Nate, did you want another . . . ?

175

You're fine? Fine. Again, Marilyn's pajama top was pushed up, her pajama bottoms down around one leg. This is not consistent with a sex maniac ripping away his victim's clothes—it does indicate hurried sexual intercourse.

Marilyn was a lovely young woman. Mildred Dodge was not. Would it be fair of me to describe Mildred as an unusually unsightly female? Unkind perhaps, but accurate. Such women are understandably resentful of female beauty, and often are insecure in their own romantic relations, shall we say. Almost certainly she suspected what was going on between her husband and their attractive neighbor.

If on the night in question Mildred discovered at some point her husband had left the house, she might well know where to look for him. She would likely walk there, and it would be natural for her to take along a flashlight. That flashlight would have been in her hand when she arrived at the house. Whispers and noisy bed springs from the second floor could have easily encouraged her to climb the stairs. If she turned the flashlight beam on Marilyn and Marshall, what she saw could be cause for murder— the kind of frenzied murder the physical evidence tells us took place.

The wounds inflicted upon Marilyn could well have been inflicted with a metal flashlight, and by beating with fists. Mildred, by the way, is left-handed. Marilyn's fatal injuries are consistent with the strength of a woman—more so than a man. And the number of blows is consistent with the act of a woman flooded with jealous hatred. . . . Oh, thank you, Dolly. What a darling girl you are.

Sam Sheppard's spontaneous reference to Marilyn's killer was 'they,' indicating the presence of more than one person. Marshall Dodge, ashamed and shoved aside by his wife, was in a position—when Sam charged to the top of the stairs—to deliver that blow to the back of Sam's neck.

The aftermath, with Sam unconscious upstairs, was a hurried approximation of a robbery, probably after Marshall sent his wife home to dispose of her bloody clothing. Then came Sam down the stairs, and the pursuit to the beach, with the attendant struggle, followed.

But out of all these incriminating facts, the behavior of the Dodges, after they received Sam's frantic call, is the most damning. After hearing

Sam—'Marsh, come quick, I think they have killed Marilyn!'—does he call the police? No. Does he grab a weapon? No. Does he leave his wife at home behind securely locked doors? No. Does he respond immediately? No.

Instead, he gets up and gets dressed. His wife does the same—he waits for her to do so. He takes no weapon. He doesn't lock his doors. He gets in his car and drives the one hundred yards to Marilyn Sheppard's home, a trip he's made on foot countless times. He enters the Sheppard house taking no precautions, with his wife at his side.

As for Mildred, she did not hesitate to accompany her husband. She showed no fear. She did not lock her home, even though 'they'—killers— could have been in the area. Without being told by Sam where Marilyn was, Mildred made a beeline to the second-floor bedroom, in spite of any dangers that might await.

If guilty, the couple would have known there was no danger. Marshall would know that Mildred was responsible for this tragedy, in which he was now an accomplice, and likely ordered her to come along and help him do whatever might need doing. Both would know where the body lay, without being told. They would have their car handy, if they needed to run. They would be in a position to kill Sam or Marilyn, should Sam have come to realize who had done this to him, as Marilyn, if still alive, surely would have. They would have killed her then. They placed no calls to the police until the situation had fully presented itself.

"It's a workable theory," I said.

"I believe it's more than a theory," he said, matter-of-factly. "I'm convinced the Dodges are responsible."

I sipped my gimlet as he lighted up yet another Pall Mall. "Lee, I don't work it out that way. It's trying to prove a conclusion you've already come to, which tends to exclude any evidence that doesn't fit. Frankly, it's the way Gerber and the rest of that Cleveland crowd railroaded Dr. Sam Sheppard."

He twitched a smile and smoke curled from his lips.

"You're right, of course," he said. "And if you can find a better murderer or two, by all means do so. You *are* going to take the job?"

"Yes." I grunted a laugh. "But I have to tell you, going back to Cleveland holds little appeal."

"Who really does relish going to Cleveland?"

I shook my head. "For me, it's just got too many ghosts."

His laugh was barely audible and nothing to do with humor. "Your friend Eliot," he said. "And Flo—she accompanied you on those Cleveland interviews in '57, didn't she?"

I nodded.

He chuckled. "You know, I may owe a good share of that Supreme Court win to you, Nate."

"How's that?"

"You advised me to talk to Flo. To remind her that Judge Blythin was dead, and any responsibility to protect him was past. I had no idea what you were talking about."

"I figured she'd do the right thing."

"And she did. I'm just relieved she gave me that deposition before we lost her. Did she *really* take her life?"

I sighed. "She was working on a book called *Murder One*, Lee. Due to be published next year by her friend Bennett Cerf. One of the key chapters is the Sheppard case, open-ended of course. But the big finish? She had the inside dope on the JFK assassination. She got Jack Ruby to talk. She was a wonder. So, no. She didn't really take her life."

He lifted his tumbler of bourbon. "Here's to Flo. Let's see if you can finish that Sheppard chapter for her."

CHAPTER

13

I lured Flo Kilgore back to Cleveland—in January 1964—on one of two jobs relating to the Sam Sheppard case I took on for F. Lee Bailey, prior to the investigative work in '66. Flo was eager to make the trip—what good reporter wouldn't have gone to far worse places than Cleveland for an exclusive like this?

After picking her up at Cleveland Hopkins International Airport, I shared with her what I'd learned from a private detective agency in Düsseldorf, West Germany. She already knew some of the background, but you may not, so here it is.

In December 1962, Lee Bailey received a letter postmarked West Germany. Folded up in red stationery, with "Ariane" printed in white at the top, was a check for one thousand marks—$253 American—the biggest donation to date from a single person for the Sam Sheppard defense fund.

Bailey learned from brother Steve that Sam had been exchanging letters with Ariane Tebbenjohanns for several years now, a jailhouse romance having long since blossomed. Snapshots sent to Sam showed a gorgeous blonde in her late twenties, striking various sultry poses. Maybe in reality she was a homely Brunhilda hiding behind somebody else's pictures. But somehow Lee didn't think so, considering the fancy red stationery with the white "Ariane" letterhead.

Checking on her for him, I called the A-1's Düsseldorf contact and soon had a report. Seemed Ariane was the well-known daughter of a deceased wealthy inventor of water purification systems. Purification must have been in her blood, because she appeared to be swapping the French Riviera and Swiss Alps for a prison romance in Marion, Ohio, at the minimum-security facility Dr. Sam was transferred to in '61.

The sort-of English-speaking operative told me on the phone, "She is what you call vild. Can drink good vodka all night long. Svears like a beer-barrel transporter."

I guessed that was the German equivalent of swearing like a sailor.

In '57, after a rocky six-year marriage, she'd divorced steel-manufacturing magnate Olaf Tebbenjohanns, with whom she had an eleven-year-old daughter named Iris who lived with Ariane's mother in Düsseldorf. Recently she became so bored with high society and fast living, she'd flown to Ohio to meet her soul mate. Or was that cellmate?

Somehow Ariane had wangled a visitor's pass, based on the already approved communications between her and Sam. She had arrived in mink, slinky dress, emeralds, dangling earrings and high heels—a prisoner's platinum-blonde dream-come-true. For four and a half hours, Ariane and Sam sat and talked at a table in a dreary cement-block room, guards behind glass looking on at a respectful distance—Sam was, after all, a model prisoner. By the time she left, wearing a non-emerald necklace with a dove pendant Sam had fashioned for her, they were engaged.

"A romance for the ages," Flo said.

We were on Route 10, traveling east from the Ohio Turnpike, seven or eight miles from downtown Cleveland. The weather was cold, snowy but not snowing. I had the lining in on my Burberry coat, worn over my gray Botany 500, and was sporting a fedora, which these days I only did during the winter. Private eyes post-JFK mostly went hatless. Flo was in a mink coat over a pink suit with a leopard blouse, pearls at her throat, hot pink pumps on tiny feet.

I said, "Come on, kid. You're a veteran crime beat reporter. You know these jailhouse romances are nothing out of the ordinary— convicted killers are flypaper to lonely women with ink, paper, postage, and low self-esteem. Basking in reflected notoriety, playing the mother role, ready to redeem and reform. Putting the pen into pen pal."

"That's cynical even for you, Nate Heller."

"Do you disagree?" I was turning onto Lorain Road, heading to Fairway Park.

"No," she said with a shrug. "But it makes for great copy."

The Buckeye Motel was a low-slung L-shaped flat-roofed two stories with a modernistic, Frank Lloyd Wrightish look, unless you knew something about Frank Lloyd Wright. Its fifty-two units had air-conditioning, TV, phone, and wall-to-wall carpeting. I had stayed in worse, but I wasn't sure about Ariane Tebbenjohanns. These lodgings were not quite what one might find on the Côte d'Azur.

Her room was on the first floor, her front door facing the parking stall where a baby blue Lincoln Continental roosted, looking no more out of place than a flying saucer.

I knocked twice and the door opened, nightlatch in place; a very dark brown eye—in what appeared to be an attractive if rather thin-lipped female face, topped by platinum hair that startled against tanned flesh—regarded me and my companion.

"Mr. Heller? Miss Kilgore?" The German accent was thick but the words perfectly pronounced.

We said yes.

The door closed for the unfastening of the latch, then opened wide. She was quite pretty, eyes large, nose pert, face oval with some sharp but attractive angles—she resembled Kim Novak, right down to the stingy but explosive smile. Her platinum hair had bangs in front and a ponytail in back. She wore a dark suit with white mink collar and cuffs and hemline trim; her heels were high enough to make her petite, gently curvy figure seem more formidable.

"Do come in," she said pleasantly, her voice a nice alto and not guttural, despite the heavy accent.

Our hostess took our hats and topcoats, folding the latter gently, depositing everything neatly onto a chair by the front window, then gestured with a red-nailed hand to the drably modern motel room. Two chairs had already been pulled around to face the side of the double bed in anticipation of our arrival. On the dresser, their reflection in the mirror looking back at them, were a bottle of Smirnoff, an ice bucket, a twenty-eight-ounce bottle of Canada Dry ginger ale, and some bathroom glasses, all but one wearing its paper crown.

"Would you care for a drink?" she asked. "Vodka and ginger is all I have to offer, I'm afraid."

We declined, but she helped herself, dropping in some ice. A cigarette was already going in a nightstand ashtray. She came over and settled herself close enough to the pillows to reach the ashtray and her pack of Kents, and to set her drink down. Our chairs had been pre-angled to accommodate the arrangement.

We sat.

"I have seen you on the television, Miss Kilgore. You are, if I may say so, even prettier in person."

Flo smiled that deceptively prim smile of hers. "Thank you, Miss Tebbenjohanns. But do please call me Flo."

Despite the friendliness of that, the girl reporter was already at work, the notebook out of her purse and her pen poised in a white-gloved hand.

"I would be pleased if you would call me 'Ariane.' I am afraid for anyone but a German, my last name is . . . a mouthful?" She gave me the kind of smile that could fry a man like an egg. "And you are Mr. Heller."

"Nate."

"Nate. I have read of you in *Der Spiegel*—private eye to the movie stars! Most impressive. Did you know Marilyn?"

That threw me for a second—did she mean Marilyn Sheppard or Monroe? I took a chance, taking the context of her question into consideration.

"I knew Miss Monroe rather well," I said. "She was a lovely woman. Her hair shade and yours are identical, by the way."

She dipped her head, keeping the smile going. She was almost exactly the kind of blonde any healthy man would like to share a motel room with, under different circumstances.

Flo said, "I don't want to interview you under false pretenses, Ariane. I'm here as a journalist. But you probably know I was known as the most sympathetic of those who covered your fiancé's trial."

She nodded. "I am aware of that, and I am grateful."

I said, "And I'm here representing your fiancé's attorney— Mr. Bailey. So I'll keep an eye on Flo, here. Keep her honest."

They both responded with a smile. Neither smile seemed forced.

Our hostess lighted up a Kent with a silver art moderne lighter that might have been borrowed from the set of *The Blue Angel*. "You may ask me anything you like, both of you. I am not shy. I do not easily embarrass."

"I appreciate that," Flo said. "But if I step over the line, do please say so."

She shrugged, exhaled smoke in a stream. "People have at times accused me of all kinds of things. They say it is impossible for a good-looking woman—who has been a playgirl up to now, just worrying about her next adventure—to possibly fall in love with a Sam Sheppard. They think you have to be ugly, a thousand years old and bowlegged to have human feelings in your heart, and the guts to stand up and fight for what you think is right, and good."

Flo gave me a glance that at once said she was glad she knew shorthand, with these words flying by, and gave me permission to take the lead in questioning.

I asked, "How did you get interested in Sam's case?"

Ariane tossed off a gesture with a cigarette between red-nailed fingers. "I first read of it in a picture magazine in a dentist's office.

Was this man a killer? Was his community prejudiced because of his wealth? It made me angry! I could . . . *identify* with this doctor. Successful at thirty, and the object of such jealousy! When I was a child at school, I was resented for my family's money." She shrugged elaborately. "Anyway, I knew he was innocent."

Flo looked up from her notebook. "How?"

"I could tell just *looking* at him! I could *feel* it. And I wondered how such a thing—such an *injustice*—could happen in America? My husband did not want to hear about such things, and I admit I went on and on about it. I asked an American couple, vacationing near our place on the Riviera, if they knew of the Sheppard case. They did—and they said they thought he was innocent. They said the newspapers convicted him! I wanted to write to him. I *did* write letters, but always tore them up. As a rule I never intrude on other people's affairs, but somehow, even though I was a complete stranger to him, I thought for him to know that I believe in his innocence would *help* him some way."

I said, "And you finally did send him letters."

She sipped her vodka and ginger ale, then nodded. Her legs were crossed; they were nicely tan and shapely, slipping through a slit in the skirt of the mink-edged dress.

"I waited several years before I had the courage to write," she said. "But the prison would not deliver them. For a time his brother Steve sneaked my messages in and Sam's out. Then permission came and we were able to write each other in the open and, finally, I was able to visit him."

Flo said, "Quite a step to take. Coming all the way from Germany to the States—to Cleveland."

Dark arcs of eyebrow raised momentarily. "I did come to Cleveland, during a terrible snowstorm, and for a few days stayed with Steve and his wife Betty. But I took the train by myself to Marion." She took smoke in, let it out, and her thin, very red smile became somehow private. "It was not love at first sight, you know."

"It wasn't?"

Now the smile went public. "We were already in love. It was

184

just that the meeting . . . *confirmed* for each of us our previous impressions of each other. Sam said we were in love *before* first sight."

I said, "You talked for over four hours, I understand."

She nodded several times, flicked ash into the tray. "There was much catching up to do. We held hands and he told me about prison life, and I told him of my silly, indolent existence. We talked of my daughter and his son, and our future plans."

Flo said, "*If* he is released."

"*When* he is released." She took a good slug of the vodka and ginger. "If I had any doubts about his innocence, they were eliminated during that visit." Her laugh was brittle. "The beautiful Riviera and the crazy life I led there? No longer seems important to me. Sam is the important one—not me. He's the one who should be free."

I said, "You're convinced of that."

She sat forward with an urgency at odds with her cool manner. "Not only in my mind but in my heart, I *know* that Sam couldn't *possibly* have killed Marilyn. There was no *reason* for him to do it! He was happy with her. If he were guilty, he couldn't have lived with himself all these years and be the man that he is today."

Flo said, "If he was so happy with Marilyn, why did he run around on her?"

She batted the air with a palm that split her own smoke stream in half. "Oh, I know a lot of people say, 'But he lied about having an affair with another woman.' Well, if all the men who have lied about affairs were murderers, there wouldn't be enough jails for them."

Flo smiled a little. "No argument there. But his affair with Sharon Kern is most likely the biggest single factor in his conviction."

A grave expression flattened the lovely face. "That type of thinking upsets me, because I have to fight a different kind of prejudice. In my travels I find many people hate me just *because* I am a German. Other people don't like me because, oh, I wear long earrings and eye makeup and don't dress or live as they do. So they say: 'She must be no good.'"

Ariane had unwittingly opened a door for me and I went right through it. This was information that I hadn't yet shared with Flo, but which would make the exclusive she was getting *really* worth a Cleveland trip.

"It must be difficult," I said, "explaining to some people how being in the Hitler Youth was no big thing."

Flo is a pretty cool customer, but if her eyes had opened any wider, they might have tumbled out. Ariane didn't notice.

"People are too touchy," our hostess said, with a toss of a cigarette-in-hand. "It was simply *the* organization for Germans under eighteen, like your Boy or Girl Scouts."

Flo said, "I, uh, never thought of it quite that way."

"Oh, yaah. It taught us good things. It taught us to love our country." She sighed, lifted her shoulders up and down. "We were full of idealism then."

Sitting forward, Flo asked, "But you weren't *really* pro-Hitler . . . ?"

Ariane smiled, waved that off, too. "I was *never* a Nazi. I was only fifteen when the war ended."

I asked, "Were you at your sister's wedding? When she married Goebbels, with Adolf Hitler as best man?"

Dr. Paul Josef Goebbels, propaganda minister of the Third Reich. I bet you can almost hear Flo's gulp.

"Of course not," Ariane said lightly, as if we were discussing the weather. "I wasn't even a year old then, and Magda was only my *half* sister. She was married and living in Berlin when I was growing up."

Flo's shorthand was flying.

"My father was against that marriage," Ariane was saying. "He was no Nazi—not even a Nazi sympathizer. But Goebbels and Magda visited from time to time. I remember, when I was ten, my father got into a terrible quarrel with him—over the treatment of the Jews? I heard him tell Papa, 'If you weren't my father-in-law, I would have you thrown into a concentration camp!'"

The day after Hitler and Eva Braun killed themselves in their Berlin bunker, Goebbels killed himself, his wife Magda and their children. I saw no reason to bring that up with Ariane.

Just when I was thinking Ariane had dug herself out of a hole—or maybe a bunker—she said, a manic edge coming in, "You know, the German people find the American standards of justice *horrifying* . . . with the unfair trial of my Sam a big example." The arcs of eyebrow rose and, this time, hung there for a while. "I intend to carry on a press campaign in Germany, to raise awareness of this injustice—*Der Spiegel* wants an article from me! I had planned to take this up with President Kennedy at the White House, before tragedy interceded. But I will talk to his brother, the attorney general, and appeal to *him* for justice!"

"Ariane," I said gently, "are you planning to attend the parole commissioner's hearing coming up?"

She drew on the cigarette, then gestured with it in hand as she let the smoke drift out. "Of course. It is an excellent opportunity to proclaim my love for Sam . . . *and* my displeasure with the American justice system."

Flo asked, "Do you think that's wise, dear?"

The big eyes got even bigger. "*Someone* has to speak for Sam! If he is refused his parole, I already have three television stations that want to interview me. And radio stations, and several *American* magazines. Public opinion is so important."

Flo nodded, closing her notebook and slipping it back into her purse. "Yes, it is."

Before long, after warm yet somehow cool goodbyes had been exchanged with our hostess, Flo and I were back in the rental car. I was heading downtown, to the Hotel Cleveland, where she planned to check in.

"Let's head back to the airport," she said. "I want to see if a red-eye is available."

"You don't want to stick around? I think I can get the Sheppard brothers to sit for an interview."

She shook her head. "No. I'm going to write this story, but it will be the last I file about this case, for a while—maybe ever. That screwy broad is going to sink the Sheppard ship, and you know it."

"I'm not sure that's true," I said, both hands on the wheel. The road was just snow-packed enough to require thought. "You know how I feel about jailhouse romances, but as you said, the public can be suckers for them. Next week on *The Fugitive*, Richard Kimble and a jet-set beauty fall in love, in a stirring, inspiring—"

"You can barely get that out," she interrupted, "without laughing or maybe choking. The nightly news and their cameras are going to go for her in a big way. Let's face it, she's sexy. She's got an aura—if she walks in a room, men look at her."

"I hadn't noticed."

"Right. And if I hadn't been along, wouldn't you have a made a pass at her, just to ascertain her sincerity for F. Lee Bailey's client?"

"I plead the Fifth."

Flo had turned toward me now, and was leaning close. "Look, she's a scrapper, but also a loose cannon, with zero judgment and no awareness of how her zany behavior, and ill-advised, ill-conceived public statements could backfire."

"Plus she was in the Hitler Youth," I said.

"Plus she was in the Hitler Youth," she said. "How can a guy like Lee Bailey, who plays the press like a banjo, make a mistake like this? There's no *way* she should attend that hearing!"

I shrugged. "Well, you know going for parole is Sam's idea. Lee would rather have him get a new trial through the federal courts and get his life back. Exoneration means practicing medicine again and voting and the works."

"Is Bailey that sneaky?"

"Was Hitler a stinker?"

I took her for supper at Guarnino's on Mayfield Road, the oldest restaurant in town, and a former speakeasy. We had the veal saltimbocca. Eliot had introduced me to the place.

Flo made the red-eye.

And Ariane's appearance at the hearing—and her self-styled

media blitz afterward—caused all the trouble Flo had anticipated. Not only did Sam not get his parole, in February he was told "all this publicity is unacceptable" by the director of Ohio prisons, who referred to Ariane as "a blonde bitch" and Bailey as an S.O.B. Sam said if Ariane was a bitch, then the director's wife was a whore, and Sam Sheppard was taken from Marion's minimum security back to the Ohio Penitentiary and dumped in the hole for six days, after being beaten with rubber hoses by guards.

My other interim job for Bailey was largely a PR stunt, though it had its practical side, as well.

After the 1964 district court decision, terming the 1954 trial a "mockery of justice," Sam Sheppard was released on a ten-grand bond . . . but with the sixty-day threat of a retrial hanging over him.

So on July 16, I got a call from Lee Bailey at my Chicago home. For the record, that was the top two floors of a brick three-story on Eugenie Street, a block north of North Avenue, with the bottom floor lodgings reserved for visiting A-1 clients.

The mellifluous voice said, "I'm calling from a motel in Columbus."

"The ruling's all over the news, Lee," I said. "Congratulations."

"You still have a good relationship with the *Tribune*?"

"Well, Jake Lingle is dead, but I may still have a few connections over there. Why?"

"Do you think they might like to arrange and cover a wedding for a celebrity client of mine?"

I grinned at the phone. "Is your celebrity client a groom named Sheppard? And is the bride a blonde named Ariane, who is definitely not a Nazi?"

"Yes," he said. "Steve Sheppard and I aren't crazy about this marriage happening so quickly. . . ."

"Probably doesn't seem all that quick to your client."

"No." I heard the intake of smoke and then the out-go. "He

wanted three things when he got sprung—a glass of orange juice, a rare steak, and sex with Ariane."

Not necessarily in that order.

I said, "I would think a shrewd counselor of the law like you could arrange those things."

"I could, but the last one is a problem."

"Maybe for her, handling a man who hasn't had a woman in ten years."

I could never get a laugh out of that guy.

He was saying, "I got word Louis Seltzer has his people on us like a skin-tight dress on our little Düsseldorf dish. He would like to see Sam's ass back in jail, even if it's for spitting on the sidewalk."

I got his drift. "A fornication charge."

"Still on the books in Ohio. I can sneak our boy out of here, if you can put things in motion with the *Tribune*."

"Why help out any newspaper, after what the press has done to that poor bastard?"

"Sam says, why not exploit *them* for a change?"

"I see his point."

"Let your *Trib* guy know we need a bridal suite, champagne, meals, blood test, and fees. They get exclusive wedding photos and the story that goes with them."

I made some calls. Illinois was a good move—no waiting period, and the blood tests could be processed immediately. The *Tribune* loved the idea.

Bailey and his own pretty blond wife, Wicki, accompanied Sam and Ariane in that baby blue Lincoln, which she drove—staying under the limit, since a police helicopter trailed them out of the state. Louis Seltzer would gladly have settled for a traffic violation.

They were in Chicago by midnight, driving through a raging rainstorm, slipping the *Trib*'s rival reporters in half a dozen trailing cars, and finally getting out on Michigan Avenue to be whisked to the fourth floor of Tribune Tower for photographers and a WGN-TV camera crew. Separate rooms were booked for them at the Conrad Hilton—no fornicating till tomorrow.

They were married in the bridal suite the next afternoon. Lee and his Wicki served as best man and matron of honor. I was just an observer, though Ariane honored me by coming over and whispering, "This hotel is shabby compared to our fine European ones. I had hoped for more romance."

"Honey, you're gonna *love* Cleveland."

That evening the wedding party wound up at the Pump Room, with a reception hosted by Irv Kupcinet of the *Sun-Times*, whose good side I needed to stay on.

Ariane at one point said to me, "I was worried about Sam keeping up with me."

"Keeping up with you how?"

Some rotten part of me was hoping *she* was making a pass, but instead she said, "With my drinking. But he's already way ahead of me."

Her face was smiling but the eyes in it weren't. Sam—and who could blame him—was the "vild" one now, his high-pitched voice loud and a little desperate as he threw down the bourbon. His freedom, after all, might well be temporary.

"Nate," he said, the baby face showing surprisingly little wear, but his cheeks bourbon-blushed, "thanks for everything you've done over the years!"

"I'm just a bit player," I said.

He gave me half a smirk. "Let me tell you, my friend—it's no fun being the star of this thing."

Two small footnotes.

The *Trib* stiffed Sheppard for the bridal suite. I'm surprised Bailey didn't sue them.

And for the honeymoon, Mr. and the new Mrs. Sheppard headed to New York and the Pierre Hotel, dining like the famous people they'd become, walking hand in hand in Central Park, looking for the romance that had been missing at the Conrad Hilton.

After only two days, the couple flew back to Ohio for a champagne party thrown by a New Yorker—Flo Kilgore, who'd flown to Cleveland one last time.

CHAPTER

On July 3, 1966, the Lobby Court bar in the Cleveland Hotel seemed oddly shy of customers for a holiday weekend; but this was the middle of the afternoon, when even premature fireworks were unlikely.

That is, unless the meeting with Sharon Kern that F. Lee Bailey's office had managed to arrange got heated. I'd been warned by Bailey's secretary that it had taken some talking to get "the other woman" to agree to see me. But with another trial in the offing for Sam Sheppard, Mrs. Meredith (her new last name) surely knew the star witness of the first go-round would seem destined for an encore.

I had the last of my rum and Coke. She was a little late. Meanwhile I could sit back and take in the ornate mahogany woodwork, black-and-white marble floors, lush draperies, and ceiling-to-floor windows with their view on Public Square. Not much different than in Eliot's day, when we would stop by here for his Manhattan and my . . . well, my rum and Coke. We'd done that the night Mayor Burton was reelected, in '39, after the reception in the ballroom upstairs attracted a hundred friends and supporters and more reporters than, what? The day the guilty verdict came in for Sam Sheppard?

Another ghost drifted in, but not from my life or Eliot's—Sam Sheppard's "paramour" (as his attorney William J. Corrigan had quaintly called her in court) entered from the lobby, turning her eyes loose till she found me at a table along the windows. We'd never met, but I'd been in magazines, and she'd been in newspaper clippings in the packet I'd been given by Erle Stanley Gardner nine years ago.

Sharon Kern Meredith was one of those small women who seemed almost tall, her fashion-model slenderness and high heels working wonders. As she glided over, granting me the slightest smile, I could well imagine Dr. Sam liking what he saw, ten years ago—judging by this knockout of a married woman in her mid-thirties.

Her slender, small-waisted figure looked fine in the scooped-top silver knit dress with silver belt and pearls at her throat and more on one wrist; her eye shadow was silver, too, her mascara something Liz Taylor would have been fine with. Cut well above the knee, the dress somehow seemed both mod and classic. On the Fourth of July weekend, she might have gotten away with far more casual attire, even in the Lobby Court bar; but she was every bit as elegant as the surroundings. Her brunette hair was worn Twiggy-style, vaguely suggesting the wild girl she'd once been.

My dark gray Botany 500 suit, with a two-button jacket and even darker gray tie, gave us just enough color coordination to look like a nice couple. We would see about that.

I stood, smiled. She approached, stopped, extended a hand, and we shook like two lodge members at an Elks convention. I gestured to the chair across from me, at this table for two, asked her what she'd like.

"To be anywhere else," she said pleasantly. Then she smirked just a little and said, "Nothing to do with the company."

The sound system was oozing Mantovani—"Who Can I Turn To?" At least it wasn't "What Kind of Fool Am I?"

"You haven't spent enough time with me," I said, equally pleasant, "to be offended yet. Give it a few minutes."

She liked that. She even laughed a little.

A waiter in black and white, in tune with the marble floor, took our order—she, a Manhattan. Like Eliot. I ordered another rum and Coke. Like me.

I was taking in her pretty features. She had big dark lustrous eyes and a fetching trail of freckles tickling its way across her nose, and the bruised fullness of her lips was accentuated by very red lipstick. She was nicely tanned. She lived in California, after all.

"I've read about you," she said. Her voice was high but not shrill. "You're not an attorney. You're that 'Private Eye to the Stars.'"

"Guilty, Your Honor."

"Then why do you live in Chicago?"

"Some things are just hard to explain. I do have an office in L.A., and if you need anything, drop by. But a lot of the 'stars' I've known are not famous actors. More like public figures. Amelia Earhart. Charles Lindbergh. Bobby Kennedy."

"Al Capone," she said. "Frank Nitti. Bugsy Siegel."

She had me liking her already.

I said, "You *did* read an article once, didn't you?"

"Guilty," she said. "And speaking of pleading guilty . . . may I plead my case?"

"Certainly. Though I don't know what you have to plead about."

She leaned forward. "I really don't want to be involved in this thing anymore. Again. Whatever. I have children. I have a husband. I don't want this."

I gave that a gentle shrug. "Well, F. Lee Bailey has no intention of calling you as a witness. But we can't stop the prosecution from doing that."

She took a deep breath, let it out. "Shit. Yes, I know. I'm not *that* dumb."

"You're not dumb at all. Are you still a lab technician?"

"I'm a housewife. Ten years now. My husband is a very successful sound TV and film editor. Music, mostly. Would you like to hear something funny?"

"Almost always."

"He's music editor on *The Fugitive*." Her laugh had an edge in it. "What do you think of that? Have you ever heard of a crazier coincidence?"

"No," I said, not having the heart to tell her that Eliot Ness had lived next door to Sam Sheppard, and that they both had TV shows with the same producer. And that her husband worked on at least one of them.

"So if you're not calling me as a witness," she said, "is this kosher? If you want us to get our stories straight, I can't help you. Sam and I tried that once and it didn't work out so well, did it?"

"You both denied your affair."

She nodded. "Never under oath, but it got us both in *real* hot water. Him a lot hotter, I admit. Understand, we both feared criminal charges for, you know, adultery. So what's the function of this meeting? My husband is understandably anxious when I go out with a strange man."

She was maybe trying too hard now.

"I'll tell you frankly," I said, "there's a good chance the prosecution also won't call you."

Those big eyes got even bigger. "What? Why?"

I shrugged. "Times have changed. Birth control is every girl's favorite pill, except for maybe acid. The kids are rebelling, free love is in, and skirts are so short I don't even have to bend down pretending I'm looking for something to take in a nice set of gams. 'Gams' dates me just a little, doesn't it?"

She laughed gently through the last half of that.

"Maybe," she said. "Just a little."

"Also," I said, "Lee Bailey is bound to try to keep the sex stuff out. He'll go after a ruling that Sam's infidelities are irrelevant. And, knowing him, he'll get it."

The eyes went wide again, but just for a moment, her head tilting. "Times *have* changed, all right. So, then, what's there to talk about?"

The waiter brought our drinks.

I sipped mine, then said, "Unfortunately, we do have to go over some old ground. My job is to find new evidence, and to look hard at some old suspects . . . and maybe some *brand-new* suspects."

"I don't see how *I* could be a suspect," she said, frowning a little. She kissed her Maraschino cherry into her mouth, chewed daintily, swallowed, sipped her cocktail. "I was in California. Unless you think I hired somebody to kill Marilyn."

That remark surprised me a little. But then she was surprising me a lot.

"You didn't like her? Marilyn?"

"No." Something about her face told me she was regressing, her younger self asserting itself. "I didn't wish her dead, and boy do I wish she was still alive. But she was the kind of woman who knew damn well her husband was running around, and was fine with it . . . but then if she ran into you, she'd be catty as hell. Claws would come out."

"For example?"

"Well, I was living with my parents in Rocky River, and didn't have a car of my own. Back then Marilyn and Sam and their kid were living in an apartment, half a block from us. Mornings, I'd walk over and get a ride to work from Sam. It got to where I would just open the garage door and climb in on the rider's side of his little MG and wait for him. Sometimes *she'd* come out and say he was going to be late and I should just walk or catch a bus. Other times she came right out and told me how presumptuous and rude she thought I was."

I had a hunch Sharon would react the same way if her husband gave a pretty young thing a ride, but that wasn't how she'd seen it then, so it wasn't how she saw it now.

She made a face; she was definitely in her early twenties again. "Then there was this Halloween thing, kind of an office costume party? Sam came dressed as a woman and I came dressed as a doctor, all in white with a stethoscope, and when he showed up, I took that pipe out of his mouth that he was always smoking, and stuck it in mine. We were only just joking around. But Marilyn got in a huff and called me a 'bitch,' and *flew* out of there." She frowned. "Of course, Paul wasn't thrilled either."

"Paul?"

"My fiancé. Paul Robinson. He's a doctor, too. Look, I have to tell you—you probably heard, or figured out, that I was something of a . . . wild child. I worked hard, lots of hours, very hard, and when it came time to party, guess what I did?"

"So you were engaged to this, uh, Paul at the same time you were seeing Sam?"

She nodded. "We broke up not long after that started. But later Paul and I got re-engaged, and had a ring and the date was set and everything. But, I, uh . . . I'm not proud of this."

"You were still seeing Sam."

She sighed, nodded again. "I was still seeing Sam. It wasn't as regular—maybe we'd make it, oh, once every two weeks, y'know. We had fun together. It wasn't always smart. You know, he was still in his twenties, late twenties, but twenties. I was younger than that. Marilyn was the first girl he was ever with. So when he had the chance to try something new, he tried it." She gave me a knowing half smile. "Listen, this was no great love for the ages. We'd do it in that little car of his, pulling over somewhere, when he was driving me home from a late night in the emergency room. There were apartments in Bay View Hospital, for the doctors, and we used some of those. Lucas Hardmann had one we used often enough that he would call with a signal, you know two rings, hang up, three rings, hang up, meaning he was on his way home."

"So the idea that you and Sam would marry someday—"

"Well, look," she said with a shrug. "Even in a casual affair, things get hot and heavy. Getting hot and heavy is kind of the point, isn't it? So sometimes Sam would say he loved me, and would love to marry me, but later say he couldn't leave Marilyn and Chip, 'cause he loved them, too. But every time we broke it off, in a week or two he'd call and then we were off somewhere, doing it again."

Mantovani was lulling "As Long As He Needs Me" into submission.

She leaned forward, almost whispering now. "One time I told him that I was in love with Paul, Dr. Robinson, not him. He said, 'How can you be in love with Paul and be here with me?' And I said, 'How can you be in love with your wife and be here with *me*?'"

"What drew you to Sam?"

A quick shrug, a distant look. "He was little-boy handsome, and well-to-do in a way. He would compliment me not just on my looks but, well, my intelligence, my skill at work. Having one of the Sheppards on my side at Bay View gave me freedom and a kind of status."

I sipped rum and Coke. "Then you finally broke it off with Sam and moved to California."

"Well, I was kind of pressured by the rest of the Sheppard family, but, hey, it was time. For a fresh start. Got a good lab tech job right away."

"But then Sam came out to visit you."

"Yes, and right in the middle of a month-long trip with his wife! Did I mention he can be a cheap bastard? Instead of getting a room, we shack up in the spare bedroom of some friends of his—for five days! What kind of idiot does that?"

I wasn't quite sure whether she was talking about Sam or herself.

She was shaking her head, wearing half a disgusted smirk. "Sam and me getting hitched was never in the cards. Never what it was about, really."

I had to ask.

Only I didn't, because she answered the anticipated question: "Do I think Sam did it? I can't believe that. But I would be very happy never to hear of the Sheppard case again."

We each returned to our drinks for a few moments.

Then I asked, "Can you tell me anything about this Lucas Hardmann character?"

"An odd duck. Sam liked him, but it was almost like Luke was a . . . charity case. Luke was older, he was always screwing up, he was a resident forever at one hospital after another, never getting anywhere." She shuddered. "He was always pawing at women but so *obvious* about it, he never got anywhere there, either. It was almost like he didn't want to get anywhere."

"What do you mean?"

The red smile was knowing. "Sometimes a guy seems to be overdoing it, particularly when another guy is around. Like I always wondered if under all that stupid macho crap, Luke was gay or something. You know, Marilyn hated him, Sam said."

"Yeah?"

She nodded. "He stayed with them for something like six weeks once, and he didn't make the bed or change his own linen or do his dishes or clean up after himself. After a while, she refused to cook for him or make his bed."

"Still, he was staying with Sam and Marilyn when all this went down. He just happened to be away for the night, visiting a doctor friend."

"Yes, I know. He had an overnight at Paul's."

"Your ex-fiancé Paul."

She nodded again. "That's right. Paul was Luke's alibi for the murder. Hasn't that been looked into?"

"Not yet," I said.

Kent, Ohio, on the Cuyahoga River, was a town of fifteen thousand or so, home to Kent State University and its lovely campus, and so typically middle-American that Norman Rockwell would have found it a tad too clichéd for his tastes.

Lucas Hardmann—when I called him at the home of his friend Dr. Robinson, with whom he was spending this long holiday weekend—suggested we meet at what he described as "the town's most cherished institution."

And so, in downtown Kent, I sat with the osteopath in a back booth at Jerry's, a bright red boxcar-style diner sitting on a corner with a warehouse to one side and a residential neighborhood at its back. Jerry's was doing better business than the Lobby Court bar, but then this was mid-evening and folks were stopping by for a burger and fries and/or pie or maybe a malted.

A jukebox was playing rock 'n' roll, not obnoxiously. I didn't mind. Made me think of my son, who played in a rock band. Right now it was "Paint It Black." Outside the occasional premature fire-cracker would go off.

Hardmann had been here when I arrived, a big grinning goof—not fat, just big—with a dirty blond crew cut riding an ambitiously receding hairline. His eyes had a brightness that lived somewhere between happy and hysterical, and when I came in dressed as I'd promised—in a tan short-sleeve Banlon shirt and brown trousers—he lit up with a wide smile like a jack-o'-lantern with its candle going.

He slipped out of the booth and stood in the narrow aisle, welcoming me with a curled-fingers traffic cop gesture. Thankfully he did not have a whistle. He was wearing an orange short-sleeve golfer's shirt and orange-and-black Bermuda shorts, an outfit really set off nicely by his black socks and loafers.

I pegged him at about fifty-five or so, and was immediately reminded of Sergeant Schultz on *Hogan's Heroes*. Well, if you have to hang around with a German guard at a POW camp, he might as well be an affable one.

We shook hands before sliding in on our respective sides.

"I hear you're famous," he said jovially. "But I never heard of you."

"That's all right. I never heard of you either."

He laughed at that. Of course, it wasn't exactly true, because since the first time I'd gone over Gardner's Sheppard case file, something about this guy and his story had got my attention. And not in a good way.

He leaned forward, his smile slightly maniacal. "I *thought* you'd get a kick out of Jerry's."

He said this as if we were sitting in a diner whose replica wasn't in every town in America.

"Jerry's Diner," he said in what I took to be an imitation of W. C. Fields, "where philosophers, poets, artists, folksingers and others of dubious repute often gather!"

Trying to get this back on an even keel, I said, "I really appreciate you taking time to talk to me, Dr. Hardmann—this being a holiday weekend and all."

The grin kept going. It was the kind of grin you got from a guy as he excused himself on his way to go blow his brains out. "Call me Luke. I prefer that to Lucas. And I'll call you Nate—unless you prefer Nathan?"

"Either is fine."

He gestured magnanimously. "Let me treat you to a slice of cherry pie, Nate. Or apple."

"No thanks."

"Well, you're going to have to watch *me* eat a piece."

A young redheaded waitress, who seemed considerably less impressed with Jerry's Diner than Hardmann, came over and looked sullenly pretty in spite of, or possibly because of, her heavy makeup with its green eye shadow. She took our order and went away. "Kicks" by Paul Revere and the Raiders was playing on the jukebox.

He leaned forward chummily. "Listen, Nate, I'm happy to talk to you. It's not my favorite subject, obviously, and it was such a *long* time ago . . ."

"Nine years tonight."

He chuckled. "That's right, isn't it? This is a kind of anniversary!"

That almost made it sound like a celebration—like maybe he should have ordered cake, not pie.

"You understand," I said, "Mr. Bailey has no intention of, or interest in, calling you as a witness. That will be up to the prosecution."

"It'll cost 'em."

"Oh?"

His nod just kept going. "They'll have to fly me in. I'm in San Francisco now. I mean, I'm in *Kent* at the moment, obviously, but my hospital is in San Fran—Presbyterian Medical Center."

"You've worked a lot of places."

He kept smiling but it curdled some. "Well, I keep running into people who make mistakes, then blame me for it. Politics, it's always political, wherever you work. It's like you're all the time living in a damn soap opera!"

The smile was gone now, and rage flickered in the eyes.

"I know what you mean," I said sympathetically.

His cherry pie came, as well as our drinks—milk for him, iced tea for me.

He began to eat enthusiastically, squeezing in sentences between bites. "I don't know what there is to talk about. . . . I was a houseguest, which I was a lot of times with Sam and Marilyn. . . . But I wasn't there when it happened. . . . If I *had* been, maybe I coulda stopped it. . . . Or maybe it wouldn'ta happened at all."

"Do you think Sam did it?"

He paused, a forkful of cherry pie frozen midair. His eyeballs marbled at me. "Hanky Panky" was going on the jukebox. "I would *never* say that."

"Would you think it?"

He sighed. His eyes went back to normal, or as normal as possible. He ate the bite of pie, then said, "Hard to believe."

That wasn't really an answer.

"I'm somebody poking around in the past," I said, "and talking to people I don't know about other people who I never met. So I have a limited point of view."

He chewed. "I can see that. I can see that."

"For instance, I keep hearing . . . forgive me for this, Luke . . . but I keep hearing Marilyn didn't like you much. And that strikes me as odd, because she seems to have been someone who really liked people. Relatives, neighbors, even neighbor kids, were always welcome around her place."

He swallowed the last bite, pushed the plate away. His smile had a reddish tinge now. "Here's the thing. She was jealous of me."

"Of you?"

He nodded. "See, Sam and me met in college, back in '44. He was just a baby, twenty, but I was a man, a dozen years older. So I took him under my wing. Like an older brother. Showed him the way."

"But wasn't Sam already a favorite of his classmates and professors? Wasn't he at the top of his class?"

He pursed his lips. "Yes, and I don't think Marilyn ever appreciated my role in that! How I guided him! After they got married, it was always like she was trying to inject herself between Sam and me."

I held up a gentle palm. "Again, Luke, forgive me—but my materials, and they may be inaccurate, state that when you were a houseguest, you would flirt with her. That you even made a pass at her, once, that she rebuffed."

His eyes flared and so did the rage in them. "*And* told Sam! But that's *not* how it was. I was trying to be friendly, trying to get *through* to her. And I'm a red-blooded man, and she was a good-looking woman, no question of that . . . but *frigid*! I told Sam many a time that if he wasn't getting enough at home, he needed to look for it elsewhere."

"That didn't work out too well for him, did it, Luke?"

His eyebrows shrugged. "No. The boy never was discreet. That Marilyn caused me a lot of trouble. I had a *good* job at Bay View for a while, but she turned Sam's parents against me—and his papa was the big cheese there! I went to the Dayton hospital for a while, but the politics at that place—*brother*! I went back to Bay View, with Sam's help, but again, Marilyn—she was head of the Ladies' Hospital Auxiliary there—God *knows* what she told people!"

I opened a hand. "Why would you invite yourself as a houseguest so often, when you knew how Marilyn felt?"

The eyes flared again. "Nate, Sam was like my little *brother*!"

I jerked a thumb over my shoulder. "You do know he's living over in Rocky River, don't you, out on bond? With his new wife. Waiting for judgment. Are you going over there to see him while you're in the area?"

He shook his head. Any trace of happiness was gone. Gloom had settled in. "Marilyn *ruined* it for us. Our friendship."

"Her getting murdered did, you mean."

He nodded, not grasping that I'd insulted him. "Nate, that

event put me in an awkward position. I had to tell the truth, didn't I? When the authorities asked, I told them how his brother, Steve, told Sam to get his story together. Both Sam and Steve really resented that. I overheard them when I visited Sam at the hospital that first day."

He stared in despondence at his barely touched milk. He drank some. The Supremes were singing "My World Is Empty Without You" on the jukebox.

Then he said, "Marilyn told her father-in-law I was a bad influence. That I was encouraging Sam to divorce her . . . when it was just the *opposite*! I *told* Sam to stay in that marriage! Fool around on the side, if that's what it took. But not mess up a good thing. I mean, his father and brothers would have *killed* him, if he divorced Marilyn! All those kind of people think about is their reputations."

I leaned forward, let some of the contempt into my voice. "The way you felt about Marilyn—is that why, when you got the call from the Bay Village police about her murder, telling you to come report in to them, you sat down in your friend's kitchen and ate a sandwich and a piece of pie . . . cherry, maybe? Taking your time, at a time like that?"

His face still looked like a German POW camp guard's, but not benign like Sergeant Schultz. Not anymore.

"I had just played eighteen holes of golf, Mr. Heller. I was tired. So I ate a goddamn fucking sandwich. *Sue me!*"

He got out of the booth, reached in a pocket of his orange-and-black Bermuda shorts, and tossed a crumpled couple of dollars beside the empty pie plate, which was smeared scarlet.

After he'd stormed out, the waitress returned. She seemed amused now. "Anything else, sweetie?"

"Give me a piece of that cherry pie. Scoop of vanilla."

"Your wish is my command, handsome."

Pushing sixty and I still had it.

I was just starting in on the slice when a guy in a yellow polo shirt and tan shorts slipped in across from me. He was slim and serious, with short dark hair, sharp dark eyes, and pleasantly bland features; his sideburns had some white going, and a few lines were in his face, lending a distinguished touch. The waitress might have called him "handsome," too.

"We Can Work It Out" by the Beatles was on the jukebox.

"You're Nathan Heller," he said.

"Am I?"

"I followed Luke over from the house. Waited for him to go. He's really not as bad as you think he is."

"How bad do you think I think he is?"

He sighed. "Pretty bad. He's his own worst enemy. I'm Paul Robinson."

"I was hoping to talk to you, Doctor," I said, pushing the pie away.

"Go ahead with that," he said, nodding toward the plate. "It'll melt."

I returned the pie and ice cream to their rightful position, but before having another bite, I said, "Luke's a charmer. Does your medical expertise include the term 'manic depressive'?"

"No, but I picked that up from *Ben Casey*. Look, he doesn't know anything. He didn't do anything. My house is a couple of blocks over—a duplex. The private practice is on the main floor, and I live with Dad upstairs. He's been in private practice here for years, retired now. Mom has passed, but she was around when Luke stayed over, uh, nine years ago."

Tonight.

"Dr. Robinson, several things bother me. First of all, it's an easy ride, Kent to Bay Village—an hour under the worst circumstances, and not much more than half an hour under the best. And that loony friend of yours could have killed Marilyn Sheppard and driven back to Kent and slipped into the house again. In plenty of time."

He was already shaking his head. "Probably not, Mr. Heller. I sleep like a rock—like Sam does. We used to laugh about it, grabbing naps on ER shifts. But my mother was a notoriously light sleeper, and it was warm that night, as you might imagine on the weekend of the Fourth. She had the windows open. She'd have heard him leave and heard him come back."

"Maybe he was quiet about it."

Robinson laughed softly. "You saw him. You met him. Luke's a lot of things, but nimble isn't one of them."

"Okay. Let me give you that, all of it. But just suppose you noticed he'd gone out, or heard him come in. His return would have been early enough in the morning to wake you up."

"I don't know if I like what you're implying."

"I hadn't got around to implying anything. But I am curious why it didn't occur to anybody that Luke's alibi was Sharon Kern's ex-fiancé."

His forehead tightened. "That wouldn't make me the enemy of Marilyn Sheppard!"

"No. But it wouldn't make you the friend of Sam Sheppard, either."

He shook his head, his eyes sad but steady. "I didn't cover up for Luke. And anyway he didn't do it—the police looked into it, thoroughly."

"Did they? Did they check his car or his clothes? When Coroner Gerber started talking about surgical implements as the probable murder weapon, did they check his, or yours? One other possibility bandied about for a murder weapon was a golf club. Did the police check the contents of your friend's golf bag? Or yours? Did they make an inspection of his hands for cuts or abrasions? How about his teeth? Did you know your friend went to the dentist a week later? Did you ever notice that your buddy had something of an unnatural interest in Sam Sheppard, and an intense dislike for Marilyn Sheppard?"

He had no answers. He was staring at my pie. Maybe he was hungry.

"To me it's a strong possibility," I said, "your screwball pal, during his final unwelcome stay at the Sheppards', got fed up once and for all with Marilyn's bitchy attitude toward him. So he arranged his sleep-over visit with you, as an alibi . . . not enlisting you, but knowing he could sneak out and back in again. He had planned ahead, so whatever the murder weapon was, he had it in his car, which was a new model by the way, and the killing tool could be tossed out a window on the ride back, probably with his bloody clothes. And after your round of golf the next day, when he was told of Marilyn's death, what did he do? He sat down and had a sandwich and a piece of pie."

He let some air out. His eyes could barely look at me. "Maybe you should talk to the police about this."

"What police? The Cleveland police, who would like nothing better than to railroad Dr. Sam one more time? Or the Bay Village police, and their crack staff of five officers?"

"Wild Thing" by somebody or other was on the jukebox.

He held up both hands, palms out, as if in surrender. "I didn't have anything to do with this. As for Sharon Kern, I didn't hold the affair against Sam. She just wasn't ready to settle down. If it hadn't been Sam, it would've been somebody else. She was a beautiful girl but she got around. And I don't believe Luke had anything to do with her murder, either . . . but pursue that if you like. You probably should."

The smile I gave him wasn't much of one. "Here's the problem Luke has—it's the same one you have."

"Which is?"

"Which is when Sam Sheppard is finally cleared, the cops will suddenly have an unsolved murder on their hands."

The damn ice cream had, as the doctor diagnosed, melted. I got up and left, stopping just long enough to give the little redhead a five-spot.

CHAPTER 15

I took July Fourth off.

Disrupting family holidays with questions about a murder case—even though that is exactly what had happened nine years ago—seemed a little out of line.

With the temperature in the nineties, I took in a rerelease of *Psycho* at the Vogue for the air-conditioning and a movie I knew would be good. And in the evening I caught the Indians losing a close one to the Twins, followed by a rousing patriotic fireworks display unhampered by the defeat. I may have done all of this, as well as have various nice meals at various nice restaurants, as a lonely bachelor. Or I might have met a thirty-five-year-old blond American Airlines stewardess in the Lobby Court bar who was worried that she was getting too old for the job and needed reassurance from an understanding older man who reminded her of her father, but not enough to be a problem.

Having been accused of including gratuitous and perhaps dubious sex scenes in these memoirs, I will say no more.

But I did wake up alone, as either a sad lonely bachelor or a guy whose bedmate had an early flight out, and began a long if interesting Monday talking to a variety of people. First up was a Spang Bakery deliveryman named Ronald Draper who I caught at the Barber Avenue plant, a brick building consuming several blocks of a narrow side street in an otherwise residential area.

Along with half a dozen like him, Draper was in a massive garage loading up his red truck with bread and doughnuts off a wooden rack. The warmth and scent of freshly baked goods overwhelmed any automotive odors. Draper was in his forties and wore a milkman-type white uniform with a white cap. He looked skinny enough to suggest he'd long ago gotten past the urge of heedlessly sampling the goods.

But he said he'd seen someone else sampling the goods at the Sheppard place.

"Mrs. Sheppard would leave the Lake Road door unlocked," he said, in a husky second tenor, "and we had this understanding that I'd just knock, then come on in, go down the hall, and then the kitchen opened up just to the left. I'd leave her a loaf of Aunt Mary's brand bread and sometimes some doughnuts. On several occasions she was sitting at the kitchen table having coffee with this distinguished-looking older man, gray hair, you know, suit and tie. They were friendly and kind of . . . familiar with each other. I figured it was Dr. Sheppard, but later I found out it wasn't."

"You've since identified him as Marshall Dodge."

He nodded. "That's right. They give me five pictures and I picked him right out. Funny—the Dodges were on my route, but I never saw him. Turns out he was the mayor. Of course, like I said, I never saw Dr. Sheppard, either. I dealt with mostly the ladies."

"How familiar were they with each other, the mayor and Mrs. Sheppard?"

The deliveryman got uncomfortable. "Will I have to testify to this?"

"Probably. No sense in pulling your punches."

He sighed. "Okay. Two times it was more than just a couple of people having coffee. Once, her nightgown—she was always in her nightgown when I saw her with this fella that turned out to be the mayor—it was down around her waist, and her . . . you know, her boobies was out. Her bosom. He was kissing her on her mouth while he . . . you know, was feeling her up. Caressing her, I mean."

"What about the other time?"

"Oh, she had her nightgown on, nothing showing. No funny business. But she handed him this key, house key looked like, and said, 'Don't tell Sam.' I guess that was when I first figured out he wasn't Dr. Sheppard."

"How did they react?"

"They didn't see me, either time. They hadn't heard me knock. So I went back down the hall, the way I come in, and knocked again, you know, on the near side of the door. But loud. Then I just, you know, went in and nodded and smiled at them—her night-gown was closed now, that one time—and left the Aunt Mary's bread and a box of doughnuts."

I smiled. "You don't look like you eat many doughnuts."

A grin appeared in the midst of an unhealthy-looking pallor. "I sure don't. I got the diabetes. Gotta stay away from sweets. I'm only filling in at the bakery a few days a month now. I been too sick to work full time, either here or at the amusement park. I was night watchman."

"You must have to be pretty observant for that."

"Oh, yes. I still don't miss much."

Didn't seem like he ever did.

The Huntington Water Tower, often mistaken for a lighthouse, had once been used to pump water to irrigate vineyards belonging to the long-ago industrialist it was named for. Now the looming structure was just a cream-colored clapboard fifty-foot artifact of an earlier day, its dignity compromised by an attached one-story refreshment stand as wide as the tower was tall.

We were seated on a bench to one side of the latter, with a nice view of Lake Erie, but not of the beach below, which—like the re-freshment stand—wasn't doing Fourth of July business on Mon-day the fifth. But nonetheless a steady flow of girls in their teens and twenties in skimpy bikinis were buying ice-cream cones, and scampering around giggling and licking, and making me wish I were a lot younger or they were a little older.

My companion on the bench, not looking much older than the ice-cream customers, was really an old married lady of twenty-six. Very pretty in a girl-next-door way, she wore pink-framed, green-lensed sunglasses and a pink-and-white sundress with low pink heels. She might have been my daughter.

She was, instead, Jane Carter, maiden name Sparling, the onetime babysitter of the Sheppards' son, Chip. She'd been good enough to agree to see me, and suggested this spot. Huntington Park began just down from what had been the Sheppard home. She had lived across the street from them.

"Marilyn was a lovely woman," she said, in a warm, mid-range voice. "I was a shy kid, confused about what was happening to me, to my . . . well, physicality. She always looked so fresh and sweet. I could always depend on her for advice, or a shoulder to cry on."

The ninety-five-degree day seemed almost cool in the lake breeze. "You would visit her just about every morning, I understand."

Jane nodded. "Before school. She was always up bright and early."

Her face was turned toward the glimmering expanse of blue beyond the bluff. Girls giggled and yelped in the background, animals in their natural habitat.

"Then," she said, "about six months before . . . before what *happened* to her, Marshall Dodge—the mayor? He started dropping by to see Marilyn. She said I should always call her that, not 'Mrs. Sheppard.' Anyway, whenever the mayor showed up, that was my cue . . . you know, to make tracks."

"How did you take that?"

The green lenses swung toward me, staring at me with their big round blankness. "Well, in an immature way, of course. I was kind of jealous. I would have liked Marilyn's attention, *all* of her attention. I really loved her. Not in a . . . not in *that* way."

"I know. Big sister."

"Well . . . more like a mom. I had a rocky time of it with my folks. We don't need to get into that. But later I got a little suspicious. Mayor Dodge seemed to get . . . kind of familiar with her."

Familiar—the same word Ronald Draper had used.

"And," she went on, "about a month before . . . before it *happened*, Marilyn told me, next time he dropped by? To stick around. Not to ever leave her alone with that man again. She put it like that: 'that man.'"

The sound of purring motorboats rode the breeze. "How did Dodge react when you didn't 'take your cue' as usual?"

She turned her gaze back to the lake. "Well, he didn't like it, that's for sure. Sometimes he'd just sit and have a cup of coffee and the talk would be . . . strained, I guess. From the start, he would bring special cuts of meat from his butcher shop. He would walk right over to the refrigerator and just put them in. Like he owned the place. When things got tense, or strained, if he saw me sitting there? He'd come in with one of those white-wrapped packages, with the red coming through, and put them in the fridge and nod and go out, without hardly a word."

"Did you ever see anything?"

The green lenses swung my way again; they had an oddly science-fiction look. "You mean . . . did they kiss or hug each other or do anything . . . sexual? Not in front of me, they didn't. But one of the last times I talked to Marilyn, she told me Mr. Dodge said he loved her. That he'd been arguing about it with Mrs. Dodge. Marilyn asked me whether I thought she should tell Dr. Sam about it. Imagine, *her* asking *me* for advice?"

"What advice did you give her?"

"I said she should tell him."

"Do you know if she did?"

She nodded, lowering her head to look at me over the glasses. "Yes, and she said Sam took it well. It kind of . . . shook him, though. They'd been real close, the two couples, going on vacation together, co-owning a boat, and right then Marilyn and Dr. Sam stopped seeing them so much. What she told me was, 'We decided to branch out into other social circles, and put a little distance between us and the Dodges.'"

Laughter drifted up from the beach. It had a hollow sound.

I asked, "Did that subject ever come up again?"

"No, but I wasn't seeing her quite so often. Chip got old enough that he didn't need a sitter. I was in high school now, and it became more a once-in-a-while thing, me stopping over. But there was always a closeness, y'know?"

Giggling, yelping, pale flesh, tanned flesh, young female flesh, capered and squealed. Innocent.

For now.

"Jane," I said (we'd agreed on first names). "Thanks for taking the time to talk to me."

"You're trying to come up with things that might have been missed, the first time?"

"Right."

"I can think of one."

"Please."

"I knew Mrs. Dodge, Mildred, pretty well. The Dodges had a daughter, still do, who was a classmate of mine. Name is Lisa. Jerry Dodge was a year ahead of us. So Lisa and I were friendly enough that I was there some, at the Dodges. One time Mildred, Mrs. Dodge, asked me for a . . . kind of funny favor."

"Oh?"

"I don't exactly remember when it was. I think maybe it was after Marilyn and Dr. Sam had it out about Mr. Dodge. Anyway, Mrs. Dodge . . . Mildred . . . knew I was close to Mrs. Sheppard. And she asked me to sort of . . . keep my eyes and ears open around the Sheppards. Report anything I heard or saw that had to do with them."

"Did you?"

"Of course not!"

"Didn't mean any offense."

"Sorry. I didn't think you did, Mr. Heller."

"Nate."

"Nate. You want to know the thing, the one thing, that really haunts me?"

"If you'd care to share it."

The green lenses stared blankly at me. "I . . . I stayed in that bedroom where Marilyn, Mrs. Sheppard, was killed. I slept in that same bed on three occasions."

"Why were you there overnight?"

"Trouble with my parents. Marilyn would take me under her wing when things got rough. That room she was in, that was their guest room. I guess she and Dr. Sam moved into it later, because that gave them a window on the lake."

The breeze ruffled her hair, as if to confirm that.

I said, "Mr. Bailey may want you to testify."

She shrugged. "All right, but I don't live here anymore, you know. So he'll have to fly me. I'm in Connecticut now. You caught me at home, visiting my folks."

"Getting along better with them now?"

"Twice a year, I do."

Mather Auto Sales & Used Cars, on Lorain Avenue, was a corner lot with signs on poles bragging of HIGH APPRAISALS and CLEVELAND'S CLEANEST, and flags flapping with various slogans—SAVINGS, LOW PRICES, WE FINANCE! I parked on the street and walked into the well-stocked lot past a sandwich-board sign saying IF THE HORN BLOWS, WE'LL BUY IT, down an aisle past Pontiacs and Chevies and more, big price tags written in white shoe polish on windshields—*'60 Chevrolet $898, '65 Ford $1348, '62 Dodge Dart $2195.*

He came at me like he'd been shot out of a cannon, limping slightly, his hand extended like a blade. Marshall Dodge was dumpy but his suit was a nice off-the-rack number, his tie snugged, the picture of middle-class prosperity. So his schlub quality came from the droopy face, black-circled eyes, saggy body and various competing double chins. His hair was fully gray now.

He slowed as I came into focus, his politician's smile continuing but his eyes narrowing; then the hand dropped and by the time he had planted himself in front of me, he had recognized me.

"I don't remember your name," he said, his voice soft, almost frightened. His face had fallen, the flesh hanging loose on the bones beneath.

"Nathan Heller," I said.

He looked like he might cry. "Is this about the Sheppard thing again?"

"It is. I'm working for F. Lee Bailey now, and going back to talk to the principal players."

He flinched, swallowed. "Is that what I am?"

"Why, don't you think you are?"

He gestured around him at the dog pound of unwanted cars. "Can't you see I'm working here?"

No customers were in sight.

"It's hot and the world is at work," I said. "All I want is a few minutes."

"Get it over with. But if a customer stops by—"

"I'll get out of the way," I said, raising a palm. "Do you have an office we can sit in?"

He frowned, squinted, as if the sun weren't at his back. "Let's do this out here. But I don't know what I can tell you that you didn't hear from me the first time around."

I smiled a little. "That's nine years ago, Mr. Dodge. We have catching up to do, and my memory can use refreshing. So you're in the used car business now? You own the lot?"

"No. I'm the manager, but not the owner."

"I thought you had a successful business going with that meat market of yours."

He sighed deep, let it out slow. "Mr. Heller, you don't know what that Sheppard mess cost me. I've spent years fighting rumors and fending off accusations. There are people who think *I* had something to do with that murder!"

"No. Really?"

Shaking his head, pawing at the air, he said, "Crank calls at home, at all hours—'Hey Dodge, I wanna kill my wife—can you help me?' Go over to the market and try to work there, and people would say, 'I heard this and I heard that,' blah blah blah blah. You have any idea how often I've wished we weren't even *in* Bay Village that night? Rather I was in goddamn Timbuktu or something."

"But you weren't. And you got the six A.M. phone call from Dr. Sam that put you in this thing forever."

His expression had something pleading in it. "Yes, and who has ever been second-guessed as much as Mildred and me? Why did we do this, why didn't we do that. Look, we just reacted, made decisions on the fly, like anyone would. It's easy to Sunday-morning quarterback this thing."

Of course, it hadn't been a game, had it?

"So you sold the business," I said.

"Yes. And I got this job in Cleveland, and I moved to Westlake— Bay Village can take a flying leap."

"Broke up your marriage, too."

He shrugged. "I don't know if that's so bad. We had some good years, Mildred and me, but . . . I remarried, you know. Very happy now. All of that's in the past."

I leaned back against a '64 Chevelle, $1598. "Well, Sam Sheppard's new trial is very much in the present, and you can't duck that. The prosecution will call you, no question."

"Let 'em do what they have to." He grimaced. "And I suppose that Bailey character will climb my ass."

"There are some things he'll want to clear up, yes."

His eyes got wide. "What kind of things?"

"Like whether you and Marilyn Sheppard were lovers, for one."

The eyes bulged in their dark baggy settings. "Ridiculous! That's just . . . *ridiculous*! She was a fine young woman, and we were just friends. Neighbors."

"You would drop by for coffee."

"Right."

"And cash checks for her?"

"Yes, to save her a trip to the bank." He shrugged. "I was going, anyway."

"How many times a week would you drop by and have coffee in the kitchen with her?"

Another shrug. "Not often."

"*How* often?"

". . . Three times a week, maybe."

"Do you remember the bakery deliveryman who brought bread and doughnuts around to Marilyn? And to your house, too, I believe?"

His voice was even softer now. "Maybe. I'm not sure."

"Do you remember him coming in on you and Marilyn when you were, let's call it, comforting her about something?"

His eyes popped again, like he was a rubber squeeze doll. "No! I never saw him in that kitchen."

"He says Marilyn handed you a key, and said not to tell Sam about it. A house key, was it?"

Dodge shook his head; some sweat flew. "That never happened. I told you, I never saw him in that kitchen."

"What about the Carter girl?"

"What about her?"

"Did you and Marilyn and young Jane have an understanding that when you came around, she would go?"

He leaned against a '65 Oldsmobile, $1298. "Anything that kid tells you is suspect. You want to know why? She's a neurotic little character. Always telling crazy stories about her parents. Just a nut. Forget anything she says!"

"What about that deliveryman? Is he a nut, too?"

Like an out-of-breath distance runner, he tried to keep going. "I don't know *what* he is. Maybe he has an imagination. Maybe he wants notoriety or something. How should I know?"

"I notice you still have a limp."

Another shrug. "I've had a limp since I was a kid. Bone infection. What about it?"

"Slows you down, does it?"

"Yes, some. Worse as I get older. Don't *you* have any aches and pains? You're about my age."

"Sure." I grinned at him. "My bullet wounds talk to me about the weather."

I thanked him and went back to my rental Ford. He stood in the midst of all those other cars, and might have been trying to figure out whether I'd meant to scare him with that last remark.

He kind of looked like a guy standing out in the middle of a traffic jam.

I arranged to meet Mildred Dodge at three o'clock at the Silver Grille on Higbee's tenth floor. The art deco tearoom hadn't changed much since my lunch with Flo, but this time of day the place had a cavernous feel, perhaps fifty patrons in a restaurant that held five-hundred-some at lunch or supper. I'd chosen this spot because Mildred Dodge worked at Higbee's as a switchboard operator. We were meeting on her break.

We were having iced tea, befitting the time of year, though air-conditioning made the scorcher outside a moot point. The petite woman wore a white cotton blouse with a ruffle down the front and a simple black skirt. She hadn't changed much either—her hair was still short but all-over dark now, the gray apparently banished by a hairdresser. She was back out in the workforce, so looking a little younger made sense. I still thought she was very nearly pretty with those large wide-set dark eyes, but the long nose argued against it. And the drawn-on eyebrows didn't help.

She sipped her iced tea. She was having the lemon chiffon pie with whipped cream, which I'd encouraged, to get on her good side. Skinny as she was, and as pinched as her expression could get, her having a sweet tooth seemed doubtful, but she was digging in. I had the mocha torte, if you're interested.

After several bites, she started right in. "I do remember you, Mr. Heller. Frankly, it's not that you're so memorable, but after all, you dropped by the house with a TV star, didn't you? Rest her soul."

"I did. Flo and I ate here on that trip."

She glanced around with a wistful smile on her thin red lip-sticked lips. "It's an elegant place. In the '30s, an orchestra provided background music, and you would see celebrities here—Lillian

Gish was almost a regular. Often it was writers doing events in the book department—Anita Loos, Irving Stone, even Dr. Seuss."

Or maybe Flo Kilgore, another ghost now.

The dark eyes looked at me unblinkingly. "Whatever could there still be to talk about, Mr. Heller, where that tragedy is concerned?"

"Quite a lot, actually, with the new trial coming up. You're bound to be a prosecution witness. I represent Mr. Bailey, but he won't be calling you."

She huffed, "He's quite the *show-off*, isn't he? You know, he's used the Sheppard case to take advantage of its fame, and ride its coattails—riding on his own *jet* plane, I understand! Well, I won't hold it against you, Mr. Heller. You're just trying to make a living like the rest of us."

I sipped iced tea. "Well, there are a few things that Mr. Bailey's investigators have discovered, which he shared with me. Things that didn't make it into the first trial."

She swallowed a bite of lemon chiffon. "Such as?"

"Odds and ends, really. I may jump around a bit . . ."

"I can keep up with you. Begin."

I took some air in and let it out. "Let's start with the fact that you had your fireplace going on July third, 1954. It's been speculated that the reason for that was to burn up evidence. And it does seem odd you'd have a fire going in July."

She looked down the long nose at me. "That's because most people don't know what it's *like* to live on a lake. It was windy and quite cool. Not unusual for us to have a fire that time of year, on that kind of night. We used cannel coal."

"A reporter said she saw the burned ends of logs."

Mildred didn't bother to frown. This was just a fly to flick off. "She was wrong. Anyway, what difference does that make? The things these people seize upon!"

"There seems to be some confusion about who was home and who wasn't, on the night of the third."

She shook her head. "Not in my mind, there isn't. Marsh and

I walked down to the beach about ten that night and watched the fireworks. And it *was* cool, the lake really untamed. Back at home, I watched a movie on TV, with my daughter—*Strange Holiday*—then read a magazine, till around two-thirty in the morning. Marsh went to bed earlier—we had separate bedrooms, but don't read anything into that. Marsh was just a snorer, that's all."

I nodded. "What about your son?"

"Jerry was out on a date, but came back early enough to listen to the ball game on the radio with his father."

"Wasn't he planning to stay out all night with the girl, by pretending to be on a sleepover with one of his pals? But you and your husband caught on and refused to allow it?"

Now she frowned. "Who told you that?"

"Just something one of Bailey's investigators came up with."

"Out of whole cloth! Nothing like that happened."

I sat forward a little. "But when Jerry was questioned by police, he couldn't remember what movie he and his date had seen. Or even what theater they'd gone to. Doesn't that make you think maybe they weren't at the movie at all?"

Her smile tried to be cute; it failed. "Weren't you ever in the back row of a movie theater, Mr. Heller, with a date, and didn't watch the screen?"

Ignoring that as rhetorical, I said, "Could you put me in touch with Jerry? Does he live in the area? He's a doctor now, I understand. An osteopath?"

Some pride came into her expression. "Yes. And also a captain in the Army Medical Corps. Serving in Vietnam. You have my blessing to look him up there."

She was getting a little surly. Maybe it was my questions, or maybe she'd just run out of pie.

No reason not to get into the nasty stuff, then. I told her about what Jane Carter had said about Marilyn and her ex-husband, and what the Spang Bakery delivery guy, Draper, had reported. She dismissed Jane Carter as "a dippy little nut," and Draper as a delusional fool.

"Marsh had his problems," she said, her expression severe now, even for her, "and I trust he still does—but he *never* slept with that Marilyn Sheppard. That young woman was closer in age to our *son* than to Marsh!"

"Surely you had to have *no* reason to divorce him."

Her chin came up again. "I had several. He'd started drinking, heavily, and his mental state was a mess—he threatened suicide, had a second nervous breakdown. He was making a hobby out of feeling sorry for himself. I'm a strong woman, Mr. Heller, but there are some things even a strong woman cannot abide. If you think it was easy for me, you are wrong—I had been with Marsh since *high school*."

Like Sam and Marilyn.

"I probably still love him," she said offhandedly. "But enough is enough."

"Just a few more questions, Mrs. Dodge."

"Very few." She glanced at her wristwatch. "My break will be over in five minutes."

"Why did you ask the Carter girl to keep an eye on the Sheppards for you?"

Her frown removed whatever suggestion of prettiness there'd been. "She said *that*? She *is* a kook, that one. A first-class kook!"

"Well, you did keep tabs on the investigation, didn't you? Leading up to Sam's arrest?"

She reared back. "What are you talking about?"

"You turned your living room over to Coroner Gerber as his command center, for what? Two weeks? Even served him his meals. You couldn't have missed much."

She stiffened. "Marsh was the mayor. He was the safety director. That was *proper*! He was just behaving responsibly."

As opposed to drinking to excess and threatening suicide.

I asked, "To what do you attribute your husband's nervous breakdowns?"

Her upper lip curled into a thin sneer. "That was the fault of those Sheppards—when Sam, his longtime *friend*, accused him of killing Marilyn, it *crushed* Marsh. And how hypocritical was that? *Sam Sheppard killed his wife, nobody else.*"

She stood, but she didn't go, not yet.

I said, "Some think you and your husband are good suspects in this tragedy. That Marsh was having an affair with Marilyn, and you caught them in the act—you're left-handed, right? And the beating Marilyn took was not what a young, athletic man like Sam would deliver, but more suited to the relative weakness of a woman. How do you respond to that?"

I had gone all the way with that one. I might get a glass of water thrown in my face. I might have been slapped. She could have sworn at me at the top of her lungs until the Silver Grille's rafters rang.

But all she did was smile faintly.

"Mr. Heller," she said, "I wouldn't swat a fly."

She touched a cloth napkin to her lips and strode out, head held high. Me, I sat there wondering if she had seen *Psycho,* too.

Or if maybe I'd just had tea with one.

16

Beyond the city limits of suburban Westlake, twelve miles west of downtown Cleveland, Bradley Road took me through a beautiful wooded area, mid-morning sun dappling leaves that shimmered in a balmy breeze. I stopped my rental Ford at a green cast-iron, antique-looking mailbox at the mouth of a long, gently sloping macadam drive. EBERLING & OBIE, the mailbox said. To the left was a wooded area of oak, maple and elm, to the right a bizarre assemblage of red and black pines and other, unidentifiable trees.

Pulling over, I could see what had to be my host waving as he neared the bottom of the drive.

As I got out of the car, he called out in an easy baritone, "Mr. Heller! Richard Eberling. Come let me give you the tour!"

Six-one, lanky but with a large oblong head more suitable for a heavier man, he was not quite handsome, his dark eyes small under heavy black eyebrows, his nose long and indifferently formed, his mouth a small rosebud. He wore a pink-red-and-white pullover shirt with red scarf around his throat, white cotton duck trousers and red leather loafers with no socks. His dark hair sported a Beatles cut, circa their Ed Sullivan debut, and his tan said he spent time outdoors.

I approached and we shook hands, his grip firm but brief. His smile was bigger than his mouth indicated it could be, and his expression was too happy.

"Very honored to have you stop by, Mr. Heller."

We'd spoken only briefly on the phone, as I indicated I was kind of an advance man for F. Lee Bailey on the upcoming Sheppard retrial.

"You're gracious to accommodate me," I said. "But I'm not sure it's much of an honor."

The smile turned a little sideways; his chin jutted. "Well, I've read about you in the magazines. The big ones, like *Life* and *Look*, but also the true detective variety. I'm kind of a buff in that department. You ought to write a book!"

"One of these days, maybe. You really can't see the house from here, can you?"

His smile became more of a grin. "That's just one of the things Obie and I like about it. Obie's my business partner. You'll meet him later. This way?"

I followed him on foot up the macadam drive, then he looked back and gave me a little-kid smile—he was all smiles, this one—and waved for me to follow him.

"Come on! You've got to see this."

I trailed him on a stone path through what seemed like a bunch of overgrown weeds.

"Isn't this wonderful?" he asked, as we pushed through the jungle. "I have a master Japanese gardener who tends this for me, *meigakure*-style."

"Does that mean it comes with bamboo shoots?"

He glanced back again and chuckled. "No, that means the really interesting parts are hidden away from prying eyes. This is a garden that keeps its secrets. There's a whole acre of it!"

The twisting path he led me down gave up a number of its secrets, always coming into view suddenly, at first concealed from view—a boulder here, a tall delicate plant there, a mini-waterfall suddenly before us, then finally a reflecting pool. It was all magical, and a tad creepy. The winding path emptied us to the edge of where the macadam widened into a skirt in the midst of a well-tended front yard with traditional shrubbery. A two-story house that probably dated to the previous century wore gray aluminum siding. To the right a double garage had been added.

I followed him up four stone steps to a porch with an overhang under which an array of potted plants thrived, with wrought-iron benches at left and right.

He beamed. Something about his face made it little boy and old man at the same time. "Ready for part two?"

"Pardon?"

"Of the tour! Come on in."

Said the spider to the fly.

Like the hidden garden, the old (if newly sided) farmhouse had lots of secrets on display. By the front door was a stained-glass sign that said "The Hermitage," the door itself a dark walnut with black nickel handle and black nickel door trellis on glass. Inside, he took me upstairs and then down, gesturing to a crystal chandelier, various antiques ("Reproductions," he clarified), framed landscape oils ("Those *are* antique," he insisted), and glassed-in cabinets displaying fine china and crystal. The four bedrooms were upstairs, the master decorated with framed Japanese prints and taken up mostly by a big double bed with a black spread. None of the rooms was terribly large, but there were a lot of them. The place was brimming with lush drapery, parquet floors, Oriental carpets, and walls papered in various shades and patterns of charcoal and/or red.

The effect was a fancy brothel where they didn't need to mug you, because they were already getting enough of your cash.

"Why *reproductions* of antique furniture?" I asked. "Obviously you can afford anything you want."

His serious expression was intended to convey wisdom. "I consider a new reproduction a better investment than a genuine antique. I prefer the look of the old, but the smell of the new."

I had no idea what to say to that. On the other hand, the place did smell pretty good—sort of lavender.

We were seated in the living room in a pair of red-and-black brocade chairs, angled toward each other, separated by a French Louis XIV walnut table with a tropical-birds-shade Tiffany lamp

on it. The latter was the only light on, though sun filtered in past
heavy drapes through filmy inner curtains. In terms of size, the
living room was modest, probably about what space there'd been
back in farmhouse days. Yet somehow they'd squeezed in a fireplace with a framed mirror over it, making the room seem bigger,
and four red-upholstered sofas, each with a slumbering schnauzer
curled up against a pillow like a fuzzy kielbasa ring.

I nodded toward them. "What does it take to wake them? A
rampaging cat?"

His laugh was short and caught in his throat. "Oh, don't mind
the girls. They're Obie's little darlings. But I swear, someone could
pull a van up and empty this place, and as long as the intruders left
those sofas alone, those little bitches would sleep right through."

He had already provided himself and his guest—me—with
a glass of iced tea wearing a slice of lemon. It was, surprisingly,
sweetened, Southern-style. The last I looked, this was Ohio.

He'd noticed my reaction and said, "Not a fan of sweet tea?
Took me a while, too. But that's always what's in the pitcher in the
fridge. Obie made it. He's from West Virginia and there's nothing
to be done about it."

Whether he was talking about his business partner's place of
birth or the sweetened tea, I wasn't sure. And didn't ask.

I did ask, "What's the story on this place? If you don't mind
sharing it."

"Not at all!" He folded his hands in his lap and leaned back.
"I was an orphan, you know."

"I didn't," I admitted. I felt like I'd asked someone where they
were from and they replied by starting with the log cabin where
they were born.

"Oh yes," he said, with an offhanded wave. "You know, it's
truly unfair to bring a little bastard into the world. Richard was
saddled with such *terrible* options! And yet, and yet—he came out
a winner every time."

I almost asked him who "Richard" was, then remembered *he*
was Richard.

He gazed at the unlit fireplace and his tone grew wistful. "Richard never knew who his father was. Rumor has it Frank Story himself fathered the child!"

"Story, who was chief of police?"

"Yes. Well known in the community. He was a crony of Eliot Ness, they say."

"Is that right."

His eyes lifted as he got back to his story. Not Frank Story, just his story. "Richard was a foster child sent out five times before the age of seven. When they were displeased with him, one set of foster parents would stick Richard in the dark basement and tie him up with rope. He suffered seizures as a child, fits . . . and also as an adult, but less frequently. Richard attributes the malady to being raped at age seven by another of his foster fathers."

It was like saying "How are you?" to somebody, who then shows you the X-rays.

"Then," he continued, "Richard was sent to an orphanage, and let me tell you, Nate . . . Nathan?"

"Either's fine. I'm guessing you prefer Richard?"

"Yes. Nothing wrong with Dick, but Richard sounds more . . . sophisticated, don't you think?"

"Sure."

"Next came the orphanage . . . and Nate, let me tell you in no uncertain terms—an orphanage is the equivalent of a prison! It really is. No movies, no games, no outings, just rules, rules, rules. Like prison, all you think about, hour after hour, is getting out. Then one day Richard *did* get out. A couple named the Eberlings took him on as a foster child."

"You weren't adopted?"

"No. There were three children, grown and gone, and two other foster boys already on hand. George, the father, worked those two like *slaves*. And I worked hard, too, don't think I didn't . . . but Christine, the mother, wouldn't let George crack the whip with me."

He was in the first person now, I noted.

"To me, Christine was like a real mother. I was her sweet little

Dickie bird. The other boys had to work that farm—sixty acres of fruit and vegetables and dairy cows. But I had a touch with the housework and she loved that. I had a few goats I tended, and two little gardens near the house. Christine gave me special privileges. Sometimes I got an extra piece of pie or cake for dessert. And I had my own personal subscription to *Better Homes and Gardens*. She could be affectionate, too, hugging and kissing. I was her 'baby'!"

"Loved you like a mother, sounds like."

He frowned. "Wasn't all good. Richard didn't like the way Christine wouldn't let him play with other children. If a boy or girl from school rode over on a bike, she would send Richard inside and shoo them away. She wouldn't let him play sports, afraid he might get hurt. She filled him with false hope about being a doctor someday, though Richard was only an average student, because he had the gumption to stand up to the teachers. It was like she *owned* Richard. Like he was a *possession*."

I shifted in the chair, which was at least as comfortable as a cement block. "Your full name, I understand, is Richard George Eberling. So they must *eventually* have decided to adopt you. . . ."

He shook his head; with that Beatle mop, it was like that baby-faced bass player going for a high note. "No, I was a foster child, beloved though I was to Christine. Out of respect to her, and to honor my foster father, I changed my name legally in high school—my original name was hard to pronounce, and I'd already begun my window-washing business."

"Then you didn't inherit the farm?"

He shook his head again. "No, I bought it parcel by parcel from Christine, after George's passing. When he died, I breathed a sigh of relief. He was good to me, but very strict. He had a sudden attack of cerebral apoplexy. Rumors of poisoning were bandied about by jealous relatives—well, that was just something Richard had to put up with."

Third person again.

"Why were they jealous, Richard?"

"Just a sad fact of human nature. You see, my late foster father made Christine executor of his estate. The biological spawn would get everything only after she died. But until her death, she could sell off parcels to raise cash to live on. And she only did business with me, bless her heart. Pretty soon, I owned everything. She passed, and then Obie joined me here and we turned this old haunted house into a real showplace."

One of the schnauzers was snoring.

I asked, "And you were able to buy the entire spread, a parcel at a time? Strictly from a part-time window-washing business?"

"That's right. And after high school graduation, I wasn't part time for long. Always had one or two boys with me. Had Bay Village all sewed up, homes up and down Lake Road. At my peak, I had as many as two hundred accounts and never less than one hundred—mostly homes, but also a gutters and siding company . . . they did this house . . . a metal fabricating firm, a kitchen cookware distributor, and three church parish houses."

"You were doing very well."

"Oh, yes. Richard's secret was a solution of water and hard brown vinegar—not ammonia—with a dollop of Blue Sheen carpet cleaner."

But Richard had another secret.

"Not to be rude," I said, "didn't you have another business on the side? An offshoot of the window-cleaning service?"

His smile pretended to be embarrassed. "I suppose we have to get into that."

"We do. If Mr. Bailey calls you as a witness, that will likely come out . . . not by him, but by the prosecution, trying to impeach you."

"Nathan, you must keep in mind that Richard was very young, really a remarkable success story for a high school boy, an orphan! And temptation abounded. It took years for anyone to realize that Richard was helping himself now and again to jewels and rings and money and things. These people were well-off. And they left their doors unlocked, so who was to say Richard was the culprit?"

"But you *were* the culprit. And you *are* Richard."

His smile was a shameless thing. "You called it a 'business,' but it was more . . . a hobby, or maybe an obsession. I was like a stamp collector or somebody who pins butterflies in a book. I just had hot fingers, that's all. Started in lifting small items from clients. When the police came out here, they took two truckloads away! It wasn't like I was fencing the items, though they accused me of that. The only thing I kept was money. So in that sense, it was a business, sure."

"This was mostly jewelry?"

"Other things, too. I have an eye for finer objects—bowls, pitchers, really nice wristwatches, sterling silver—not a whole set, just a spoon here and a fork there—and Royal Doulton figurines, Steuben glass. Little things, easily concealed, hardly missed. I always had my pail of wash water I could drop things in, and just take with me out the door. I did remove diamonds and other jewels from unworthy settings, which I discarded. After a client got suspicious, an uncle of mine who was a policeman came around, and Christine—she was alive then—just *screamed* at him for his suspicions. But then he got a search warrant, so what can you do?"

"I'm sorry to make you go over something so painful," I said, working hard to keep the sarcasm out, because he was really enjoying himself, essentially bragging. "But I guess you know why, in court, on the stand, things could get sticky."

He nodded. "Is it warm in here?"

"Not bad." The place was air-conditioned, but it *was* a little warm, the day heating up out there. One of the schnauzers had rolled onto its back. As he'd said, a girl.

"I'm just talking too much," Eberling said, with mock embarrassment, "and getting worked up into a lather." He put his hand on top of his head. "Do you mind?"

"Not at all," I said, not knowing what the hell he meant.

He took his hair off and set what was a Beatle wig on the walnut lamp table between us. The top of his skull now wore wispy memories of what must have once been an actual head of hair.

"Started losing it in high school," he said, meaning his hair, but that was a little ambiguous. "I have a whole shelf of wigs and toupees, actually. Pay top dollar for 'em! Just another fashion accessory."

Was he trying to distract me? Change the subject?

I said, "When your 'hobby' came to light, it was, what, about seven, eight years ago?"

He nodded, but suddenly didn't seem to have anything else to say on the subject.

"How," I asked, as casually as possible, "did you happen to have Marilyn Sheppard's engagement ring? And a cocktail ring of hers? The Sheppards were clients of yours, right? Did you pick those things up while doing a job for them?"

He shook his head; no suggestion of a Beatle going for a high note now. "They were my clients. But that's not where or how I got the rings. I'd seen the cocktail ring before, out on her dresser, when I was up there cleaning? Nice item. One diamond, surrounded by diamond chips, worth hundreds."

"If you didn't get it at the Sheppards', then—"

"Oh, I got it at the Sheppards, all right . . . just not *those* Sheppards. The two rings were in a box on a shelf in the closet at Richard and Dorothy Sheppard's place. My service did more than just clean windows, we did walls, too, including closets."

His idea of cleaning a closet was different than mine.

He was sitting forward, his hands folded almost prayerfully in his lap. "I saw a box that said 'Marilyn Reese Sheppard—Personal Property' on it. Just an old cardboard box. But those rings were in there. So I took them. As a kind of . . . memento."

"Of what?"

"Of her. Of Marilyn. I didn't do the first job at Dr. Sheppard's place, two of my boys did. But they came back saying, 'Wow! What a dish!' Thought I'd have a look myself, so I went over to get payment personally and she had this California look—tight little brief shorts and a very little blouse. She was immaculate, all in white. Only a few years older than me."

"How many jobs did you do there?"

"Half a dozen. I only met Dr. Sam once. He was at the breakfast table with Chip and her. She introduced me to him and I hardly got a nod, certainly not a word, but she had me join them, sit there with them. That man was arrogant, thought he was a gift to mankind."

"But Mrs. Sheppard was nice to you."

"Yes, if a little . . . distant. Not full of herself like her husband, but she was one of those golden girls from the East Side, with the qualities of a well-groomed lady. One day, when I was working, she brought out a tray of brownies and milk onto the porch for me to share with her and Chip. It was almost like we were a little family."

"The rings were intact? You didn't remove the stones from their settings, which was your standard way?"

"I did remove the stone from the engagement ring, but I held on to the setting, too. The cocktail ring, like you said, I didn't fool with. I kept the rings separate from other things I'd gathered, tucked away."

"Why?"

He frowned. "They started to bother me. The stones had belonged to a dead girl, you know?"

"How many thefts did you admit to?"

"Oh, over a hundred. In Bay Village, Westlake, Rocky River. I talked to lots of detectives from here and there, and tried to help. One asked me why my blood was found in the Sheppard house—I learned later that was just a lucky guess. Anyway, I told them how I cut my finger taking out a storm window by the kitchen sink. When I went back to work, I inadvertently dripped blood in various parts of the Sheppard house."

This had turned Eberling into a suspect in a supposedly solved murder. Part of why I was here was to see whether he made a better witness for the defense or suspect for the murder. The blood was key, because a trail of blood, unable to be typed, had been said by the prosecution in the first trial to be dripping from the bloody weapon as Sam Sheppard wandered about the house, in a post-homicidal haze, getting his act together.

"They wanted to do a polygraph with me," Eberling said, "but Bay Village couldn't afford the cost, so they tried to palm it off on Cleveland. That Coroner Gerber came and talked to me for almost four hours, and decided I was innocent and blocked the test."

"But later Bay Village *did* give you a polygraph."

"Yes, I guess they scraped the money up from somewhere. And I passed it, without a hitch. Listen, if I had been the slightest bit guilty, they would have pulled me in."

The door opened and a slightly stocky, boyish man in amber-lens wireframes rolled in. His full, tousled hair and skimpy mustache were black, and he wore a blue-green-yellow Madras short-sleeve shirt and light blue shorts well above the knee. He had a Rolex and a tan.

"Ah see we have comp'ny," he said in an easy Southern drawl, and walked straight to me as I stood. We shook hands—another firm, brief one. His smile was a dazzler.

"Oscar B. Henderson," he said, "but call me Obie. Has my business partner here been chewin' your ear off?"

Speaking of chewing, the four schnauzers had roused themselves and were bounding from the couches to dance around Obie enthusiastically, like Indians attacking a circled wagon train. *Woo woo woo woo, woo woo woo woo. . . .*

"Nathan Heller," I said with a nod. "Doing a little pre-interview for Lee Bailey."

"Pleased to meet you, Nathan. Dick, would you feed these girls for me, and put 'em outside? Thanks, brother."

Eberling, saying, "Outside, outside," led the four bearded girls down a hallway.

Obie took his partner's chair and I sat again, too.

I said, "Richard's been very open about his past. That's a good thing, because we can't have any surprises on the witness stand."

"You might keep in mind, Nathan, that not everything my buddy tells you may be strictly true. Oh, he's a hell of a guy, Dick— we live here together, and travel, Mexico, Ireland, Japan, throw parties together, buy property together. But there's something you need to know—we do *not* have a homosexual relationship."

"I didn't assume that," I lied. "Anyway, it's none of my business."

"Good to hear, 'cause I'm a live-and-let-live kind of guy myself."

Eberling was coming up the hall, and apparently had heard some of that, because as his footsteps echoed, so did his voice, as he said, "Obie does the laundry, I do windows and clean. We take turns on supper. He pays utilities, I buy groceries, so there's no money spats. We just share."

My host pulled another brocade chair from somewhere and positioned himself in front of and between us.

"Oh, we have a tiff now and again," Obie said, "like any couple." He seemed to realize how that sounded, and added, "Of friends."

"The list of women," Eberling said, shaking his head and grinning, "who are after Obie here? It's as long as, well, it's long."

Obie said, "Y'see, Nathan, we both have sadness in our pasts where the fairer sex is concerned. I was married when I was young, unhappily, and have a son who suffered for it. So that's a road I don't care to go down again. The girl Dick loved died tragically, in an auto accident he had."

That must have been a road Dick didn't want to go down again.

"So," Obie was saying, "let people think what they will. Y'know, Nathan, just because we're interior decorators doesn't mean we're a couple of faggots."

"Not at all," I said. "Is that what you are now—interior decorators?"

Both men nodded, but Obie said, "After Dick had that little problem with klepta-mania, his window-washin' concern kinda went by the wayside. But he still has a way with the ladies . . . the *older* ones, widows? And cleans and does household chores for several, regularly."

"In the meantime," Eberling said, "we're taking on more and more interior decorating clients. This house has been our best public relations move—we're on the Westlake Garden Club unique homes tour, and that got us all sorts of press write-ups. What was it that one columnist said, Obie?"

Obie grinned, his mustache coming along for the ride. "'The Hermitage displays the elegance of a nineteenth-century salon.' I think he hit 'er on the nose."

"No argument," I said.

We chatted some more—Eberling, as a fan of true detective magazines, had questions about various jobs of mine, and after all that he'd spilled about himself, I felt he'd earned some stories from me. They invited me to stay for lunch and I politely declined.

Obie was on his knees playing with his dancing dogs when Eberling walked me to the door.

"Nate, when do you suppose the trial will be?"

"Probably early in the fall."

"And you think I'll be called as a witness?"

"Good chance of it."

After all, Lee Bailey had all but ruled him out as a suspect. Eberling had passed a lie test successfully, and no matter what Dick and Obie said, they were obviously gay. Of course it was possible one or both were bisexual, but I didn't think so, at least not in Eberling's case.

Marilyn Sheppard's murder had been a sex crime, either a rape or more likely—considering the way her pajamas had been arranged—consensual sex. The way it looked to me, Richard viewed Marilyn as the mother in an idealized family, the kind denied an orphan boy. A bastard.

Richard Eberling had stolen a lot of things in that oddball life of his, but a piece of tail from another man's wife in the early morning hours?

I didn't think so.

17

I spent Tuesday afternoon talking to several of what you might call the "bushy-haired" witnesses. These were people who had seen things in the predawn morning of July 4, 1954, that seemed to back up Sam Sheppard's description of the intruder he claimed to have wrestled on the beach.

These included a Cleveland attorney with a client who'd seen a man running on the beach, said client having been reluctant to come forward because it would reveal a tryst with a "respectable lady" who wasn't his wife. Imagine something like that happening in Bay Village.

A woman who'd been on a bus near Bay Village, headed east, said a nervous man with bushy hair had boarded the bus, shortly after the estimated time of Marilyn Sheppard's murder. A husband and wife had seen a bushy-haired man alongside the road and so had a guy coming back from a fishing trip, a suspicious-looking character "six feet tall with his hair standing up."

These individuals were so generous as to see me at my Hotel Cleveland suite and were informed this was just a preliminary meeting. Mr. Bailey or one of his legal associates would likely be speaking to them later.

Or maybe not. The nameless "bushy-haired intruder" as murder suspect did not hold much appeal to Bailey. He felt the answer lay among the Dodges, Lucas Hardmann, or Richard Eberling, and

I didn't disagree with him. Part of my mission here was to see if I could hone in on which of these suspects to like best.

The only key person I hadn't seen this trip was Sam Sheppard himself. Of course, I had only been in Cleveland a few days, and somehow making contact over the Fourth of July weekend seemed in questionable taste. I had called that morning and left word with Ariane that I would stop by this evening, when I'd finished my interviews with the bushy-haired bunch.

"It will be good to see you," she said, as if we were old friends when we'd only been around each other twice.

Rocky River, the western suburb beyond Bay Village, was another bedroom community, where Ariane had leased a five-room brick townhouse while Sam was still in the Ohio pen. I parked in the drive behind a purple Thunderbird—a gift to Ariane from herself, while she gave Sam her old Lincoln—and was soon going up the three steps to the small landing under a modest white overhang supported by slender pillars.

I was poised to knock when I noticed the door was ajar. Since I was expected, I pushed it open a ways and was about to call out when I saw Sam Sheppard, stretched out in a T-shirt and boxer shorts, on the living room sofa. He was out. Whether passed out or sleeping, I couldn't tell, but the detective in me deduced the former, since a bottle of Johnnie Walker and an empty glass were on a nearby coffee table.

So was a .38 snubnose revolver.

I went in quietly. I had not been here before. As surprising as that gun had been, the real shock was the decor. Having survived Eberling and Obie's decorating style this morning, you might think I would not be easily surprised.

You'd be wrong.

Not that the royal purple color scheme didn't go perfectly with the eighteenth-century furnishings. How Sam could sleep, or even stay passed out, on that under-stuffed, spindly-legged shades of lavender button-tufted sofa, I couldn't hazard a guess.

Ariane must have shipped over her favorite furnishings from

Germany. In addition to the Louis XV furniture, touches included an oversized light purple vase with purple artificial flowers, and a shelf of knickknacks dominated by an ebony statue of a curvy nude woman seated in a pose with hands behind her head and elbows winged, like Marilyn Monroe's famous calendar shot. Over the couch were two framed original paintings of Parisian beauties of a type I'd seen at George Diamond's Steak House hanging with the Keane waif masterpieces—these were waifs who'd grown up nicely, as their big floppy chapeaus and wispy fashions showed. They were benign angels floating above the balding baby-faced man in his T-shirt and shorts with a bottle of Scotch and a .38 within reach.

Also downstairs were the kitchen and a den, both empty of Ariane or anyone else. I went upstairs where two rooms were off a short hallway. Standing open was a door to what appeared to be a guest room—framed photos of Marilyn Sheppard and son Sam Jr. (Chip) were on the wall. The furnishings here were contemporary, more 1952 Holiday Inn than eighteenth-century French. The other door was shut—presumably the master bedroom.

I knocked, very softly.

Then, my voice barely a whisper, I said, "Ariane? Ariane . . . ?"

Nothing.

I went in. Again, the furnishings were early Holiday Inn. Only the living room was a showplace. On the bed were two yawning-open suitcases, Louis Vuitton, with their signature monogram canvas and tan leather trim; in them were piles of haphazardly folded designer dresses and such. Across from the near side of the bed were closed double slatted closet doors.

I went over and opened them. Ariane Sheppard née Tebbenjohanns was crouched on the floor under now-empty hangers. She was hugging herself as if it were cold, and the air-conditioning was doing its job, all right, but that wasn't why she was shivering. Her big dark eyes were bigger than usual, her white hair up in a stylish beehive, her slender, shapely form in a dark blue dress with white polka dots, bare arms and a scoop neckline. Her earrings were white suspended balls, almost as big and round as her eyes. She was fully made up, her mouth a red wound.

"Nathan," she said, shuddering, looking up at me like a puppy hoping another beating wasn't on the way. "Nathan. What am I going to *do?*"

I held a hand out to her, like she was a wallflower who was lucky to have a guy offer her a dance. She got to her feet, smoothed her dress, which wasn't a mini but showed plenty of nice tan leg, and then she came out and hugged me.

Nothing sexual about it. Well, not much, anyway. She slipped out of my arms but stayed close, and, with an arm around her waist, I led her to the double bed, where she sat on the edge, the Vuitton bags framing her.

"Looks like you're going on a trip," I said.

She swallowed and nodded. I found a chair somewhere and sat right before her. She reached out for one of my hands and I let her take it.

"Going home," she said firmly but softly. "Back to Düsseldorf."

"What does Sam think about that?"

She shook her head, the global earrings swinging. "He doesn't know."

"Are you coming back?"

She shook her head again and the earrings swung some more. "I don't know."

"Let me guess. You thought you'd take a hike while Sam was nice enough to be dead on his ass on the couch."

She frowned a little. "Take a hike? *Leave?* Dead on his ass? *Unconscious?*"

"Nicely translated from the semiliterate to actual English. Why don't you tell me about it?"

Her eyes narrowed and she shared a secret: "He's been drinking."

"Really."

She nodded. "Pills, too. He's been irrational. A maniac!"

"Has he struck you?"

"No."

"I thought you two were happy as clams."

"Clams?"

"Well, happy, anyway."

Her eyes drifted from my face to nowhere. "I tried to make a go of this marriage. Really I did. I knew, *of course* I knew, Sam was under a terrible strain. And I thought it would work itself out. But we fight all the time."

"I thought you two were getting along fine." That's what Bailey had indicated.

Her eyebrows lifted as the eyelids came to a weary half mast. "At first, yes. Sam would give me rubdowns using all of his medical knowledge. He would shave my legs, massage my feet, trim my toenails—my devoted servant!"

More like slave. And slaves have a tendency toward uprisings.

"Every day at first," she said, "he would drive me to the beauty shop to wash and style my hair. And we would go out to dinner, then come home and Sinatra would sing to us from the phonograph. Sam would drink. So would I. I like to drink. But then . . . he began earlier in the day. And continued. And continued. At first, so much sex . . . you are a man of the world, aren't you, Nathan? I can speak frankly?"

"Yup."

Something wistful came into her expression. "He would talk of his desperate love for me. Once, toward the beginning, we made love ten times in one day."

I shrugged. "Well, he was in prison that many years. Things build up. At my age, twice is a miracle."

I was trying to make her smile, but she was in a kind of waking trance, saying, "He stole personal things from me, perhaps to take them to the . . . pawnshops? To 'hock' them? Are those the right terms?"

"Yes."

"He stole money from me, and denied it or said, 'So what?' I paid twenty-five thousand dollars to your lawyer friend, Bailey, for Sam! He sold my Lincoln Continental, behind my back! Why does he *need* money? I have paid all of his bills—I sold my major interest in a company in Germany to do it. Once, in Boston, he got mad at me and threw me out of the car in the rain. I had no money and had to walk a mile to the hotel. Soaking wet. He carries knives and sometimes a hatchet and *always* a gun. He needs medical help!"

"You say he's never hit you."

She shook her head, sighed. "No. But last night, in the middle of the night, I woke up. I felt something cold against the side of my head. He had the gun, its little nose, pushed against the side of my head, and he looked right at me, so cold, and said I was a thief. *I was a thief!*"

An armed uprising.

I asked, "You didn't call the police?"

She reared back as if I'd said something absurd. "No. You can't call the police and still live with your husband!"

"Is that what you want to do? Keep living with him?"

"I don't know, Nathan."

"Do you still love him?"

"I care for him. I believe in him. I *do* love him, still. And I *know* he is innocent."

"You know that even after he put a gun to your head?"

She shrugged. "He didn't fire it."

I nodded, as if she'd made a good point.

"I'll tell you one thing, Ariane. If you repeat any of this in public, or share it with the police, Sam doesn't have a prayer in the new trial. You know the expression, his goose will be cooked?"

She nodded. "I do not wish to cook his goose."

I squeezed the hand she'd given me. "If you leave him before the trial, before the verdict, all the effort, all the money, will've been wasted. File for divorce or separation now, and the world thinks *you* think Sam is guilty. You can go back to Germany for a while with an excuse you give the press—you're off to visit your daughter and mother, or to wrap up some business matters—but you have to be back well before the trial. Do you understand?"

She nodded. "Will you talk to Sam?"

I nodded. "You want some help with those bags?"

Soon we were moving slowly and near silently through the purple living room and out the door. I moved my car out of the way. We loaded up the Thunderbird, and she gave me another hug, and a sisterly kiss, then got behind the wheel and backed out of the driveway, smiling, looking almost giddy. When she was out of sight, I went back in.

I lifted the coffee table carefully, just a few inches off the wall-to-wall carpet, and moved it away from the couch and set it back down. From the coffee table I took the .38 and dropped it in my pocket; I left the bottle of Johnnie Walker there, but out of reach. Somehow I found a chair worth sitting on to pull over and arranged it before the slumbering Sam. I unbuttoned my suitcoat and slipped out of it, then draped it around the high back of the fancy schmancy chair, and sat in shirt-sleeves and shoulder holster. I told you I always carried the nine millimeter in a murder case, no matter how moldy the murder.

I kicked the side of the couch.

Nothing.

I kicked it again.

Again nothing, but the third try roused him. He sat up like a driver who fell asleep at the wheel, only to have a trucker's horn scare him the hell awake. He tasted his mouth, a snack I didn't envy him, and tried to make his eyes work—they could barely manage a blink. He ran a hand over his short-haired, balding head. I could have helped him sit up, but letting him do that by himself let him wake up a little. Also, it amused me some.

"Your wife has gone back to Germany," I said.

The baby face scowled, teeth clenching, cheeks reddening. Then he relaxed. He reached out absently, probably for the Scotch, maybe for the .38. He blinked some more, really coming around, saw where I'd moved the coffee table and apparently felt it too challenging a trip.

"Nate Heller," he said, in that somewhat high-pitched voice. If I were a woman, that sound alone would have been enough to make me leave him.

"Right."

He tried to bring me into focus. "You were . . . you were coming over tonight."

"I was. I did. I am."

He squinted, un-squinted, tasted his mouth again. His expression said, *Yucchh*, then he said, "What was that you said about Ariane?"

"She left. Went to Germany."

"Good riddance. Fuck the bitch. For good?"

"She didn't say. I told her if she didn't come back for the trial, or if she went public with your shenanigans, you were deader than your first wife."

His expression turned indignant. "What shenanigans?"

"Oh, I don't know. Stealing money. Selling her car. Waking her up with a gun to her head. Little things. Of course, they say the little things mean a lot."

He frowned. "Did I do that?"

"All three or one in particular?"

"I . . . I thought I dreamed that."

"You didn't."

His frown turned pouty. "Well . . . she drove me to it. She smothers me. I don't have a single male friend, Nate. She, she boxes me in! Crowds me too much. Really bugs me."

"That's tough, her being such a bitch, in between paying your bills and fucking you ten times in a day."

That startled him. "What's she been telling you?"

"I'm a private detective. If you want dirt on your wife, you'll have to hire me. What was last night's fight about?"

Shrugged, shook his head. "Nothing, really."

"I know. But, still, it must have been something."

"I called her Marilyn at dinner, by mistake, obviously. Just a slip of the tongue. You know. And she got mad."

"Imagine."

"She says, 'Thank you,' and doesn't speak to me for the rest of the evening."

"She said you gave her a little thirty-eight-caliber wake-up call."

The eyes widened, then un-widened. "Probably not the smartest thing. She's been talking about a divorce a lot lately."

"I wonder what Louis Seltzer will do with that, heading into the new trial?"

His mouth dropped open, and again the eyes were wide. "I really . . . really can't let that happen, can I?"

"No. You can't. But I don't know if I, in good conscience . . . to the degree I have one . . . could advise Ariane to stay in a marriage, even temporarily, with an asshole who puts a gun to her head."

He got up and got the Scotch and the glass. Sat again, filled the glass, put the bottle between his bare legs and against the front of his boxers. He guzzled a little from the glass.

Then he said, "She'll come around."

"I'll take your word for it. I get paid whether the state of Ohio calls you a murderer again or not. Would you like to know what I've been up to? Besides taking in an Indians game with a stewardess?"

Damn. Let it slip.

"Please," he said. "You want something to drink?"

"No."

"Beer? Coke? Seven-Up? Some of this Johnnie Walker?"

"No."

Filling him in on my witness/suspect interviews took a good hour, with him sobering up enough to ask the occasional smart question. And he made that one glass of Scotch last through my whole spiel. That was encouraging. But we were a long distance from the thoughtful pipe smoker I'd met at the prison.

He was shaking his head. "I don't remember meeting this Eberling character."

"He says it was only once, at breakfast. He seems to have known Marilyn a little. He was there half a dozen times on jobs or collecting payment. She gave him brownies and milk on the porch with your son, he claims."

"Sounds like Marilyn. She was always taking in strays. He sounds like a kook, but that doesn't make him a killer. My opinion? It was Mildred. Marsh was having an affair with Marilyn, got drunk and came over and Mildred caught them in the act."

"Do you know for a fact Marilyn and Dodge were having an affair?"

He shook his head. "No, but it was possible. Everybody in town knew Marsh was sweet on her. Plus, well . . . I don't know if I should get into this."

"Into what?"

He looked into the glass of Scotch. "It's something I did privately for Lee. We've kept it under wraps."

"I'm working for Lee. You can tell me anything that you feel is useful. I'm covered by your client confidentiality with him."

He sighed, nodded. "Okay. You know as well as anybody how much effort Lee Bailey put into getting me a polygraph, which he was never able to get approval for. But once I was finally freed, awaiting the new trial, too much time had passed for that kind of test to be considered reliable. So a top authority on hypnosis, a Dr. Bryan in Los Angeles, who is also a lawyer, regressed me to the night of Marilyn's murder. Bailey was right there—he can tell you better than I could."

"Well, he isn't here. Do your best, Sam."

"Okay. I guess I relived the experience very realistically, even violently. At one point I threw myself to the floor and missed a heavy piece of furniture by a couple of inches. Under hypnosis, I remembered Marsh assaulting me, and I also remembered another voice, I think female, saying, 'Shall we kill him too?' And I also remembered the person I chased through the door on the lake had a slight limp."

A perfect fit.

"None of that's admissible, Sam."

"Okay, but it tells us a lot."

"Sam—had Lee developed his theory about Marsh and Mildred being the murderers, before you were hypnotized?"

"Well, yes."

"And were you aware of it?"

He shrugged. "Yes."

"Well, you could have faked being under and said what Lee wanted to hear."

His eyes flared; nostrils, too. "*Goddamnit*, man—"

I held up a palm. "Easy, Sam. Under hypnosis, you could have been influenced by Lee's theory and reported that as if you remembered it. *Unintentionally*, but influenced."

Now he finished his Scotch.

Then he said, "There's something else."

On this damn job, there always was.

He was saying, "It's the reason I got bent out of shape last night."

"Okay."

"Client confidentiality, right?"

"Right."

"Well, Lee told me yesterday that a source tells him an old 'friend' of mine from the state pen is trying to work out a clemency deal through the new trial's prosecutors."

I grunted a laugh. "Let me guess. This friend is using you as a bargaining chip."

He nodded. "His name is Armand 'Frenchy' Foor. He's a repeat offender, a bank robber, a strongarm thug really, but also a guy rumored to be a snitch. I got close to him in stir. There was nothing about what I was doing for him to snitch about, and he could handle himself. So I paid him for, you know, protection. He was a buffer between me and people who thought I had money or that I could get them narcotics because of my hospital privileges. Frenchy was a good guy to know inside."

"Only outside he isn't."

He smirked. "No. He's made up a couple of stories about me. It's really *one* story, but he's used different characters. In one, I bribe a guard to get Frenchy transferred to a minimum-security facility, and he breaks out. You see, I've hired him to grab Lucas Hardmann, and make him write a confession about murdering Marilyn, after which Frenchy kills him, faking a suicide. For this I'd supposedly give him a bunch of money and some plastic surgery—Frenchy doesn't like the way his ears stick out. The other story just substitutes Marshall Dodge as the kidnap victim who writes a suicide note confessing his crime before killing himself. And when I got out, I was to give Frenchy an ear bob."

"The prosecution is buying this?"

"Seems so. The Dodge version is what the prosecutors are supposed to be going with. Bailey thinks they'll hold Frenchy for a rebuttal witness after I testify."

I frowned at him. "You're planning to testify?"

Fist in the air. "Damned right I am!"

"Sam, you may want to reconsider. You testified last time and it didn't go so well. And now that you've told your story a dozen more times, going on the stand would open you up to punishing cross-examination on each and every one of them."

He was shaking his head. "Bailey has assured me I'm going on the stand."

I shrugged. "He knows what he's doing. What kind of pills have you been taking?"

He looked hurt. "Who says I've been taking pills?"

"Who do you think?"

He tasted his mouth again—now it only tasted like Scotch, apparently, because this time he didn't make a face. "Barbiturates."

"Washing them down with booze?"

"Of course not. A doctor knows better!" His shrug was elaborate. "Sometimes a man needs to sleep. Sometimes I need to take the edge off the anxiety. Don't you think I have a right to feel anxious, after all I've been through?"

"Yes," I admitted. "But I wouldn't be surprised if your wife is feeling a little anxious herself. You might keep that in mind, if she comes back from Germany to give this star-crossed romance another try. And give you some support."

He swallowed. Nodded. "Your words aren't falling on deaf ears, Nate. I promise you that."

"I hope not."

I stood, went over to the coffee table, emptied the slugs from his .38 and left them and it there.

On the way back to Cleveland, I mulled over the various suspects for Marilyn Sheppard's murder who I'd questioned over the past several days.

Including the one in Ariane's brick townhouse.

Back at the Hotel Cleveland after a long day, I was just getting ready to climb out of my clothes, turn on Johnny Carson, and crawl into bed. I'd be lucky to make it past the monologue. I'd just climbed under the covers when the bedside phone rang and startled me a little.

"Mr. Heller?" a reedy voice said.

"Yes. Who's calling?"

"Somebody from a long time ago. Could you meet me down at the Harbor Inn? You know, in the Flats?"

"Yeah, I know the Flats, and the place. And you know me, and you say I know you. Try running a name past me."

"Gary," he said. "Gary Weed. Remember?"

The newsreel of my memory began running footage of a skinny, sideburned kid at the DeLand, Florida, jail. Wearing a checked jail-house shirt with his cuffed hands in his lap.

"I remember," I said.

"I heard you was in town talkin' to people about the Sheppard case."

"Where did you hear that?"

"Never mind how. Thought maybe you'd like to talk to me again."

"You have something to say I haven't heard before?"

The thin voice had a fat smile in it. "Could be I do. Could be somethin' you'd like to hear. Or anyways, you should. I'm at the Inn right now. Why don't you come on down and buy me a beer or somethin', and we can do some catchin' up."

". . . Half an hour, Gary."

I cradled the phone.

I got back in my things, including my nine-mil in its shoulder holster. Put on the suitcoat, skipped the tie. Even in clothes worn all day, I'd be overdressed at the Harbor Inn, where I could have thrown on a sportshirt and fresh slacks, to fit in better with the natives. But I didn't have a sports jacket along tailored to accommodate hardware, and I'd have been underdressed without the Browning.

After all, the last time I'd been to the Harbor Inn, I'd never made it past the back room where some barely post-puberty punks had required me to teach them a lesson. I almost wondered if Weed was somehow linked to that nasty little crew, that maybe this was some long overdue try at getting even with an out-of-town private cop.

But I decided not. The Harbor Inn was a natural meeting place for the likes of Gary Weed, and sometimes a coincidence is just a coincidence.

I parked on the street under the Center Street Swing Bridge, its shadow doing little to cool the warm night. Industrial sounds rumbled like big dangerous animals in the darkness. I headed across a deserted street to the nondescript brick building on its West Bank corner. Supposedly a saloon since 1895, the joint wore minimal lighting and an ancient Coca-Cola sign, the familiar red button riding white rusted metal with HARBOR INN in faded blue.

The inside of the dive sported the same brick as outside, a long, narrow, cavernous place with a gray and pink tile floor that had faded from black and red. As deserted as the street had been, the dingy joint was well populated. A well-worn, well-stocked bar with an ancient cash register had, behind it on the wall, a rugged ship's wheel amid neon beer signs. The hefty stubble-puss bartender looked like a bouncer shanghaied for the duty.

Though the jukebox played "Time Won't Let Me," confirming

it was 1966, this might still have been 1957, or maybe 1942; the workaday crowd, including a good share of dockworkers, had changed little from decade to decade. The beer was cheap and cold and that was all it took to keep the regulars happy—on a week-night, anyway. A little stage toward the back, and posters here and there, indicated rock bands came in on Friday and Saturday, likely drawing kids from all social strata. But right now, this was Hourly Worker Land.

In addition to a row of pinballs singing their tuneless tune, a bowling machine stretched along a wall, a group of guys going at it, dime after dime. Athletes with beer bellies and drooping ciga-rettes, eager to compete.

Gary Weed sat alone at a table-for-four against a brick wall op-posite the bar, a human collision between the '50s and '60s—the dark sideburns now accompanying dyed-blond bowl-cut Rolling Stones hair, his pack of Luckies tucked into the rolled-up sleeve of a white T-shirt, emblazoned with a comical, big-foot fella on the move under a bold cartoony "Keep on Truckin'." Weed's rolled-cuff dungarees were pure Marlon Brando out of *The Wild One*, but the pointed-toe black boots were strictly Beatles.

He had a beer and a fag going, the latter adding to the curtain of cigarette smoke, and was glancing around somewhat conspicu-ously, watching for me to come in the front or side entrance. When I came in the side way, his eyes caught me, and lit up. His grin was missing a bicuspid. Despite his youthful apparel, he looked older than just nine years later—more like a weathered forty-some than early thirties. The sunken-cheek skinniness that before had sug-gested youth shouted druggie now.

Cigarette dangling in a smile as thin as he was, he waved me over with two hands, as if bringing in a small plane at an airfield.

I joined him. A pretty shag-hair brunette waitress in a Harbor Inn T-shirt with no bra and black hot pants came over quick, took my order for a beer, and walked away slow. I watched her go. There was no law against it. Some men my age felt like this whole sexual revolution and youth culture thing had passed them by. They didn't have Hugh Hefner and *Playboy* on yearly retainer.

"I bet she's a dyke," Weed said, by way of greeting.

"Why is that, Gary?"

"She's got short hair. All the dykes got short hair."

"I'll file that one away. How have you been? Incarcerated mostly, I would guess."

He grinned. That missing tooth gave him charm. Not really.

"Funny you should say," he said. "Guess who my cellmate at the state pen was?"

"Robert Stroud?"

He frowned stupidly. "Who?"

"Inside joke." I should have known *Birdman of Alcatraz* references would be too hip for the room. Maybe if I'd said Burt Lancaster. "Who was your cellmate, Gary?"

"Frenchy Foor. Armand Foor?"

The back of my neck tingled.

Weed was saying, "Frenchy was Doc's muscle boy in stir. But I bet Dr. Sam wishes different about now."

The jukebox started in on "The Ballad of the Green Berets." Bowling-machine players were yelping and yowling, and the drone of conversation, working up over the jukebox blare with occasional highlights of laughter and shouts, seemed to ride the tide of cigarette smoke.

"What are you getting at, Gary?"

He leaned forward, sharing his missing-tooth grin again. "I know all about Frenchy snitching on Doc. About the story he's ready to tell that would put Doc back inside."

"Doc," as you probably figured out, was what Sheppard had been called by his fellow prisoners.

"What story is that, Gary?"

He frowned, as if I'd hurt his feelings. "You *know* what story. How Doc was gonna grease some wheels to get Frenchy transferred to Marion Correctional—the honor camp? And then Frenchy would strong-arm some guy to write a confession about killing Doc's wife, then fake a suicide. *That* story."

My beer arrived. I smiled at the waitress. She smiled back—I was old, but looked like money. At least in here I did.

"Let's say," I said, "that story does seem familiar. Trumped up, but familiar. Why does that make stopping by the Harbor Inn worth missing *The Tonight Show?*"

His eyes narrowed. "Just answer me one simple question."

"Do my best."

Now the eyes glittered. "That ten-grand reward the Sheppard family put up—is it still available? They stand behind that, after all this time?"

I shrugged. "I think so. I could easily confirm it with a phone call."

Another grin. "Why don't you go *do* that. There's a booth around the corner. *Then* we'll get into the long and short of it."

Shook my head. "No, Gary, I don't think so. You tell me what you have in mind, and I'll decide whether calling Sam Sheppard's brothers is worth the trouble."

Gary thought about it. That took a while. Then he leaned his skinny frame forward and said, "I'm still tight with Frenchy. I can get word to him to *take back* that story—it'll mean the Frenchman servin' the rest of his time, almost two years . . . but he would do that for me."

"Is that right."

He shrugged. "There's no obligation 'less Doc gets off. Once he's cleared, that ten grand would be the payoff. But I need *five* up front."

I sipped the beer, gave him an easy smile. "If Dr. Sam doesn't get off, do we get a refund?"

He'd clearly not thought that through.

Then he blurted, "Hell no! It's a guarantee, like. But you wouldn't have to pay the *other* five grand—you know, the balance. I mean, think about it—if that story got out, in an official type way? From the cops or a DA? Doc'd have not only his wife's murder hangin' around his neck forever—but a evil setup to frame and *kill* a guy, too! Who wants *that*?"

"No."

His eyes narrowed again. "Nobody wants that, you mean?"

"No. I mean, no as in no. No deal."

He looked astounded. "It's a genuine offer!"

The jukebox helped out with "Don't Bring Me Down" by the Animals.

"I'm sure it is," I said. "But the ten-thousand-dollar reward is for information leading to the arrest and conviction of the real killer. That's not what you're offering. It wouldn't even lead in that direction. All it does is make some lying fucking con stop lying for a while."

His eyebrows went up. "What if it's *not* a lie? What if Doc really *wanted* to put Frenchy in motion like that?"

"No," I said.

I got up, waved the waitress over and gave her a five, which I told her to keep. She liked that and she liked me. What generation gap?

"That's just for mine," I told her. "Brian Jones here is on his own."

She reared back and grinned. "*You* know who Brian Jones is?"

"Doesn't everybody?"

She'd never guess my son, who was about her age, was in a rock combo, and that I'd picked up a few things by osmosis.

I was almost out the door when I felt the hand on my arm. I looked back at Weed, who smelled of it.

His smile wanted to be nasty but it was only desperate. "You're makin' a *mistake*, Heller."

I shook my head sadly. "When you were younger, Gary, you used to call me *Mr.* Heller. Sign of the times, I'm afraid."

Back out in the warm night, I stood and watched the winking, vari-colored lights on the Cuyahoga River, and beyond. Crickets were trying to be heard but boat whistles would frequently stomp them out. The deal Weed offered had too many bad possibilities attached to it—for one, it might be a sting, designed to make Lee Bailey look like he was buying off a witness. And ten grand didn't sound worth Frenchy serving out two years more of a sentence, even without splitting with Gary.

Tomorrow I would call Bailey and report the meeting—if nothing else, it indicated Frenchy was likely in league with Weed, giving the story he was trading to the prosecution the whiff of a scam—a playing-both-ends-off-the-middle type of scam, at that.

But Bailey also needed to know—if he really was thinking of calling his client to the stand—what kind of shape I'd found Sam Sheppard in tonight.

I'd finished my inquiries in under a week on my July Cleveland trip, but in late October I returned for the Sam Sheppard retrial. Lee Bailey wanted me around in case something unexpected came up during the proceedings where I might be needed. Though he had no plans to call me as a witness, I was being held in reserve, should what I'd seen and heard in 1954, 1957, and earlier that year require my testimony.

I sat in on several meetings with Bailey and his client, whose wife was back in the country and often at his side. She was prominently around to make a lie of the truth of their separation/divorce conflict, which had leaked to the press, thanks to the big mouths of both. Out of their earshot, Bailey had taken to referring to the couple as "the bitch and the blockhead."

The Sam/Lee tension came from money squabbles, which I talked to Sam about in the hallway outside the Statler Hilton suite where Bailey was staying.

His eyes flaring with indignation, Sam said, "That mercenary bastard made me sign over the *movie* rights to my book!"

A ghostwriter was still working with Dr. Sam on an "autobiography" that would be published after the new trial allowed a final chapter to be written. Producer Robert Evans had paid $125,000 to make *The Sam Sheppard Murder Case* out of it.

I put a hand on Sam's muscular shoulder. "Have you forgotten Lee has represented you since '61 for no fee? And look what he's done for you."

He nodded, his baby face in a pout. "But you have to admit, Nate, the man has an overwhelming greed for money."

I just nodded back. That was the last I tried to reason with him on the subject.

But I did say, "For now, you need to put any hard feelings aside. With the trial starting next week, you two have to come together. You're outnumbered—you two are on one team, with the state of Ohio, and particularly the city of Cleveland, on the other."

He nodded again, the pout gone, but red coming into his cheeks. "You're right, Nate. Twelve years ago they put me away when I hadn't done a damn thing. Put me away in the face of evidence that I had a fractured neck!"

Now I had both hands on his shoulders. "Take it easy, man. Suppose they do convict you? That doesn't seem likely, but even so, you'll immediately be eligible for parole."

"You think they'd give that kind of break to *me?*"

"I do. It would be better for them, easier for them, than dealing with an F. Lee Bailey appeal. So cool it, okay?"

He sighed. "Okay."

"And for God's sake, lay off the booze and pills. Get it together before you testify."

"At least," he said, mostly ignoring my advice, "that's one thing that money-grubbing bastard and I can agree on—that I'm going to testify on my own goddamn behalf!"

Bailey had been loudly letting the press know that his client would take the stand and exonerate himself through his own lips.

Later Bailey, warned by me of his client's attitude and generally flaky condition, said, "I told you he was a blockhead. Jesus Christ, I've spent fifty grand making fifty-plus trips to the fair city of Cleveland since 1961, all out of my own pocket. You may have noticed the conspicuous absence of Sam's brothers—he's alienated both of them with his paranoia and talk of Mafia contacts he made in prison who he can turn to."

"Lee, you know what I'd do if I were you?"

"What's that?"

"Walk out on him and let him find some public defender or ambulance chaser to take over. Is this worth it, just for a little front-page publicity and the cover of *Time*?"

Bailey gave me a funny look, then smiled his sly smile. "Point taken."

On October 24, Sam Sheppard returned to the dreary gray courthouse and the second-floor courtroom where he'd been sentenced to life just shy of twelve years before. I was in the gallery with the kind of reserved seat a reporter would kill for.

Oh, there were reporters all right, but Judge Francis J. Talty—a young-looking magistrate in his mid-forties—was putting up with no press circus this time around. All news cameramen and photographers were ordered to remain outside the building. Only fourteen seats were assigned to the press, with just two non-local media reps allowed, AP and UPI. And the lawyers were under a gag order not to give interviews till after the trial.

The carefully selected jurors—seven men and five women—were sequestered at a hotel for the duration, with no TV, no radio, and all outside calls supervised.

When the prosecution began presenting its case, the witnesses for the state were mostly a rerun of the '54 trial, with the notable absence of Sharon Kern. The prosecutors weren't playing the Other Woman card this time—instead, the murder motive seemed to be a spontaneous argument over Sam's general infidelity that turned homicidal.

I skipped the jurors' visit to the crime scene. I'd been there before and, anyway, the house had been remodeled and refurnished by new tenants, so the old World War Two saying came to mind: "Is this trip really necessary?"

The prosecution's first witness was former homicide cop Robert Schottke, who now worked robbery detail. He repeated his previous testimony, including Sam lying to him about his affair with Sharon Kern. This made Sam a philanderer and a liar without making the Other Woman the motive.

Then Bailey had at him.

"Sergeant Schottke, when you interrogated Sam in his hospital room, you knew he was there because of possible serious injuries. That his neck had been X-rayed. Did you make inquiry as to just how badly he had been hurt?"

"No, I did not."

"You know that if these injuries were serious beyond the point where they might have been self-inflicted, then Sam could *not* be guilty?"

"Yes."

"Then it appears, does it not, that you accused the doctor of murder without troubling yourself to determine whether, in his condition, he *could* be the guilty one."

The detective only managed a nod. If he had been a crisply professional Joe Friday on the stand in 1954, he was now the faintly ridiculous Jack Webb of the '60s *Dragnet*.

Butcher-turned-car-salesman Marshall Dodge testified and so did his ex-wife, Mildred. Marsh limped to the stand, his skin looking as gray as his hair, and timidly answered the prosecutor's questions, doing his best to mirror his 1954 testimony. This included the bombshell of brother Richard asking Sam if he "had anything to do with this."

On cross, Bailey pounced, getting Dodge to admit he'd visited Marilyn Sheppard three times a week or more. The defense attorney hammered the usual questions: When Sam called and said, "They've killed Marilyn," did Dodge know who "they" was? No. From this came the questions about Marsh and Mildred going to their neighbors without a weapon or any apparent concern that danger might await.

Dodge said of his odd, apparently reckless behavior, "I just . . . I didn't give it any thought."

Asked if he'd ever seen a Spang Bakery deliveryman at the Sheppard place, he said, "Quite possibly."

Mildred coolly described the crime scene for the prosecutor: "Her hair was a tangled mess of dried blood, and it was lying in a large area of bloodstain, and her face was completely covered with blood. Her pajama top was up under her chin. A sheet was pulled up to about her hip, and her arm was extended out."

Bailey got Mildred to confirm her husband's nervous breakdown, and the coal fire she'd started in her fireplace on the early morning of the Fourth. Bailey asked her if she was aware that national weather reports put the temperature that night no lower than sixty-nine degrees Fahrenheit. She was not.

Dr. Samuel Gerber, now sixty-eight, took the stand knowing he would have to face Bailey, who in recent years had asked him repeatedly to debate the Sheppard case in public. Gerber had always declined. That would not be an option today.

The small, white-haired, well-dressed coroner—not the star witness of the prosecution, this time—was called basically to establish for the state a handful of key points, particularly that Marilyn's pillow showed the impression, in blood, of an object used in the murder. The prosecutor was careful not to get into the controversial opinion Gerber expressed in the first trial—that the bloody impression was of a surgical instrument.

Bailey was eager to take down the man who, more than anyone—even more than Louis Seltzer himself—had been responsible for the wrongful imprisonment of Sam Sheppard.

Walking back and forth between the witness box and the panel of jurors, with his shoulders emphasizing already emphasized words, Bailey—a predator in a three-piece suit—stalked his prey.

"Doctor, when you interviewed my client on the morning of the murder, at Bay View Hospital, did you believe he had been injured?"

"Not seriously, no."

"You examined him, then."

"I took his pulse."

"When you were practicing medicine, Doctor, did you make determinations and diagnoses without examination of your patient?"

"No, I did not."

"Why didn't you examine Dr. Sam Sheppard?"

"I didn't think he was hurt very badly."

Bailey's quick tempo seemed to pull the witness in, causing him to answer the questions at that same tempo, without due consideration.

"Dr. Gerber, did you determine that he had no injury to the back of his head by taking his *pulse*?"

"No. I had no right to examine him further."

"Doctor, did you tell a fellow doctor that you were going to 'get' the Sheppard family?"

This sudden shift seemed to startle the witness.

"No! Whoever said that is a liar. I deny it."

Quickly Bailey selected the bloodstained pillow from the table of exhibits. Back in front of Gerber, he creased the pillow and asked, "How do you suppose this impression was made—by the folding of the pillow like this?"

"No, sir."

"Would you explain to the jury how you are satisfied that it was *not* made in that fashion?"

"I'd be glad to. Do you mind . . . ?" The coroner reached for the pillow.

Bailey bowed, just a little, as he graciously handed the pillowcase to the witness, saying, "Do whatever is necessary to explain it please, Doctor."

"This impression of an object is similar to a pair of pliers, or something with two blades that opens in a fulcrum, or a surgical instrument."

From my seat in the gallery, I could clearly see all of the prosecutors at their table lowering their heads, as if in prayer. Gerber had used that dreaded phrase, "surgical instrument."

Bailey smiled at his victim. "You have indicated that the murder weapon might be a surgical instrument?"

"I have."

"Do you have such an instrument available for us to look at, Doctor?"

"No, sir."

"Doctor, could you tell us where we could find one of the instruments compatible with what you believe you may see there?"

The witness shrugged. "Any surgical store."

"Would you tell the jury the name of the surgical instrument you see impressed in that pillow, please."

"I can't give you the name of it, because I don't know what it is. It could be one of many, but it's something that weighs about eight, nine, ten, eleven ounces."

"Now, you know Sam Sheppard is a doctor, don't you, Doctor?"

"Yes."

"And you knew it at the time of the first trial?"

"Yes, sir."

"And you testified then that it was a surgical instrument, didn't you?"

"I did."

"And you never produced one, did you? *Did* you?"

"No."

"Produce one now, if you can."

"I can't. But they have names—cast spreader or bone spreader."

The attorney's surface courtesy and his underlying tenacity were throwing Gerber off badly.

"Did you ever find anything that fit that impression?"

"No."

The prosecutors were not even trying to hide their dejection. None seemed able to bear to look at the witness stand.

"You could never find one in twelve years?"

"I found plenty of things close to it, but . . . no."

Bailey put on a mask of sympathy. "When you testified at the last trial about a surgical instrument, you didn't suggest that just because the defendant was a *doctor*, did you? Doctor?"

"Oh no. Oh my no."

"Of course, you *have* been a surgeon *yourself*, haven't you, Doctor?"

"No."

"Do you have such an instrument back at your office?"

Gerber shook his head.

"Have you ever seen such an instrument in any hospital, or medical supply catalogue, or anywhere else, Dr. Gerber?"

"Oh, I've looked all over the United States."

"My goodness, then please, by all means, tell us what you found."

". . . I didn't find one."

The rest of the trial was Bailey's, too.

He got Gerber's assistant, Mary Cowan, to admit the assailant was left-handed; Sam, of course, was right-handed. An osteopath testified that, two days after the murder, Sam's X-rays showed a fracture of the third cervical vertebra and a bruise of the spinal cord. Dr. Paul Kirk, brought in from Berkeley, shared the story told by the blood patterns in the murder room—that Marilyn was slain by a person whose O-type blood was different from Sam's A-type; that the killer was left-handed; that blood on Sam's wristwatch—which Cowan claimed came from "flying blood"—had reached it by direct contact.

During a recess, in a side room, Bailey spoke to Sam and gave him some bad news: "I'm not calling you, Sam."

The defendant's eyes showed white all around. "Goddamnit, man, you *have* to!"

"No. We have everything to lose and nothing to gain. We have this thing sewed up—Gerber sewed it up for us. It's too big a risk for you to go on the stand. If you do poorly, we're screwed. If you do well—or probably if you just testify *at all*—the prosecution has Frenchy Foor in its pocket as a rebuttal witness."

"He's a fucking liar!"

"I don't doubt that. But do you really want this trial to end with testimony saying you tried to hire a fellow convict to frame and kill Marsh Dodge?"

Sam looked at me with that baby-about-to-cry look.

"He's right," is all I said.

Apparently it was enough.

On November 16, Sam Sheppard was found not guilty of the murder of Marilyn Sheppard.

CHAPTER 19

On the courthouse steps, Lee Bailey—standing beside his grinning client, Sam Sheppard, whose son Chip was on his left, with wife Ariane (a blonde in sedate black) on his right, an arm around either—answered a few press questions. A small retinue, including myself, hovered behind them. On this mildly chilly Wednesday evening, topcoats weren't necessary.

"My client was found not guilty and that's what he should have been," Bailey said, "but neither of us will be satisfied until the real killer or perhaps killers of his late wife are brought to justice. Nathan Heller, the well-known investigator, is still on retainer, and on the case. Stay tuned."

In the back of a limo, I sat next to the confident attorney in his usual three-piece suit, and said, "What's the idea? Do you really want me to stay on this thing?"

"Possibly."

"What does that mean, Lee?"

"It means I intend to compose a letter to the police chief of Bay Village detailing the evidence you've already gathered on Marshall and Mildred Dodge. If that jump-starts an official investigation— perhaps with a grand jury impaneled—I may ask you to dig further."

"Who's your client in this? Sam Sheppard was found not guilty."

"But not innocent. Think of the publicity finding Marilyn's

killer would bring. The American public has a memory of about six weeks. We need to jog it by tying a bow on this thing."

"Why, so the movie about the case has a better ending?"

He smiled that sly smile of his, which could delight or infuriate. "Now that you mention it."

No great victory celebration followed, at least not one I was invited to, and by ten that night I was in my Hotel Cleveland suite packing my things in preparation for checking out in the morning. I'd called the airport and had a reservation for a plane back to Chicago in about twelve hours, the same length of time it had taken the jurors to reach their verdict.

When the phone rang, I half expected it to be Lee or Sam inviting me for a drink or something; but the reedy voice belonged to neither, though I recognized it at once.

"Now that you helped get David Janssen off," Gary Weed said, "maybe you'd like to bring in the One-Armed Man and really get some ink."

The One-Armed Man, of course, was the TV *Fugitive's* version of Sam's bushy-haired intruder.

"You obviously know where I'm staying, Gary. Maybe you'd like to drop him off at the front desk."

"Come see me and let's talk. Same place."

"When?"

"What do you think? Right now."

"Is this going to be worth my time? Last time it wasn't."

"You come see."

He hung up.

I stood looking at the phone receiver, like maybe it could explain to me why this case, this job, wasn't over yet. Gary Weed was a drug-addled opportunist and not very smart. Should I even bother with this?

And yet there I was, parking under the Main Avenue viaduct, in a neighborhood smelling of industrial smoke and exhaust fumes. A fall crispness was in the air and leaves nobody was bothering to rake up were in view pretty much everywhere. Even the Harbor

Inn—with its narrow sidewalk in front and along one side, parking lot in back and vacant lot next door—had a backdrop of skeletal trees having spilled their leaves. I hadn't shed the suit I'd worn all day at the trial, though I'd added an accessory: the nine millimeter was under my arm.

Again, Weed was at a side table opposite the bar, in the midst of dinging pinball machines, too-loud conversation, and a jukebox blasting "Last Train to Clarksville" by the Monkees, who were to the Beatles what Richard Kimble was to Sam Sheppard. My buddy Gary wore a blue corduroy peacoat and matching captain's cap snugged on his dyed blond bowl-cut hair; also a sweater of wide blue and red stripes and faded denims. He appeared more prosperous, a hippie who came into money. The Beatle boots, though, were unchanged.

Nor were the sunken cheeks and eyes with reddish whites. He looked like Herman of the Hermits if Herman had a drug problem.

The working-class crowd at the Harbor Inn had been infiltrated by long-haired boys and girls in their late teens and early twenties. The dockworker types gave the boys nasty looks and the girls longing ones, but right now nobody was causing trouble.

Except maybe Weed, for me.

One of those girls, a redhead who was working here, took my drink order—a Hamm's on tap. This was the land of sky-blue waters, after all. Gary had a beer already, and was lighting up a cigarette.

I said, "We have to stop meeting like this."

"What would you say," Gary said, through exhaled smoke, "if I told you I have the grip."

"I'd say, 'What fucking grip?'"

He flicked ash off into a tray; his smile gave him a skeletal look. Like the trees.

"I dug it up," he said. "The grip. You know, *the* grip. With the bloody clothes? And the hunk of pipe?"

And it came back to me—the story he'd told in the sheriff's office in DeLand, where he had a grip stuffed with the murder scene clothes and blunt instrument, and buried them in the woods near a construction site.

I stayed cool. "Where you buried them, Gary? Found the exact spot after all this time?"

"I didn't bury them. Frenchy did."

My eyes were burning from the smoke in the joint; pretty soon I would have reddish whites like Gary's.

"Frenchy Foor," I said. "Armand Foor. The state's favorite rebuttal witness they didn't call."

"Right. I know Frenchy going way back. When I said we was cellmates, I wasn't lying. But I give you the wrong, you know, impression. We was cellmates in Florida, a long time ago. That's when, that's where, he told me about killing that Sheppard bitch."

His smile really was an awful thing, yellow and crooked, here and there. It added a British Invasion flavor to his look.

I didn't say anything. He was, after all, a lying little drug-fiend prick. But back in DeLand, he knew things.

"That's how come," he went on, reading my mind, "I could 'confess' that time. How come I knew things."

"You were in Cleveland that night, Gary. We confirmed that. Now you're saying you wound up with a cellmate somewhere in Florida who also just happened to be in Cleveland that same night?"

He nodded. "Only it wasn't no coincidence. Frenchman was with me in Cleveland. Hangin' out with me. Now I didn't do the crime with him, but we linked up later that night—morning. I was gettin' out of town with him. I was with him when he buried that grip."

He was a liar, all right, but chances were that some truth was swimming around there in the bullshit soup he was serving up. Sam's impression that two people had been responsible could mean Gary and Frenchy were both upstairs at the Sheppards' that night. Morning.

"What do you have in mind, Gary?"

"Same-o, same-o. That ten-grand reward. Dr. Sam and them

brothers of his, they want to be back in the doctor business together, right? Gonna be tough goin' in a town where most people
don't care two shits about that verdict today. Most people in Cleveland think Dr. Sam did it."

He wasn't wrong.

"So the reward," Weed said. "I want five grand down. Five grand
on delivery of the grip. You look the shit in the grip over, decide for
yourself, is it legit. Then you turn it over to the cops, leavin' me out
of it. And I get the five grand, and another five when Frenchy gets
taken down for the wife's murder."

What the hell was this really about? Some of it could be true.
Certainly all of it was meant for Weed getting his mitts on that five
grand.

"Can you get the cash together," Weed asked, "by tomorrow?"

"Yes," I said.

"Groovy. Meet me tomorrow night somewhere."

"Here?"

His grin still lacked a bicuspid. "Right. I'm gonna haul in a suitcase of bloody clothes and a bloody iron pipe, and you're gonna go
over the stuff right out in the open. Maybe here at this table, huh?
Hell no! Someplace, you know, secluded."

Somewhere where Weed and a confederate or two could kill
me and take five grand home for their trouble.

"No," I said. "Somewhere in public. Not a busy public place.
But not some dark alley, either."

"Where?"

"I need to get the money together. You call me at my hotel tomorrow about this time. I'll set a place. If you don't like it, then
you don't have to pick up the five thousand."

"No cops? No tricks?"

"No cops, no tricks. How about you, Gary? Any tricks?"

"No tricks."

I got up, threw a few bucks on the table, said, "That's for the
waitress, Gary," and went out to the rental car. Back in my room, I
called my partner in Chicago, Lou Sapperstein.

"I need you to wire me five thousand from petty cash," I told him.

"Five thousand isn't all that petty. What's left to do in that town now that you and Bailey got Sheppard sprung?"

"Maybe something, maybe nothing. But worth the gamble, and I'll either hold onto the five K or we'll get reimbursed. We have contacts in law enforcement in both Ohio and Florida, right?"

"We do."

"I need to know *tomorrow* if Armand 'Frenchy' Foor was ever imprisoned or even just jailed in Florida, and when. He's in the Ohio pen right now, on a bank robbery rap. But see if you can find out who his cellmates have been since he was jugged. Also, see if Gary Weed, that's W-E-E-D, has been in the Ohio pen at the same time as Foor. See if there's any overlap between them in either state."

"Okay. What are you up to?"

I told him.

"That sounds risky as hell. You want me to arrange backup with our sister agency in Cleveland?"

"No. But call somebody who would know where I can get an unregistered handgun in Cuyahoga County. Pawnshop, probably, but I'd rather not go randomly shopping."

"Nate, you get yourself killed and business will suffer."

"Your concern touches me. Can you do all that?"

"Of course."

Next morning, I was up and showered and shaved and in a fresh suit when Lou called with information on what pawnshop to try. He would be working on the other info throughout the day. I should be back in my room by late afternoon by the phone. I said that was fine.

I went out and bought a nine-millimeter Browning, a newer one than I carried, the sentimental value of which—my father had killed himself with it, and it served as the only conscience I had—meant I didn't want to lose it on some half-baked venture like I had in mind. In addition, I purchased a Smith & Wesson model 36 and a five-shot snubnose .38 revolver, with a leather ankle holster to go with it.

"You ever use one of those before?" the white-bearded pawn-broker asked me, pushing the holster across the counter. He was about my age, with a gut, but also icy blue eyes that said ex-military. So did his camos.

"Yeah. But I don't regularly pack an ankle gun."

"To get at the thing, you have to drop to a kneeling position. You right-handed?"

I nodded.

"Then you'll wear it on your left leg on the inside."

I thanked him. I knew all that, and I also knew if you regu-larly carried an ankle gun, you ought to practice your draw till you overcame any slowness of response. But I also knew dropping to a kneeling position wasn't necessary, if you could stand on one leg while you lifted the other. After all, male dogs could do it—of course, they had four legs.

I picked up a second snubnose—Smith & Wesson M&P .38— and purchased ammunition for both of the snubbies. I already had nine-millimeter cartridges. At a nearby hardware store I purchased a roll of gray duct tape. At a men's shop I bought a brown suede jacket with a darker brown fur collar and nice deep pockets; also a dark brown sweater and some black jeans. The shop had a shoe department and I got some black sneakers, too.

At the Western Union office on Euclid the five thousand dol-lars was waiting; the clerk counted out all hundreds, which was fine. Fifty crisp bills would fit nicely in a business-size envelope.

Back in my room, Lou called. Foor and Weed had never been in prison in Florida together. That, of course, meant Foor couldn't have fed Gary the facts about the Marilyn Sheppard murder—or they really had been together on the murder night, probably as accomplices? They had been in the Ohio pen at the same time, but never as cellmates. What that meant, if anything, I wasn't sure.

Then I drove out to the location I had in mind for the exchange. The park I'd chosen was too cold to attract many visitors, and I didn't have to wait long to find the right spot for me to hide the Smith & Wesson M&P, using the duct tape to secure it.

Then I took a bench for about three hours, well into dusk, timing the police patrol cars making their circuit. The municipality was small, so their run was only half an hour. Passing by every quarter after and quarter to.

I had a light supper at Kornman's on Short Vincent, where I'd once had many a meal with Eliot, who liked standard steak-and-chophouse fare. For some reason his ghost lingered with me today, perhaps because my preparations vaguely resembled my friend preparing for a raid. Of course Eliot wouldn't recognize Cleveland anymore, or America itself, for that matter, with its long-haired boys and mini-skirted girls, anti-war demonstrations and raucous rock 'n' roll that made the jazz of his day seem restrained. Of course you could say the same for Sam Sheppard, who had missed a lot during his ten years behind bars.

I somehow managed a nap—the Kornman's version of a light meal perhaps helping me sleep—but I was awake on the first ring, right at ten o'clock.

"Where?" Weed said, with no preamble. "When?"

"Back where it all started," I said. "Huntington Park in Bay Village."

"Why there?"

"It's public, but at two twenty-five A.M.—when we meet—any cars passing by will be infrequent. The cops make a half-hour circuit. Gives us twenty minutes to do business. Plenty of time for a transaction this simple. But close enough to the residential neighborhood for anything noisy to be noticed."

"But why *there?*"

"I just told you."

"Plenty of other parks in this town."

"I like this one. Nice view of the lake. And of the city skyline across it."

"Are you kidding?"

"Maybe. But it somehow seems right to me. You're coming alone?"

"Yeah. You?"

"Yeah. I *will* have a gun with me."

"You won't need it, Heller. I don't go for guns. Anyway, this is gonna be a friendly transaction."

"We're not friends, Gary. But we can do business."

"Where in the park?"

"There's a picnic table looking over the beach, near the bluff. That's the nice view I was talking about."

A long pause. "Okay. The park. Two twenty-five. Be there!"

"Or be square," I said pleasantly.

I hung up, then got into the sweater and the rest of the newly purchased clothes. I stuffed the plump envelope of hundreds in a deep suede-jacket pocket, the left-hand one. I'd already put the ankle holster on, wearing it when I went out to eat, to get used to it. But only now did I snug the snubnose in its berth. Its brother was duct-taped under that picnic table.

If it came to that, I would still prefer the nine mil, but all that artillery seemed wise, since I didn't know exactly what I was getting into.

I drove directly to Huntington Reservation, as it was officially known, leaving the rental car in the narrow graveled parking lot between the street and the park itself. I sat in the car with the heat on, waiting for the next run by the Bay Village cops. The patrol car glided by at eleven fifteen. Seeing that single car in the parking area didn't seem to rate a look much less a slowdown and a pass of a flashlight.

Then I shut off the car and moved to a bench near the street. The night was cold enough that I kept my hands in my pockets— no gloves, because I didn't want to impede my dexterity. Now and then I smoked a cigarette, having picked up a pack of Chesterfields in the hotel lobby. At a quarter till eleven, the fuzz rolled by again, and neither cop even bothered to look my way. I returned to the car and moved it to a curb in the residential section nearby.

With the nine millimeter in the deep right pocket of the suede jacket, I prowled the whole park. The leaves were a crunchy carpet under my feet, which was another reason I'd picked a location like this—anyone approaching would likely be heard. I'd thought some necking or copulating couple, maybe with a warm sleeping bag, might turn up; but apparently nobody was that frisky tonight. The night was clear but dark, with only a fingernail clipping of moon. I repeated the circuit and convinced myself that Gary and whoever might be with him were not here. Had not jumped the gun, at least not yet anyway.

The beach below was not the thin strip of sand behind the Sheppard place—it was a good-sized, real beach, at least for the middle of Cleveland, Ohio. And the skyline view *was* impressive, its geometry cutting the horizon, its lights glimmering on the lake before the shimmer of the modest moonlight took over.

I took a position at the picnic table, which in addition to that great view of Lake Erie and the Cleveland skyline had an opposite view, if somewhat limited by interfering trees, of the parking area, if Gary was dumb enough to park there.

Turned out he was. He pulled in just a little after two, parking his Chevy Corvair, a small car but somewhat sporty, bright blue and new under the streetlights. About right for a drug dealer, which was my guess for Gary's occupation when he wasn't selling bloody clothes and secondhand blunt instruments.

Possibly Weed knew his way around Huntington Park, because he came right toward me, crunching leaves as I expected he would. He was in the same attire as last night, the blue peacoat and captain's cap, but now he was carrying a beat-up old suitcase, not much bigger than a briefcase.

He approached, slowing, grinning nervously. "You're early."

"So are you, Gary. The cops just made their circuit."

"I saw 'em, from where I was pulled over for while."

That was stupid. In this kind of affluent neighborhood, an unknown vehicle—even a late-model one, like the Corvair—might

rate a look, and even a glimpse at the long-haired driver could signal a drug deal.

But the officers on patrol hadn't even slowed down. Even in a
neighborhood where one of the most famous murders in America had happened, the Bay Village boys had become complacent.
Human nature.

I'd been sitting sideways on the picnic table bench. Gary came
around, sat across from me, feet under the slatted table, as if ready
to dig into some potato salad. I did not assume a similar posture—I
stayed turned to one side, the lake and its beach and the bluff,
lined with trees and bushes, at my back.

Gary said, "Let's see the color of your money."

"Let's see the color of your blood-spattered clothes."

He shrugged. "Okay. But put the cash on the table first. I won't
touch it till you say."

I nodded. With my left hand got the well-stuffed envelope out,
which wasn't sealed shut, just had its flap tucked in. I set the envelope on the table and opened it enough for the fat wad of money
to show.

"Fifty hundreds, Gary. Now the grip."

He plopped the grip onto the table. The thing had dirt on it
and it was an old brown thing, scarred and faded. It was like we
were sitting down and about to share the worst picnic ever.

The snaps were on his side. He clicked the thing open and
swung it around, his face hovering above the lid, his dilated and
bloodshot eyes peering over at me. Right on top was a piece of iron
pipe as he'd described it over almost a decade ago in that sheriff's
office—a length of pipe maybe a foot long, curved at the top. It had
dark crusty red on it, and rested on some half-wadded, half-folded
old clothes, a plaid shirt, some worn denims, and they too were
spattered with red.

Too red.

And the smell that wafted up was sweet, not coppery. Sugar,
not blood. Ketchup, not gore.

Gary or somebody had liberally doused the clothing with ketchup, like they were fucking french fries, and then left them out somewhere to get appropriately dried and crusty.

So it was just a scam.

And I didn't like the way that lid partially blocked my view of Gary—he could be behind there with a gun. I was reaching toward the lid to slam it down when someone coughed.

Only it wasn't a cough: it was the sound of a silenced gunshot and above and between Gary's eyes a third eye appeared, but there was nothing spiritual about it, just a black hole with some modest spatter making a psychedelic design of it.

My hand, already reaching toward the grip, went to the iron pipe, thinking that cough had been right behind me, almost over my shoulder.

And I was right—a figure in a dark shirt and dark trousers with a lot of hair, Afro-style, was just a few feet away and in its left hand was a .22 automatic with a homemade silencer, giving it a long silver snout.

He had apparently stepped out from behind the nearest tree and now the limited moonlight caught him. The Afro was blond and his face was contorted with rage and fear. With a gun deep in my jacket pocket, and one on my ankle, and yet another duct-taped beneath the table, I already had my hand filled with the blunt instrument, and I lunged and swung it and caught him on the forearm on the gun-hand side, the clumsy .22 pitching somewhere. He howled and backed up and that was when I recognized him.

He was older, almost ten years, and I had a hunch a lot of drugs and maybe booze had turned him old before his time, but I still recognized the kid with the close-set eyes—the friend of Larry Dodge who had helped find the green cloth bag of evidence.

And in a fraction of a second, much less time than it takes to tell it, Denny Lord's presence told me a story—a story of hormone-happy teenage boys who got drunk in the predawn morning hours of the Fourth of the July, kids who had hung out at the Sheppards, played ball with Sam, who flirted with and lusted for the cute young wife in the short white pants

and halter tops, and who, drunk and horny, had wound up in Marilyn's
bedroom, only to be rebuffed, and impulsively use a heavy flashlight or
maybe the missing table lamp to batter that prick tease and really teach
her a lesson. Maybe just Denny, maybe one of the other dozen boys, too.
But somehow, in that slice of a second, I knew Denny was the one, the
one who had lost his temper, the one who heard Lee Bailey talk about me
being on the trail of the real killer, a real killer who somehow had gotten
in league with the late Gary Weed, sprawled on the grass with his feet up
on the picnic bench and his three eyes staring up through the skeletal trees
at the barely existent moon.

Screaming, Lord threw himself at me and that hunk of iron
flew from my hand, too, and then we were wrestling and punching
and rolling around on top of each other like humping teenagers.
Finally I shoved him off of me and I was on one knee, clawing
at my pant leg to get at the ankle weapon, but he got to his feet,
all the way up, and kicked me with the flat of a sneakered foot,
shoving me more than hurting me. He had spotted where the pipe
went, and it was at the edge of the bluff. He was scrambling for it
when I swung my right fist up and caught him on the side of the
jaw. He went backward, and then realized where he was, with his
back to that drop-off, and his arms did the windmilling thing, but
it did him no good when I shoved him.

He went tumbling down the rocky slope, the equivalent of
thirty-six steps all the way to the beach, where he ended up on his
back, limbs spread like a starfish.

I wasn't going down that bluff on foot, no way. So I walked
over to the wide cement stairs with their metal railing, which came
in handy for a guy pushing sixty who was very out of breath and
mildly beat up. I didn't have to walk over very far—the nine mil in
hand now, just in case—to where he lay. His head was at a funny
angle. Or anyway his neck was. He'd broken it on the way down
and now he was looking up with eyes as empty as Gary Weed's.

I knew how he'd been able to sneak up without the leaves
alerting me—he'd walked down the beach, from his parents' place,
and likely scaled the bluff much more slowly and carefully than

he'd just come down. Or maybe he'd even taken the stairs I had. Anyway, he'd slipped behind that tree and waited.

Now he was dead on the beach, the struggle with the murdered woman's husband on the Erie shore finally over, the lake not so angry tonight, just a lulling, lapping thing that on this bigger width of beach didn't come near him. Still, though the water appeared gentle, I knew it was cold, and unforgiving.

Back up in the park, I searched Gary Weed in case he had something on him, a scrap of notepaper maybe, that might connect me to him. I wiped the iron pipe clean, then pressed it into Gary's limp hand. I took the dummied-up suitcase with the Heinz ketchup gore, which I would dump somewhere out of the neighborhood. And of course I collected my .38 from under the table and the five thousand dollars in fifties on top of it.

The dead were on their own.

Then I went to the rental car and drove out of the park, positioned as it was between Eliot's house and Dr. Sam's, each with their own ghosts.

CHAPTER

I had checked out, but remained in Cleveland, with an early evening flight out to Chicago. I felt it only right to make a stop on my
way out of the city, and I pulled up to the townhouse in Rocky
River and left the car at the curb.

My second knock was answered by a worked-up Sam Sheppard.
He was in a T-shirt, boxer shorts and bare feet; he needed a shave
and what little hair he had was askew. His eyes were wild, and you
didn't have to be a doctor to know he was high on something.

Standing there looking like a baby with five o'clock shadow,
not worried about who saw him in his underwear, he said, "Thank
God! I tried your hotel and they said you'd checked out. And Bailey's
in the air on his way back to Boston. Jesus, am I glad to see you."

He had a newspaper in his right hand, like a newsboy about to
shout, *"Extra! Read all about it!"*

I guided him back inside. Then he moved through the royal
purple living room and into the kitchen, where on the counter
was a bottle of Scotch, a glass, and a cluster of pill vials. Nothing
seemed to have changed, other than his .38 revolver's absence.

"Where's Ariane, Sam?"

"She's, uh . . . taking a break. The reporters were camped out
outside last night and she freaked out. She's in a motel room. But
she's coming back. She *is* coming back."

"Good," I said, and sat at the table.

He was on his feet, pacing, animated, pausing at the refrigerator. The newspaper in his left hand was rolled up now, like there was a bug to swat or maybe a disobedient child who needed spanking; his arms were heavy with the musculature earned by prison cell push-ups. "You want a beer or anything? Damn, but I'm glad to see you, Nate. I've been going off my *nut*!"

"Why is that, Sam? No beer, thanks."

He flung the paper on the table between us. With two hands he spread it out for me to see the front page of the *Press*. It wasn't the headline, but below the fold was:

DRUG DEALERS DEAD
IN HUNTINGTON PARK

"You've seen this, right?" he asked, grinning, eyes glittering.

"I have."

He leaned over the table, thumped the newspaper with a forefinger. "Let me tell you something you don't know. One of the dopers who died is the *Lord* kid—he was tight with Jerry Dodge, Marsh and Mildred's boy? Those two kids were the ones who found the green bag of stolen things from my house!"

I gestured to the paper. "I read it. It says Lord had a record of selling illegal narcotics on the Case Western campus, dating back to when he went there and ever since he dropped out. That he still hung around the campus and college hangouts, as kind of a permanent unenrolled student who peddled pot and probably harder stuff. Got busted more than once."

He slammed his fist on the story. "That's right! He was a *rotten* kid. Always was a rotten little shoplifting kid."

"The other dead dope dealer was known as the Weed Man. That's all anybody knew him by, at least that's come to light so far." Gary Weed had not been identified. I doubted he ever would.

"Don't you *get* it, Heller! Don't you *get* it?"

"Get what?"

He was waving a hand. His eyes were dilated, like Gary Weed's.

"Those kids," he said, his voice high, whiny, "those teenagers that hung around my place! That were always *drooling* over Marilyn! This little Lord S.O.B. is a *suspect*!"

"A suspect of what?"

"*Goddamnit*, Heller! Of killing Marilyn. And so is the Dodge kid. There were *two* of them that night! One battered Marilyn, the other hit me from behind."

"Why the Dodge kid?"

"They were friends, those two! Lord and Dodge. Like I said— they found that bag of things stolen from my house! Could have been a plant! Once I talk to Lee, this whole thing is going to bust wide open."

"No it isn't."

His mouth dropped open, his jaw slack. "What? Why?"

"Over a dozen boys used to hang out at your place, back when Uncle Miltie and Howdy Doody were still a big deal. And I don't know *how* many girls. Lord happened to be a kid who got into pot and other shit—not exactly a rare breed these days. Far as I know, none of those other twelve or so kids have killed anybody lately."

"If it was the Dodge kid—"

"If the Dodge kid was there on the murder night, maybe on a very ill-advised holiday toot, he'd have been a sort of . . . guilty bystander. He'd be the one who hit you, just because he *had* to. 'Cause things had got out of hand. The other one, say the Lord kid, would've done the killing and later played tag with you on the beach."

He held up his palms in momentary surrender. "Okay. That makes sense. We'll tell Lee. Or the cops! I can call Fred Drenkhan, he's chief of the Bay Village police now—he's a pal."

I laughed. "Oh, yeah. He was a real pal of yours."

Sam leaned forward again, his head moving side to side. "Think about it, Nate! The Dodge kid being involved explains so much! It makes his parents' behavior finally make sense—suppose their boy came home and confessed to them! Before I ever called! They'd have done everything, anything to cover it up! Think about them inviting

Gerber in, to use their living room as his headquarters! Man, it's *all* making sense!"

I kept my voice soft, and calm. "Let me tell you about the Dodge kid, who I only met once, but who I don't make as a suspect. But for the sake of argument, let's say he was pulled along on a stupid stunt by a buddy who got out of control. You know who Jerry Dodge is today? A doctor. An osteopath, like a certain neighbor he really admired. You know where he is now? Vietnam. A medic, a captain. There's no reason to think you're right about him, but, Sam—if you are? He's turned out pretty good. He's redeemed himself. And I doubt somebody with the kind of character it takes to become a doctor would be part of something like this in the first place. But that didn't stop some people from saying a doctor named Sheppard killed his wife. You *really* want to put some honest young doctor through that kind of mill?"

He looked like he might cry. "Goddamn, Heller! Why don't you see this as the break it is?"

"I don't know." I shrugged. "Maybe I was there last night."

He reared back, that endless forehead frowned. "Wh-what?"

"Maybe," I said, "I went to the park with a wad of cold cash to buy some evidence from the Weed Man . . . only this grown-up kid called Lord jumped from behind a tree with a gun. Maybe he shot the Weed Man in the head, to have all the dough to himself, and then maybe he and I struggled. Like you and the bushy-haired man, Sam."

His eyes seemed to be trying to eject themselves from his face. "What are you *saying*?"

Another shrug. "I'm not saying anything except 'maybe.' Maybe I killed Lord in the struggle. Knocked him over the bluff and he tumbled down that rocky slope and broke his damn neck. Then maybe I cleaned up the scene because just maybe it would have been very bad for a respectable private investigator to get involved in something like that. Particularly since it would reflect on the controversial lawyer who hired him, and would look even worse for their client, who just got found not guilty of a murder charge."

Rage and frustration fought for his expression. "Are you *screwing* with me, Heller?"

"No. I'm being straight with you. You go to Lee with this, I deny it. You go to the cops, I deny it. Nothing there links me to it. Suppose that wild story I just told you is true—you of all people think I want to explain myself to the *Ohio* authorities? Do you want an investigator working for you and your lawyer to admit to killing a suspect in the case? The night your verdict came in? That could come back on you in a very nasty way."

He was slowly shaking his head. "Why are you telling me all this?"

"I haven't told you anything but 'maybe.' With Lord dead, the name of his accomplice—very possibly an unwilling, unwitting one—died with him. And what I can tell you for sure is that I have no intention of risking a manslaughter rap, or having a very successful private investigation agency go down the tubes because of my efforts on your behalf."

His cheeks were getting red, the baby-faced man on the verge of a tantrum. "What if I come forward with what you've told me?"

"I'll deny it."

Through clenched teeth he said, "Or . . . or would you just kill *me*, too? Or maybe have one of your Chicago mob buddies do it for you."

"No need." I got up to go, nodding toward the pill containers and bottle of Scotch. "You're doing a good enough job of that yourself."

He watched from the front doorway, still in his T-shirt and shorts, a ghost haunting his own house, as I walked to the car, got in and drove away.

I encountered only a few of the players in the Sheppard affair over the coming years, but I kept track of several, and checked up on a few before writing what follows.

F. Lee Bailey (as promised) sent a fifteen-page letter to Bay

Village police chief, Fred Drenkhan, in which he detailed the evidence supporting his theory that Marshall and Mildred Dodge murdered Marilyn Sheppard. This led to a new investigation and the convening of a grand jury in 1966, with Marshall Dodge testifying. No indictment resulted. Nor did any connection between the drug dealer deaths in Huntington Park and the Sheppard case come to light.

Bailey and Sam Sheppard then filed separate civil suits for damages on Cuyahoga Coroner Samuel Gerber and *Cleveland Press* editor Louis Seltzer. Both suits were dismissed in 1968, the dismissals upheld in 1970.

Bailey's theory about the Dodges did make its way into the film based on Sam's ghostwritten biography, *Endure and Conquer,* a movie initially planned to be titled *The F. Lee Bailey Story,* with serious talk of Bailey starring as himself. The resulting fictionalized film, *The Lawyer,* directed by Sidney J. Furie of *Ipcress File* fame, starred a dynamic Barry Newman as the Bailey-like lawyer (spun off into a TV series, *Petrocelli).* Dr. Sam, however, was not impressed—he disliked the film intensely, much like his response to *The Fugitive* on TV.

The two-part final episode of *The Fugitive* aired in August 1967. More than 78 million people tuned in to see Richard Kimble finally catch "the One-Armed Man," making it the most-watched TV series episode of that time.

For a while, Sam Sheppard—like Marshall Dodge—sold used cars for a living, as he sought to have his medical license restored. When it was, he joined the Youngstown Osteopathic Hospital. His career, and his marriage to Ariane, seemed back on track—in a Sunday-section article, anti–comic book shrink Dr. Frederic Wertham wrote of the success of this unusual marriage, and explained why it would surely last.

But two wrongful death malpractice suits in 1968 found Dr. Sam "resigning" from the hospital by year's end, with a third malpractice suit following in 1969. Sam had already been served with divorce papers, which aired Ariane's charges of his drug and alcohol abuse, as well as her fears for her safety. The latter resulted in a restraining order against Sam Sheppard where his soon-to-be-ex-wife was concerned.

For a while Dr. Sam opened an office as a general practitioner in a strip mall in a suburb of Columbus, referring any surgical patients to other physicians. Always a physical fitness buff, Sam began to work out with a new friend, professional wrestler George Strickland. Sam had been a wrestler in high school and college, and now he began a new secondary career—as a professional wrestler. His stage name "Killer" Sheppard was, he said, black humor. He aimed to be "the cleanest, meanest, damnedest wrestler you ever saw." His signature move? The Mandibular Nerve Press, inserting two fingers into his opponent's mouth and pressing two nerves beneath the tongue, "inducing a temporary paralysis that would render a foe helpless."

In October 1969, he married Strickland's nineteen-year-old daughter, Colleen, in Mexico. Dr. Sam now practiced medicine, on a limited scale, out of the living room of his father-in-law's ranch-style home, where he and Colleen also lived. His relationship with his brothers became strained to say the least, but now and then he saw his long-haired son, Sam Reese Sheppard (no longer "Chip").

On April 6, 1970, Sam Sheppard died on the kitchen floor, the way Eliot went. His rambling last words included a claim that he knew who killed his wife, and could prove it. He provided no details.

Pills and booze were blamed, the official verdict "liver failure." He wore sunglasses in his casket, his medical instruments beside him. Richard Sheppard and a "visibly shaken" Lee Bailey were among the pallbearers. Sam's son was in Europe, unable to attend, and so was Steve Sheppard, studying psychiatry in London.

Ariane attended as well, and embraced the third Mrs. Sheppard, two of Sam's three wives crying together.

The second Mrs. Sheppard, as of 1977, lived in Fort Lauderdale, Florida, then moved to New Jersey a year later, and back to Germany in 1979. In the early '80s Ariane was in Rocky River again, in a rented home where she lived with her mother. In an on-air 1984 interview on a Cleveland newscast, she said at the time of the re-trial, Sam was already "far gone with drug and alcohol addiction," and made bitter by his time in prison. Still, Ariane claimed never to have doubted her late ex-husband's innocence.

Steve Sheppard became a psychiatrist in California. **(EDITOR'S NOTE: At this writing, Dr. Stephen Sheppard, 97, lives in Oakland, California. His brother, Dr. Richard Sheppard, is deceased.)**

Dr. Lucas Hardmann practiced in Sweden for a while, then in 1975 opened a clinic in Southern California. He moved to San Jose and worked as an anesthesiologist, dying in 1987 of a heart ail-ment. The only contact he had with Dr. Sam after the second trial was by way of a telegram to his old friend, encouraging him to resume surgery and tennis. Luke's friend Dr. Paul Robinson con-tinued his father's family practice in Kent, Ohio.

Sharon Kern remained in California, and by century's end was a mother twice, and a grandmother four times. I have no idea what became of pretty onetime babysitter Jane Carter, but I hope she's had a very nice life. The Lords left Bay Village and moved to Clearwater, Florida. I don't know what became of them, after that. Marshall Dodge also wound up in Florida, and married for a third time; he died in 1981. Mildred, still in Ohio, died a year later. She had become a kind of buff on the case, obsessively filling a trunk with magazine and newspaper articles and books on the subject.

Their doctor son, Jerry, died in Vietnam in 1968.

F. Lee Bailey became the top criminal defense attorney in America, his clients including Ernest Medina (of the Mai Lai Mas-sacre), kidnapped heiress Patty Hearst, and yet another accused wife killer, O. J. Simpson. I witnessed many remarkable masters of cross-examination in my years, including Clarence Darrow, but Bailey was easily the best. **(EDITOR'S NOTE: Mr. Bailey is, at time of publication, a polygraph and investigative consultant in Maine, having been disbarred in Florida and Massachusetts over monetary matters that he disputes.)**

Dr. Samuel Gerber, elected Cleveland's coroner thirteen con-secutive times, led a largely distinguished career. A star ever since

Eliot's Torso Murders case, Gerber was first to link alcohol consumption to traffic accidents, and was a pioneer in the study of crib death, as well as a founding member of the American Academy of Forensic Sciences. He is, however, remembered more for his mean-spirited blacklisting of Dr. Paul Kirk from that organization, Kirk's "blood splatter" forensics work having helped clear Sam Sheppard. The highest honor in the criminalistics section of that professional organization is now named for Kirk, who died in 1970.

Thirty years to the day after Eliot's passing, Gerber died in 1987 in Cleveland Heights, best known today for his dogged and often unethical pursuit of Sam Sheppard for Marilyn's murder. The state-of-the-art Coroner's Center that housed labs, offices, morgue and college auditoriums was torn down at the end of the '90s to make way for a parking ramp.

Louis Seltzer remained unrepentant—even proud—of his role in the first Sheppard trial. "Mr. Cleveland" self-published his autobiography; he died in 1980, the *Press* dying two years later.

Erle Stanley Gardner retired from the Court of Last Resort in 1960, the organization withering without his participation and leadership. While *The Court of Last Resort* television series lasted only one failed season, *Perry Mason* enjoyed nine successful ones— Gardner on camera playing a judge in the final episode. Raymond Burr returned as Perry Mason for twenty-seven TV movies that ran from 1985 until the actor's death in 1993. Gardner never again became involved in the Sheppard case, but in interviews spoke out against the miscarriage of justice perpetrated by Gerber and Seltzer. He died March 11, 1970, on his ranch.

And what of everybody's favorite suspect, Richard Eberling?

He and his pal Obie Henderson continued to ingratiate themselves in Cleveland social circles until finally Obie was hired by the Republican mayor as his personal assistant. Obie and his partner Richard were then hired to decorate the home of the mayor's wife; the Eberling-Henderson interior decorating business skyrocketed, as they snagged richer and richer clients and hosted frequent over-the-top parties at the Hermitage. Finally, in 1973, they were contracted to restore the historic Cleveland City Hall; their arrogance and over-spending, however, got them fired by the next mayor. Meanwhile, Eberling continued to pursue his "other" business—befriending and defrauding elderly women.

Eberling became a nurse's aide for a widow, whose sister—who vocally disapproved of Richard—was brutally battered and strangled in her bed in 1962, a murder somewhat echoing Marilyn Sheppard's. By the 1970s, Eberling was a trusted and well-paid presence around the mansion, where he devised a new will for his beloved charge, who in 1983 was found on her belly on the floor by ambulance attendants Richard had summoned. Identifying himself as the comatose woman's nephew, Eberling reported that she had stumbled and taken a nasty fall.

Richard's "aunt" died six weeks later in the hospital, never waking up. X-rays showed a fracture near the second vertebra, not unlike the one Sam Sheppard suffered in the early morning hours of July '54. In July '89, Eberling and Obie were convicted of her murder as well as on forgery and theft charges, and both were sentenced to life.

Having been the Sheppards' window washer, and the thief who'd taken Marilyn's rings (from Richard Sheppard's home), Eberling was apparently inspired to tell various other inmates various other things about the Sheppard murder. He seems never to have directly confessed, but teased others (including Dr. Sam's son) with his inside knowledge. He also concocted wild stories, such as Sam Sheppard and Marshall Dodge being homosexual lovers who killed Marilyn together. He died in prison of cardiac arrest in 1998. **(EDITOR'S NOTE: A paroled Oscar B. Henderson died in 2016 in Texas.)**

The late Eberling was nonetheless a major presence in a third Sam Sheppard trial. In 2000, Sam Reese Sheppard—who had grown from a long-haired hippie war protestor into a bald anti–capital punishment activist—sued the state of Ohio for wrongly convicting his father of his mother's murder in 1954. Sam R. Sheppard's attorney offered up Eberling as a real-life "one-armed man,"

DNA evidence from the crime scene suggesting someone with a genetic profile closely matching Eberling's had also been in the house.

But the defense bobbled the DNA evidence, with a heavily accented Pakistani expert who was tough to follow, with exchanges that didn't explain the DNA science well enough, allowing the opposition to dismiss the testimony (in a vaguely racist manner) as "mumbo jumbo." A former FBI crime profiler made the same points to the jury that Eliot had to me back in 1957, labeling the murder as displaying all the earmarks of a domestic homicide. The old circumstantial evidence of the dog that didn't bark and the disputed neck X-rays of Sam's injury were trotted out. The verdict, returned in under five hours, found for the state, in effect endorsing the original 1954 guilty verdict.

In the run-up to the trial, both Sam and Marilyn were exhumed for purposes of obtaining DNA samples for blood testing. Sam's remains were then cremated, and at his son's request, the doctor and his wife were reunited with their unborn child in a red-carpeted, marble-walled mausoleum.

Like the shell of a man who emerged after ten years of false imprisonment, Cleveland itself was no longer the "Best Location in the Nation." Factory towns in America were not what they used to be. Hardly anybody shopped downtown anymore. The population was down fifty percent, since 1954. The Cleveland Indians were politically incorrect, and the "Mistake on the Lake"—a lake fed by a river that once notoriously caught fire—became best known as the home of the Rock 'n' Roll Hall of Fame.

And maybe as the town where Eliot Ness failed to bag a butcher, and where a doctor once killed his wife on the Fourth of July.

Just ask anybody in Cleveland.

I OWE THEM ONE

Despite its extensive basis in history, this is a work of fiction, and liberties have been taken with the facts, though as few as possible—and any blame for historical inaccuracies is my own, mitigated by the limitations of conflicting source material.

My usual practice, in the Nathan Heller memoirs, is to use real names as much as possible. That remains true with the police, lawyers, reporters and other non-suspects in the Marilyn Sheppard murder. But the only suspects here who appear under their real names are Richard Eberling, Obie Henderson and Sam Sheppard himself.

While they have real-life counterparts who students of the Sheppard case may recognize, a number of players here are fictionalized, their names fictional as well, and the author has no intention of laying any crime at the feet of any of the real people. This novel, for all its research, is a work of imagination and has tried to bring to life various existing theories to this enduring mystery and explore a possible new one as well. Not every fact or clue is introduced or dealt with.

I changed my mind about the identity of the killer or killers half a dozen times during the research for this novel, and if you dig into the available information, you are likely to have the same experience. An ultimate resolution to this crime, at this point, is about as likely as definitively determining who Jack the Ripper was. What cannot be doubted, whether innocent or not, Sam Sheppard got a very raw deal from the justice system as it was dispensed in Ohio in the 1950s.

Those characters who appear here under their true names must also be viewed as fictionalized. Available research on the various individuals ranges from voluminous to scant. Whenever possible, actual interviews with the subjects, and transcripts of courtroom appearances, have been used as the basis of dialogue scenes, although creative liberties have been taken.

Flo Kilgore was introduced in the Heller novel *Bye Bye, Baby* (2011), as a composite of journalists Dorothy Kilgallen, Peter Hyams, James Bacon, and Florabel Muir, reflecting their respective roles in the investigation that followed Marilyn Monroe's death. In *Do No Harm*, Kilgallen is the sole historical counterpart for Kilgore, although the fictional character does not entirely parallel the real person (Kilgallen, for example, was a Catholic and married only once). The Heller novel *Ask Not* (2013) explores the circumstances of Kilgallen's death and possible murder, touched upon only briefly here. Reference on "Kilgore" came from *Kilgallen* (1979), Lee Israel; *The Reporter Who Knew Too Much* (2016), Mark Shaw; and *Murder One* (1967), Dorothy Kilgallen, which includes a chapter on the Sheppard case, in particular the first trial.

F. Lee Bailey material is drawn from his autobiography (with Harvey Aronson), *The Defense Never Rests* (1971), which includes a lengthy Sheppard section. Also consulted was the 1971 biography *F. Lee Bailey* by Les Whitten. Bailey's later book, *When the Husband Is the Suspect* (2008), with Jean Rabe, also deals with the Sheppard case. In addition, I viewed the 1967 episode of *Firing Line* with F. Lee Buckley interviewing Bailey, a rather crackling exchange, as well as Bailey's stunningly effective cross-examination of Mark Fuhrman in the O. J. Simpson murder trial.

A major research tool was the 11/23/66 letter from F. Lee Bailey to Chief Fred Drenkhan of the Bay Village Police in which the attorney spells out the "Marshall and Mildred Dodge" theory, which prompted a grand jury inquiry. This is available online, at the

Cleveland State University website, along with a Sam Sheppard timeline, a Who's Who in the case, and transcripts of testimony from the first two trials.

Normally when I have researched a famous crime or mystery for the Nathan Heller memoirs, the books on the case at hand have ranged from excellent to lousy, with many stops in between. I have always been frank in these end notes, and have tried to guide interested readers to the best works on the subject. Unusually, the vast majority of books written on the Sheppard case are first-rate.

The seminal works are by *Chicago Tribune* reporter Paul Holmes, who covered both trials and published the first three books on the subject: *The Sheppard Murder Case* (1961); *My Brother's Keeper* (1964), with Dr. Stephen Sheppard; and *Retrial: Murder and Dr. Sam Sheppard* (1966). Holmes developed the theory about "Marshall and Mildred Dodge," which greatly influenced F. Lee Bailey, who has credited Holmes.

Dr. Sam: An American Tragedy (1972) by Jack Harrison Pollack is similarly excellent, a highly readable account that benefits from having been written after Sam Sheppard's death. My favorite book about the case, however, is *Summer of Shadows* (2011) by Stephen Knight, who cuts back and forth between the Sheppard case and the Cleveland Indians' race for the American League pennant. This unusual juxtaposition, which feeds an overview of Cleveland itself, makes for a unique read, and the book was a big influence here. I do have a complaint: there is no index, which makes its use as a research tool a frustrating one.

Tailspin: The Strange Case of Major Call (2002) by Bernard F. Conners presents a theory about another possible suspect in the Marilyn Sheppard murder. Though I chose not to go down this path in my novel, I did find the book interesting and occasionally helpful.

To really understand—or even try to understand—the Sheppard case, three of the most recent works are crucial.

The best single, complete overview of the case is *The Wrong Man* (2002) by James Neff, which covers in depth all three Sheppard trials as well as the major theories of whodunit. Neff believes Sheppard is innocent and makes a good case for it.

Mockery of Justice: The True Story of the Sheppard Murder Case (1995) by Cynthia L. Cooper and Sam Reese Sheppard is in many ways the best book of the bunch. With the participation of Dr. Sam's son, the heartbreaking aspects of the tragedy become clear, though never is the book self-pitying. It explores every major theory and covers just about everything. On the other hand, it's not where to start—it jumps around as it intersperses Sam R. Sheppard's timeline with flashbacks to the first two trials. To really get the most out of *Mockery*, a familiarity with the case is best—even necessary. So first read *The Wrong Man*, *Dr. Sam*, or the two Holmes books on each trial.

Mockery of Justice—and to an extent, *The Wrong Man*—is the reason the Richard Eberling theory has become so prevalent. You may well be convinced that Neff and Sam R. Sheppard are right. (The Onyx paperback edition of *Mockery* is "updated with stunning news developments.")

Dr. Sam Sheppard On Trial: The Prosecutors and the Marilyn Sheppard Murder (2003) by Jack P. DeSario and William D. Mason presents the anti–Dr. Sam point of view, the only book that does. Read in the context of at least one other book—possibly *Mockery of Justice* or *The Wrong Man*—it helps bring numerous things into focus. Without that leavening influence, *On Trial* is one-sided, co-written as it is by Mason, one of the prosecutors at the civil suit trial in 2000.

Ironically, the weakest and least helpful book on the case is *Endure and Conquer* (1966) by Dr. Sam Sheppard, ghostwritten by William V. Levy, who interestingly has gone on record saying he thinks Dr. Sam did it.

Erle Stanley Gardner material came from *The Court of Last Resort* (1952), Erle Stanley Gardner; *The Case of Erle Stanley Gardner* (1947), Alva Johnston; and *Erle Stanley Gardner: The Case of the Real Perry Mason* (1978), Dorothy B. Hughes. "Court of Last Resort" coverage, initially by Gardner and then by Gene Lowell, appears in

Argosy magazine, June, August, and October 1957; November 1960; May 1962; May and October, 1963; April and November 1964; and February 1967.

Other coverage consulted includes *Confidential Detective*, May 1962; *Lowdown*, April 1955; *Whisper*, August 1955; *Inside Detective*, November 1954 and August 1958; and *Man's Magazine*, October 1955. *Murder in Mind* issue #28 (1998), a UK magazine, devotes an entire, photo-filled issue to the Sheppard case.

Other books referred to include the WPA guides to Ohio and Florida; *Images of America: Cleveland's Flats* (2005), Matthew Lee Grabski; *Justice USA?* (1967), Howard Feisher and Michael Rosen; *Popular Crime* (2011), Bill James; and *The Years Were Good* (1956), Louis B. Seltzer.

I sometimes wonder how I ever wrote Nate Heller books without Google. I will not even try to share the names of every website I visited during the writing of this novel. But here are a few articles you can Google and find yourself: "Cleveland's Oldest Bars," John Petkovic; "Did Sam Do it?", Adam Ross; "Famous Trials," Professor Douglas O. Linder; "Infamous Dr. Sam Sheppard Wrestled at Akron Armory," Mark J. Price; and "The 17 Oldest Places and Things in Cleveland," Brittany Rees. Thank you to these writers and so many more on the Net.

Several movies were screened, including *Guilty or Innocent: The Sam Sheppard Murder Case* (1975), directed by Robert Michael Lewis, and written by Harold Gast and Lou Randolph; and *My Father's Shadow: The Sam Sheppard Story* (1998), directed by Peter Levin, and written by Adam Greenman. The former is a fairly straightforward retelling of the case, taking no real stand on whether or not Dr. Sam was the perpetrator; George Peppard does an admirable job as Sheppard. The latter, adapted from *Mockery of Justice*, is an odd piece in which the spirit of Dr. Sam (well played by a somewhat miscast Peter Strauss) and his son Sam Reese Sheppard have philosophical conversations while the son evolves into an advocate for his father's innocence. *The Lawyer*, as mentioned in the novel, is a fictionalized but superior film version of the case, with Barry Newman's strong, energetic performance as the film's engine.

I was able to speak to Mr. Newman several times about his approach to the film, and how much time he spent with Bailey (not much—a question-and-answer session and a photo shoot). The film takes a *Rashomon* approach, with various versions of the crime shown on screen, a tactic carried over into the well-regarded *Petrocelli* TV series, for which Mr. Newman was nominated for a Golden Globe and Emmy. He was both helpful and gracious in answering my questions and discussing the case.

I also watched "The Killer's Trail," a 1999 PBS *Nova* episode, written and directed by Marian Marzynski and Joel Olicker, focusing on Sam Reese Sheppard's efforts to get his father's name cleared by the state of Ohio. Also viewed was *True Crime Scene: Fugitive Justice* (2008), director and co-writer (with Gary Lang), Agnieszka Piotrowska, as well as various YouTube clips from newsreels of the day.

My longtime research associate, George Hagenauer, drew upon his knowledge of Cleveland (his wife's hometown) to help in matters of geography and more. Only I, however, am to blame for any geographical inaccuracies. George also provided vintage "true detective" magazines. His research with me on the Eliot Ness novels of thirty years ago or so—much of it at the Case Western Reserve library— influenced the Ness material herein.

So did A. Brad Schwartz's research for *Scarface and the Untouchable: Al Capone, Eliot Ness and the Battle for Chicago* (2018), a nonfiction book by Brad and myself. Brad—an indefatigable researcher—was helpful throughout the writing of this book, not only where Ness and his various cronies in Cleveland government are concerned, but in the matter of the proximity of the Ness house and the Sheppard house—a fact gone unnoted previously. I will not enumerate the sources for the Ness material here but will instead recommend *Scarface and the Untouchable* (and its extensive bibliography) to my Nate Heller readers, in hopes they will increase Brad's royalties (and mine).

Fifty Years of the Playboy Bunny (2010) by Hugh Hefner, John Dante and Josh Robertson provided much of the Chicago Playboy Club reference, as did vintage issues of *Playboy*, which were also plumbed for advertising and fashion information.

Thanks to my friend and agent, Dominick Abel, who always goes above and beyond; and editor Claire Eddy at TOR/Forge, for her warm support and enthusiastic encouragement.

Barbara Collins—my wife, best friend and valued collaborator—as usual read and proofread each chapter emerging from an office that began spotless and ended a disaster area, as is always the case. That she was working on her draft of our next "Barbara Allan"–bylined novel never dissuaded her from acting as sounding board, cheerleader and editor. Nate Heller and I love her very much.

MAX ALLAN COLLINS was named a Grand Master in 2017 by the Mystery Writers of America. He has earned an unprecedented twenty-three Private Eye Writers of America Shamus Award nominations, winning for his Nathan Heller novels *True Detective* (1983) and *Stolen Away* (1991), and his short story "So Long, Chief" (with Mickey Spillane). He received the PWA Eye for Life Achievement (2006). In 2012, his Nathan Heller saga was honored with the PWA Hammer Award for making a major contribution to the private eye genre.

His graphic novel *Road to Perdition* (1998) is the basis of the Academy Award–winning Tom Hanks film, followed by two acclaimed prose sequels and several graphic novels. His other comics credits include the syndicated strip *Dick Tracy*; his own *Ms. Tree*; and *Batman*.

His innovative Quarry novels—the first hitman series in mystery fiction—was recently adapted as a critically acclaimed TV series of the same name by Cinemax. He has created a number of other suspense series, including Mallory, Eliot Ness, Jack & Maggie Starr, Reeder and Rogers, and the Disaster novels. He is completing a number of Mike Hammer novels begun by the late Mickey Spillane; his full-cast audio novel, *Mike Hammer: The Little Death* with Stacy Keach, won a 2011 Audie for best original work.

For five years, he was the sole licensing writer for the popular TV series *CSI: Crime Scene Investigation* (and its spin-offs), writing ten best-selling novels, four graphic novels, and four award-winning video games. His tie-in books have appeared on the *USA Today* bestseller list nine times and the *New York Times* three, including *Saving Private Ryan*, *Air Force One*, and *American Gangster*.

An independent filmmaker in the Midwest, Collins has written and directed four features, including the Lifetime movie *Mommy* (1996); and he scripted *The Expert*, a 1995 HBO World Premiere, as well as the film-festival favorite, *The Last Lullaby* (2009), based on his novel *The Last Quarry*. His documentary *Caveman: V. T. Hamlin & Alley Oop* (2008) has appeared on PBS and on DVD, and his documentary *Mike Hammer's Mickey Spillane* (1998/2011) appears on the Criterion Collection DVD and Blu-ray of *Kiss Me Deadly*.

His play *Eliot Ness: An Untouchable Life*, was nominated for an Edgar Award in 2004 by the Mystery Writers of America; a film version, written and directed by Collins, was released on DVD and Blu-ray, and appeared on PBS stations in 2009.

Collins lives in Iowa with his wife, writer Barbara Collins; as "Barbara Allan," they have collaborated on sixteen novels, including the successful Trash 'n' Treasures mysteries, *Antiques Flee Market* (2008) winning the *Romantic Times* Best Humorous Mystery Novel award of 2009.